DELICATE
Storm

Contents

Author's Note

This book contains subject matter that some people may find triggering. A list of the main potential triggers can be found on Katherine's website:

http://www.katherinejayauthor.com

Please note, triggers are not listed here to avoid spoilers for the book.

DELICATE STORM'S SOUNDTRACK

Delicate - Taylor Swift
Stargazing - Miles Smith
Risk - Gracie Abrams
Something Just Like This - The Chainsmokers, Coldplay
Now I'm In It - HAIM
Made You Look - Meghan Trainor
I Can Do It With A Broken Heart - Taylor Swift
Demons - Imagine Dragons
Ocean Eyes - Billie Eilish
Someone You Loved - Lewis Capaldi
Glad You Exist - Dan + Shay
Love Me Now - John Legend
Shivers - Ed Sheeran
Wolves - Selena Gomez, Marshmello
Love Me Back - Max McNown
APT. - ROSÉ, Bruno Mars

To my amazing readers who have been with me from the beginning... Easton wrote himself. I hope you enjoy him.

And to anyone holding back because their life is too messy, I hope this encourages you to take a leap, or to risk your heart, because you could be missing out on something truly incredible.

PROLOGUE

PAIGE

Christian stalks toward me, his hands outstretched as though he's ready to wrap them around my throat. A game we used to play until it stopped being fun.

"You're a goddamn menace, you know that?" he scoffs as he shakes his head.

"*Me*," I yell. "I haven't done anything."

"Just tell me what you know."

"I told you." I step forward, getting in his face. "I didn't see or hear anything." I'm lying, of course, and he probably knows that, but without proof, he's got nothing. Like me.

Christian stares, his pupils dilated, as a few seconds tick by. And just when I think I'm going to have to repeat myself, he releases a quick breath. "Either way, we're done."

"Fine by me." A shiver runs down my spine, but I keep my posture straight, confident, refusing to let him see how rattled I am. "Feel free to leave."

"It's funny that you think it's going to be that easy." He laughs sadistically. "I'm not going until you pose with me. For old times' sake."

My skin crawls but I put on a smile. He's right—we need to do this or we'll be gossiped about for months. "Where do you want me?"

"Our favorite spot." He dons a fake smile of his own before stepping out onto my balcony, expecting me to follow without a word. And I do. Because I want this over with just as much as he does.

He perches on the edge of the hot tub, positioning himself with the sparkling New York skyline as his background, beckoning me over. "Come on, baby. Let's show the world we're amicable." He smirks, rolling up his sleeves to show off his arm candy. And God knows, his arms are *candy*. Everything about this man used to make my mouth water with hunger. Chiseled jaw, peppered with the perfect amount of stubble. Dark piercing eyes. Perfectly plump lips. Abs made of steel. He's the definition of Adonis.

But he's a dick and I'm done with his games. And the rest of it.

I'm ready to make my own moves.

I gloss my lips as I walk over and sit beside him, letting the split in my skirt fall open as I angle my legs toward his. A signal of comfort. I'm happy, he's happy, we're all *goddamn* happy. Plastering a signature smile on my face, I lean in and laugh. "Ready when you are, *babe*. But don't ever call me 'baby' again."

Christian raises a brow in challenge and I look away. "You love when I call you baby, but"—he grabs my chin as he leans closer, turning me to face him—"consider it retired."

Dropping his grasp, he reaches for his phone and positions it in front of us, wrapping an arm around my shoulder. "Say... best friends."

"Best friends," I repeat cheerily, the lie tasting bitter in my mouth.

"Okay. One more now. Three, two, one. *Smile*."

Socialite Paige D'Angelo and Billionaire Christian Mikkleson confirm their split after months of speculation. The pair shared the news together on their social media platforms, claiming the split was a mutual decision.

EASTON

I stare at my sister, a rage simmering under the surface of my skin. *She's the messenger. She's the messenger. She's the messenger.*

"Don't kill the messenger," she pleads, raising her hands in the air, alerting me to the fact that maybe my rage isn't as hidden as I thought.

"How are we only just finding out about this?" I question, working hard not to aim my anger her way.

"They were worried you'd try to shut down the show," she says, a little defeated because...

"Rightly so. This is bullshit, Keeley. I didn't sign up for that."

I didn't sign up for *any* of it. During what was the *biggest* season of our football careers, the Storm owner—or ex-owner now—decided it would be a good idea to welcome the filming of a TV show centered around the team. It was met with backlash from day one, but they persisted, and when episode one aired, *after* we won the Super Bowl, it quickly soared to the number one spot.

Everyone's watching it. My mom, my sister, supporters, players from other teams...

And Isaac.

I never imagined showing him would be an issue considering I don't share anything about my personal life. Or him. But it turns out, someone else did it for me.

"I'm just as pissed as you are, East. But technically they didn't do anything wrong. It was Zane that brought it up."

That little fucker. As if it's not bad enough that my teammate slept with my girlfriend—now ex—the mother of my child, but he has to share the news with the world. Claiming I attacked him *unprovoked* when he was trying to come clean.

"Is there any way we can convince them to cut that storyline?" I ask since she's the media liaison for our team and worked closely with the crew.

"I doubt it; it airs next week."

"Next *week*? They never even asked me to comment."

"Actually they did." She cringes. "You refused."

My mind drifts back to the filming. They asked me for a lot of things and I pretty much denied them all. Toward the end, I didn't even listen to what they were saying.

"Fuuuck."

"Yep."

"Can Amelia do anything?"

"Unlikely. She doesn't work there anymore, remember?"

Amelia *was* the director of the show, and while I barely knew her, I trusted her to keep my personal business out of the spotlight. Hell, I even trusted the director that took over when she left to have a baby with my teammate Luke. But the producers... I didn't trust them for a second and I was right.

"Fuckers."

Keeley frowns sympathetically. "I wish I had better news. But I did tell you—"

"I know." I cut her off, not wanting to hear how she told me I should cooperate. Again. It doesn't change anything now.

How the fuck am I supposed to shield Isaac from the shit show between his parents if it's forever immortalized on a TV show starring his dad? What the hell was Macy thinking? Of all the guys she could have chosen, she had to go for Zane. The only guy who cares more about his cock than his teammates.

"I need to get away. If I'm here when that episode airs, they'll be all over me. I can't do that to Isaac."

I should be riding the high of my first ever Super Bowl win. I *should* be feeling on top of the world. Unstoppable. Instead, I've been forced into the shadows. *Again*. The first time being when my separation from Macy leaked. And now this.

Fuck my life.

I suck in a deep breath as Keeley shakes her head. "You can't leave Isaac with Macy."

My jaw drops and the panic in Keeley's voice has my anger growing. "Do you think I'm stupid? He's been begging me to spend more time with Mom. I'm sure she'd love a week with him. And no one knows where she lives."

Keeley grimaces. "Sorry. You know I don't think you're stupid, but I wasn't sure what the two of you had decided. For custody and all that."

Custody... I'd love it if we were discussing that. Then maybe I'd believe Macy actually cared. But she doesn't.

"She'll be fine with Isaac staying at Mom's." She'll welcome it. She doesn't want the responsibility.

"Good. Because you're right; Mom will love it. Where do you think you'll go?"

For the first time since I opened my door to Keeley, I smile. I know exactly where I need to be. But I'd prefer to keep it to myself.

"All you need to know is that it's far away from here."

It's the perfect place and I'm ready to cause absolute destruction.

The San Francisco Storm controversy continues in the latest episode of STORM CHASER. The episode highlights the tension between star wide receiver Easton Wilder and his rookie teammate Zane Fitzpatrick. We revealed last month that Easton split from his long-term girlfriend and mother of his child, and now we know why.

CHAPTER ONE

PAIGE

NY socialite Paige D'Angelo spotted at JFK airport. Sources say she's on the run, but if they know why, they're not talking.

If running away from your problems was a crime then I'd say... *Lock. Me. Up.* I'm as guilty as they come. But it's okay, because I look damn good in orange.

Luckily, I also look good in my comfy travel pants and sneakers that I specifically put on because I thought I was being stealthy, sneaking into the airport unnoticed.

I was dead wrong. I've already found four different photos of myself online, all with similar headlines.

It's only now that I'm settled in the lounge that I can relax. *I hope.* You never know who's lurking around the corner, waiting for their chance to make a dollar.

Taking a deep breath, I pull out my book and make myself comfortable, tapping my foot as though it'll speed up time.

I'm early.

And I'm *never* early. I'm that friend you give a fake start time to, an hour ahead of schedule, knowing I'm always late. But I'm here now, two hours before my flight, because I'm desperate to get out of this state. Hell, if I could leave the country for a while, I'd do it. If I didn't think my mom would cut me off. She already threatened to write me out of her will simply because I was moving to California.

Not that it would matter. *Much*.

I may have been born with a silver spoon in my mouth, but I've always worked hard for my money. From a young age, my parents were sure to instill the value of every dollar. Dad came from a modest income family and worked his ass off to build his business. Mom came from one of New York City's wealthiest families and yet she always had a job and made my dad pay back every cent she ever loaned him. Which wasn't much to begin with. My brother and I used to joke that Mom and her family were only wealthy because they Scrooged their money away. That was until we were old enough to realize we never went without. We were always dressed in the latest fashion, always had the most up-to-date technology. Whatever we wanted we got. But the second we started acting like the spoiled brats that we were, the money disappeared.

And because of that, I made sure to forge my own path. I may not be a self-made billionaire. Or even a millionaire for that matter. But if my family wealth was to suddenly dry up, I'd get by. Comfortably. And I'm proud of that notion.

When I'm almost certain no one is watching me, I relax into my latest read, and after I've been reading for an hour, my phone buzzes with a text from my dad, making me smile.

> Daddio: You know I trust you completely, but please put your old man at ease and let me know you're on your way to the airport. Your flight leaves in a little over an hour

He thinks he knows me so well, but I'm a changed woman.
I had to be.

> Paige: I'm in the lounge with a coffee and a book. If you need photo evidence, I'm sure the Internet will provide

I'd laugh at my own joke, only I'm not sure that it is one. But it will make my dad smile. He's been making headlines almost as much as I have lately.

Daddio: I'll have a car waiting for you when you
land. Love you, Kid

I don't respond because I'm not big on "love yous." Not yet anyway. And he won't be expecting a reply, so I'm safe.

Dad and I haven't always gotten along. I wasn't a huge fan of him putting work ahead of his family, and took Mom's side when they divorced. But over the last few years, things have been better, and now—after a few months of him asking me—I'm moving across the country to live with him.

It's going to be interesting to say the least, but the timing feels right. I'm ready for a new adventure, and I'm ready to take a break from my New York City life.

It's time to give California a go.

I toss my phone on top of my bag, and it lights up again with another text.

Airline Announcements: Your flight has been delayed. Your revised flight departure time is 11:05

Goddammit. Another hour to wait. If I'd been late as usual, I wouldn't be stuck here for as long.

Blowing out a breath, I stretch my arms out in front of me and scrunch my nose. I'm about to start reading again when an attendant stops to collect my empty glass and I smile. "Don't suppose you know any way I can kill a couple of hours? My flight's been delayed."

I roll my shoulders as I speak and her eyes zero in on it.

"You could go for a massage," she says, pointing to where I've just grabbed my neck, making me pause as my eyes light up in anticipation.

"You wonderful human, you. Thank you. That's perfect. May you always be blessed with green lights when you're running late."

The attendant laughs as I jump up and grab my bag. *A massage.* Why didn't I think of that? I smile as I pass and walk toward the front doors, a bounce in my step until she calls out.

"Miss, wait." I turn and she winces as she points behind her. "It's that way."

"Of course. Thank you." I would probably know that if I wasn't always running late for my flights. I never get time to use the facilities here. Which is a shame because then I would have known that everyone on my flight was going to have the same idea. By the time I arrive at the day spa, there are at least ten people in front of me. Not that I let it derail my happiness. I have time and I'm getting a massage.

How can I not? It's the perfect way to begin my new life.

My body may be well and truly relaxed, but I am *not* feeling the zen. I lost track of time as I waited for my massage, and when they called me in, I followed without question. I was beyond ready to rid myself of the built-up tension I'd been stockpiling over the past few weeks. And now, as if to remind me that I am still in fact the same Paige D'Angelo that I was yesterday, I'm late.

"Sorry." I rush through the hall, expecting to be greeted by a bunch of angry expressions as I board the plane, but instead, I'm blessed with smiles.

"Welcome, Miss D'Angelo. Please take your seat and we'll be with you shortly to offer some refreshments."

I smile and nod, graciously thanking them as relief fills me. But the second I locate my seat—already occupied—the smile fades and I internally groan. If I ever needed proof that being early sucks, here's exhibit A. If I was late, I wouldn't have thought to get that *damn* massage.

I move slowly down the aisle and pause next to the first class seat assigned to me.

The man who's laid claim to my sanctuary for the next seven hours doesn't look up as I loom over him, his bald head reflecting the cabin lights into my eyes.

Tapping my foot, I clear my throat, but he continues his laser focused stare on the screen of his phone, reading what looks to be emails.

My eyes flicker to the man seated by the window seat beside him, but he too is ignoring me. I blow out an audible breath just as the window seat guy flexes his hand, drawing my attention to the veins in his forearms, and... *Hello, hottie.* My gaze momentarily shifts to his face shadowed by his baseball cap, pulled low, to see his rigid jaw tighten as his lips purse. Like the bald guy beside him, he has his eyes on his phone, and it's safe to assume that he's not happy about whatever he just read.

But I'm choosing to pretend he's angry on *my* behalf, and it makes my next move easier.

"Excuse me." I gently tap the bald man's shoulder. "I'm really sorry, but you're in my seat."

I sense the window-seat *hottie* glancing up, but before I get the chance to look his way, he huffs and goes back to his phone. Meanwhile, I don't even get an eye roll from the guy whose attention I actually seek.

"I know it's annoying," I continue, taking a sympathetic approach. "I'm not sure what happened, but my ticket says—"

"All the seats are the same, *Miss*," he snaps, finally looking up at me. "Just sit *somewhere else*." He waves a hand before wriggling to make himself comfortable, hitting me with a patronizing smirk.

Oh-kay.

I make a show of searching the cabin, but he couldn't be more wrong. "The only free seat is a *window* and I purposely *booked* an aisle." *And as an added bonus, I happen to be very partial to attractive forearms, so this seat is a must. There's no way I'm moving.*

I toss him a sarcastic smirk of my own, but he doesn't even flinch.

"Look, Miss. I—"

"Hey man, I get it," window-seat hottie cuts in, and I frown. "You're settled and comfortable," he adds while the guy in my seat widens his smirk, only for it to drop from his face in an instant as the man beside him continues, "but be a *goddamn* gentleman and get the hell out of the lady's seat."

His eyes widen along with mine, but instead of arguing, he undoes his belt and makes a show of grabbing his things, muttering something about famous people.

He stands, and while I've left plenty of room to let him past, he purposely knocks into me, grunting as though it's my fault.

"Ex—"

"Hey asshole." Window guy snaps, his body half out of his seat, ready to get up. "What the fuck are you doing?"

The bald guy holds his hands above his head and scoffs, showing no remorse. "Leave it alone. It was an accident."

My eyes bounce between the two of them in a standoff as my heart races. I'm about to change my mind and walk away when a flight attendant joins us. "Everything okay here? We need you to take your seats."

"That's what I'm trying to do," bald guy curses under his breath before walking the three steps it takes to get him to what was presumably his assigned row, knocking the person next to him as he pushes past to the window.

I smile at the flight attendant as she walks away, shoving my bag into the overhead locker before sitting down.

"Thank you for that." I turn to look at the guy beside me. "I really appreciate your help." Armed with a smile that's clearly fake, he glances my way and holy shit... His forearms are merely an appetizer for the delicious meal that this man is. If looks could kill then I would happily take my last breath for the panty-melting blue gaze that's staring back at me.

And his beard. My God. I've always focused my energy on clean-cut suit guys, and I fear I've been missing out.

"What?" he grunts, snapping me out of my ogling as I straighten uncomfortably in my seat.

"I was thanking you." I smile again, but it does nothing to melt his icy stare.

"Don't mention it." He looks away and I pout at the loss of my view, but when I'm offered a white wine, all is good in the world again.

Until the plane taxis on the runway and my body tenses.

No matter how many times I fly, I will never be comfortable with it. I wouldn't say it's a fear, but my nervous system does not like it. At all.

Curling my fingers over the end of the armrests, I grip tightly but try to remain calm. Taking a deep breath, I lock my legs so they don't bounce, but the second we speed up, I lose control, gritting my teeth in annoyance.

"Are you okay?" I hear from beside me and freeze, assuming I imagined it. Though sure enough, when I chance a sidewards glance, window-seat hottie is staring back at me.

"Oh. Yep," I lie. "I'm good, thanks." *But you're going to regret asking me that because you just became my distraction.* "How about you?"

"I'm fine." He frowns but before he has the chance to turn away again, I rush out another question.

"Are you on your way somewhere or on your way home?"

He pauses as though my question confuses him, or perhaps he's deciding whether or not to engage in my chitchat. Either way, after the longest beat, he sighs. "Home."

"Nice. Me too. Sort of." *It's about to become my home.* "Business or pleasure?" I ask next and he sighs even louder.

"You don't have to do that." He stares at me blankly with a slight shake of his head. "In fact, I'd prefer that you didn't."

"Do what?"

"Make small talk because I helped you. You don't owe me anything."

I frown until a small laugh escapes me. "That's not what this is."

"Ohh-kay."

"It's not. I promise." I laugh again and grimace. "I talk *a lot* when I'm nervous, and flying always makes me nervous. Add to that I'm moving away from New York for the first time and I'm a ball of stress. A stress ball. But not the useful kind that you can squeeze to make yourself feel better. Nooo. This stress ball will only make you feel worse when I slap you in the face for inappropriate touching."

"The *fuck*."

"Sorry." I shrug, not really sorry at all. "It's—"

"The nerves. I get it. Do you know what helps with my nerves?"

I smile and a giddy feeling wells up inside me. He wants to help. "No. What?"

"Talking to myself. In my head. In silence."

"Really? That—" I cut myself off, briefly closing my eyes as I snort. He's joking. Actually, he's not joking. He's telling me to shut the hell up. "Noted. I'll give it a try."

I bite back a smile and turn to face the front of the plane, grabbing the airline magazine from the pocket, mindlessly flicking through the pages.

I try hard to stay still, but before long, my legs are bouncing while I tap my fingers on my knees, and barely a minute passes before my window-seat hottie groans.

"Okay. Fine. I'll bite."

"What?"

"Are you traveling for business or pleasure?"

Huh? My brows furrow, but with his arresting gaze boring into mine, waiting for a response, I don't question him again. "*Neither.* I'm moving to California for...a change of scenery. What about you?"

"I was visiting a friend." He's quick to answer, and it's safe to say that small talk is not his thing.

"Visiting a friend," I repeat. "In New York? I wonder if I know them." He stares at me deadpan as if to say "seriously" and I laugh. "What? It's possible."

"I was in Scotland. This is my connecting flight."

He speaks with no emotion while my eyes light up. "Scotland? *Wow.* I've never been but I hear it's beautiful." I smile and picture the vast green landscape I've seen in movies, until a shiver runs through me when I think of the weather. "It's cold, right? Was it cold?"

"It was fine."

"Fine?"

"If it was cold, I didn't notice." *Interesting response.*

"What sights did you see? Anything you'd recommend?"

Window hottie tenses and the frustration is clear in his posture, but he releases a breath and continues amusing me. "I spent the week breaking shit."

"Breaking shit?" My voice rises, giving away my excitement at that prospect. I would love to break shit right now.

"Yep. It was needed."

"In Scotland?"

"Yep," he repeats, popping the *p*, and I find myself watching his lips until they purse, snapping me out of it. Again.

"You know you can do that here, right?" I know that because I've done it. *Maybe it's time to do it again.*

"Break shit? I do. My ex does it all the time."

His ex what? Oooh. I laugh out loud though I'm not sure he meant that to be funny. "I meant you could break shit for a release. Assuming that's what you were doing. You know... You could crush a truck, smash a glass, destroy dinnerware."

"Destroy dinnerware?" He raises an eyebrow and frowns. "Like a plate?"

"Sure. Or a bowl." I shrug and I think I see the hint of a smile, but I don't draw attention to it, though a small part of me makes it my mission to see a full-on grin before we land.

"As I said...my ex was good at that."

"*Wait.* I thought you meant that metaphorically. Like she breaks hearts or promises."

My new friend huffs out the smallest of laughs—if you could even call it that—and folds his arms over his chest, leaning back into his seat to create some distance between us.

"Nope." He gives me nothing else, so I quickly move on.

"I find it's better to do it in a controlled environment," I say though I'm not sure he cares.

"That's definitely a wiser move," he humors me by answering. "Tell me. Have you ever destroyed dinnerware?"

"No."

"I see."

"I smashed a truck," I deadpan, staring into his eyes, trying not to smile.

My response catches him off guard, and I hold my breath as his lips curl into a genuine smile. *Yes.* I knew I could do it. Biting back my victorious laugh, I raise a brow and wait for his response.

"A truck? Was that in a controlled environment? Or did you take a baseball bat to an ex's pride and joy?"

I burst out laughing until the image of that works its way into my mind and my happiness fades. *If only.*

"I wish it was option B. God knows he deserves it. But alas,"—I put on a grin—"it was option A. And let me tell you, it's incredibly satisfying. But I guess you know that already. What did you destroy? Do you have any photos?"

"Photos?"

"Of your wake of destruction?"

"Ah. No. I'm not really a photo guy. Do *you* have photos?"

"Of the truck? Definitely. Loads of them. Sometimes I look at them to remember that high. It's only second to..." I trail off. While it doesn't seem like the gorgeous man beside me has any idea who I am, I'd prefer not to get too personal. Instead, my gaze moves to the food cart as it makes its way toward us. "Thank God. I'm starving. What about you? I'll bet, being the big guy that you are, you're always hungry. Am I right?" He stares at me like I'm crazy, and I'm confused until I replay what I said, barking out a laugh. "Never mind. I didn't mean that as a negative—"

"It's fine." He reaches out toward me but then seemingly changes his mind. "I didn't take it the wrong way. And you're right. I'm often hungry."

"Good. How about I grab us lunch?" I joke, bouncing my eyebrows, hoping for another smile. But instead, I get a quasi-nod snort huff thing which I think might be a suppressed laugh. Either way, I take it as a win.

CHAPTER TWO

EASTON

The woman beside me beams when I huff out a laugh, and I have to give it to her—she's a little funny. *Annoying, but funny.* If she's aware of my lack of interest in our conversation, or conversation in general, she's completely ignoring it. Though I doubt she's that oblivious. I'm not exactly subtle when it comes to that.

She keeps talking, her confident smile back in place now that we've moved on from whatever topic she was avoiding, and when it's time for our meals, she pauses only long enough for the attendant to offer us a drink and then her mouth is moving again.

A mouth I've found myself drawn to one too many times already. I can't help it; she has a perfect little pout.

"Did you do anything else while in Scotland?" she asks, her voice light. "Or was the trip purely for destruction purposes? What did you destroy, by the way? I don't think we established that."

Nope, we didn't because I don't want to talk about it.

"I had no other plans. The trip was purely for destruction purposes and it was a castle."

She gasps. "A cast—"

"Before you lecture me. It wasn't some old relic. Well, it was. But I helped with some demolition so they'd be able to do a rebuild and—"

Jesus. Why am I justifying myself?

"And?"

"That was it. Period."

"So you just needed the release?"

"Something like that." *Moving on.*

The last thing I want to do is rehash how fucked-up my last few months have been. She's a stranger. She doesn't need to hear about my teammate sleeping with my girlfriend, Macy, the mother of my three-year-old child. Or that before that, we'd barely spoken in weeks, with her checking out of the relationship earlier than that.

This stranger doesn't need to hear that I got my first official warning for attempting to "beat the shit" out of said teammate in the locker room after my ex decided to tell me about her tryst...in detail. Or that my problems were then fed to the public via a TV series showcasing my football team during the biggest year of our careers, when I didn't even want to be a part of it.

Last, she doesn't need to know that instead of facing my issues head-on, I've spent the past week hiding away, shirking all responsibility.

For nothing.

My beautiful stranger may have been right. The release of endorphins *was* momentarily freeing, and the rush intoxicating. But the second I boarded my flight home, the feeling was gone. I don't need to talk through it; I need to let go.

It's time to get back to reality.

And my reality is a mess of epic proportions.

We thankfully move on to more *stranger*-appropriate topics like the weather and favorite TV shows, with my seatmate chatting away for five minutes to every ten seconds from me. I'd say it was convenient that she was a talker since I don't like to talk, but the point is... I. Don't. Like. To. Talk. Period. And she's failed to realize that despite my many clues.

She asks me if I watch reality TV and what type of music I listen to. She asks if I prefer to be hot or cold. She asks if I've ever been to Alaska. For someone that was starving, she barely touches the food in front of her, spending the time talking instead.

The conversation bounces around more than a pigskin during a football game, but she never once asks what I do for a living. Something most would consider a go-to question when engaging in small talk, but I consider it a win.

I could tell from her very first glance in my direction that she didn't recognize who I was. And that's a rarity. Especially since winning the Super Bowl. Hell, I was stopped in Scotland for a goddamn photo with an

Australian tourist. Yes, I'm fifty percent sure my friend set it up to piss me off, but there's still a fifty percent chance I'm wrong. Of course, he'll never admit it. He's not much of a talker either or a jokester for that matter, which is why in this situation he made the perfect companion. If he was anything like my seatmate here, I would have been on the next plane home.

After the flight attendant collects our trash, the woman falls silent beside me, and I take the opportunity to turn on a movie, making it clear that our sharing time is over.

Thankfully, she takes the hint, at least until the seatbelt sign comes on as the captain prepares to land.

"You said San Francisco was home, right?" she asks, further proving my point that she doesn't know me, her perfectly sculpted brow lifting in question.

"I *did*." I drag out my response, hesitant as to why she's asking, hopeful this isn't leaning toward more personal topics now that we're almost saying goodbye.

Her eyes light up and she swivels in her seat to face me, giving me a proper view of her face for the first time, and fuck me because I was wrong. She's not just a pretty mouth; she's goddamn beautiful. *Annoying, but beautiful.*

"That's great," she says, beaming again, drawing my gaze to her lips once more, momentarily distracting me. "Any good restaurants I should know about?"

I internally relax. Restaurants I can do. While I love cooking, I don't get a lot of time to be creative, so I rely on my favorite restaurants to satiate my taste buds. "I know a few. Any particular area?"

She mentions neighborhoods that I'd consider too close to home but I don't let on, instead giving her a few options for each until she hits me with a satisfied smile.

"Thank you. I've vacationed there, but never for more than a few days. It won't take long to find my feet, but I'm grateful for the head start."

I hold back from saying "anytime" because that would be a lie. She caught me in a situation I couldn't escape from; otherwise, I would have found an excuse to hightail it out of there.

"Good luck," I say, giving her a small nod, ending the conversation.

"Thank you. I'll leave you alone now. Give you some peace before the chaos begins."

Chaos? She has no idea. And yet, I have never wanted to get home so badly in my life. Mess aside, I can't wait to see my son.

I open the windows in my truck to keep myself awake and call my mom on the drive, letting her know that I'm on the way. I should have slept on the plane, but Miss Chatterbox beside me wouldn't let that happen. Not that I tried to stop her. The second she flashed me her adorable but pleading smile—a look I don't think she realized she was giving—I was done for. Before my son was born, that wouldn't have affected me. In fact, it probably would have had the opposite effect and repelled me. But now, it's safe to say he's softened me a bit. Though I *had* thought my weakness was only reserved for him... I guess it's expanding.

My mom tells me that Isaac's napping, so I stop by my house on my way, instantly regretting it.

A guy in an over-the-top pinstripe suit hovers in my driveway as I come to a stop behind him, his eyes widening when he registers who I am. I'd question why, if I hadn't passed the obnoxious for sale sign littering my front lawn.

Macy is selling the house.

My ex is selling *my* house.

I've only been gone for a week. Can people really get things moving that quickly?

The guy recovers and smiles, waving as he steps away from his bright red sports car, moving toward me. My gaze drops to my gear shift. I could easily change into reverse and get the hell out of here. But what's that going to achieve? I can only escape for so long, and it's not going to change the outcome.

I slowly step out of my truck, greeting my houseguest with a glare.

"If it isn't *the* Easton Wilder." The agent pretends not to notice my annoyance. "Nice to meet you." He rushes over, failing to hide his confusion...or is he equally as annoyed?

"Macy didn't mention you'd be here," he says, checking his phone.

Of course she didn't. She didn't mention we were selling the house.

"How's the interest?" I ask, and it pains me to play pretend, but I refuse to bring another stranger into my business.

"It's good. Great. Lots of people want a house owned by a Super Bowl champion."

"I'll bet." It's a struggle not to roll my eyes or shield my gaze from the glow of his white teeth, but I force a smile and nod.

"It's a beautiful home," he adds and I have to stop myself from punching him. "*It's a beautiful home?*" I *fucking* know that. That's why I chose it. It's my dream home. Private. On the beach. There's a gym, a pool, no nosy neighbors. It's gated. Has a decent kitchen. It's big but not in-your-face obnoxious. It's perfect for me.

And she's goddamn selling it.

"Are you waiting for Macy?" I ask to change the subject, hoping he can't sense my frustration. Since she's not answering my calls, this might be my best chance to catch up with her. "I've been on a plane for the past two days," I continue. "Sorry, I'm not up-to-date with everything." I wave my hand toward the house and force another smile.

"No, sorry, sir. She asked me to handle everything. Said she'd be out of state."

She said what? That's probably something I should have known.

"God, I'm an idiot. I knew that," I lie. "It's been a *long* day."

"Of course. I'm sorry to bother you. I have two clients coming today, but I promise to stay out of your hair."

"That won't be a problem. I'll only be here for a few minutes. Do what you need to do."

He nods, and it takes everything in my power not to tell him to fuck off, but he's lucky the world knows enough about my life at the moment. I don't need this guy knowing more than he should. Plus, I have places to be and those places do not include my home while new buyers wander through it.

Fuck my life.

Actually no, *fuck Macy.*

I saac's still asleep when I arrive at my mom's, and while it's later than usual, I don't wake him, needing to talk to her first.

"He hasn't been sleeping very well," she tells me, tightening my chest with guilt. "Knowing he'll see you soon must have put his mind at ease."

"I shouldn't have gone. *What was I thinking?*" I whisper the question under my breath, but Mom catches it and frowns.

"You were putting yourself in a better headspace for your son. You were *thinking* about Isaac."

"I know, but—"

"No buts. I won't hear it."

I smile, but it's surface level and Mom sees right through it.

"East—"

"Did Macy visit?" I cut in, not wanting to make this about me.

Mom's face falls as she shakes her head, a sheen of mist coating her eyes. "No, and she hasn't called," she whispers, her gaze flitting over my shoulder, making me turn to find the hallway empty. "Isaac's been asking about her and I hate lying, but I also can't break his heart."

A rage simmers inside me, but I fight to quell it. "I'm sorry you had to deal with that," I snap, but it's not directed at her. "That shouldn't be your responsibility."

Macy had *one* job while I was away. To be a decent mom and visit her son. I said I'd call him every day—because I was going to do that anyway—as long as she saw him *once*. It was the perfect plan—she'd get to spend time with him knowing there was no chance of running into me—and yet she still couldn't do it.

I let her stay in the house. I gave her my goddamn credit card. She fucking cheated on me and I've been the one trying to keep things civil between us. For Isaac's sake. But it ends here. "I wish you'd told me. I would have come home and—"

"We've talked about this. You needed the break. You're about to dive headfirst into single parenting. And we had fun. He asked about her occasionally, but for the most part he preferred to talk about you. He's a great kid." A genuine smile lights up her face, and it hits me in the chest. "I'm not just being biased—"

"I know. He is a good kid. I'm lucky—"

"It's not luck. Yes, he's his own person, but you're doing a good job, Easton. Don't ever doubt that."

"I'm trying but he needs a—"

The pitter-patter of little feet cuts me off, and I turn to see Isaac round the corner, his eyes half closed as he scratches his head. My heart races in anticipation, and I couldn't stop my responding smile if I tried.

"Nana, is Daddy—" He pauses when we lock eyes and his face lights up as he snaps out of his sleepiness, taking off in a run. "*Daddy.*" He launches himself into my arms, and in an instant, the tension leaves my body as the world around me ceases to exist. It's just him. Nothing else matters.

"Hey, Little Buddy. I missed you."

"I missed you too." He tightens his hold around my shoulders as I choke back my emotions. "Are we going home?"

"No, not yet," I rasp. "But I'm staying here. With you. What do you say? Do you think Nana will let me stay?"

Isaac rushes out a yes as he curls into me, all while my chest warms. Mom was right. I needed to go away for *me*, so I could be a better father to Isaac, but God was it hard to be away from him.

And now that I'm back, I'm going to make his life better, and I'm going to fix the mess his mother made.

I have to.

Isaac and I play until dinner time and then it's not long before he's tired again. Maybe Mom's idea that he's more relaxed isn't far off, but instead of easing my mind, it makes me feel worse for leaving.

We snuggle in bed as I read him his favorite bedtime story, but I'm only partway through the fifth page when his breathing slows, and with a soft smile gracing his lips, he drifts off to sleep.

At first, I can't bring myself to leave, but the second I close my eyes, a metaphorical brick hits me in the face, making me drowsy, and I long for bed. I haven't slept properly for over twenty-four hours and I'm at my limit.

After saying goodnight to Mom and thanking her again for all that she does, I settle into the spare room just as my phone goes off with a string of messages. I don't have to look to know who it is and I internally groan.

My teammates or as I like to call them... Fuckers.

Reed: Anyone heard from East?

Dylan: No, but I know he's back

Luke: You know? Is there something you want to tell us? That sounds stalkerish

Dylan: He was photographed at the airport, dick

Luke: That doesn't help your cause

Dylan: Summer saw it online

Luke: Sure, it was Summer

Dylan: Fuck you, man

Luke: I love you

Reed: Now, now. Let's not fight. Thank you for letting us know, Dyl. Maybe one of us should call him

No. Jesus.

Easton: Don't fucking call me. I'm fine

Luke: Good job, Team. It worked

Fuck. I walked right into that. A few of my teammates started this stupid group chat when Luke was going through something last season. I was included in case he needed parenting advice—not that I ever gave him any through texts. If he truly needed me, he'd have to grow some balls and ask.

Now that he's happy, the group chat has been changed to *my* support group because apparently they want to help me with all the crazy going on in my life. Spoiler alert...they can't. No one can. It's between me and Macy and it's staying that way.

So, like always, I show them how much this group means to me and *leave.*

But less than a second later, my phone chimes again. Just like I knew it would.

LUKE ADDED YOU TO THE GROUP

Fuckers. It's the same routine. All the time. I can't escape it.

Luke: See you next week, East

I roll my eyes, but I can't complain. I could easily block them, but a little part of me—a part way, way in the back of my mind—likes knowing someone cares about what I'm going through. Even if I don't want them to. They've been checking in on me since the season ended, and while I've never responded until today, I know they've got my back.

And now that Macy's on the run and practice is about to pick up again... I'm going to need it.

CHAPTER THREE

EASTON

"The man of the hour is back," Luke Bennett, cocky tight end—and the reason for the damn group chat—calls out, and I pause at the threshold of the locker room, hoping like hell he's talking to someone else. But of course, he's not.

I had planned to arrive early so I wouldn't have to engage in any bullshit catch-up talk, but life decided it had other plans so I'm walking directly into the firing squad.

When I look up, all eyes are on me and I internally groan. It's the first time I've seen anyone since the TV series aired, and I know what they're waiting for. But I refuse to give them another show.

I refuse to give my teammate Zane any more of my time or energy. He slept with Macy. I said my piece and now I'm moving on. She's no longer my problem and neither is he.

Beelining for my locker, I only pause to nod at our assistant coach, then I'm on my way again, dropping my bag with a thud after making it without comment.

"Where'd you disappear to?" Luke says from beside me, making me cringe. Guess I thought too soon. "We missed you on the group chat."

I quietly groan, ignoring him, as always, but as I'm throwing my phone into my locker, it lights up with a text.

Luke: You can't hide forever

Dick. I'd love to say he's changed since becoming a dad, but he really hasn't. Yes, he's dropped the playboy persona and become a loyal puppy when it comes to his wife, Amelia. But he's still a cocky motherfucker and he's still goddam annoying.

> Luke: We know where you are

He sends another text and I imagine him saying the words in a creepy, stalkerish voice, grimacing with secondhand embarrassment. If only I could escape him. Escape all of them for that matter. But I can't.

Although... I wonder if Isaac wants to visit Scotland? It's peaceful there. No cocky football players, no group chat, no ex. Maybe it's time I consider retiring. Too bad I love it so much.

> Reed: Luke, that was creepy. East, it's good to have you back

Thank you, Reed. The sensible one in the group. I hold up my phone and turn to face Luke, making a point of switching it off without responding, and of course, he laughs.

I'm thankfully left in peace to get changed, but the second my cleats hit the turf, my luck runs dry.

"Wilder, you're running drills with Fitzpatrick," Coach calls out.

The fuck. With Zane? He can't be serious. Sure, I'll have to play with him eventually, but day one. *Minute* one. Really?

"Coach, I think—"

"I don't care what you think, Wilder. You and Fitz need to sort your shit out today or I'll drop you both. We've got plenty of time to find replacements."

He's bullshitting. He won't drop us. At least he won't drop *me*. But that's not the point. He's right. We're a team and Zane's likely to step up into Dylan's position as receiver now that he's retired. May as well get this over with.

"Fitzpatrick, you're with me. Let's do this."

Zane smirks, and the urge to punch the grin right off his face has me clenching my fist. But Reed notices, and subtly shakes his head as I stifle a sarcastic laugh. That guy sees everything. Only I wasn't actually going to punch him. *I don't think.* Not today anyway. I'm smarter than that.

After taking his sweet-ass time to meander over, Zane stands a few feet in front of me and holds his arms wide. "Should we get this over with?"

Keeping a straight face, I grab a ball as I answer. "I don't know what you're talking about."

"You want to deck me," he explains even though we both know I was lying. "And I'd love to stop walking around waiting to be decked."

"You think I'm going to deck you?"

"Aren't you?"

"Believe it or not, I don't dwell on the past. I couldn't give a fuck about you and Macy. I'm here to play football. You're my teammate. I'll be civil. But make no mistake, if you cross me again, I won't hesitate to fuck you up. Or maybe I'll leave you hanging. I like the thought of you 'waiting to be decked.' That sounds more fun."

Zane laughs, but there's a hint of something else simmering beneath the surface, and I can't tell if it's nerves or regret. But before I can figure it out, his expression turns.

"I'm not going to apologize, if that's what you're thinking."

"Wouldn't dream of asking. Like I said, I don't care. It's done. Let's focus on the game. It's a new season and we've got another Super Bowl to win."

Zane's eyes narrow as he processes my words. I'm only half lying. I don't care about Macy cheating anymore. In fact, it was a blessing. The push I needed to officially end things with her. And maybe that's why she did it. She wanted to leave. I wanted her gone, but I also wanted her present for Isaac's life and was willing to fake it indefinitely. But when our business became public, I couldn't take it anymore. And that's the part I hate. I'm not delusional; I chose a career in the public eye. But I never chose *that*. I never asked for that. So if I was going to deck him for anything, it would be because he decided to talk about my personal life on that damn TV show.

"Okay," Zane nods as he finally steps closer. "Moving on."

"Nope," Luke cuts in, stepping beside me, coming out of nowhere. "I'm not moving on."

"Luke—"

"Hear me out. Is it any of my business—"

"*No.*" It's really fucking not. I glare his way but he chuckles.

"That was rhetorical; I wasn't finished. I know it's none of my business, but if this fucker..." He points to Zane. "If Zane's going to be a starter this year, then we can't have you two pissed off at each other."

"I'm not pissed, I'm—"

"Bullshit. You're fucking ropeable."

"What the hell is ropeable?" I turn to Zane, and for once I think we're on the same page because he too is clueless.

Luke laughs again. "It's cool, huh? I learned it from Hayley, Amelia's friend," he adds like we haven't all met his wife's Australian friend. "It means you're furious," he continues while we both stare at him. "I imagine it to mean you want to wring his neck, you're that angry."

What the fuck? He's using Australian terms now. As if he wasn't annoying enough.

I stare at him deadpan while Zane laughs. "I like it. I'm going to steal that word." *Jesus, he's just as bad as Luke.*

"If I'm ropeable about anything, it's this goddamn conversation. Luke, I'm sure you're needed somewhere else. Zane, let's go."

Luke grabs my arm before I've taken a step and pulls me to a stop. "Wait." He turns back to Zane. "Grow the fuck up, Fitzpatrick, and apologize so we can all be a happy family again."

"I have nothing to be sorry about. I didn't know she was his girl."

That's not the point but I keep quiet. I wasn't kidding; I want to move on.

"If you accidentally trip over someone, do you say sorry?"

"Yes, but it's not the same."

"God, you're a fucker." Luke shakes his head incredulously and I almost laugh. I remember calling him that many times before, and now look at him, trying to make things right. This could be a proud moment for me...if I cared.

"Okay. Jesus." Zane turns to me and takes a deep breath. "I'm sorry I *accidentally* found myself with my dick inside your girl. It won't happen again."

I'm so far past the point with this drama that I actually laugh.

"Okay, great. Glad we got that out in the open. Can we practice now?"

"What? I don't get a thanks?"

"Fuck no. But you can rest assured, your face is safe. I won't try to rearrange it."

Luke smiles triumphantly as though he just changed the world before jogging away, leaving Zane and me alone until our receiver coach arrives.

"You two work out your differences?" he asks with his brows raised.

"Of course. Like Luke wanted... we're one big happy family."

"That's what we like to hear. Now, line up for some tracking drills. Thomas is on his way over."

As if waiting for an introduction, our quarterback, Thomas Kelly, joins us with a smile, grabbing my arm as Zane runs off to get in position.

"I'm sorry you have to work so closely with him," he says, his eyes locked on Zane. "I wouldn't fault you if you *accidentally* kneed him in the balls."

I've always liked Thomas. He's a solid captain but still keeps mostly to himself. It's a good combination. "Thanks, Kelly." I offer him a smirk. "I'll keep that in mind."

After practice, Coach Pearce announces that our new team owner will be here to meet us on Friday, and a few of my teammates groan. To say I was shocked when our previous owner sold the team is the understatement of the year. We'd just won the Super Bowl. We were champions, he was the face of the team... and he left? Seems crazy to me.

But it turns out, he'd been planning it for years, wanting to get into movie producing—hence the reason for our TV show. No one knew he was the puppet master for that little production.

The only thing I know about the new owner is that he's the youngest to ever buy a team, and he's here to "shake things up,"—Keeley's words not mine—whatever that means. I haven't looked him up yet, and unlike her, I don't tend to stalk people's social media presence, so I have no idea what to expect. But I figure, as long as I do my job and do it well, I've got nothing to worry about.

I actually doubt anyone on the team needs to be worried. Why would you change a championship roster? You'd be crazy. At least wait to see how this season goes. If we make a mess of things, then sure, shake it up, but for now, he'd be better to just let things play out.

But who am I to talk about big business decisions?

"Do you think the management team will change?" one of the guys on our defensive team asks from behind me, concern clear in his voice.

I don't wait for anyone to respond, because a second later, we're dismissed, and I'm out of there. One day down, and it wasn't as painful as I thought it would be.

The group chat lights up on my drive home, and I don't have to look to know they'll be covering one of two topics—my talk with Zane or speculation about the new owner. Since I have more important things to concern myself with, I mute the chat and focus on the shitstorm I'm coming home to. My phone rings as that thought enters my mind and Macy's name flashes on my screen—making me deal with the storm sooner than I would have liked.

"Is this a dream?" I ask by way of an answer and immediately regret not calling it a nightmare.

Macy laughs sarcastically. "Come on, Easton. I've known you for years; you're no comedian."

"Really?" I scoff. "Now that's funny, because our entire relationship was a joke."

"Ugh." Macy sighs as I pull up at a red light. "I didn't call to get in another argument."

"Then why did you call *today*, when I've been calling *you* all week?"

"I had some free time. Are you back?"

For fuck's sake. "I am."

"Have you been by the house?"

"I have. Don't you listen to your voicemails?"

"No. I never do. You know that. If you want me, you need to text me."

I roll my eyes and take off as the light turns green, putting my foot down harder than I should. "*Or*," I snap in frustration, "you could return my goddamn calls."

"That's what I'm doing."

"*Fuck*. Okay. Where are you?"

"Like you, I needed a break. I'm spending some time at a wellness retreat in Arizona."

"And that couldn't wait until I was home so that one of us was here for Isaac."

"Your mom was there."

"He needs a parent."

"Come on; she's a better parent than I ever was."

That's not a lie but... "She's not *his* parent. She's mine and no matter what I think about your parenting skills, Isaac doesn't see it that way. He wanted *you*."

"I'll be back. Soon. I just need—"

"*Don't*." I cut her off before she hits me with excuses. "I'm sick of the games. If you want out, tell me, and it'll be easier for us to move forward."

"Aww, you miss me."

The fuck? "What the hell did I say to make you come to that conclusion?"

"Easton. I don't know why you're so angry. I never wanted this. It was all you. But I've tried. I really have."

My fists tighten on the steering wheel as I suck in a breath, trying hard not to raise my voice. "Do you want to be in Isaac's life or not?"

"Of course I do. I couldn't bear the thought of never seeing him again."

My teeth clench as I groan. "That's not the same thing, Macy."

"That's all I've got right now. I'll call you in a few weeks."

"A few weeks?"

"Yes, they frown upon using phones here and—"

"We need to talk about the house."

"Don't worry. Paul is going to get a great price for it."

"I don't want to sell it."

"What? I didn't think you'd want to live there after, you know..."

She trails off and my entire body stiffens. "After what?"

"You know?"

"No, I don't. Enlighten me." My mind reels with what she's about to say, and if I'm right in my thinking, I'm going to need to destroy more than a castle.

"I thought you knew."

Fuck. "You took Zane to my house?"

"Zane? No. That was at the Chambers Hotel."

I instantly relax and yet... "I don't need the fucking details. Who else did you cheat on me with."

"Brant Webster."

"Who?"

"The guy that painted the mural on the Westerly Hotel."

"The graffiti guy?"

"He prefers to be called an artist."

"I'm done. Tell your agent he's dealing with *me* now. It's my house. I call the shots. And if you don't speak to your son within the next couple of days, don't bother calling him at all. Ever. Happy? I made the decision for you. Bye, Macy."

I hang up as I pull over to the side of the road, something I probably should have done when I first answered. My heart pounds as a tightness fills my chest.

I never planned on giving her an ultimatum, but enough is enough and she pushed me to the edge.

My priority in all of this is Isaac. He deserves better. He deserves the world, and I will fight anyone that says otherwise.

But if she doesn't call...if my plan backfires... What the hell do I tell Isaac?

Chapter Four

PAIGE

A MONTH LATER

We've got the first pics of Billionaire Christian Mikkleson and his new mystery girl in what appears to be a hotel jacuzzi. Now we know he's well and truly moved on but has anyone heard from Paige?

The phone drops from my hand as I suck in a breath. Another day, another headline. Another piece of false information.

That's not Christian's new girl. It's *me*. It was taken almost a year ago. And the only reason no one has figured it out is because I'm wearing a wig. Another game of ours.

God, I feel icky.

I hate that my name is still being associated with Christian's, but I guess it could be worse. At least I wasn't identified. *For now.*

Staring down at my phone, I consider calling him again to complain, but he didn't answer my first three calls, and I seriously doubt he's behind this. Especially now that there's photo evidence, and it's not exactly a flattering image. He's too vain to have released that.

Whether or not it was him, we need to talk. For the last two weeks I've been hit with headline after headline about my sex life with Christian—the games we played, the money we spent. A false version of events anyway.

And while no one has mentioned me by name, it won't be long before someone puts two and two together, and I need to stop that from happening.

Lying back against my pillows, I close my eyes just as my phone buzzes with another alert. I'd love to be the type of person who could ignore it, knowing it's likely to be something I don't want to see, but I can't do that. Social media is my life; I'd be a nobody without it. And while I really wish that wasn't the case, I can't change the fact that it is.

Leaning over the edge of the bed, I curse and grunt as I stretch to reach my cell, the tips of my fingers brushing the edge. Just a little bit—

"Goddammit."

I fall to the floor with a thud, my shoulder colliding with the frame of my bed, making me cry out in pain. All for a stupid gossip headline.

I rub at the dull ache, which will surely be a bruise come morning, and pick up my phone, finding a text from Christian instead.

And a photo.

Not the same photo that's already been leaked online. Another one. One that clearly shows my face mid-orgasm with Christian's head nestled between my legs.

And again, I'm nauseous.

> The A-hole: I don't know how they got this, but you know what they're like. (Shrug emoji)

A goddamn shrug emoji? Like it's no big deal. And who are *they*?

> Paige: Who? And why the hell does a photo like that still exist?

> The A-hole: Relax. It's harmless and they're not going to release it. I just thought you should know that they've seen it

> Paige: Who the fuck is THEY?

> The A-hole: My family. I thought you knew they were behind the leaks

What the hell?

His family. *Jesus.*

Does that mean the leaks have been for me? Are they threats? A way to ensure my silence. *Who does that?*

And if it was them, are they willing to sacrifice their son? I mean, they practically gave him a loaded weapon for his own demise without him even realizing it. That photo will ruin his business reputation just as much as it will ruin mine. You'd think they'd want to keep their son's life private. Although it's safe to say, in the media, Christian's been painted as a hero in our breakup, so he'd probably come out of it unscathed. While I'd be called a whore. The tramp that tried to deprave the innocent young businessman.

Which, coincidently, is actually what his parents already think of me. It's been their opinion of me from the get-go. Never mind that it was the other way around. I was the innocent and naive one when we met.

I can't win.

I want to scream.

I want to post Christian's tiny dick pic all over the Internet and tell the world he gets his size from his dad. But I can't do that. I have to be the bigger person and take it like the proper young woman I was raised to be— with poise and grace.

But that doesn't mean I have to be nice to Christian. It's time he learned what his parents are really like.

My fingers run wild as I type a response, pointing out exactly what he and his family can do with their photos and their stories. As I'm halfway through, my phone buzzes again and I pause, second-guessing myself.

Dammit.

> The A-hole: Should we meet up to talk about it all? I'll be in LA next week

Is he kidding me? Meeting up is the last thing we should do.

> Paige: Or you could tell your parents to drop it and then we agree to never see each other again

> The A-hole: I'm going to ask you again... Do you know anything?

Jesus. The short answer is yes, but the long answer is so much more complicated than that. I have information on them. That's what the threats are about. But I have no idea what to do with that information or if I even want to do *anything* at all.

I'm not blackmailing them. I'm not holding it over their heads. I left and I took the information with me. They should have let it go.

> Paige: I don't know what you're talking about. I just want a fresh start

> The A-hole: Good enough for me

Great. But will it be good enough for your parents?

I throw my phone onto the carpet and drop my head against the bed, blowing out a slow breath. I barely get a second of reprise when there's a soft knock on my door, and my dad calls out, not waiting for a response before he pops his head in.

"Only me."

I snort out a laugh as he enters. "I know, Dad. Who else would it be?"

He smiles until he spots me on the floor. "What are you doing down there?"

"Yoga?" I lie, putting on my most innocent smile so I don't have to explain why I fell off the bed.

Dad chuckles as he nods. "Makes sense. Are you ready to pick up your keys?"

Ready? I've been ready since the day I arrived.

The time between me finally agreeing to move and me packing up my entire life was a lot shorter than Dad had anticipated. The second I agreed to his offer to join him here, he bought me an apartment in the same building as his, but then he decided to have it renovated to include some of the luxuries he thought I couldn't live without—like a steam shower and a walk-in closet. Neither essential but offers I'd never say no to.

Because of that, I've been living with dear ole Dad while they finish. And now it's done.

I get my own space again. I'm free. Within the restraints of living in the same building as the man that half raised me.

"I was born ready." I smile wide, making him scoff in return.

"Come on, I don't cramp your style that much."

"You don't," I agree. *For the most part he was working.* "But I like my own space."

Despite only just turning twenty-five, I've lived on my own for over six years.

I love my mom, but she can be a handful, and she knows it. Plus, she practically kicked me out by presenting me with the deed to her old Fifth Avenue apartment when I turned eighteen. I suppose I could have had a friend move in, so I wasn't alone, but I liked the solace. That apartment was the only place I was able to truly be me.

"I get it. I would have done anything to have lived by myself at eighteen," Dad notes and it's my turn to scoff.

"You were only twenty, Dad. You weren't that much older."

"I know, but I worked hard for that apartment. Plus...a lot can happen in two years."

"I worked hard too. I grew up being raised by you and Mom; I deserve more than an apartment."

"You're right. You deserve two. And now you have them. One in New York and one in San Francisco. And you say you're not spoiled."

"I never said that. I'm well aware that I am. And I graciously thank you for it. But I promise I have plans to start paying you back as soon as I've got my footing again. I could afford to move out now and live somewhere a little less *extravagant*, but I know you want me close, so I made the sacrifice."

Dad bites back a grin. "What a darling daughter you are."

"Always."

I'm sunshine and lollipops until I have the keys in my hand and it all becomes real. I'm making a home here. In San Francisco. When I always assumed I'd end out my days in New York.

"You're doing the right thing," Dad says, cutting into my thoughts as I stare down at the new life sitting in my palms.

"That may be true, but it feels wrong."

"You need to put New York behind you and focus on your life here. It's going to be a big year, and the D'Angelo Foundation needs you."

"*Mom* needs me." I may not have lived at home, but I saw her every other day. I may complain about her constantly, but we were close.

"She doesn't need you. She pretends to need people so they don't leave. Trust me, this will be good for her. And you."

"You don't have to be an asshole. You loved her once."

"*Once*? Paige, honey, I *still* love her. And I have no doubt I'll love that woman until I'm old and gray. She's the one that walked away, remember?"

My heart seizes but I ignore it. "That may be true, but you love your work more. Always have."

"Not all of us earn money simply by breathing, Paige." His words sting. I know he's talking about Mom, but I was born into money all the same. On both sides. Yes, my father worked hard for his, but at the end of the day, it's still money that *I'll* get 'simply by breathing.'

"You didn't exactly come from nothing," I snap, a little embarrassed. "You weren't broke. Grandpa would roll over in his grave if he heard you saying that. And you know I'm in the same situation, right?"

"Wrong."

"Wrong?"

"About *you*. You're earning your money by working. You've been a spokesperson for the Youth Voices charity since you were a teenager. You're a model, a business owner, and an incredible artist." He pauses with a brow raised, waiting for me to comment, but I let it slide. I don't like talking about my art. It's the only part of my life I've been able to keep secret. "You may have those opportunities because you were born into wealth, but *like me*, you've paved your own way and I'm proud of you. Always have been. Even when you refused to talk to me."

Guilt gnaws away at my insides. Especially considering I only agreed to move here for my own benefit—and he knows it. To his credit, he hardly ever mentions it. Until now. Though, he's joking.

"Relax, I'm—"

"Kidding, I know. You've forgiven my *brattiness*."

"You weren't being a brat. You were misinformed. I should have worked harder to ensure you knew the truth. But this is the world we live in. It's impossible to know what to believe. Even when it comes to family."

He's not wrong. Christian's family is proving that right now. And I have to admit, I kind of like having two sides to my family again.

"You know, I might actually miss living with you. A little," I say honestly before quickly adding another "*might.*"

"Well, I *know* I'll miss you. I'm not going to pretend otherwise. Why don't you come to the stadium tomorrow? The team has a preseason practice session. You could watch from my suite."

"From your suite? You mean I can't stand on the sidelines?"

"Not a chance. If I could put a restraining order on the entire team and force them to stay at least a hundred feet away from you, I would."

"Come on, they're not *all* bad."

"No, they're not but I heard what you said. You may not have explicitly told me, but I know that asshole hurt you. I don't want to be responsible for someone else doing the same."

He knows because the world knows. Only my ex painted a very different picture. *My* truth was getting in the way of *his* story. So, he rewrote the narrative. Kind of like the heroes across history. And I let him. I needed a reason to disappear, and he gave it to me. We'd been on the rocks for months. He traveled often, so it was normal for us to go weeks, sometimes months, without seeing each other. We'd share "I miss yous" on social media to keep the dream alive. But toward the end, we barely spoke. I'm not naive; I know he had women in multiple countries, but in New York, in America, he was mine, and I was okay with that. It was a relationship of convenience. But it ran its course.

As much as I want to support my dad, now is not a good time to be thrust back into the public eye. And while I may not be a fan of sports per se, I know the change in ownership of a team is a big deal, and it's a bigger deal when it's on the back of a Super Bowl win.

The media will be everywhere. All the time.

I'm already in the gossip columns on a daily basis; I don't need to add fuel to the fire. And Dad doesn't need that either.

I can see it now. *Has Paige D'Angelo moved on with one of her father's players?*

I'd rather avoid that if I can.

Plus, I have no intention of dating anyone at the moment. Things are complicated enough.

"I think I'll pass this time. Maybe another day?"

"Sounds good."

I settle into my new apartment, and by seven p.m., I'm starving for something my dad didn't have pre-stocked in my fridge. A sweet treat.

So after throwing on a more respectable outfit, I go in search of cookies, and call my mom on the way, missing the sound of her voice.

"Hi Sweetie," she answers nicely, and then... "When are you coming home?"

"*Mom.*"

"I'm kidding. I'm kidding." *She's not.* "Have you found anyone special yet?"

I don't bother hiding my groan as I answer. "As I told you last time we spoke, I'm not *looking* for anyone."

"I know you said that. But it wouldn't hurt to put yourself out there again. Christian's moved on and—"

"I look like the poor little girl that got left behind?"

"No. Of course not. Never. No." *That's a yes.*

If she was standing in front of me, I'd give her a death stare. But since she's not, the man walking toward me in the lobby is bearing the brunt of my gaze.

And now he's stopping. *Dammit.*

I hold up my phone to signal that I'm busy, but he doesn't take the hint, asking me if I'm Paige from the Internet, his voice in a whisper. I shake my head no but he doesn't believe me. And when I take a step out of his way, he follows.

A shiver runs through me, and I'm about to tell him to politely fuck off, when a man comes into view, with a newly familiar glare, and my pulse spikes.

"Oh my God!" I gasp out loud. "I'm sorry," I tell both the stalker guy in front of me and my mom on the phone. "I just saw a long-lost friend," I lie. "I have to go." I walk away without a backward glance and lower my phone, my mom's rushed "What?" the last thing I hear before I hang up.

My lips pull into a smile and *I* become the stalker, following my new "friend" until he stops in front of the elevator, only then calling out, "Window-seat guy!"

To my surprise, he turns, his expression doing nothing to hide his shock.

What are the chances?

I glance over my shoulder to make sure my stalker hasn't followed and breathe a sigh of relief as I rush to catch up to the only person I know in this city other than my dad.

And he just unknowingly came to my rescue. Again.

I owe him a drink.

CHAPTER FIVE

EASTON

I stand frozen as the woman from the plane jogs over, her expression full of excitement. "You turned?" she asks, the surprise in her voice mimicking my thoughts.

I did turn. But why? I have no idea, because... "You called me window-seat guy?" It's like I recognized her voice.

"Yep. That's my name for you." She beams and if I was any other human, I'm sure it would be infectious. "Got a problem with it?" She raises an eyebrow and pops her hip, making my lips twitch. But I don't smile.

"Would it matter?"

"Nope. I like it so it's going to stick until you give me something else to call you. Anywho... What brings you here?" She bites her lip and it's not my mouth that twitches this time. It's been a while for me, and my cock is in need of some attention. Attention it's not getting from a stranger I met on a plane. "Were you looking for me?" she adds.

"What?" I snap out of my thoughts and frown. "Why would I be looking—"

"I'm joking. Since you have bags of food in your hands, I'm guessing you either live here or you're visiting someone. Someone that is *not* me."

"Good guess."

"You're not going to tell me which one, are you?"

"Nope." Though I am curious as to why *she's* here.

"Okay. Well, I live here." She laughs, answering my silent question and *what the hell are the chances?* "I'm on the twelfth floor," she continues. "I just moved. Sort of. It's a beautiful building. Don't you think?"

"It's alright. I guess. Anywho..." I use her term though my tone is significantly less peppy than hers. "I need to get this upstairs." I point toward the elevator and fake a grin. "Nice seeing you again."

"Paige," she offers.

I didn't ask, but... "Paige. Nice seeing you again, *Paige*."

The doors open and I move to step into the elevator, hoping to get away, but when she follows, I stop, an awkward tension settling between us. I stare her way and she raises her hands into the air. "I'm not following you. I was going out for cookies but then there was a creepy guy following me so I thought I should go home. I live here. Remember?"

"Yep. I do." And now I'm stuck on the creepy guy following her. *Is the fucker still here?* I glance over my shoulder, searching, and completely forget she's still standing in front of me until she speaks.

"Are you looking for him?"

"What?"

"The creepy guy. Are you looking for him?"

"No," I lie, my eyes drifting back to hers, finding her bottom lip trapped between her teeth as she bites back a smile.

"Okay." She nods. "My mistake. But ooooh... I almost forgot." She does that finger gun motion as her smile widens. "I owe you a drink."

"What?" I'm getting whiplash with the way this conversation is changing. "Why?"

"For helping me."

"When did I help you?"

"On the plane, you came to my rescue with that jerk in my seat, and then again just now."

"I didn't—"

"Believe me, you did. So drink?"

Like always, the answer no pops into my head so fast you'd think I'd set it as a default response. But unlike other times, today my thoughts go to war. *Why not have a drink? Isaac's usually asleep by now and... Isaac...that's why. My life is complicated enough and I'm playing catch-up. But it's just a drink. A* thank you *drink. Why am I making a big deal out of this? She might be one of those people that always needs to settle debts. I know I am. I hate the thought of owing people. But in this situation, that's a* her *problem, not a* me *problem. Plus I do have food in my hands. No. It's a no.*

Decision made.

"I have to get this upstairs." I subtly nod toward the elevator. "Maybe another time?" *Maybe another time? What time? I barely have time to scratch myself.*

"Another time it is. I'll hold you to that. I'm sure we'll run into each other around the building, since we both live here." Her eyes widen while my brows furrow. *Maybe I should have said yes and gotten it over with. It's too late now.*

"I'm sure we will."

"I *knew it*!" Paige fists pumps the air and smiles brightly, confusing the hell out of me. "Thank you."

"For what?"

"You weren't going to tell me if you lived here or not, remember?"

Releasing an exasperated laugh, I shake my head. I wasn't going to tell *anyone* I lived here. It's supposed to be short-term, but it's now week four and I've yet to decide what the hell to do next. I want to find a house and give Isaac a solid base, but I don't want to rush it. Right now, all my decisions are coming from a place of panic, and I can't afford to put housing into that mix.

Paige stares at me in anticipation and my shoulders drop. "Well done," I deadpan. "Great detective work. You win."

She bites back a smirk and raises a single brow, trying not to laugh. "Was that a joke? Mr..."

"Window-Seat Guy."

Her jaw drops before she bursts out laughing, and I can't help but smile. *Who the hell am I?*

"Window-seat guy... I can't *wait* for that drink. You have layers. I like it."

"Good to know."

"Alright. I won't keep you any longer. See you around."

She lifts her hand in a wave as though she didn't *just* tell me some guy was stalking her and is expecting me to walk away. I'm not.

I fold my arms over my chest and stare at her, waiting for her to catch up.

"What's going on right now?" she asks, pointing to my tense stance. "What are you doing?"

"I'm waiting."

"For what?"

I tilt my head and raise my brows. "Get in the elevator. You were going home, remember?"

"I—" She cuts herself off and nods before moving past me to press the button. "Of course. Let's go."

When the doors open for a second time, I gesture for her to go first, and this time, instead of hitting me with her usual bright over-the-top grin, she smiles shyly and thanks me under her breath.

"No problem." I nod, forcing myself to look away when a tightness fills my chest. I've got enough on my plate; I don't need to start worrying about a stranger too.

We're both silent as we travel toward our floors, and when the elevator stops on level twelve, I cut in before she can thank me again, needing to change the weird tension that's settled between us.

"I guess you owe me another drink now," I say, keeping a straight face.

Thankfully she laughs.

I text my mom when I'm in front of my apartment asking if it's safe to come in. It's after Isaac's bedtime, so if I go inside and he's not *quite* asleep, she'll kill me for making him excited. I hate not seeing him, but at the same time, I know it's important to give him a proper routine when everything else in his life is up in the air.

Like our goddamn living arrangements. I don't want him to get used to this apartment, but at the same time, I don't know where I want to live. My old house is a no-go zone now that I know it was ruined by Macy, and if I'm honest, even the neighborhood's a little tainted.

Especially considering I've since discovered she slept with one of our neighbors as well. Three guys and counting. Something I wish I'd known *before* giving her an ultimatum. Because she goddamn fulfilled it, calling Isaac the next day. And now instead of having her out of our lives for good, she's stringing him along, when we both know she's not in it for the long run.

But what do I do? She's his mom and clearly going through something.

So, while I refuse to help her, I can't exactly cut her off completely. Isaac loves her.

It's a catch-22. I don't want to hurt him by pushing his mom out of his life, but by keeping her around, it's setting him up for devastation.

I need to focus my energy, but at the moment, I'm spending all my time just staying afloat.

My phone buzzes, and I'm thankful I didn't have to wait long for my mom to text back.

Mom: You're safe. He's asleep

Taking a deep breath, I open the door and smile when her weary eyes meet mine. "How was he?"

"We had a good day. He only asked about the witch once."

"*Mom.*"

"Don't '*Mom*' me. I don't call her that in front of Isaac, but I'm not holding back when it comes to you."

"Fair enough." He'd been asking about her a little less every day, but it only takes one call and she's back in his orbit again. God, I wish I knew what was best for him. "Did he ask about me?"

"No."

I frown and she laughs. "But he did talk about you nonstop. You're definitely his favorite person."

"Feeling is mutual." I smile as my heart pounds in my chest. In Isaac's mind, I'm a hero. In my mind, it's a very different story, but I'm working on it. "Anyway, how are *you* feeling?" I ask. She was more tired than usual when she arrived this morning, and I know it's because I'm asking for too much. "Are you ready for me to get a nanny yet?"

"Never. I told you that. In a few years, Isaac won't want anything to do with his Nana. I'm cashing in on it now. While I can."

"You'd tell me if it was getting hard though, right?"

"Probably not."

"*Mom.*"

"What? You need me. I'm here. It's what moms do."

My mind conjures up an image of Macy and I huff out a laugh. "Not all moms. Some leave the state."

Mom's face drops and she walks over, pulling me into a hug that I don't reciprocate. I don't need sympathy; I need to sort my life out.

"It's going to be okay, East. I promise it will all work out."

Mom leaves not long after our chat, and it seems like barely any time has passed before she's back the next day, ready to help out again.

Since it's preseason, I have a little more time on my hands, but I know once the season begins, something has to change. I can't expect her to keep driving across town every day to help out.

"I've been thinking," she says after breakfast when Isaac's out of earshot. "Since Wednesday seems to be late for you and Thursdays are usually early, what if Isaac comes to my place on Wednesday for a sleepover each week? It will give you time to yourself and save me on travel."

My eyes flash to Isaac as he crashes two wooden trucks into each other and my chest tightens. It makes sense to help Mom out but... "I don't need time to myself."

Mom's brows furrow and she frowns. "You've never been a good liar."

"I know." I sigh. "I just don't know if I'll be able to stay away from him. I already miss out on seeing him during away games. But I can drive him to your place more. That's not an issue."

"What about we try it next week? It might be good for all involved."

"Go! Go! Go!" Isaac calls out as two of his trucks race across the floorboards, hitting the wall on the opposite side of the room.

"It would be good for him to have a bit more space. And a yard to run around in."

I grew up on a decent-sized property in North Carolina, with lots of space to run around. Without it, I probably wouldn't be the football player I am today. When I paid for Mom to move here a few years ago, I insisted she have a yard, despite her arguments. I thought she'd regret it if she had grandchildren and nowhere for them to play. I was thinking about Keeley, or my older sister, Addison, when she visited. I never considered I'd be the first to bless her with a rugrat. But here we are.

"So that's a yes?" Mom asks enthusiastically.

"That's a 'let's give it a try.'"

"Deal. But I think you'll find you love it."

"You might be right."

"I usually am."

She sets about making Isaac lunch while I say goodbye.

"Little man, I have to go into work again, but Nana's here." We've been playing all morning which means this could go either way. Some days he pushes me out the door because he's ready for someone new, and on other days he gets upset because we've been spending so much time together and he doesn't want to let go. I pause, my breath caught, as I wait.

"Okay, Dad. Lub you."

The air leaves my lungs as I bend down to pull him into a hug. "Look after Nana, okay?"

"Yep."

He jumps up and runs into the kitchen while I sigh in relief. It's never easy leaving him, but saying goodbye when he's crying makes it so much harder.

"I'll see you in a few hours, Mom. Let me know if you need anything on my way home or if anything—"

"We'll be all right," she cuts me off, lifting Isaac into her arms. "Off you go."

"Bye, Daddy."

Pulling my cap low on my forehead, I throw my bag over my shoulder and walk to the door, calling out as I leave, "Love you, Isaac."

"Lub you."

Isaac's voice remains in my mind as the tension of each goodbye swirls in my gut, and I'm still in my head as I take the elevator down to my truck.

How am I going to do this when the season begins? How am I going to travel with the team, knowing he's at home without either of his parents? My mom's great, but she's not *me*. Or even Macy.

For all her faults, and Macy has many, she was always home while I was away. That was a deal we made. And until she decided she'd had enough and cheated, it was working. Although I guess I never really knew what they got up to. He always seemed happy, but was she really looking after him?

Either way, she's keeping us in limbo now. Keeping *Isaac* in limbo. And it's *my* fault.

The elevator comes to a stop on another level, and I'm snapped out of my head as the doors open. Dropping my gaze to the floor, I step back and watch as a woman joins me inside, her long legs covered in tight black leggings that appear painted on, paired with red strappy shoes complete with a heel that could kill a man.

It's fucking hot.

And I don't have to see her face to know who the legs belong to.

"Hey, you," Paige's voice enters my mind as I glance up, her expression bright as she settles in opposite me, leaning back against the mirrored wall. "We meet again."

"We do." I nod before lifting my cap higher so I can see her properly, taking in the rest of her outfit. And immediately regretting it. She's wearing a white lace top that's basically a long bra made to look like clothes, revealing a strip of toned skin across her navel.

She's clearly dressed to impress and it's working. Though I wish it wasn't.

"Where are you off to on this fine day?" she asks, drawing my attention to her painted red lips as I watch her mouth move.

She looks like she belongs in a magazine rather than an apartment elevator. And I want out.

"I'm going to work," I answer swiftly, not bothering to elaborate. "You?" *Dammit. Why did I ask?*

Paige blows out a breath, appearing stressed, but her signature smile remains plastered on her face. "I've got a hellish day. I'm already running behind. I have a photo shoot for *Silver and Stripes* magazine in my apartment. Have you heard of it? They mix high-end fashion with business. What am I saying? Everyone's heard of them." I haven't... But that's not what has my brows furrowing. I'm wondering...*is she a model? A businesswoman? Or is she the photographer?* "Anyway," she continues, thankfully stopping me from asking since we're almost at the lobby, "I've got that, and then I'm meeting my dad for dinner—not dressed like this, obviously. I mean, I love it, but not for my dad. Then after that, I plan on curling up on the couch with a glass of wine and a good book. That's the part I'm most looking forward to. Do you read?"

"Ah—" When my mind catches up, I'm about to tell her that I do when the elevator dings and the door opens to the lobby.

"Ooh. This is me," she says before I have a chance to answer. "I'm meeting the crew here to take them upstairs. Have fun. Don't work too hard."

She waves as she walks away, and I can't stop myself from watching her leave, my gaze drawn to her every move until the doors shut again, cutting off my view.

And I literally shake off my thoughts.

What was that? She threw me off with the outfit and the talking...

She's doing that a lot. Throwing me off.

When I reach the parking garage, I jump in my truck with thoughts of Paige running on repeat in my mind. And I actually smile. Pausing with my hands on the steering wheel, I almost laugh.

She distracted me. I was spiraling, and Paige pulled me out of my head with her endless chitchat and perfect legs.

She rescued *me*.

Does this mean I owe her *a drink now?*

Chapter Six

PAIGE

"Can we try one more by the window?" the photographer asks and I move toward the window. "Actually, stop. No, that won't work. What about something a little edgy? In the bath?"

I laugh and follow her into the bathroom. I'm not sure how sitting in a bath is *edgy* but—

The photographer's assistant turns on the tap, testing the temperature of the water as he fills the bath, cutting me off mid thought.

She wants me in the water. That makes a little more sense. Especially when I glance down at my white top and instantly regret my decision to go braless. Pick your own clothes, they said. *Dammit.* This is about to get interesting.

"I'm ninety-nine percent sure this top will be see-through when wet. How does that work for the magazine?" I ask, while also contemplating how that's going to work for *me*.

"It's fine with us. If it turns out to be your best shot, we'll cover your tits with some text."

Okie dokie. "Great." I smile again. I've been photographed almost naked before, and suggestively naked, but I've never actually shown anything.

But since my motto has always been *never say never*, why not? They might end up being the photos I'm most proud of. You never know.

When the bath's full and the water is confirmed to be at the perfect temperature—whatever that means, they're not cooking a turkey—I slide in and make myself comfortable.

My already tight clothes cling to my body, and as expected, it takes barely a moment for my nipples to show through. I bite back a laugh, imagining the reception they would have received if the bath had been cold, and thank my lucky stars that it's not.

The crew takes turns assessing the new visual in front of them—me—and while they update the lighting and decide on the best angles, I don't feel self-conscious, like I thought I would. Instead, a sense of strength runs through me. And I own it.

"How do you want me?" I ask, waving my hands in the air, exuding the confidence I suddenly feel.

Then it begins.

We spend the next thirty minutes running through a series of poses—adding extra water when the bath turns cold—and when they're almost done, the photographer asks if they can pour water on my head.

Since I'm all in now, I don't have to consider it before I happily agree, knowing full well my mascara will run, assuming that's the look they're going for.

We continue on for another few minutes, and it's the most fun I've had on a photo shoot. The photographers are easygoing and open to suggestions. The crew is great. The interview—which takes place with me wrapped in a plush dressing gown—flows like a conversation with a friend.

It doesn't feel at all like work.

But I'm getting paid for it.

Yeah, I can fend for myself. Look at me. I'll be paying my dad back in no time.

Call me "boss girl."

My phone rings as the crew are packing up, and when I see that it's Dad, I frown. We're due to meet for dinner in an hour, so there's a good chance this is an "I'm sorry, Kid. I got caught up at work" call.

You'd think I'd be used to them. Calls like that were a regular occurrence during my childhood. It was an "I'm sorry" call that ended my parents' marriage. The final straw.

Yet, here I am, my chest tight, my fight response activated. I refuse to let him get away with it now that I'm here. He wanted me to come. He better damn well act like it.

"Hi Dad," I answer, ready to snap.

"Hi Kid, how was the photo shoot?" He seems cheery but he always was. He never saw it as an issue.

"It went well, thanks. Where are you?"

"I'm about ten minutes away. I know I'm early, but do you want me to pick you up on the way? So you don't have to walk."

What? My heart races as everything I was expecting throws my mind into shambles.

"Ah. Yes. Yeah. Thank you. That would be great. But I need to fix my hair and makeup. I might be a bit longer." I step back and bump into the couch, snapping me out of my fog for long enough to see my expression in the mirror.

"That—"

"Actually, I *will* be longer. Maybe thirty minutes."

Dad chuckles at my interruption. "Works for me. It'll give me time to get changed. It's been a busy day. Maybe I'll even shower for you."

A smile pulls at my lips while my mind whirs. "I'd appreciate that."

"Everything okay?" His voice softens, his tone reflecting his concern. But he doesn't need to worry, because he's already eased my mind.

"It's perfect. I'll see you soon."

Talk about an overreaction. I've been here for a month and Dad hasn't let me down.

But the team has been in the early stages of preseason. Things are ramping up now and—

I clearly have daddy issues. Maybe I need to work on that.

Thirty minutes later, I look somewhat presentable just in time for Dad to knock on the door. When I let him in, he fakes a gasp at the mess we made today.

"I could have sworn I asked the builders to make you a walk-in closet," he jokes, waving his hands at the clothes piled up on every spare surface of furniture. "I'll have them fired at once. Who do they think they are leaving my darling daughter without a space to hang her designer clothes?"

"Wow." I smile as I shake my head. "You really went all in on that joke."

"What can I say? The D'Angelos never do anything by halves."

"Oh, I know. I'm a D'Angelo and I find it quite unfortunate to have that ingrained into me. I'd love to slack off every now and then."

"You did. In high school."

I burst out laughing because he's not wrong. I spent most of my high school years rebelling against expectations. In my own way. It was my rite of passage. But at the end of the day, I was a good, easy kid and he knows it.

"Are you ready to go? Or do you need to clean up the mess first?" Dad asks, his gaze once again scanning my apartment.

"I'm good. It will still be there in the morning."

Dad scoffs out a laugh. "You are so much like me, it's scary. Your mom would never have left the house like this."

"Yes, but it's not like she would have cleaned it herself. Her house wouldn't look like this to begin with. She has fairies that ensure that doesn't happen."

"Ah yes, how could I forget about her cleaning fairies?"

Since it's a pleasant night, we ditch the car, choosing to walk the few blocks to the restaurant, and I have to admit, it's nice. Yes, we lived together until yesterday, but we fell into a pattern of merely existing. Now, we're really talking.

"How are things with the team?" I ask as the traffic whizzes past. "Do you think they have what it takes to win again?"

"They certainly think they do." Dad smiles. "But they've lost a few key players this year with Mathers retiring and Jenson out with an injury. It will be hard to fill those spots. You know how it is."

"Nope, I do *not* know. I don't follow football, remember? The last time I saw a game was when you took me to see the Giants when I was around ten."

Dad's jaw drops. "I thought you dated that college football player when you were nineteen."

"I did. But we didn't talk about football. We didn't talk much at all, really." I bounce my eyebrows and laugh when Dad's face pales.

"Paige Lucia D'Angelo, you're talking to your father here."

"What? We went to the movies. Or out dancing. What did you think I meant?"

I meant *exactly* what I was alluding to but I'm not going to tell Dad that. Though I do love messing with him since he wasn't around for all those years. And I'm clearly still fucked-up over it. "The point is...I don't know anything about football. You can say any name you want and I'd believe they played on your team."

"We need to change that. As soon as possible. But for now, all you need to know is that our star wide receiver, Ryan Gosling, is killing it this year and our quarterback, Clint Eastwood, is still a powerhouse despite his age."

He winks and I bite back a laugh. "You're really cashing in on dad jokes these days."

"Get used to it, Kid. I'm making up for lost time."

A sadness settles inside me, but this time, I'm not upset because of my own issues; I'm hurt for my dad. Yes, he made his own choices when I was younger, but he's trying now, and God knows, my mom wasn't the easiest to live with.

"I think we both have some lost time to make up for," I say, moving the conversation into dangerous "feelings" territory. "I held on to a lot of anger when you left, and I even questioned if you were calling to cancel tonight."

"God, I'm—"

"Wait. I'm not telling you this so you'll feel guilty. I said I forgave you when I moved here, and I meant it. But I'm still getting used to having you around. It'll take time."

"I know. But I promise you, you're my number one priority. I'm not going to pretend I won't be busy, because I know I will be. But if you call, I'll be there. You just have to ask."

Dad pulls me into a side hug, and while it's awkward and unfamiliar for the two of us, it's still kind of nice. And a little part of me thaws because of it.

When I first moved here, I wasn't sure I'd made the right decision, but today, after the shoot and my talk with Dad, I'm confident in my choice. I think it will be good for me.

Welcome to my new life. I'm a California girl. It's time to embrace it.

After dinner, Dad calls us a car and we go in search of ice cream—the cute little parlor by our building closes early midweek so we need another option. When our driver stops to drop us off after we finish our dessert, my gaze locks on a familiar figure, and I smile as window-seat guy slows from a run.

Dad chats with his driver while I lose all train of thought, watching as window-seat guy lifts his tee to wipe sweat from his face, giving me a clear view of his sculpted abs.

Abs I have imagined many times before while never truly picturing the perfect specimen he is.

As I ogle him from the comfort of my hiding place, he locks his palms behind his head and his biceps bulge, leading me to imagine his arms braced on a bed as he hovers above me, my legs wrapped around his back, our bod—

"Are you ready?"

"What?" I choke on thin air, my face paling as my dad's question snaps me out of my fantasy. My gaze whips around to check if he noticed what... or who I was staring at. But his warm smile suggests that he didn't.

"I can't get out until you do." He chuckles, gesturing to the door.

"Sorry, yes. I was in my own world."

"I could tell. You were staring into space."

Space? That will do. I'd rather he assume that I was lost in my head than discover I was perving on some guy in our building.

I take my time, slowly grabbing my bag before opening my door, and by the time I get out of the car, window-seat guy's gone and I'm both relieved and disappointed.

There's no reason to hide him away from my dad, but at the same time I wouldn't know how to introduce him.

Saying "Dad, this is a random guy I met on a plane. He's a little grumpy but intrigues me enough that I think we could be friends" doesn't quite feel right.

We're not friends, acquaintances, or even actually neighbors. But there's something there, hovering between us, because every time I see him my smile widens involuntarily and an excitement takes over me. I can't explain it, but I'm determined to find out what it means. Whether he likes it or not.

One can never have too many friends, and God knows, I could use a friend around here.

CHAPTER SEVEN

EASTON

For the next few weeks, I see Paige more than I've seen anyone else in my building. If I had a regular schedule, I'd seriously question if she was stalking me. But since I'm barely keeping up with where I need to be or when, I doubt she is. And if by chance she *was* up-to-date with my whereabouts, I'd have to consider hiring her as my personal assistant because my life is a mess.

I still haven't done anything about our living arrangements, and with football season ramping up, I'm hesitant to change too much because I won't be around to help Isaac settle in. Meaning...apartment living it is.

On the plus side, Isaac is loving his Wednesday-night sleepovers with his nana, and the extra time to myself doesn't hurt either.

Mom suggested I use the time to meet new "friends." Her way of suggesting I start dating again. But right now, dating isn't in the cards for me. Sex isn't even in the cards for me, and God am I suffering because of it. My hand can only do so much.

An image of Paige works its way to the forefront of my mind, like it always seems to do when I think about my poor abandoned needs, and I can't help but laugh. She's not the first attractive woman to talk to me and she won't be the last, but for some reason she's the only person in a long time that I've actually thought about after she's gone.

When I was with Macy, I never once strayed, even after we mentally separated, staying together only to keep up appearances.

Did we have sex during that time? Yes, regularly. But it was more to satisfy a *need* rather than a *want,* and I guess that wasn't enough for her in the end.

I wish we'd called it quits sooner.

Since then, I've had plenty of offers—women willing to help ease my pain now that the world, or at least America, knows I was cheated on.

They all think I'm suffering. That she left me. That it came out of nowhere. But the truth is we both checked out of our relationship *way* before the thought of cheating entered her mind.

And the other more unfortunate truth is that I've never wanted any of those women. Not even once.

Yet I can't stop thinking about Paige.

I'm convinced it's because she's everywhere. I can't escape her while other women simply come and go.

In the space of a weekend, I saw her in the lobby, the bar, the courtyard. I saw her in the damn street when I was walking home. She's *always* there, and I find myself waiting to see her...*expecting* it. It's driving me fucking crazy.

What is it about her? I'm a private person, while she tells me everything. I think before I speak, and she doesn't have a filter. She's younger than I am. I think. She's a model. Or a businesswoman. I haven't figured that out yet, but I'm leaning toward the former based on her stunning looks and what appears to be a designer wardrobe.

But even then, what the hell would I know?

The only thing I'm certain of is that she has no idea who I am. Every time we cross paths, she calls me Window-Seat Guy, and on the one occasion she saw me posing for a photo with a group of kids, she frowned, confusion clear in her expression.

And I like that.

It doesn't happen often and it means she has no idea about my life...or Macy. I'm just some guy she met on a plane.

I like being that guy. At least, for the few minutes I'm in her presence. I don't want to be him forever; I'd miss Isaac too much.

After checking my phone to find it message free, I step onto the treadmill and stare at myself in the mirrored wall of the gym, my mind whirring during one of the rare times I get to be alone.

I jog for a few minutes, trying hard to get out of my head, but it's no use. Alone time means time to think, and time to think can be dangerous.

I increase my pace to a run, hoping that will help, but I've barely made it a mile when the door beeps, signaling someone's entry, and I groan. Out loud. I'm not at all worried about them hearing how annoyed I am. No one ever uses the gym at this time. In fact, hardly anyone uses the gym. Period.

There goes my solace.

With another sigh, I continue to run, pretending I'm not staring at the entry, hoping it's a cleaner or someone that's never watched a game of football in their life and has no clue who I am.

And when the door swings open, I'm safe. On the football front anyway. But I'm in trouble for a whole other reason.

As I was saying, Paige is everywhere, and today for a change of scenery, or to make things worse, she's at the gym.

I don't look away in time—probably because I can't stop myself from checking her out—and our eyes lock in the mirror. Her jaw drops before her ever-moving mouth pulls into a grin. "Okay, the universe has to be messing with us. Don't you think?"

"Nope," I lie. While I don't believe in that crap, it is strange that she's everywhere I turn. Showing up whenever I'm thinking about her. "We live in the same building; it makes sense that we'd see each other often." I'm not sure if I'm trying to justify the logic to her or myself, but I'm going with it.

Paige thins her lips as she contemplates my response. "Do you regularly see your neighbors?"

"Yep." *Fuck no.* And even if I did, I sure as shit wouldn't notice them. I don't think I'd recognize any of them if they knocked on my door asking for sugar.

"You could be right." She shrugs, no longer pushing me. "I'm used to living in New York. Everyone was always so busy there. No one ever stopped for long enough to get to know one another, me included. People move at a slower pace here."

"Not if you come from a small town." *Dammit*, why am I still talking? She hooks me in every time. I never let anything interrupt a workout. Ever. Except Isaac. This is *my* space. My escape and yet...I've fucking stopped running. *When did I even push the pause button?*

"Ooh." Paige's grin widens, appearing positively giddy. "Are you a small-town guy?"

Fuck. "I was. Now, I live here."

"What's that like?"

"Being from a small town?"

"*Yes.* We had a house in the Hamptons, but I don't think that's really the same thing. There's always thousands of people there when I go and—"

"It's not the same. My town had *hundreds* of people, not thousands."

"Oh. Sometimes I wonder if that would have been a better way to grow up."

"It was fine. I guess it depends on your circumstances. It was hard for me to—" I cut myself off and laugh. *What am I doing?* I hate talking about myself.

Paige's brows furrow and she steps forward. "To what?"

"Never mind." I make a point of checking my watch and grimace. "I better keep going. I have to be somewhere in an hour."

"Of course." She smiles, bouncing on her toes, not a care in the world, and it hits me in the chest. What I wouldn't give to be that happy all the time. "Don't let me stop you," she continues. "Enjoy."

She spins on her toes and heads over to the weights, laying down her yoga mat before launching into a series of stretches.

In my direct line of sight.

Her body curls into unnatural positions—her moves slow, purposeful. Incredibly distracting.

For the next thirty minutes, I burn more energy restraining myself from watching her than doing my actual workout.

Paige is dangerous at the best of times, always sucking me in, but in Lycra shorts that sculpt her perfect ass and a sports bra that accentuates her perky breasts, she's lethal.

And judging by her confidence as she moves around the space, she knows it.

I'm staring at my feet, doing my cooldown, as a timer goes off somewhere in the room. And when I look up, Paige is standing by my treadmill, her yoga mat tucked under her arm and a bead of sweat dripping down her chest, making its way toward her— *nope.*

"How was your workout?" I ask to distract myself.

"Good. Great, actually. It's nice having the gym to ourselves."

"It sure is." *That's why I usually come at this time.*

"Mind if I join you again?"

I consider telling her I *do* mind. Because this is my time to myself.

There's no family drama. No teammates fucking around. No reporters. No fans. It's just me. And it's been that way since I moved in. I don't know how it's played out like that, but who am I to question it.

Now, I have to decide whether I want my sanctuary invaded. *By Paige.*

She's a distraction I don't need. With her bubbly personality, her constant chatter, her flushed body, her heaving breasts and *God-fucking-dammit.*

"I can't really stop you, can I?"

"Nope." She pops the *p* and smirks. "But at the same time...I don't think you want to. Deep down. And I mean deep, *deep* down." She runs her finger from my heart to my navel, and I have to fight to stop my abs from tensing. "I think you like having me around."

I bite back a groan, refusing to let her see how much she affects me. It's only because of my drought. *And* the fact that I can't escape her. Right?

"Tell me, Paige..." I begin, refusing to let her get to me. "How exactly did you come to *that* conclusion? Did you discover that from our few interactions?" I raise a brow, projecting a confidence and relaxed attitude that I do not feel.

"Five," she says, confusing me.

"Five what?"

"Five interactions." *Has it really only been five? It feels like more than that.*

"And no," Paige continues, drawing my attention back to her mouth. "I got that from the slight bulge in your shorts."

Holy shit. My eyes widen as she lets out a breathy giggle before walking away. Only looking back to smile over her shoulder, catching me watching her.

"See you tomorrow." She lifts her hand and wriggles her fingers in a half wave while my jaw hits the floor.

Mic drop.

Lethal.

The second she's gone, my gaze flits to my pants, and I snort laugh. She fucking lied. She couldn't see anything.

And something about that makes me want to show her what she's missing. I want her to see that if I was hard, there'd be nothing slight about the bulge, and she wouldn't be smiling. She'd be begging me to fuck her.

I don't go to the gym the following day like Paige expects, or the next, but that doesn't stop me from thinking about her.

Especially when I'm in the shower a few nights later, my palm wrapped around my throbbing cock, picturing her on her knees, her smart mouth open, ready to take me in.

My length twitches, but I hold back from giving in to my urges. Because if I do this now, where does it end? When I'm slamming into her as she begs me to make her come? Or when she's yelling at me to leave because I can't give her what she wants?

I'm closed off. I have no space in my head for anything more than a quick fuck. And while I barely know Paige, I know she deserves better than that.

But maybe she doesn't want more.

My thoughts clash in a war of chaos as I picture her hands taking over from mine, imagining her red lips as they glide along my length, sucking me into her mouth, her tongue rolling against my tip.

She cries out as my length hits the back of her throat, her eyes filled with tears while she smiles up at me, enjoying every second of me fucking her face.

What I wouldn't give... No, I can't and, "Oh fuck. Oh God."

I pump harder, my hand braced against the wall as I picture her nails digging into my ass, the vibrations of her whimpers sending a spark to my shaft and, "*Fuck. Jesus. Fuck.*"

I grunt as my orgasm hits, my cum shooting out onto the shower wall, my body convulsing in spasms.

That wasn't supposed to happen. But fuck, my hand has never felt so good.

If only I didn't have to lock Paige in a box marked "too good to damage" because a little part of me would give anything to ruin her.

Who the hell am I?

What is she doing to me?

God, I need sleep. I'm delusional.

The next morning, my phone rings when I'm about to leave for the gym, and I groan at the interruption. That groan only intensifies when I see that it's Macy.

"Hi," I huff, pulling my shoe on with my phone wedged between my shoulder and ear.

"Hey, it's me," she responds, her voice light and fluffy, like we didn't part on bad terms, and it pisses me off.

"It's Monday, Macy. Isaac's with my mom, remember? They just went for a walk. If you want to speak to him, you'll need to call tomorrow. Or you can call her." I'd rather she didn't, but I'm offering because I know that she won't.

"Ugh," she whines. "That's not going to happen. She hates me."

I wonder why.

"Anyway, I called to talk to you."

"Why?"

"I'll be in San Francisco this weekend and I want to take Isaac out for the day Saturday. I could take him to the zoo or the museum, or run around at the beach. Some mother and son bonding time. Wouldn't that be nice?"

"You want to take him out?"

"Yes, why do you sound so skeptical?"

"Because you never once took him out while you were here."

"We had a big house on the beach, so we didn't have to go out; we had plenty to do."

"Okay." I'm dubious, but if she's trying, I have to give her the benefit of the doubt. I want him to have a mom that makes happy memories with him. That's why I haven't cut her out of his life. "What time?"

"Eleven?"

"The zoo opens at ten."

"That's too early. I have dinner plans on Friday night and I'll be out late."

"Okay. You do you. I'll have him ready at eleven. But he needs to be home by six for dinner."

"I can give him dinner and have him home in time for bed."

"Fine. No later than seven, then. He needs to be in bed by seven thirty."

"God, so many rules."

"He's three, Macy."

"So? A little change in routine never hurt anyone. You should try it one day."

Her verbal jab hits me exactly where she wants it to. I'm a creature of habit. It's one of the things we always argued about. But I have to be. It's my job to keep in peak fitness, to get plenty of sleep, to fuel my body when it needs it. And doing all that on top of raising a son—alone—requires a routine that works.

"Help me out here, Macy. It's important for Isaac."

"Fine. I'll have him home by seven."

"Thank you." My lips twitch but I refuse to smile. Not yet. I'll smile when I see Isaac's face light up after spending time with his mom. I may cringe at the very sight of her, but he loves her, and if he's happy, I'm happy. As long as she's making his life better. "I'll see you Saturday, Macy. Bye." I move to hang up but she calls out.

"Wait."

"Yep."

"I'll need some money. To pay for everything. The zoo isn't cheap and there's food on top of the entry cost. I don't want him to miss out on anything he might want during the day."

God, I'm a dick. This isn't about Isaac at all.

"Of course. I'll pack him lunch and some snacks and I'll pre-order zoo tickets for you both. Dinner is on you."

"What if other things pop up throughout the day?"

"Pay for them."

"I don't have any money at the moment. Staying at the retreat isn't cheap and—"

"I'm paying for the retreat. I gave you half the sale of the house. Where's the rest of that money?" My voice rises and I'm thankful Isaac isn't here.

"I bought a house. I can move in next month. Did you think I was going to live on the streets?"

"Get a job."

"I had a job, remember? But you wanted me to stay home and look after Isaac. It's not that easy to reenter the workforce."

Goddammit. Guilt eats away at me because she's right. I wanted her home for Isaac. Yes, she always complained about her job, but I knew she never wanted to be a stay-at-home mom and I begged her to do it.

"I'll give you some money for dinner and emergencies. But Macy, you better not fuck this up. Isaac loves you and he needs his mom. Be a mom. Think of someone else for once."

I hang up without waiting for a response and pace the room, my fists clenched as my frustrations rise to the surface.

Tossing my phone into my gym bag, I throw it over my shoulder and slam the door as I leave, my anger building the longer I'm alone with my thoughts, biting my knuckles to stop myself from screaming.

If she messes this up... If he doesn't come home over the fucking moon about his day, I'm going to... I'm going to... *Fuck*. What can I even do? As long as she's making an effort, it will be impossible to keep her away from him.

I'm fuming as I enter the gym and pumped to work out my frustrations, but come to a halt as I reach the threshold.

I'm not alone.

Paige is here. Again. And the first thing I see is her ass in the air as she bends over, her hand and knee on the bench beside her, while she lifts a dumbbell, working her triceps. If she heard me come in, she doesn't acknowledge it, continuing to pant as she finishes her set.

I watch her like a stalker, picturing my hands on her waist as she gasps, imagining what it would be like to work her into a sweat. To let her distract me like she's always trying to do.

I internally groan.

It's safe to say I have *never* wanted to fuck someone so much in my life. Not even my ex.

And I don't think I can hold back any longer.

CHAPTER EIGHT

PAIGE

My arms burn as I finish my push-ups, and when I stand, my gaze flits to the door, just like it has for the last few days, waiting. Hoping that my Window-Seat Guy will suddenly appear so I'm not doing this alone. Again.

But of course, he doesn't.

I'd wager he's avoiding it—me—on purpose.

If I wasn't so self-assured, I'd probably get a complex. It's obviously my fault.

I make him uncomfortable. I know that.

It's written on his face every time we run into each other. But I'm not convinced that's a bad thing. I look at it like pushing him out of his comfort zone, and we all need a little of that sometimes.

At least, I do.

Every time I think about what I said at the gym last week, I can't help but laugh. *I mentioned his cock.* We're barely even friends, and yet, I felt comfortable enough to go there. Because his grumpy ass needed to hear it. He's wound so tight all the time that someone needs to help ease the tension.

And I love pushing his buttons. I can't even explain the joy it brings to my life, watching his nostrils flare or his eyes widen. I love to see his lips twitch like he wants to smile but refuses to admit something or someone makes him happy.

I'm not stupid; I'm aware that he's dragging around some heavy baggage. That much is clear. But a little teasing never hurt anyone.

And I was clearly joking. I hadn't really looked at his pants to see if there was a bulge. But after the words left my mouth, I wanted to.

I still want to.

That man... God, every time I see him, I want to mount him like a horse. There's something about his manner that has me desperate to attract him. And it's not only because it's been too long since a man last touched me and he's gorgeous. It's more than that.

Only I can't explain it.

Ignoring my disappointment at the empty room, I move on to my next set, and by the time I'm working my triceps, I'm exhausted.

I don't usually push myself this much, but I had the crazy idea to sign up for a charity run early next year. And now I'm suffering the consequences.

But it was time to make a change. To try something new. To drink that drink I've never tasted, compete in that event I've never entered, fuck that guy I've never fucked...

I chuckle to myself. That one isn't new, but Window-Seat Guy is definitely not the polished businessman I usually go for. And for some reason I have my sights set on him.

The door buzzes while I'm still grinning and my smile drops so fast that a nervous energy takes over me.

I continue my workout, keeping my eyes locked on the wall in front of me as I pretend I haven't noticed that someone has joined me.

My heart races as my breathing intensifies, and it has nothing to do with physical exertion.

It might not even be him, but anticipation is rife in the air. My chest is tight. My insides are twisted, and I'm working hard not to clench my legs because my mind is going exactly where it shouldn't.

The door clicks shut but no one speaks or moves. The only sounds filling the air are my ragged breaths.

Is he here? Watching me. Or am I deluded because of how badly I want him?

What I wouldn't give for him to wrap his arms around my waist and make me feel what I do to him. If I do anything at all.

What am I saying? Of course I do. I've seen it in his expression. He may not understand it, but he wants me just as much as I want him.

I know it.

The silence continues and I almost turn around, but don't.

God, this is some messed-up kind of foreplay. But I think I might like it.

He's done nothing, and yet I am well and truly ready for him to take what he wants because I want it too.

My arms are dead when I finish my set, and I can't keep up the ruse any longer. After standing tall, I turn slowly to find Window-Seat Guy a few feet behind me, his eyes ablaze with fire, his gaze locked on my heaving chest.

I want to tell him it's all for him, but I can't bring myself to speak.

For all I know, everything I'm feeling could be one-sided. He might be married—but no ring—engaged, or in a serious relationship. He might not be experiencing the same pull I do for him—it wouldn't be the first time I'd deluded myself.

Testing the waters, I bite my bottom lip, tugging the flesh into my mouth, and watch as his throat bobs and he stifles a groan.

My lips switch into a triumphant smile, but I turn away before he can see it, only looking back when I've schooled my features. I'd usually launch into a cooldown after a workout, but I'm no longer convinced it's the workout that has my heart racing but rather the man standing in front of me, staring at me like I'm his next meal.

And God, do I want to be.

He takes a step forward, and my heart stops beating until his expression changes and I catch the moment his internal war begins, resistance in his gaze, fighting for control.

And I can't have that.

Not now.

Shaking his head, he drops his bag to the floor and walks toward the treadmill. His movements slow. Hesitant. Refusing to look at me.

Telling me everything I need to know.

He feels it too. But he needs a little push to do something about it.

Knowing he has a clear view of the changing rooms, I engage my "try something new" attitude and pray that it works.

My chest heaves and I step through the threshold and wedge my foot against the door, holding it open. Turning around, I wait until Window-

Seat Guy glances up before slowly removing my sports bra, letting the top fall to the floor as I curl my fingers into the waistband of my shorts.

If he doesn't want me, now is the time for him to bow out. All he has to do is turn away or tell me to stop, and I'll give up on this crazy idea.

Because it is crazy.

He hasn't said a word since he walked in. We've only had a handful of interactions. He's never indicated that he wants anything from me. And yet, I'm practically throwing myself at him.

In a public gym.

So desperate, I can't hold back anymore. Not that rational decisions and holding back have ever been my strong suits.

Taking a breath for courage, I slide my shorts down my legs until I'm standing in nothing but my panties. My gaze hardens, a challenge set in my expression because it's now or never, Window-Seat Guy, and it's your move.

He closes his eyes and I panic, but instead of turning away like I expect, he releases a guttural groan before stalking toward me, ripping his tank over his head as I gasp.

I wanted this. It was my plan. But now that his wanton gaze is locked on mine, I'm nervous. Because I have no idea what type of guy he is.

What if he wants a girlfriend. I'm not that girl and—

He reaches the changing room and pushes me inside, slamming the door behind him. In two quick strides, he has me locked against the counter, his arms braced on either side of me, his expression feral.

"Is this what you want, or are you a tease?" His raspy words have my core pulsing as I confidently meet his state.

"I'm almost naked. I want this."

"Well, we better fix that."

"Fix wha—" He drops to his knees, gliding my panties down my legs so fast, I almost squeal. I had imagined and hoped he'd be the take-charge kind, but I wasn't convinced of it. And God, am I happy he is.

His eyes lock on mine as he tosses my thong onto the floor beside my clothes, his gaze roaming my body, setting me alight without ever once touching me. My nipples stand to attention, my core throbs between my legs, and I can't remember a time I have ever been this turned on, this desperate for a man's touch.

And I'm not above begging. "Please."

"*Jesus*. Tell me what you want. Tell me what you were thinking about when you stripped for me."

"I want you. Anything. Everything." *God, what am I saying?* This guy could be a serial killer.

"*Fuck*," he groans, and the surprise in his voice suggests that he's not, though right now, I'm not sure I'd care.

He sets his gaze on my pussy before rising to his feet and spinning me around in one movement, bending me over the counter with my ass in the air.

Our eyes lock in the mirror, and I melt into him.

"I don't make a habit of bringing protection to the gym." He pauses, his deep voice and intense stare making my legs jelly. "But if I did, I'd be sinking into this pretty pussy faster than you can say 'take me.'" He cups my center and rocks into me, letting me feel how much he wants me.

And he's rock-hard.

Leaning forward, he moves my hair away from my ear and whispers, watching me as he speaks, "I hope you don't mind settling for my mouth. I'm a little rusty, but something tells me you won't hesitate to correct me if I get it wrong."

Oh God.

Arousal pools at my center, and my head spins as he kicks my feet apart, spreading my legs before dropping to his knees again, not wasting any time as he runs his tongue between my folds.

And I buckle.

My legs give way as I fall against the counter, holding on for dear life until two strong hands grip my thighs, holding me upright, while he continues his assault.

The last few days have been hell for me, with friends and my family telling me I'd made a mistake by leaving. That I was selfish. My uncle even called me a brat, telling me I'd regret it. But if this is what regret feels like, then I'm going to be the biggest brat they've ever seen because...

"Oh. My. God." I jump. "Yes. Oh. Don't fucking move from that— *Jesus*."

Window-Seat Guy's mouth disappears, and I groan as my angry gaze darts to the mirror. "What the hell?"

"Get out of your head, Paige. Then I might listen."

"What? How did—" He groans and I quickly shake my head. "Not important." I can process how he knew that some other time. "As you were. I'm here. I'm ready."

"Good girl."

"Thank you."

Gliding me back until my ass is higher in the air, he bites my clit before swirling his tongue through my heat. I buck against his face, my head falling to the counter as I let the pleasure take over me.

This guy is *good*.

I lose control as he works me into a writhing mess, his tongue lapping at my center, his thumb rubbing circles around my clit, his fingers brushing my hole but never going in. He has me panting and moaning and thanking the heavens that this beautiful man knows how to set me on fire, because...

"God, this. Jesus. Don't stop."

His tongue disappears before the tip of his finger sinks into my heat and I buck again, the fear of falling gone thanks to his strong hold on my leg. The pressure builds low in my belly until I'm teetering on the edge, struggling to hold on to the rush...desperate for a release but also never wanting this to end.

I cry out again, rocking my hips, waiting for him to push in that little bit farther. "Yes. God. Please." He curls his finger, but before I have a chance to react, he stops. Again. And I almost cry.

"Wha—"

Ignoring my words, he flips me around until we're face-to-face and lifts me onto the counter, his gaze locked on mine. I watch with rapt attention as he lifts my legs and positions my feet on the fake marble, pushing my knees to my chest as he groans.

"What are you doing?" I pant, feeling more exposed than ever before. Sex has never been a big deal for me; I'm generally up for anything. But I have never had a man look at me like he's looking at me now. It's primal, possessive, and my God do I want him to do whatever the hell he's thinking.

And I don't even know his name.

"Hold your knees," he says, snapping me out of my head as he raises an eyebrow.

"What?"

"Hold your knees and keep your legs spread. I want you to watch as your pussy weeps for me."

"Oh. God."

Barely a second passes before he's buried between my legs again, his tongue lavishing my center, his fingers teasing my entrance but never giving me exactly what I need.

"I think it's time I told you my name." He glances up at me, suppressing a smirk as his fingers continue their ministrations.

"Why?" I rush out, my chest heaving while my core pulses. "We've made it this far without it." I'm desperate to know what to call him, but there's no way I'm going to admit that.

"You're right. But you need to know what to scream while I'm making you come."

He doesn't wait for me to respond before sucking my clit into his mouth as he finally plunges a finger inside me. Then two and—

"Oh God. Oh God. Oh God."

He pulls back, licking his lips, and my eyes follow the journey of his tongue as it travels across the flesh, my breathing out of control.

"Or you can keep calling me God." He shrugs and I'd laugh if I wasn't completely at his mercy and desperate not to break the spell.

He pumps harder, his fingers working in sync as he stares up at me, waiting, his piercing blue eyes making me shudder.

"Jesus. Okay. What's your name?"

"I thought it didn't matter and I kind of like 'God.'"

"Tell me. Now." My voice comes out rushed, frantic, full of want but I couldn't care less. He's tearing me apart and I want to scream out his name. No, I *need* it. "Jesus, I'm close. *Please.*"

He smirks again, and if I thought grumpy looked good on him, it's nothing compared to the cocky expression he's hitting me with now. "Only because you asked so nicely." He slows his moves, a spark in his eyes that makes me fucking melt. "Call me Easton."

Easton. He licks me again and I buck against him, fucking his face as I ride his fingers, chasing my release.

"Yes. Easton. Oh fuck, yes."

He bites my clit at the same time he curls his fingers inside me, and I lose my goddamn mind, screaming his name over and over as my body spasms against him.

"Easton. Easton. *Easton.*"

He slows his pace while my body convulses, and when I'm finally able to control my breathing, he pulls back, staring up at me.

"Jesus, Paige," he huffs almost breathlessly, shaking his head. "This pussy and that mouth are a dangerous combination on their own. But you screaming my name from those pretty pink lips is downright fatal."

CHAPTER NINE

EASTON

Who the fuck am I?

I don't hook up with random women in public places. Not anymore anyway. I left that behind in college.

But now... I'm wondering why.

Paige giggles as I lick my lips again before wiping my mouth.

My cock strains against my shorts when I stand, but I ignore it as I help her off the counter, holding her close until her feet hit the floor.

"Your turn." She bounces her eyebrows, and my cock twitches when I step back.

"You don't have to do that."

"*Easton.*" She says my name slowly, her deep brown eyes boring into mine, and I'm transfixed by the way her lips move. I've never thought about someone saying my name before. It happens every day; it's not newsworthy. But with Paige. Fuuuck. When Paige says it... God... I want to eat her again.

"I don't make a habit of doing anything I don't want to do," Paige whispers, stepping forward to palm my shaft over my shorts, curling her fingers around the girth as her eyes widen. "And you have no idea how badly I want to make you come. I don't think I've wanted anything more in my life."

"Jesus, Paige. If you keep talking like that, you won't get the chance. I'm already so turned on, I might come in my pants."

Paige smiles, but before I get the chance to laugh at the words that came out of my mouth, she releases me from my shorts and drops to her knees, biting her lip as my cock bounces between us.

"I knew you'd be big, but Jesus. Although my last boy—"

I cover her mouth before she can ruin the mood and glare down at her, making her laugh as she pulls my hand away. "I was going to say he was small."

"Doesn't matter," I growl. "I don't *ever* want to hear about another man while my cock stands to attention in front of you."

Paige nods before leaning forward and licking the pre cum off my tip. My head falls back and I groan, but the second she sucks me into her mouth, my body jerks and I have to work hard to refrain from rocking into her, needing her to set the pace.

She pauses, pulling away, her puzzled gaze staring up at me. "You're holding back." It's not a question. She knows. Just like I knew she was in her head. "Don't do that," she continues. "I'm not a delicate flower. I want you to fuck my mouth."

Jesus Christ. Never mind me questioning who the fuck *I* am. *Who the fuck is Paige?*

"What if I hurt you?"

"You won't." Her confidence shines in her conviction, and I'd love to know if it sparks from her knowing she can handle anything, or if she trusts me not to push things too far. Either way, I admire her for it.

"Okay. No holding back." The lie tastes sour as the words slip from my mouth because we just met. I can't lose control with her before knowing what she can take.

Not that she's going to make it easy for me. She's a little minx with mischief in her eyes as she sucks me into her mouth, swirling her tongue around my tip, while her fingers massage my balls.

And I'm like a fucking school kid again, ready to explode when she's barely begun. Luckily, I've learned a few tricks over the years, so I can hold out a bit longer.

Wrapping her free hand around the base of my shaft, she pumps me in sync with her mouth, and my body jerks. Curling my hands in her hair, I help her move as I stare down at her, and fuck, if it's not the most beautiful sight.

She raises an eyebrow as she takes me down her throat, making me choke out a mix between a laugh and a groan. I tug on her ponytail, reminding her that I'm still in control, and she rewards me with a whimper as her expression turns to hunger.

I watch as she squirms beneath me, needing another release, but I'm too close to change this up. Too far gone.

"Touch yourself," I demand, loving it when she moans against my cock as her body melts. At first she squeezes one of her breasts and sighs. But while that's a sight to behold, it's not what I want her to do.

"Uh-uh." I shake my head. "Lower. Touch your pussy."

With her gaze locked on mine, she does as I ask, lowering her hand, the hint of a smile in her eyes. *She's loving this.*

"Yes. That's it. I want you to come with me. I want to feel the vibrations from your mouth as you coat your fingers and try to scream my name."

Staring up at me, she reaches between her legs and closes her eyes at the first touch, moaning something against my length, almost sending me over the edge. "That's it. Good girl."

She rocks her hips, fucking her hand while I fuck her mouth. And if I thought the sight was beautiful before, it's nothing compared to now.

"Faster," I grunt. "I'm almost there."

I'm seconds from exploding when the door of the gym buzzes, but I can't move. Paige is gripping my ass so hard that her nails dig into my flesh.

"Fuck, Paige. We need to stop."

She shakes her head and grips me tighter, forcing my cock to go deeper, gagging when my tip hits the back of her throat. Her body spasms against her other hand and she cries out, the sensation sending me flying as tears fall from her eyes. "Paige," I warn, but she doesn't listen. "I'm going to—"

She nods and I come in her mouth, watching as she swallows every drop, her watery gaze never leaving mine. And when I'm done, she stands and mimics my move, licking her lips as she smiles.

"God, that was hot," she whispers, her eyes flicking to the door. "Every part of it. Watching you lose control. Your forceful tone. And then knowing someone could hear us or walk in at any moment. Thank you, Window-Seat Guy."

"Who are you?" I shake my head with a chuckle, in awe of the woman standing in front of me.

"I'm Paige." She giggles with a shrug, like it's no big deal. Like *she's* no big deal, but I beg to differ. "I was going to ask you the same thing," she adds as she bites her lip.

A strangled laugh escapes me. "I honestly have no fucking clue anymore. Like I said, I'm rusty."

"You call that rusty? You just destroyed me for all future men."

Holy fuck. "Happy to be of service."

With another giggle, Paige cleans herself up, and I turn around to give her some privacy, securing my cock back in my gym shorts.

By the time I turn back, she has her ass in the air as she glides her silk thong slowly up her legs and I'm goddamn hard again.

When she's dressed, Paige walks out first, seemingly unperturbed about finding someone in the gym. But when her laughter filters through the air, I know that it's empty.

"Coast is clear," she sings, spinning around to face me, and a tension fills the space. Although judging by Paige's relaxed demeanor, I might be the only one of us that feels it because... What comes next?

Maybe we should have had that talk before crossing the line, but it's too late for that now.

Guilt works its way into my chest, and while I don't regret it, I have some concerns. I lost control and I shouldn't have. She deserves better than a quickie in the gym's changing rooms. But I can't give her anything beyond that.

Taking a deep breath, I'm about to make a mess of the "talk" when Paige grabs her yoga mat and water and smiles. "Thanks for the extra workout, *Easton*." She says my name slowly again, and I bite back a groan. "Sorry you missed yours."

Huh? "I'm not sorry." I huff out a laugh. But that's not the point. "Paige?"

"I'll be seeing you." She sashays toward the exit and waves. "Have a good day."

Then she's gone, leaving me staring at the door, a little confused but also extremely relaxed, and completely at odds with my feelings.

I've had one-night stands before, but that was something else. And it's not only because it happened during the day.

Or is everyone *that* in sync these days? Maybe I have some catching up to do. Maybe sex is like that now.

But also—

Jesus. What the hell am I doing? If Paige isn't questioning things or making it into a big deal, why am I? We had sex. We fulfilled an urge and she walked away, happy and satisfied.

I'm going to consider it a little break from reality, and now it's time to get back to my life.

Thank you, Paige. I feel good.

After getting in a bit of a workout, I'm on a high for the rest of the morning, and at practice, I'm a formidable machine. Even when they team me up with Zane again, I barely flinch. Nothing could affect me right now. I thrive on this feeling of power.

Mom leaves as soon as I get home, and I fill Isaac in on Macy's plans for the weekend, noting that the sting I usually get when I talk about my ex is conveniently missing.

Turns out, I needed a distraction... A certain release that the gym or football couldn't provide me, because right now, I'm unstoppable.

"Can we get ice cream, Daddy?" Isaac asks while I'm tidying up, his small hand tugging on my shorts. "Nana said I couldn't because I had some yesterday, but we only had vanilla."

"Vanilla. Ew." I pull a face and Isaac laughs. "We need to get some more flavor in your life. You run to the bathroom and I'll grab my wallet. Let's meet back here in five. Go."

Isaac laughs as he rushes off, and I smile knowing he's about to ask for help.

While I wait, I glance down at the time and almost do a double take at how late it is. It's five forty. I'm supposed to be getting Isaac's dinner and getting him ready for bed. In an hour I'll need to—

"*Ready*," he calls out, interrupting my spiral, making me pause. It's one night. Yes, I just told Macy she couldn't do it, but maybe I could skip the bath tonight to make up time. "I'm coming," I call back, moving in search of my son. And when I find him, his face lit up like it's Christmas, I can't say no. "Okay, Buddy. Let's go."

With Isaac's hand in mine, we rush through the lobby, his infectious laughter echoing through the space. "Faster, Daddy. It's almost nighttime."

I check the time again and curse under my breath. He's right—the ice cream parlor closes in nine minutes, and with Isaac in tow, we're at least six minutes away. Something I didn't consider when I agreed to this plan. "I promise, we'll make it."

Without stopping, I grab his hands and spin him around, lifting him over my head until he's positioned on my shoulders. He holds onto my hat and ducks down when we reach the doorway, as do I, in a move we've perfected since moving in here.

We've just stepped through the threshold and straightened up when I almost slam into someone, rocking back on my heels as I brace the wall for balance.

"Jesus, sorry."

Paige spins to face me, and I rush out something between an incredulous laugh and a groan.

An image of her panting in the gym has me shaking off my thoughts and internally cursing. This is *not* the best time for our next face-to-face. And it's not just because we're running late.

Her eyes widen and I wait for her to launch into her usual chatter, but instead her gaze flits to Isaac before she mutters a quiet "excuse me," and shifts around us, disappearing into the building without offering her signature smile.

And I frown.

That was weird. I glance back in the direction she went, but before I can process my thoughts, Isaac shakes my head. "Giddyup. We've gotta go."

Taking off on a run, I dodge the crowds of people enjoying a walk in the early evening air, and we make it to the parlor with a minute to spare.

Isaac chooses strawberry and mango flavors, and after making a mess of eating it, we head back for a quick dinner.

"I lub you, Dad," he says when he's tucked in bed and I've read him a story. "Can you take me to the zoo instead of Mom?"

My heart seizes but I keep a smile plastered on my face. "How about I take you to the zoo another time. So you get to go twice. Your mom really misses you."

My stomach knots as I speak. Macy better fucking come through on Saturday because if she made me lie to my son—

"Okay, Daddy." He cuts into my thoughts. "We can go together the next day."

Isaac smiles brightly and I can't help but laugh. "We'll go soon. I promise."

Pressing a kiss to his forehead, I say goodnight and switch off his lamp. After turning the monitor on, I make myself a drink, and by the time I sit down, he's asleep.

Only fifteen minutes after his usual time. And God, am I relieved. I'm not quite ready to completely change our routine. Especially after I just told Macy she couldn't. But I'm okay with a few minutes here and there.

For the rest of the night, I can't stop thinking about my encounter with Paige, trying to analyze her expression. Was she pissed off? Upset? Hurt? Or was that a look of indifference?

I'm not sure which is worse, but I have to know or it will eat away at me.

Only, God knows where I'd find her. She always finds me.

CHAPTER TEN

EASTON

After spending Tuesday with Isaac, I break my routine on Wednesday for the second time this week, and surprisingly, it doesn't kill me. While I'd usually head to the stadium for a weight session after dropping Isaac at Mom's, I shoot off a message to the group chat—giving them a bullshit excuse—and make my way to the apartment gym instead.

I've just grabbed the door handle when my phone buzzes with replies.

> Luke: Your truck won't start? Really? Who is she and why is she still in your bed?
>
> Reed: Do you need help? My friend owns a dealership and they have mobile mechanics
>
> Luke: You believe him? He has a brand-new top of the line vehicle
>
> Reed: Why would he lie?

I groan as I toss my phone into my bag and swipe my pass to unlock the gym, impatient to see Paige.

But she's not there.

My shoulders drop and I let out a frustrated sigh, until someone taps my shoulder and giggles erupt behind me. "Looking for me?" Paige asks, her voice rife with mischief.

"Yes." Relief fills me as I turn. "I wanted to explain."

"Explain what?" She leans her shoulder casually against the wall and waits for my response.

"Explain what you saw."

Her brows furrow as she glances away, lost in thought. "What did I see?"

Rather than answering, I start with the reason I ditched my regular training to find her. "I'm not cheating, if that's what you thought."

"What?" Her eyes widen before confusion really takes over.

"When we ran into each other Monday night, you couldn't get away fast enough."

"Was I supposed to act differently?" Her lips purse before she laughs. "You seemed to be in a hurry." I was. But...uh... *What the fuck am I doing?*

"I thought..." I trail off because it only just occurred to me that she probably doesn't care.

"Thought..." She waves her hands, willing me to continue, but when I shrug, she answers for me. "You thought I'd be worried about seeing you with a kid?"

"I did. The kid's my son."

"I figured that." She scrunches her nose but her expression comes across as shy. "I'm guessing you didn't want me to know about him."

"What?" I thought she'd be pissed off and jumping to the wrong conclusions. I didn't even consider that. "No, it's not that, I just don't—" I cut myself off. I didn't come here to talk about Isaac. "I didn't want you to think you were the other woman. That I was using you for some reason. But I'm single. And a dad."

Paige smirks before ducking under my arm and pulling me into the gym, closing the door behind us. "Weren't you using me though, a little? We had sex and I didn't even know your name. I didn't have any expectations beyond that. Did you?"

"No, not really. But I don't like the idea of you thinking I left you and went home to someone else."

"Technically, I left you. But why?"

"I don't know. I'm not that guy. I—" *Fuck.* She doesn't need to know I was cheated on and that I'd never put someone else through that kind of pain and humiliation. I'm a dick. I should have left it alone. "Ignore me. My life is a complicated mess at the moment. I didn't want you to think I'd dragged you into it."

I turn to leave, but Paige stops me, gently wrapping her hand around my wrist, her hold quite the contrast to the way she squeezed me last time we were here. "My life isn't messy as such, but it is complicated and... complicated is enough of an explanation." She shakes her head and it's obvious she's holding back, but I guess, so am I. "We were both in need of some tension relief and I sure as hell got it."

"You weren't the only one." I smile.

"So... I'm thinking... Should we continue to use each other?"

"What?" My jaw drops. I was expecting her to tell me she doesn't do "messy" and walk away. But this is...interesting. "How would that work exactly?" I raise an eyebrow as my thoughts run wild.

Somewhere in the back of my mind, something tells me I shouldn't be entertaining this idea, but that something can get fucked.

Paige perks up, perhaps expecting me to run at the suggestion, and she'd generally be right. But things are different when it comes to her. "We'd have to keep it simple," she begins. "No strings. No commitment. No feelings. Just sex. A release. We don't need to get to know each other. Don't need to engage in regular conversation. We can look at it as though we're getting a high from pleasure rather than breaking shit." She winks and I release a sarcastic laugh. *Touché.* "I think you need it. I know I need it. It's a win-win."

"That easy, huh?"

"Yep." She smiles confidently. "It's that easy. Do you think because I'm a girl, I can't do casual sex?"

"Not at all." That thought hadn't occurred to me... "I meant the 'no conversation' part. You've failed on that during every one of our interactions."

Paige bursts out laughing, grabbing my arm as she buckles over. "You're not grumpy all the time, are you? It's a front."

I'm not sure that I'd call myself grumpy just because I'm not bubbly and forthright. "I'm just me, Paige." I shrug. I don't really know what else to say.

Paige smiles, but it's not her usual grin. This one holds a little intrigue. "You know, I'm starting to see that. But who knew you were so funny? It makes you that little bit hotter."

"Thanks." *I think.* My voice lifts in question and I wait to see if she'll bite. And of course she does.

"You seem confused. Or are you fishing for more compliments? You're hot and you know it. Actually, you're a dangerous level of hot because there's also a mysterious air about you that sucks people in and..." She trails off when I smile.

"What?"

"I knew you couldn't do it."

"Do what?"

"Go without conversation."

"But you—"

"All I did was say thanks."

"*Dammit*. Okay, let's take that one out of the rules. It wasn't all that important anyway."

I consider that for a moment. We've made it this far with conversation and it's mostly surface level anyway. Plus, it might be nice to have another adult to talk to that isn't my Mom, sister, or one of the guys on the team.

"Fine, but when my cock is buried deep inside you, the only words I want coming out of your pretty little mouth are the ones telling me how good I'm making you feel. Deal?"

Paige falls silent and I laugh.

"You've gone quiet? You don't have to do that yet; my cock's currently secured in my pants. You're safe. What happened?"

"Deal. And we need to change that. Stat."

"Stat?"

"Please." She drops to her knees and curls her fingers into the waistband of my shorts, ready to suck me right there in the entryway of the gym.

She likes it when I tell her what to do. And what a coincidence, so do I.

Stepping back against the door to stop it from opening, I lower my sweats just below my ass and release my length, both of us watching as it springs up between us, rock-hard and ready to go. "You wanted this? Now wrap that perfect little pout around me and suck."

Paige opens her mouth and leans forward, but just before she touches my tip, she stops and glances up at me.

The vision alone has me twitching but when she speaks... *Fuuuck.* "As much as I love this." She licks her lips as her gaze lowers to my cock again. "Next time we meet, bring a damn condom; I need to feel you inside me."

Christ... I almost come on the spot.

"Earn it." I wink, loving it when her eyes widen and her lips part in a gasp.

Where did this woman come from? She's going to be trouble. I can tell.

I think I'm going to like this agreement. A lot.

CHAPTER ELEVEN

PAIGE

I sit silently in my dad's car as he talks on the phone, my mind drifting to my second session of mind-blowing fun with Easton. This time when we'd finished, he'd slapped my ass as he walked toward the treadmill and winked when I waved goodbye.

It really was that easy. We didn't exchange numbers, didn't set up another time. It's perfect. I can focus on my life, and he can focus on his. And when we see each other... fire-freaking-works.

"Fix it," Dad yells, cutting into my thoughts. "This is ridiculous," he continues and I feel for the staff member on the other end of the call. "I've only been gone a few months. How—" He cuts himself off and groans. "You know what? Never mind. Just fix it."

He hangs up and his palm clenches around the phone.

"I'm sorry about that." He cringes, sheepishly glancing my way. "As if I don't have enough of a mess to clean up with the Storm, I now have issues coming at me from New York."

He calls out to his driver before I'm able to respond. "Jeffrey, can you please detour to a coffee shop? I need a strong coffee."

"Don't they have coffee at the stadium?"

"I need something before I step a foot inside those walls."

His shoulders tense and my brows furrow. When he asked me to come to his team's practice session today, he was upbeat and excited about it. Now you'd think the team was a burden. "What happened?"

"The new manager I hired for D'Angelo Construction just lost us one of our bigger clients because he didn't agree with his political views. That wouldn't generally be an issue, except that he thought it was a good idea to voice his opinion when he was drunk at a corporate function."

"Shit."

"Yep."

"And that was him?"

"Hell, no. If that had been him I would have pulled over and asked you to step out of the car. You do not need to hear the words I have for that man."

"Oh." I cringe. "I'd hate to be him. But also...you were an ass to whoever you were talking to."

"Oh, that was Chris."

"Chris?" God, remind me never to get on his bad side. "Your assistant, Christine?"

"What?" His eyes widen and he shakes his head. "No. That woman is a saint. I'd be struck down on the spot for even raising my voice to her. It was our COO. He's the one that recommended Brock for the role. So he can fix the mess."

"That's fair. And the team?"

Before he can answer, we pull into a drive-thru coffee shop and Dad places his order. We're silent until he has the liquid gold secured in his hands and has taken his first sip.

"Better?" I ask when he groans.

"Much. What were you asking?"

"The team? You said that was a mess too." I don't know why I'm so interested in the goings-on of his business, except that it feels nice to be included in this *very* adult conversation. Not that I don't have business conversations—I ran my own charity back in New York—but this is different because it's Dad's business.

Business that Mom always referred to as a boys' club. She said that one of the reasons they drifted apart was because he never talked about his work, making her feel like she wouldn't understand. And now that he's talking to me, I'm wondering if maybe he just didn't want to talk to her at all. She can be very opinionated on matters that don't necessarily concern her.

Dad groans again, but this time it's not the mmm-this-tastes-good groan he had with his coffee, it's more of a I-wish-I-didn't-have-to-deal-with-this-shit groan. The shit being the team.

"I knew what I was getting into. I'd crunched the numbers. Done my due diligence. But I never factored in the previous fuck-face ensuring the team never made a dime from that damn TV show. He—"

"I know this is serious, Dad. But you left yourself wide open for this one... If he's the previous fuck-face, does that make you the current one?"

Dad chuckles and his entire body physically relaxes. "Thanks, Kid. I needed that. And you bet your ass it does. And now this fuck-face"—he points to himself—"has to make some serious changes around the team. And they're not going to like it."

"I'm sorry, Dad. That can't be easy."

"It's not. But it's easier with you by my side."

"And why exactly am I here? You're not making those changes today, are you?"

"Not yet." He laughs. "You're here so I can show you off. And show off the guys. They're a great team. It's not their fault everything is chaotic behind the scenes."

"So, you're using me to humanize yourself before you screw them all over."

"What?" Dad's face drops, his expression showing he's positively offended. "Is that really—"

"No, Dad. I don't really think that. Though, it's not a bad idea. It would make it harder for the players to side with whoever is working against you."

"Wow. You are ruthless. Remind me never to cross you—" He cuts himself off and chuckles. "Wait. You cutting me out of your life makes so much more sense now."

"Yep. Mom was the smart one. She cried. A lot."

"While I hid my pain and remained strong."

"Exactly."

"Damn. Have you ever thought about running D'Angelo Construction? I'm going to need someone to take over when I retire and—"

"No, thank you," I rush out. "But I appreciate the offer."

A huge glass structure comes into view and beyond that, the concrete walls of the stadium. My chest tightens as we turn into a side street and pull up to the underground parking garage. I have no reason to be nervous. All I'm doing is saying hi to the team before retreating to a suite to watch them practice. Or if I'm being real, I'll be retreating to the suite to play on my phone or read a book. *Why would anyone be interested in watching a football team practice?*

"We're here," Dad announces when the car comes to a stop near glass doors. "Are you ready?"

"As ready as I'll ever be," I say honestly, but hit him with a smile because he's excited about this. "Let's go."

I get it. I freaking get it.

I've been watching the team practice for all of ten minutes and I'm a convert. Give me all the football practices and the games because damn, these guys can move.

After we'd arrived at the stadium, Dad escorted me to a boardroom before disappearing for a few minutes. When he came back, there was a change in plans. The meet and greet would take place after their practice. Meaning I couldn't escape early if I wanted to.

I was disappointed at first, but now... I could sit here all day.

My phone rings while I'm watching, and I have to search through my bag to find it. I haven't needed it once since I got up to the suite. I check the screen to find it's my old friend Cassie, the only friend that isn't pissed at me for moving away from New York City because she's living in Paris herself.

"Hey babe."

"Paigey, girl. How are you?" she yells above the background noise and I wince. "I'm at the club; hang on, I'll close the door." I laugh as a loud bang echoes through my ear like she dropped the phone, and then seconds later the chaos softens and she's back on the line.

"Better?"

"Much. But you could have done that before calling me."

"Very true. Only I never think about those things. You know that.

Anyway, I'm calling because I came across a very risqué photo shoot in a well-known magazine featuring my hot bestie."

"You saw it in Paris?"

"I have a subscription. But that's not what's important. Paigey got her beautiful tits out."

"I did." I laugh while my cheeks warm. "And I'm obsessed with those photos," I admit.

"Me too. I framed one in the club."

"You did not." My jaw drops because I wouldn't put it past her.

"You bet your ass I did. You'll forever be immortalized on the walls of a Paris nightclub."

"Thank you?" I think. I mean, I agree it's a freaking great photo, but I'm not sure I'm ready for it to be on display.

Cass laughs. "Don't worry. I used the image without your face."

"Noooo. How will I ever be famous if you cut off my recognizable assets?"

"Flash them; they'll soon figure it out."

"Oh, Cass. I've missed you."

"Same, girl. Same. How's Californian life?"

I lean back in my chair, putting my feet up on the armrest in front of me while I fill her in. "I'm currently in a suite watching a football team practice."

"Oh God. Do you need me to save you? I wouldn't mind saying hello to your dad while I'm there."

I roll my eyes even though she can't see me, and yet, if she'd asked if I needed saving before I got here, I would have begged her for it, despite knowing she thinks my dad is hot. I feel the same about her brother so I can't complain.

"You need to see this. If it wasn't my dad's team and I wasn't already sleeping with someone else, I would be all over these guys. They're such... men. Rough and rugged and... I don't know. That's the best way to describe it. Nothing like the businessmen I usually spend time with."

"Rough and rugged, you say?"

"Yep."

"Get on top of that."

"I can't." I laugh. "Didn't you hear me... I'm kind of already sleeping with someone."

"Kind of? Are you married?"

"No."

"Engaged?" Her voice rises to a mocking level. She knows I'm not.

"We're not even together."

"Then I don't see a problem. If he's like any of the men I know, he's probably out there fucking someone else as we speak."

"He has a kid."

"Oh, my mistake. That definitely means he doesn't juggle women." She laughs, her tone dripping in sarcasm. "Are you crazy? Have you had the 'let's be exclusive' chat?"

"No, and I don't want to have that chat. But not because I want to fuck around. Because it's casual and I want it to stay that way."

"Ugh, fine. I guess I can fly over and do it for you."

"Do what?"

"Screw the guys on the team. You can live vicariously through me."

"You're so kind."

"I know. That's the type of friend I am. Speaking of friends... Are those bitches still giving you grief?" I laugh, but it's not even remotely funny. They're not giving me grief. They've just cut me out of their lives. And while it hurt at first, the regret I felt didn't stem from losing my friends, but the realization that I'd done the same thing to my dad. He left my mom even though he loved her, and I cut him off. I left New York, even though I love it there, and now... New York has done the same to me. If you're not seen at all the parties or keeping up with the lunches, you're no longer a part of the group.

I chat with Cass until my dad arrives about halfway through the practice. And when it's almost over, we make our way down to the field.

No one pays us any mind as we step onto the turf—the guys all off in their own conversations—and it gives me a chance to check them out now that I'm close. God, there are some hotties on this team. Cass would love it here. She'd—

I freeze mid-thought as my eyes lock on a face I'm all too familiar with, his expression bordering on annoyance, like it usually does. I'd smile if things between us weren't about to completely blow up. And not in a good way.

Easton's a goddamn football player. Not just any football player. A guy on my dear ole dad's team.

And I'm fucked.

How the hell didn't I know that? I mean, I haven't bothered to learn anything about my father's recently acquired team but that's not the point. Easton is mind-blowingly hot. I'm confused as to why there aren't more people talking about him. Or has my head been so far up my ass with my own problems that I missed it. I really wish I had Internet access right now.

How could this happen? I've joked to myself many times before that Easton is everywhere, but this is next-level.

I can't believe we decided to hook up because our lives were messy and complicated while having no idea our connection was about to became a shitstorm of epic proportions. *A storm*. How fitting.

Dad says something into a microphone and before I know it, all eyes are on him as he brings the crowd to attention. I slip in behind the coaching staff and try to pay attention, but my thoughts are so scrambled it's a struggle.

I don't want our time to be over. I've always had a pretty healthy sex life, but Easton is a god. He's possessive and demanding and sure of himself.

And he doesn't play games. The way he...

Dammit, I'm doing it again. Now is not the time. Especially considering he's going to see me in about thirty seconds and then our relationship—whatever it is—will be over.

I'm not sure how much time passes before I'm shuffled to my dad's side, a wide—albeit fake—smile on my face.

Dad introduces me to the team and I do my thing, humanizing him, before tuning out, not paying attention to anything he says beyond that. Yet somehow, I manage to tune back in the very moment he says the words I was dreading.

"I'm sure I don't have to tell you that my daughter is off-limits." He wraps an arm around my shoulder as if to highlight I'm the daughter he's referring to. "She's here because I wanted to show you all off. And so she'd believe me when I say I'm kind of a big deal."

The guys laugh while I force another smile, making the stupid mistake of scanning the crowd.

I try hard not to look for him, but like a beacon, my eyes meet Easton's stare a second before he turns away. And it's impossible to miss that he's fuming, if not also a little confused. I'm sure he thinks I betrayed him somehow. Like I knew.

But I'm not stupid. I know better than to get involved with anyone connected to my father.

Only now that it's already happened, it's going to be harder to take it back.

Chapter Twelve

EASTON

We said no strings, but there are so many fucking strings we could be at a kite festival.

What are the chances? And why are those words constantly rolling around in my head when it comes to Paige? If I believed in fate, this would be the moment I discovered it was out to fuck with me. She's the owner's daughter. Salvatore D'Angelo's pride and joy. The woman he jokingly—or not so jokingly—told us all to stay the fuck away from *after* I'd already tasted her.

This is not going to end well for me.

"Anyway, I won't take up any more of your time," he continues while I spiral. "I trust you'll all be as welcoming to Paige as you have been with me. Thank you."

I wonder if he'd consider my time with Paige as welcoming. I did assist her with her needs.

But *Goddammit.*

"Sorry, one last thing." Sal grabs the mic again and everyone falls silent. He seems like a genuine guy, but we haven't figured out if he's to be trusted yet, so everyone's on their best behavior around him. "I'd like another Super Bowl win this year if you can work on that," he adds, making the guys all crack up laughing again. Except me. "Thank you. As you were."

He walks away and the general chatter picks up. While I stand frozen.

Paige is off-limits.

I finally found someone to take my mind off the crazy in my life and she's about to be taken away from me.

We lock gazes again and her expression confuses me. Is that guilt? Did she know?

All this time I was sure she had no idea I played football, but was she playing me?

I'm lost in thought, my anger simmering, when someone slaps me on the back.

"Wilder, you're looking more pissed off than usual. What's going on? What did Zane do this time?"

Luke-fucking-Bennett.

He smirks and I want to punch him. "Is that actually funny, Bennett? You know, I thought you'd grow up after having a kid."

His face drops and he steps closer. "Sorry, man. It's been a day and humor is my go-to. But you know we're here for you, right? In all seriousness, you were there for me when I needed it, and I'll always be happy to return the favor."

The sincerity in his eyes throws me a little because as he said, humor is his go-to, although Amelia must have seen something in him so maybe I can give him a shot. "Thanks, man. I'm fine. Just having a day myself."

Luke and I walk back to the locker room together but keep the conversation on football. Despite his offer, I can't see myself opening up to him, or anyone for that matter. It's just not something I do.

Ever.

Though I can see the benefits. When Luke spoke to me about his situation with Amelia, he managed to come to some kind of epiphany after something I said. That could happen to me. Or...it could be no help at all and instead, I have a teammate feeling sorry for me. Actually, *sorrier* for me, because they already think I'm broken after Macy's cheating scandal with Zane. And that's more annoying than the cheating was.

Sal walks past us when we reach the door of the locker room and my stomach knots, half expecting him to call me away so he can personally tell me I need to end things with Paige. But of course, he doesn't. Instead, he smiles and lets us know it was a good practice.

Again, he's genuine. There's just something about the way the management acts around him that has us all on guard. But maybe, like us, they're just getting used to the change.

T he next day, I run into Paige three *goddamn* times, but never get the chance to talk to her. The first time, I was driving out of the parking garage as she was walking past. The second was in the crowded lobby in the middle of the day. And the third was at the swimming pool while I had Isaac with me. She was getting out of the water when we arrived, and it took everything in my power not to stare at her dripping body. Thankfully, I had a little reminder tugging on my shorts, keeping things innocent in my mind.

After Isaac falls asleep that night, I try to distract myself with TV and music, but it doesn't work. My head is a chaotic web of issues that I can't control, and it's impossible to determine what's worse—my imminent chat with Paige or Macy's arrival tomorrow. Or more specifically, Macy canceling tomorrow and me having to pick up the pieces of my son's fragile little heart. *Again*.

I'm calling this her last chance. If she fucks it up, I'm done. I'll have no guilt finding the best, most expensive lawyer out there so I can ruin her.

I'm sure Luke knows a guy. I remember him mentioning he had to rush Amelia's divorce so they could get married. I had to listen to that fun little story while seated next to him on the bus to our last away game. At the time, I was hating life, but now, he might be useful.

And he said he wanted to help.

I try another tack, reading in bed, and I must fall asleep at some point because when I next check the time it's four a.m and I feel groggy. Macy isn't coming for hours and our practice isn't until the afternoon, so I have no reason to be awake this early. But since it took me hours to fall asleep last night, I can't imagine it's going to be any easier now.

Accepting my fate, I get up and workout on my balcony so I don't wake Isaac, but at around five thirty there's a soft knock on the glass door, and his sleepy little smile greets me as he waves.

"Good morning." I smile back after walking inside. "Are you hungry?"

"Yes."

"What would you like? Pancakes, waffles, or eggs?"

"Pancakes." He runs into the kitchen and crawls up onto his stool near the counter.

"Okay. Done."

"Annnd waffles and eggs," he adds with a pleading smile, making me laugh.

"Woah, Buddy. That might give you a stomachache before the zoo."

His face drops at my response. "Is Mom really coming?"

Fuck. This kid is barely three and yet he's acutely aware that he has a shitty, unreliable mother.

I swear to God if she cancels—

"Do you think I'll see a snake eating today?" He changes the subject before I'm able to respond and it's lucky he did, because it stopped me from having to lie to him. The truth is that I don't know if she's coming. But for her sake, I hope she does.

While I make pancakes, Isaac and I talk about all the animals at the San Francisco Zoo, with him telling me his favorites and the ones he thinks Macy will like. My chest burns when he gets her favorites wrong because it's just more proof that she doesn't see him enough to bond with him.

"When we go, I'll let you see the wolves. I know you like them." He smiles and it warms my heart. Of course, he's right. Because I've told him that. Because we spend time together. And bond.

God, she makes me crazy.

As Isaac's pickup time arrives, so too does my headache. The clock ticks over to eleven and then eleven ten and eleven fifteen, while my heart slams in my chest, waiting, pretending everything is fine, while Isaac plays happily.

When the time ticks over to eleven twenty, I've had enough.

"I'm just going out to the balcony for a minute, Isaac. I'll be back." I keep my voice light, but I'm beyond pissed off. Only, I've just stepped outside to call Macy when my intercom buzzes.

She's here. God, I hope that's a good thing.

I don't say anything to Isaac until our concierge confirms it, then it's go time and I suddenly feel worse.

"Come on, Buddy. Your mom's here."

Isaac smiles brightly and I both love and hate it for him. He deserves to be happy, and I'm glad Macy stuck by her word. But a little part of me hoped she'd mess up because how long can he handle the ups and the downs before it scars him for life?

No matter what, Isaac is my priority. I know kids need their moms but not if they're messing with their kids' mental health.

After grabbing Isaac's bag, we meet Macy in the lobby before traveling down to the parking garage. The code to the garage was all I was willing to give her. I wasn't going to tell her which floor I was on, and I definitely wasn't letting the concierge buzz her up.

I chat with Isaac as we go, and it's not until he's settled in his seat that I turn to Macy with a forced smile, my credit card in hand. "If he doesn't come home with the biggest fucking grin on his face," I grate almost under my breath, "you will never get another dime from me."

"We're going to have a great day." Macy smiles cheerily back at me, and we both wave when Isaac glances our way. "You don't have to worry about us."

Understatement of the year. That's all I'm going to be doing. She may not have been a bad mom in the early days, but now, I don't trust her at all.

After walking over to the driver's side, Macy shoots me a wink, which I glare at until I remember what I had to tell her, my mood lifting. "Oh, and Macy, I reduced my credit card limit. You've got three hundred for the day; use it wisely."

Her jaw drops as I suppress my smirk and turn away, waving at Isaac one last time before Macy drives away with my world in the back seat of her rental, the high of ruining her plans fading away.

God, I hope I made the right decision. She's his mom and if she's trying, I have to respect that, for Isaac's sake. But what if I messed up?

My head aches and I'm feeling dejected as I step into the elevator from the parking garage, and when it stops in the lobby, I internally groan. I just want to get home. I've only got a couple of hours before I have to be at the stadium, and I need time to detox from Macy before I leave.

Resting my head against the mirrored wall, I release a slow drawn-out breath and close my eyes.

They're going to have fun. Macy's going to be a good mom. He's safe. He's cared for. He's—

"Are you okay?" A familiar voice seeps into my consciousness, drawing my attention. And when I open my eyes, I find Paige's beautiful gaze staring back at me.

A breathy laugh rushes from my lungs though I'm not sure this is a funny matter. "I should have known," I say, my voice more gravelly than I expected.

"Known what?" she asks, her expression puzzled.

"That you'd appear. You always do."

"Just think of me as your guardian angel." She thinks she's joking, but she's not that far off. Lately, when I'm having a shitty day, she's there. Chatty as always. Cheering me up. Though this time, she's part of the reason I'm so fucked-up.

The doors close and when we're the only two in the elevator, Paige sighs. "Since we only have a short ride together, let's get right to it."

"Okay. Did you know?" I hit her with the burning question, and when her body deflates, I feel a little bad.

"I knew you'd think that, but honestly, I had no idea. I'm sorry to say I don't follow football. I'm not really a sports girl at all." She cringes and I laugh.

"That's what I liked about you."

"Oh, too bad." She smiles. "Because that's how I felt until yesterday. Now, after watching your team practice, I think I'm missing out."

"Figures." The first time I find someone I can be myself around and now she's on the bandwagon.

"What does?"

"Nothing, never mind. Back to the issue at hand. You're the team owner's daughter. And now off-limits to me."

"Apparently so."

The elevator stops and when the doors open to no one, I assume it's Paige's level and hold the doors open so we can finish our chat.

"I guess it would be crazy to keep seeing each other," she continues, her expression pinched as she looks to me for answers. "Right?"

It pains me to say it, but... "Right."

"It's messy."

"And things are fucked-up enough at the moment." *For me at least.*

"Exactly." Paige snaps her fingers like that's some big revelation. "Goodbye then?" Her face contorts. She's clearly not happy about this outcome. And neither am I. But it is what it is.

"Yep. Goodbye."

"Unless we happen to run into each other," she adds before I can release the doors. "I can say hi, right?"

"Sure."

"And if we happen to be in the gym at the same time, you could help me stretch."

I raise an eyebrow and she smiles. "I guess. If you need it."

"Thanks. And if by some strange coincidence we end up locked in a storeroom together with no way out and nothing to do?"

The fuck? I stare at her deadpan until she laughs. "What? You never know."

"Then in that case, I would fuck your brains out until you don't know what day it is let alone how long we've been trapped."

"Okay." Her pitch rises. "Thank you. It's good to set boundaries. You know. Just in case."

"Of course."

Paige moves to step out until we both realize it's my floor. She never pressed the button. I pause for a second and then without departing, I press the number for her level and watch as the doors close before turning to face her.

"I missed my stop," she says coyly, biting her lip.

"You did."

"And you didn't get off," she states the obvious.

"I didn't."

We stare in silence until the doors open again. This time at level twelve. Paige's floor.

I hold my hand across the entry and allow her to pass by, drinking her in, her scent lingering after she's gone. And I make a split-second decision to follow her.

We can't keep this up. Whatever it is. But one last time can't hurt anyone. Can it?

Paige doesn't say anything as I trail behind her, but her body stiffens when I get close.

When she finally stops in front of what I assume is her door, she spins to face me. "When I first got in the elevator, you had this pained expression, like you were...broken." Again, it's not a question—she knows something is not right.

"I've had a rough morning," I confirm, giving her nothing more.

"Want to talk about it?" She smiles wide in anticipation and I huff out a laugh.

"Definitely not, but I could use something to relieve the built-up tension." I step forward, walking into fire, but ready to feel the burn. I've already crossed the line.

Paige shrugs, trying to appear unaffected, but her heaving chest gives her away. "Mmm," she says, curling a finger through her long brown hair, her eyes locked on mine.

"Know of anything?" I ask in challenge.

Paige raises a brow and I know instantly that she's about to sass me. "There's one of those destruction places around the corner that—" I slam my lips to hers, cutting her off as I push her against her door.

I might take her up on that the next time I'm seeking a release, but for now, Paige is the only thing I need. And there's no way I'm going to resist it.

Chapter Thirteen

EASTON

Paige fumbles with her bag as our tongues swirl, and when she locates her key, she pushes me back. "Found it. As much as I love the thrill of being in public, with current circumstances in mind, we should go inside."

"You won't hear any arguments from me; I don't want to have to hold back at the risk of making you scream too loud."

"That's a much better reason." Paige opens the door and drags me over the threshold before connecting our lips again. Her hands roam my body as she nibbles on my bottom lip, eliciting a low grunt from the back of my throat.

Pressing her against the closed door, I nudge my knee between her legs and rock into her, letting her feel how much I need this. *Want* this.

When her movements quicken and she starts to pant, I break our kiss and drop to my knees, sliding her leggings and panties down before my eyes lock on her pussy. "Goddammit. I don't have a condom."

And I really need to fuck her. Especially if this is going to be the last time.

Paige suppresses a smile, shaking her head when I gaze up at her. "Lucky for you, we're in my apartment. And I have a stash."

"A stash?" I question, working hard not to groan. She can do what she wants. Doesn't mean I like thinking about it.

"Yes, a stash," she states matter-of-factly as she steps out of her clothes. "But I don't mean that in the way you're thinking. I have a box, and it's full. Do you want to keep talking or should I go and get one?"

"Get two," I say, spinning her around and giving her a slight tap on the ass to get her moving. "I've got an hour before I have to leave."

Paige peers over her shoulder, her lip pursed as she hides her lust. "I'll get one," she says with a smile. "I'm expecting a call in thirty minutes."

I want to complain, but thirty minutes is better than nothing, so I'll take it. And the second she's back, I'm ridding her of her tightly fitted tank top, my eyes raking over her almost naked body.

Taking my time to worship her, I release one of her breasts from the cup of her bra, teasing her nipple with my tongue before moving to the next one. When she's squirming at my touch, I kiss a path up her neck, only stopping when I reach the sensitive skin below her ear.

"Since you've limited our time to thirty minutes, you only get to come twice," I whisper, gliding my palm along her skin, feeling her shiver. "But Paige..." I add, trailing off as I cup her heat, waiting until she stares up at me, panting. "Your first better be quick, because I want to take my time fucking you for the second."

I massage her clit and she cries out, her head falling back against the wall as she rolls her hips, silently asking for more.

I start slowly, teasing, working her until she's ready for me. And when she starts to whimper, desperate for my fingers, I plunge one inside her, pumping it a few times before adding a second, my thumb continuing to tease her until she's a beautiful, chaotic mess.

Grabbing her wrist in my free hand, I raise it above her head and lean into her, pressing her into the door while she rides my fingers. Her movements pick up along with her breath, and it's not long before her body starts to quiver. I curl my fingers inside her, rubbing her walls while I continue to work her clit, and she cries out again, thrashing against my hand as her first release hits.

"Oh God, Easton."

She bucks and shakes as she coats my fingers, and I wait until she stops screaming my name before I let go of her hand, drop my pants to sheath my length. While she's still catching her breath, I lift her off her feet until she wraps her legs around my back, then lower her onto my cock, slowly, my eyes locked with hers, both of us groaning when I'm buried inside her.

"God, your pussy was made for me, the way it wraps perfectly around my cock. Such a shame about your dad."

Paige clenches as she giggles, and then as though she's punishing me for my comment, she grips my shoulders and lifts herself up before slamming down again and rolling her hips, until I buck uncontrollably.

"Jesus. Paige. Give a guy the chance to settle."

"We only have thirty minutes, remember? Twenty now. And I need you to fuck me good."

"That I can do." I squeeze her ass and pump up into her at the same moment she pushes down, meeting me thrust for thrust. And we've just found our rhythm when she adds, "I want you to leave a mark, East. Make me remember you long after you're gone."

"Christ." My cock twitches inside her as a possessive need takes over me. "Does that mouth ever get you in trouble?"

"All the time."

She giggles, and God, I don't doubt that. She has me wanting to tattoo my name on her inner thigh so that any man coming after me knows that I was here first, that I'm the reason they will never be enough for her.

Releasing my hold on her ass, I curl my hand around her neck and tilt her head, settling for sucking the flesh of her breast until I've left a pink blemish. Her breath hitches and she tries to look down, but I don't let her, tightening my hold until I've made an identical mark on her other side.

My cock swells as I stare at her chest, and I pump harder, letting go of her neck so I can kiss her again, possessing her mouth until she's moaning against my lips.

Curling her fingers into my hair, she tugs my head back, pulling me away for only long enough to rush out her request.

"You're good but I know you've got more. Fuck me harder, East. Ruin me."

She crashes her lips back to mine as I hitch her higher and slam into her, bracing her against the wall so I can rock my hips, fucking her with abandon.

"Yes," she mumbles against my mouth before tugging my head away again. "I'm so close," she rushes out. "But I need more, please."

Without responding, I raise my thumb to her mouth and press it against her lips, telling her, "Suck."

Her eyes widen and she lets out a lust-filled moan before doing as she's told, opening her mouth, her beautiful lips wrapping around my thumb.

With a whimper, she rolls her tongue across my skin, and her pleading tone, along with the sight of her at my mercy, has my balls tightening as my release looms.

The longer she sucks, the louder she moans, and the vibrations on my hand travel straight to my cock while I pump her harder, giving her everything I've got.

My thumb properly coated, I pull it from her mouth and lean back, staring down at our connection while I press it against her clit. She bucks against me as she cries out, and when I roll my thumb, her body spasms, her walls tightening while I grunt out her name, no longer able to hold back.

"Fuck, Paige. Yes."

I spill into her as my release hits, and I tighten my grip on her ass, holding her up as she loses control, both of us coming together seconds before her phone rings.

"Jesus," I rush out. "That was well timed." I slow my movements, my body still jerking, as I try to catch my breath.

Paige's head falls back against the door as she moans breathlessly, her beautiful tits rising and falling in my face as her second orgasm takes over her.

"Do you want to—"

"Let it go to voicemail," she pants, and I can't help but chuckle.

We stay connected for another minute, silent until her breathing evens out. And it's not until her feet are firmly on the ground that she speaks again.

"Well, Easton Wilder." She pats my chest. "That was one hell of a goodbye."

I raise an eyebrow at her use of my full name and she laughs.

"As if I wasn't going to look you up when I found out you were a football star. Admit it, you researched me too."

"Nope." I can honestly say that I didn't, but now that she mentions it, I might. "All I know is that you're my team owner's daughter and as your father put it... off-limits."

"Ugh. He had to go and put a downer on the situation. But a fact is a fact. And that's exactly why we're doing the right thing and staying away from each other. Keeping our hands to ourselves." As she says that, she runs a finger across my abs, her gaze following the movement, her teeth tugging on her bottom lip.

"So you agree we still need to end this?" I ask, and the words taste like poison in my mouth. It's such a shame. Especially when she's looking at me like that. "Paige?" I question when she doesn't respond.

"Yes. I do." She blows out a raspberry. "It will be easier that way."

Since we have a preseason game tomorrow, we only had a few short meetings today, so I have too much time to kill before Isaac gets home. I'm itching to call Macy, but that's likely to send her into a rage, and I don't want that until Isaac's home safely.

Like always, my mind drifts to Paige, but I cut off that line of thinking before I picture her naked. That's not conducive to my moving-on plans. I need to find something else to take my mind off things. Something that isn't football related and unfortunately, Paige now fits that bill.

After twiddling my fingers for way longer than anyone should twiddle, I grab my phone and call my mom, hoping she'll help me pass the time, quickly realizing that was a mistake.

"What's wrong?" she rushes out, making me startle.

"Who answers a call like that?"

"Me. When you call."

"I just called to say hi."

"As lovely as that is, I saw you yesterday and I'm seeing you tomorrow, so sue me for being curious."

"Well, I'm good."

"How's Isaac?"

"I don't know. I'll let you know when he gets home."

"I'm sure he's having a blast. Oh, Keeley just arrived."

"She's there?"

"Yep."

My brows furrow because she hardly ever visits; she's a caller. Always claiming she's too busy to see people. Something must be going on. "What's wrong?" I ask, concern obvious in my tone.

Mom bursts out laughing, and it's a good fifteen seconds before she responds. "You two are so alike it's crazy."

"What does that mean?"

"Well, what's wrong with you?"

"Nothing. I already told you that."

"Exactly. And there's nothing wrong with her either." Mom laughs again and I picture her rolling her eyes. She's not stupid; she knows there's something up with both of us, but thankfully, she's not one to push it.

"Is that East?" Keeley asks in the background before the phone crackles and she comes on the line. "Can we come over?"

"What, why?"

"I want to use your pool."

I'd normally say no, but since that will definitely kill time and mean I have someone to keep an eye on Isaac while I talk to Macy, it seems like a good idea. "Fine. Come over. I'll make dinner. Hope you like steak."

"Are you okay?" she asks, and it sets Mom off laughing again.

An hour later, Mom, Keeley, and I are sitting by the pool, all our issues —our unspoken issues—temporarily benched while we enjoy the sunshine. Keeley stretches out on the lounge chair beside me and yawns, while my gaze flits to the water. "I thought you wanted to use the pool?"

"This is me using the pool. Where else do you expect me to soak up the warmth in my bikini?"

"*Your* balcony? At *your* apartment."

"Oh shush. You're happy I'm here. We both know you need the company."

"As do you."

"Touché. Now let me enjoy what little time we have."

Mom pays us no mind as she reads her book in a separate cabana, opting to stick to the shade like the clever person she is.

I consider swimming, but instead lay my head back, taking a moment to breathe.

I've just closed my eyes when the door bangs shut and I jump along with the person who just came through, eliciting the smallest of smiles from my lips. From my position on the other side of the pool, I have a clear view of Paige as she walks in, her bikini-clad bronzed skin reflecting the sun, like she's wearing some kind of shimmery lotion.

She makes herself comfortable on a lounge without noticing any of us and unfolds a large spiral notebook. My brows furrow as I watch her— the book is too big for writing in—but when she pulls a pencil out of her bag and starts drawing with small strokes, it all makes sense—she's an artist.

Something about that has me smiling, but I shouldn't be surprised that she's creative. There's no denying I'm curious about her. But unlike her, I haven't done any research. Yet. Though I have to admit, she's tempting me.

While my mom and Keeley are oblivious, I sneak glances at Paige, my mind crowded with thoughts about what she could be drawing and what else she does in her spare time. She has me wanting to pull out my phone and search her name, only I'm worried that any movement will break her concentration, and I'm not ready to shift my gaze. I'm enjoying the view too much.

Twenty minutes pass in silence until my mom coughs, and Paige blinks as though snapped out of a strong daze before she glances up and gapes, clearly surprised.

My lips curl into a grin, but instead of smiling back, she looks away, fumbling her things as she attempts to subtly close her sketch pad before securing everything under her chair.

When she looks my way again, I tuck my hands behind my head and raise an eyebrow, smirking when her gaze shifts to my abs. I'm just about to flex when I'm interrupted.

"Is that Paige D'Angelo?"

Jesus. If I had any liquid in my mouth it would have just burst out of me. I internally cringe before slowly glancing at Keeley, preempting her teasing expression. But when I look over, her eyes are firmly locked on Paige as she stands.

"Paige?" she calls out, drawing the attention away from me. "I'm Keeley. We didn't get a chance to meet yesterday, but I work for the Storm football team."

Paige straightens in her seat, her eyes briefly flashing to mine, before she glances at the cabana Keeley and I were sharing, alone, since Mom's on her own in the shade. I picture her mind whirring and cringe. Nope... that's my sister. I need to clarify that ASAP.

"Hi Keeley." Paige waves, standing when Keeley reaches her, a warm confident smile in place. "I remember seeing you, but God, I met so many people."

"Oh, totally understandable. Do you live here?"

"I do. Do you?"

"Me? No. I wish. I'm here with my brother." She points to me over her shoulder, and I flash Paige an awkward smile when her gaze follows. "He's on the team. But you may not have seen him because he was likely brooding away in the back. It's kind of his thing. East!" she calls out. "Come over here. It's Paige."

The excitement in Keeley's tone piques Mom's interest, and the next thing you know she's sitting up and looking between me and the girls.

"Who's Paige?" she asks quietly with a frown, as though Keeley and I are keeping some big secret.

"She's our new owner's daughter. We were all introduced to her yesterday."

"She's pretty."

"I better go over," I say, ignoring her comment. "I don't want to be rude."

"Since when?"

"What?"

"That's never bothered you before."

"Yes, but when it comes to the big boss's daughter, I have to make an effort."

At that her face falls, and I internally cringe for worrying her. "Is he making changes?" she asks, and though I shouldn't, I take that as my out so she doesn't ask more questions.

"We haven't figured that out yet, but better to be safe than sorry."

CHAPTER FOURTEEN

PAIGE

Easton gets up from his comfortable position on the lounge chair, and my eyes drop to the sketchbook peeking out from underneath my recliner. I'd been contemplating sketching him next, purely by memory, and apparently that conjured him to reality because here he is, walking toward me.

The lady he was talking to calls out and he barely turns around, waving her off. From my position across the pool, I can just make out her features, but there's something familiar about her, and since his sister is standing in front of me, it would be safe to guess it's his mom. God, it's one big family affair this week.

"So... before he gets here,"—Keeley waves a hand toward Easton with a bored expression, rolling her eyes as she lowers her voice—"I should tell you that we don't usually promote our brother-sister relationship. Easton's choice, not mine. Meaning...he's likely to be pissy. But since you're here, you're in on the secret. It's an exclusive club. You'll love it." She smiles at her joke and I have to stop myself from commenting, an image of a pissy Easton making me smile.

"Good to know," I say just as Easton joins us, and I don't miss the unimpressed expression he flashes Keeley's way.

"Easton,"—Keeley claps her hands together, ignoring him—"this is Paige and Paige, this is Easton." She officially introduces us and I once again bite my tongue. "Easton is one of Storm's wide receivers. And my little brother. Well, you know...younger, anyway. He lives here, and I'm crashing his personal space so I can use the pool."

Keeley turns to Easton expectantly and he rolls his eyes before offering a quick, "Hi."

"That's it?"

"What do you want me to say? You said it all. Should I mention what I had for lunch? Or my dinner plans?" He sneaks a glance my way and a smile tugs at my lips. I'm pretty sure he had *me* for lunch. Sort of. He may not have used his masterful mouth this time, but we were together around then.

And something about that makes me want to giggle. Secrets are fun. As long as they're not hurting anyone.

Keeley smacks Easton's arm, bringing me back to the present. "Don't be a dick," she snaps. "Just be nice."

"I'm always nice," he scoffs, his gruff tone turning me on before he's even looked my way. . "Hi, I'm Easton." He subtly raises a brow. "It's a pleasure to meet you."

"Hi, Easton." I control my knowing smile. "I'm Paige. Daughter of your new owner. I live here too. And I skipped lunch. I was *busy*. I currently have no plans for dinner, and it's nice to meet you too."

Easton's eyes widen, and I can tell his mind went exactly where I wanted it to go. If I have to think about it, about us, then so does he.

Keeley laughs at my comment and bumps shoulders with Easton, brushing her auburn hair away from her face. "Ooh, I like her. I bet you keep your dad on his toes."

"I try."

"You know the team is all talking about what your dad's going to do," she adds, making Easton groan.

"What the fuck, Keeley?"

"What?" She spins, hitting him with a glare. "Was that a secret?"

"No, but I don't need that information coming from me."

"It's not coming from *you*; it came from me."

"I won't say anything," I cut in before they get into a sibling argument, while also trying not to think about the conversation I had with my dad and the issues with the team. "Believe it or not, I can keep secrets from my dad. I do it all the time," I joke to hide the awkwardness I feel until I realize I'm not in fact joking at all. "I'm currently hiding a doozy."

Easton's face scrunches like my admission pains him, and I get it. I'm teasing. I too was enjoying our tryst and could have happily continued on. But life happens.

Keeley, who's thankfully none the wiser, laughs. "Sounds like me."

"Bullshit." Easton scoffs. "Mom knows everything."

"Mom, yes. Dad, no. Anyway." Keeley turns to me and I notice Easton's eyes flash to my body before I shift my gaze to smile back at her. "Sorry for interrupting your work," she says, confusing me until I remember my sketchbook. "I just wanted to say hi."

"Oh, I wasn't... that wasn't. It's not a bother. It was really nice to meet you both."

Keeley smiles, seemingly letting me get away with my little stumble of words, but Easton's not so forgiving, eyeing me curiously before his gaze drops to my things. Sorry, East, but that's not something I'm ever going to share.

"It was great to meet you too," Keeley says, drawing Easton's attention. "I guess we might see you around the stadium."

"Yes, you might."

"Enjoy the sunshine." She waves as she walks away, and when her back is turned, Easton raises a brow, his thinned lips suppressing his expression.

"Nice meeting you, Paige." He says my name slowly before nodding and starting to turn. "See you around."

Like his sister, he waves as he leaves, and I can't help but chance a quick glance at his ass. Such a shame he's a football player. He could have been anyone else and it would have been fine.

Making myself comfortable again, I stretch out onto the recliner and close my eyes. I was going to use this time to sketch before meeting my dad, but I've never been opposed to relaxing, and what better place to do it than by a luxury pool in beautiful weather.

I sigh in contentment, but my bliss only lasts about thirty seconds before my mind drifts into dangerous territory.

To Easton.

As I lie still, my mind conjures up a vivid picture of him staring at me from across the water, his piercing blue eyes drinking me in. His throat bobbing as he swallows, imagining all the things he would do to me if we were alone. If our circumstances were different.

My legs squirm, but I hide it by pretending I'm repositioning myself as

I internally curse. This isn't me. I don't fantasize about guys who give great orgasms. And yet...what I wouldn't give for—

Someone splashes into the pool, and my eyes flash open to find Keeley in the water. And when I sneak a glance Easton's way, his eyes are on me, exactly as I imagined. He shifts on his lounge, much like I did, and the movement draws my attention to his abs. Inappropriately, I wish I was over there with him, despite the fact that I'm pretty sure his mom is reading barely a stone's throw away.

God, what is wrong with me?

There's something about him that draws me in, and the fact that he's now somewhat forbidden makes it even more alluring.

With his cap pulled low on his brow, Easton holds my stare until the woman shifts in the cabana beside his, breaking his trance.

Closing my eyes again, I bite back my smile as a buzzing energy runs through me.

On top of making me hot, he makes me giddy, and that's a dangerous combination.

I'm not sure how long I lie still while my mind whirs with image after image of Easton, but when it feels like a reasonable amount of time has passed for me to leave, I jump up and grab my things, in desperate need of a cold shower.

What is this man doing to me?

I make it to the bar where I'm meeting my dad at six fifty, twenty minutes later than planned, but surprisingly he doesn't call me out.

"Hi, Sweetie." He smiles, standing up as I walk over. "How was your day?" He presses a kiss to my head before pulling a chair out for me to sit down, and it gets me thinking...

"Do you ever date?"

"What?" He chokes as I burst out laughing. "Where did that come from?"

"You pulled out my chair, so I wondered."

"It's how I was brought up. Sorry for being a decent man." He shrugs, a little embarrassed, and my brows furrow.

"Did I hit a nerve? Are you hiding something from me?" It would be good if he was, because then we'd be even.

"I'm hiding plenty." He grins comically, making me laugh out loud again. "But rest assured none of it concerns you."

"Good. Likewise."

His eyes narrow but he laughs.

"So why am I here?" I ask, changing the subject.

"I wanted to see my daughter."

"You saw me two days ago for take-your-daughter-to-work day."

"Okay. You caught me." He raises his hands in the air. "I want you to work with me and the team."

Now it's my turn to choke. "You want me to *what* now?" My voice rises and my lips part in surprise. I did *not* see that coming.

Dad chuckles while simultaneously rolling his eyes at my overexaggerated response. A response that would make more sense to him if he knew I'd been fucking his star wide receiver. *Past tense, of course.*

"I want you to come and work with me," he repeats. "On a charity event with the team." He tries to explain further but it doesn't sound any more appealing the second time I hear it, especially now that he's added more detail.

I can't help but frown and he laughs again. "Do you need me to write it down?"

"Very funny. Who are you and what have you done with my 'I want you to stay away from the players' father?"

"Now who's being funny? I'm still me. I'm asking you to spend time with the guys in a professional capacity, not jump into bed with one."

I burst out laughing, sounding just as guilty as I feel, and Dad notices.

"I can trust you, right?"

"Yes." I roll my eyes again because it's what we do when the other is acting crazy. Not that he is, but it's best if I make the idea appear insane. "I have no plans to 'jump into bed' with anyone on your team. That's not my thing." I smile as a fine layer of guilt seeps into my chest. While it's not exactly a lie—Easton and I usually get creative with other surfaces—it's still a huge misrepresentation of the truth. But really, how am I supposed to answer that?

Dad smiles and I'm relieved to see it's genuine. "Good," he says as he pats my hand. "Then this couldn't be more perfect. After the controversy surrounding the TV show, the event I have in mind will bank us some goodwill and positive vibes, *plus* it will keep you busy."

"Why do you think I need to be kept busy?"

"Because, Paige, I'm your father. And despite the fact that we haven't been that close since the divorce, I know you."

"That may be true, but I haven't exactly been curled up on my couch with nothing to do. I've been working. I've already had two photo shoots since I arrived and—"

"Please don't remind me of your photo shoots." He groans, making me laugh. "You know I'd never hold you back from anything, but there are some things a dad should never see."

"Right back at you, Daddio. Or are you forgetting I saw you half-naked on the cover of that sports magazine."

"I was twenty and your mom showed it to you. You didn't come across it while out shopping for food."

"A chest is a chest."

"Okay. You win. What was the other thing you were going to say?"

"Oh. I've offered to help out the California office of the charity I was working with in New York. We're planning a ball to raise money for youth services."

Dad's eyes widen. "You are going to be busy."

"Told you. There really isn't time for me to—"

"Please."

"Ugh." I throw my head back and fake a groan. At least, I make Dad believe that it's fake when in reality, it's as real as they get. How am I supposed to work with the players and not make it obvious that I'm imagining Easton's face between my legs? "Okay. If you really need my help, I'll do it. But don't blame me if some of the guys try to get in my pants. It's your fault I'm attractive; I got my genes from you."

Dad half laughs, half coughs, and I consider that a win. "You may get your looks from me, but you definitely get your confidence from your mother."

"I know. Remind me to thank her." Especially considering it was that confidence that led me to strip naked for a stranger and look at what that got me—incredible sex with a football star. Thanks, Mom.

"I've set up a board meeting to introduce the D'Angelo Foundation to the team this week," Dad continues, bringing me back to the conversation. "I want you there to pitch some ideas for the event."

"This week? Nothing like throwing me into the deep end before I can swim."

"What are you talking about? You do this all the time. Reuse your old ideas if you have to. They've been done in New York but not here."

"I'm sure everything has been done here," I mumble under my breath. I've worked with lots of different charities, and celebrities for that matter, but I've never worked with sports stars. I tend to stick with companies that align with my personal interests. Although, one could argue that I now have an interest in football.

"Thanks again." Dad ignores my comment and moves on, telling me more about the drama at his New York office, and when his phone rings sometime later, he cringes. "Shit, I lost track of time. I have to go. Are you free for dinner Tuesday night?"

Now this is the dad I remember. Having to leave midconversation. Although, I've got to admit, he's doing it a lot less these days, and this was a last-minute thing. It's not like he walked out on a dinner. "Tuesday? Sure. It's a date."

After pressing another kiss to my forehead, Dad rushes off. He got what he wanted while I'm left staring at the door he raced out of, wondering what the hell I just got myself into. Easton and I may have come to terms with the fact that I'm the daughter of his team's new owner, but working closely with his team is another hurdle entirely.

CHAPTER FIFTEEN

EASTON

Where the hell are they? I pace the hall near the front door, my body tense as I stew over what I'm going to do.

We agreed on seven p.m. How hard is it to make a fucking phone call and—

"They're here," Mom announces, confusing me.

"What do you mean, they're here? I'm at the door."

"Yes, but Macy doesn't know what floor you live on; the concierge just called."

"They did?" My gaze shifts to the intercom near where she's standing and I frown. I didn't hear it.

Mom hits me with an expression to match my own and steps closer. "Want me to go down?"

"No, I need to do it." Mom scrunches her face, and I know what's coming next so I get in first. "I'm not going to make a scene in front of Isaac. I know better than that."

"I wasn't suggesting you would. I just think you need a second to—"

"Please don't tell me to calm down. It's eight p.m. and my son's been missing with someone I trust less than a weather forecast. I'm allowed to be tense."

"You're right. You go down. They'll be waiting."

I stare at her for a few seconds before taking a deep breath in, rolling my shoulders, and releasing it, watching as Mom's concerned expression morphs into a smile. "Better?" I ask.

"Yes. Thank you."

"I'll be back."

The elevator ride is slower than usual, and I find myself wishing I had someone here to distract me. But Mom doesn't need to get wrapped up in my drama, and Keeley left as soon as she got out of the pool. She didn't even stay for dinner. Just used me for my facilities and disappeared. Which, honestly, was for the best. I don't need her opinion on things with Macy.

The elevator stops on level six, and I glare as an old man takes his time getting in. Isaac spent the day with Macy. A few extra seconds isn't going to make a difference to him, yet I'm anxious as hell. What if he hated it? What if she spent their time together the same way she spent our relationship—focused on herself—forcing him to tag along in his stroller.

When we finally reach the lobby, the deep breath I took to calm myself is a distant memory as the tension coils around my middle. If Isaac isn't the happiest kid on the fucking planet when I see his face, I'm going to expect answers.

The doors open, and my heart stops until the crowd parts and Isaac's eyes meet mine. His face lights up and he takes off in a run, almost knocking into a man that cut in front of him.

"*Daddy.*"

I race forward to meet him halfway, lifting him into the air as he crashes into my arms. "Hey Buddy. Did you have a good day?"

"I had a chocolate petsel for dinner." A chocolate pretzel? *The fuck?*

"You're a lucky boy, aren't you?" I smile through my anger. Macy only quit full-time motherhood a few months ago and she's already forgotten how to do it.

Speaking of the devil, Macy joins us and hands over the stroller and Isaac's backpack, greeting me with a wide smile, making me fight not to give her a piece of my mind.

"Macy." I nod instead, my body tense from holding back.

"Easton. How was your luxurious day to yourself?"

My what? Clenching my fists, I smile at Isaac before letting it drop when I face her. "I had a busy day and I missed this little man. You're late."

"Relax. It was an hour. We were having fun. Weren't we?"

Isaac nods but stays curled into my chest.

"Fun eating pretzels?"

"Yep. They're delicious." Macy laughs, and it pisses me off that she doesn't even show an ounce of regret. She probably did it on purpose, knowing it would wind him up before bedtime.

"Okay. Well, are you ready to go up?" I move on, needing to get away from the woman that has the ability to drain the energy from my body—good and bad—with a simple look. I'll tell you who has regrets. I do. I should have sought full custody the second she told me she didn't want to be a mom instead of hoping she'd change her mind. I'm an idiot, but I can't dwell on that now. "Nana's waiting for you," I add, a warmth spreading through me when Isaac's eyes widen in happiness.

"Nana! Yes." He spins around to face Macy and waves. "Bye, Mommy."

I know I shouldn't, but I take satisfaction in the fact that he seems more excited about my mom than he does about his own. Something she brought on all by herself.

I turn to walk away without acknowledging her any further, but she calls out to stop me. "I'm not sure when I'm visiting next, but I'll call again in a week."

Yay. How nice of you to keep your son hanging on when you truly couldn't give a shit about him. "Thanks. Isaac will love that."

Maybe I should have asked Mom to come down with me so she could have watched Isaac while I took a moment to set some ground rules with Macy. Like I'd originally planned. But I forgot when she was late. Now, I still have no idea what her angle is and— *Shit.*

"I need my card back."

"What?"

"My credit card."

"Oh. Yes. Of course." She reaches into her designer purse and reluctantly hands it over as though I'd gifted it to her and had suddenly changed my mind. But I've got news, Macy. That's not how this works. Isaac gets my money, while you get fuck all if I can help it.

"Thanks." She grins.

Without another word, I walk away again, holding my breath until we're in the elevator, and it's only then the stress finally eases.

"Are you tired?" I ask Isaac when he yawns.

"Nope." He yawns again, making me smile.

"Okay, and you had a good day, right?"

"I *told* you," he complains but he didn't really—he only mentioned the pretzels—but as desperate as I am to know, I let it slide.

"I'm glad you had fun, but it's good to have you back. I missed you."

"I missed you too."

We definitely go longer without seeing each other when I'm at away games, but this felt different and I'm not sure why.

"What do you say, you have a quick book with Nana and then it's time for bed?"

"Two books?"

I stare at him deadpan and he laughs, knowing that's my thing. "Fine. Two books. But they have to be short ones."

"Okay, Daddy." He curls into me again, resting his head on my shoulder, and I bask in the warmth until the negativity seeps into my mind. *How the hell am I going to give this kid the life he deserves when I'm already failing? And what do I do about Macy?*

Mom's on the couch watching the TV in silence when I walk out of Isaac's room. I've barely made a sound when she looks up. "How'd you do?"

"He's asleep. *Finally*. And it sounds like he had a good day." I drop down onto the couch beside her and lie back, closing my eyes. After initially only talking about the food he ate, he finally opened up about the rest of his time. Macy took him to the zoo as planned, and they saw all his favorite animals. And mine. His little smile never left his face while he was talking. And while that should have made me happy, it broke my heart. Because how long does he have to wait until he sees her again? And does he make her as happy as she's making him? He's still bathing her in unconditional love, but is she giving it back?

"You make it sound like that's a bad thing," Mom says, and I internally groan before opening my eyes to look at her, contemplating my response. I've just formulated a lie when she calls me out.

"Don't even bother."

"What?"

"If you don't want to talk to me about it, that's fine, but at least go for a walk or something. You'll never sleep unless you get rid of all that built-up tension."

An image of Paige works its way to the forefront of my mind, but I cut that shit off before it turns to a picture of her on her knees.

Mom's right. I do need to let off some steam, but Paige is not an option anymore, plus... "Don't you have to go?"

"Not yet." Mom pats my leg. "I can wait until you get back."

"Why don't you stay? Please." I always offer and she never says yes, but it's getting later and—

"I'm not kicking you out of your bed. I've told you that."

"I wasn't offering my bed. I've got a perfectly good couch."

She knows I'm joking, and yet, no matter what, she'll say no. "Maybe some other time."

"Okay, but I'm dropping Isaac at your place tomorrow. You're not driving home just to come straight back in the morning."

"Thank you. That would be helpful. Now go. You're being nice, and that generally means you're about to explode with anger. Get out of here before you do."

I scoff "okay" even though she's not wrong... I want to break something. And I don't mean hearts and promises.

The season is about to begin. My life is about to be taken over with football, and this year, Isaac doesn't have a mom to look after him. My mom is great, and so is Keeley, at times, but neither of them should have to take on that responsibility. So do I quit? Retire? Change careers for something less demanding? Something that keeps me at home more often. Or do I go against my mom's wishes and hire a nanny like some of the guys do? I'm sure they've got recommendations.

Whatever I decide, it has to happen soon, because every day brings me a day closer to reality.

Taking Mom's advice, I wander the streets of San Francisco, keeping my cap low and my eyes on the ground. The last thing I want to do is be recognized, and since our Super Bowl win last season, that's happening a lot more often.

When I've been walking for the better part of an hour and my muscles hurt from how tightly they're wound, I give in.

We have a preseason game at home tomorrow which always works to distract me, and then come Monday, I'll kill myself at the gym. Something I once told Luke he *shouldn't* do to forget his problems, but desperate times call for desperate measures.

A woman stares at me as I wait to cross the street on my way back home, and I offer her a tight-lipped smile before turning away to avoid her gaze.

There's a newsstand in my line of sight, and seconds after I spot Zane on the cover of *Sports Unlimited*, my eyes lock on a magazine I've never seen before. Or more specifically, the woman on the cover.

Is that Paige?

The woman—Paige's twin—is draped seductively in a bath with her hair falling strategically over her shoulders, covering her breasts. She's not naked, but it's easy to note that her white top is completely see-through based on the clear view I have of her skin. And I'm standing a few feet away. Imagine the detail when I'm up close.

I study the image before a thought hits me. Of course it's Paige. That looks exactly like her bathroom, and she said she had a photo shoot when I saw her a few weeks back but— She's wet and practically *naked*.

Someone knocks me from behind, snapping me back the present to find it's my time to cross the street.

Only now I don't want to. I can't. Not until I know for sure.

Pulling my cap lower on my brow—as though that will make all the difference—I take a step closer to one of the few newsstands still in existence, and grab Zane's sports magazine even though it pains me. I pretend to look at other items on the shelves—candy, cigarette lighters. I even risk drawing attention to myself by looking at a packet of football trading cards. But my gaze barely lingers more than a few seconds before it flits back to where it so desperately wants to go.

To Paige.

I need answers.

What kind of magazine is that?

Is she naked inside?

Do they sell those kinds of magazines right here on the street?

"She's hot, right?" The guy working the store cuts into my thoughts, unwelcome. "You know, I think she lives near here. I swear I've seen her around. Although I've been staring at that cover for so long that maybe I'm imagining it."

"What?" I snap. "Are you talking to me?"

"Who else would I be... Wait...you look familiar."

I still, and the tension already coursing through me thickens.

"You're that actor, right?" He snaps his fingers and I almost sigh in relief.

"That's me. And I'm not in the mood. I'll take this one." I hold up the sports magazine still in my hand, and the guy fucking laughs.

"Yeah, okay." He rolls his eyes and lifts Paige's magazine off the stand. "Here, I know you want this one too. I'll put it in a bag so your girlfriend doesn't see it." He puts on a voice and I almost deck him. *What the fuck*?

"I want what I goddamn asked for. Nothing else."

"*Jesus*. Okay." He takes Paige's magazine out of the bag and grabs the cash from my hand, mumbling to himself about asshole actors.

And I instantly regret my outburst.

I want that magazine.

No, I *need* it.

But at the same time, I need to chill and walk away.

So what if it's her. She can do whatever she likes. Paige is *not* my business.

At all.

So why do I care?

CHAPTER SIXTEEN

PAIGE

I've been staring at my notes for so long it's beginning to look like foreign handwriting, but for some reason nothing is standing out. I initially dove headfirst into this event like I would for any other. But at around three a.m., my brain decided to remind me of one tiny little difference—my dad is relying on this event to help save the team's image.

What the hell kind of pressure is that?

He didn't even make a big deal out of that piece of information, and yet, my mind has turned it into a goliath of an issue. Yes, he only meant it in the form of the team needing some positive exposure, but that's still something I can fuck up.

It wouldn't be the first time my name has been thrown around negatively.

Hell, I'm going through that right now, only no one's discovered that it's me the stories are referring to.

But it sure as hell pisses me off.

In the past two days, I've seen three separate gossip sites reporting on the alleged leaked letters about a New York socialite. The letters are written as though they've come straight from a teenager's diary, which is leading the said sites to assume it's someone younger than me. À la *Gossip Girl* style. But my guess is that someone paid someone much younger to write them, like someone's much younger dog walker that's been trying to get noticed by that someone for years.

That someone being Christian's mom.

The latest...

Gossip Central has your exclusive look at the newest mystery letter from New York's high society. "*Dressed as a Succubus, she set her sights on a wealthy pirate and his superhero friend before sucking them both into her web. They disappeared for hours and when they returned, a young fairy was crying over her boyfriend's seduction. She's what people call a man-eater, and she's not to be trusted.*"

Keep reading for more.

A man-eater. A succubus that sucks men into her web? I mean, what the hell? It was a freaking costume party.

I can't argue that everything they wrote is garbage because I remember that party and I *did* disappear for hours with two guys. But the rest? Lies. For one, both guys were single at the time. Actually, one of them—the pirate—was *my* boyfriend. Not the crying fairy's. And the superhero still hasn't had a girlfriend to this day.

Pirate—a.k.a. Christian—had split from his college sweetheart months earlier but like with me, he held off making it public. Was she a fairy? Maybe. But that part of the letter is still bullshit.

The entire story is bullshit. Or at least, the reasons behind it are.

At the moment, Christian's parents haven't released enough to justify me panicking and telling them what I know. I still haven't decided what I'm going to do with the information I have, but I can't stay quiet.

Christian's father and uncle are stealing from their clients. And I know this because I overheard a conversation between his mom and his auntie. If the truth comes out, my ex's family is ruined. It will destroy their business and life as they know it.

But I don't have any proof. Yet. Though I do have someone working on it.

The thing is, I assumed they'd leave me alone once I left New York. I assumed wrong.

But for now, the threat of people thinking I had a threesome is nothing compared to what Christian will go through if this all comes to light. And even though we're not together anymore—and he's a dick—I can't do that to him until I know with absolute certainty that I'm right.

Shaking off my thoughts, I push my personal life out of my head, *like always*, and flick back and forth through my folder, trying to decide on an idea for the charity event—a ball, a celebrity tennis match, a silent auction, a *not* so silent auction where the players are the prize, a garden party. *Ugh.* Nothing is jumping out at me, and if I can't think of anything soon, the board will decide for me and I'll have to roll with it. No matter how boring it is. I'm about to throw something—namely this ideas folder that has no freaking ideas—at the wall in front of me when a ringing saves me from my madness.

Oh bless you, sweet calling soul. I rush across the room to grab my phone from the charger and freeze when I see the ID.

Goddammit. Why did I have to think of Christian and his goddamn family? I could ignore the call, but he's likely to fly over here for a visit if it's something important, and nobody wants that.

"Christian," I answer plainly.

"Paige. What the hell do you think you're doing?"

"Excuse me?"

"The magazine," he exclaims. "You're naked."

A laugh bursts out of me, and I have to bite my cheek to calm down. "I'm not naked, Christian. I'm clearly wearing clothes."

"Yes, but they're see-through."

"They are? Shit. No one told me that. Oh God. Oh God. Whatever will I do." While my words scream panic, my lackluster tone says otherwise, and judging by the scoff, Christian is not impressed.

"Cut the crap, Paige. You're practically naked in *Silver and Stripes* magazine. And—"

"Since when do you read fashion magazines?"

"I don't. But—"

"Okay, since when do you care about that stuff?"

"I don't, but—"

"What the hell is the problem?"

"You were *naked* in a very popular *business* and fashion magazine and you mentioned my name in the accompanying article. It caused a lot of issues for me. Not to mention it gives my parents more ammunition for their stupid vendetta against you. Are things that bad that—"

"Stop. Before you say something that makes me fly home to mess up your pretty little face. What *I* do with *my* body is up to me. And I barely mentioned you. It was a throwaway comment. Your parents aside, I don't see how that could have caused you any—"

"I'm engaged."

"You're what?" I pause, my mouth hanging open. Does time run slower in San Francisco? I could have sworn I'd only been here a couple of months.

Christian sighs. "I didn't want you to find out like this. I was going to talk to you in person, but we've run out of time. I know our relationship was an unconventional one, but according to the people...we were together a long time, so I'm aware we might have an image issue and—"

"Wait," I cut him off, and while I'd really love to address his "to the people" statement, that's not important right now. What's more important is... "My image will be *fine*; everyone will just assume you cheated."

"I never fucking cheated."

I fold my arms over my chest and hit my phone with so much sass I'm hoping it magically transports over to him.

Christian groans deep in the back of his throat and it makes me smile. Maybe my silence did the trick.

"Fine," he grates. "I cheated, but we were never exclusive exclusive, so it doesn't count."

"The *'people'* thought we were."

"Jesus, Paige. I need you to work with me here. Please."

I don't have to look at him to know he's nearing his breaking point. If he was in front of me right now, I have no doubt his hands would be in his hair and he'd be tugging at the strands.

"Why did you call, Christian? What do you want from me?"

"My fiancée and I will be in LA late next month, and I want you to meet us for a drink."

"What? Why the hell would I want to do that?"

"So that we can be seen together. A photo will leak, and the media won't have any lies to spread about our time together. You told the magazine we were still friends. This isn't a stretch."

Dammit. I should have known that would come back to bite me in the ass. That's all I said. That we were "still friends," and I only said that so they'd stop asking for more juicy details. But lying about being friends is easy. Spending time together is not.

"What are you worried about?"

"That they'll assume Nicola and I were together before you and I broke up."

"So they'll *assume* correctly. We only broke up a few months ago, Christian. How are you engaged?"

"Does it matter?" he snaps. "Do you care? Am I breaking your frozen heart? You never really wanted me. Yes, we had an amazing sex life, but it never moved beyond that. If I'd felt even a spark of something real between us, I never would have strayed. I cared, Paige. I cared and I deserved better than that."

Holy-fucking-hell. Talk about a slap to the face. "My heart's not frozen." *I don't think.*

"Are you kidding me? I told you I loved you three times, and you never once said it back."

"You said it during sex. I thought it was just one of the games we played. The game of pretending."

Christian's loud, unrestrained laugh echoes through the phone, and I start to question my memories of our time together. "The difference between you and me, Paige, is that I only played pretend when we were role-playing in the bedroom. *You*, you were pretending for our entire relationship."

Jesus. My dead, frozen heart starts pounding in my chest. I thought we were on the same page. Did I miss something?

"I'm—" I cut myself off before saying sorry. He might be telling the truth, but our relationship had many issues; the feeling or lack of feeling argument is merely one of them. "I'll meet you for a drink. But—and there's a big but—you need to tell your parents to quit leaking stories about me. About us. What do you think will happen if your fiancée finds out? How will she feel having to read about our sex life?"

Christian grunts and I wait for his argument. "I don't control my parents. You know that just as well as I do. If you have an issue with them, you need to work it out. They won't stop until you do."

"What kind of response is that? Just tell them it's ruining your career or something. Better yet, how about I get it all out in the open so they have nothing more to share. I could do a tell-all in a men's magazine. I'll put all my bits on display while mentioning your name over and over. And your parents' names. And..." I trail off, not wanting to bring up what I know.

"And what, Paige. And what? You won't tell me. My parents won't tell me. What *is it*?"

Oh. So that's why he won't help me with them. Because it's driving him crazy to be out of the loop. "If I tell you, I'm going to have to k—"

"Yeah. Yeah. I get it. Telling me would be like opening up, and you've never been the type to do that."

Jesus. He's really digging a knife into my chest. But he's dead wrong. I cared. I may not have loved him, but I cared. It's the reason I'm not telling him about his parents. Because if he truly has no idea, he's going to need that plausible deniability.

"For this, I am sorry," I say honestly, because I am. As for the rest... "I'm not meeting you for a drink. But feel free to tell the world we're civil."

"Paige, please?"

"No."

"Fuck, okay."

I move to hang up but he cuts in before I do. "Please don't do a men's magazine. God knows you've got the body for it. But it's not you."

I roll my eyes and laugh. "Thanks, I'll take your opinion into consideration. Bye, Christian."

"Bye, Paige."

I hang up and fall back to the couch before massaging my temples. That was not a conversation I ever saw coming. I'm not closed off to feelings or whatever the hell he was implying. That was just never in the cards for us. And I thought we both understood that. But I guess I was wrong.

No matter the case, I wish I wasn't still so caught up in the Mikkleson family. I was supposed to be in California for a fresh start.

And since I'm currently questioning things going on in my life, why does everyone keep saying I was naked? You could see my nipples through a wet top. That's it. People wear see-through clothes all the time. God, it's even become a fashion statement on the red carpet. It's not the big deal everyone is making it out to be. I'm so damn proud of that magazine spread, and I won't let anyone ruin it for me.

But I was joking about the men's magazine. I know my limits. And I've already met them. Doesn't mean I think poorly of anyone that does pose for those magazines. I'm all for people being able to do what they want with their own bodies, but that also means they shouldn't be forced into parading themselves around if that's not what they want to do. Which, unfortunately, means the player auction is off the list. A shame really because I could have bid for Easton all in the name of charity. I could have told my dad that Easton was the safest choice because he had a kid and was grumpy all the time. It would have been the perfect alibi. But it's not to be.

If only I knew what was.

I spend the next few hours rolling ideas around in my mind until I have two plans in place. A conservative or boring option and something a little bit out there. And when the clock strikes six a.m., I'm exhausted and ready for bed.

But also a little confused. I usually find this so easy. What's so different this time?

God, why did I sign up for this again?

Oh, that's right... I had no choice.

CHAPTER SEVENTEEN

EASTON

It's been days and I'm still thinking about that goddamn magazine. And what's worse is that I went from seeing Paige all the fucking time, even when I didn't want to, to her being nowhere in sight.

And it's driving me crazy.

"I think Reed and Bria had a fight," Luke says, sidling up to me when we get onto the field for practice, his words confusing me as they cut into my thoughts.

"What?"

"I think Reed and Bria are fighting," he repeats and I wish I'd never asked.

"Who the fuck is Bria and why do I care?"

"Bria is Reed's bestie. You know. The girl he went to college with."

Huh? I stare at him confused. "How the hell would I know who he went to college with? And again...why do I care?"

Luke shakes his head as though I'm being a dick and keeps talking. "You should care because he's moodier than usual and he needs our help."

"So, help him. You don't need me."

"Yeah. I do. I'm not good at that stuff. You helped me once; I know you can do it again. Let's get a drink after practice. The three of us. I could even call Dylan. We can get the support gang together."

"Call us the 'support gang' again, and you'll be the one needing help. I've already got plans."

"Tomorrow then," he counters. "Or Saturday."

"For fuck's sake." *He's relentless.* "Don't you have a wife and kid to go home to?"

"Yeah. I do. But this is important, and my wife would understand that."

"Yeah, well, I'm not as lucky."

Luke grimaces before running his hand through his hair. "Fuuck. I didn't mean—"

"I know," I cut him off. "Coach is calling you to line up," I lie, watching as Luke turns in the direction we last saw Coach before I walk away, leaving him alone. Fucking "support gang." We're not friends. I've left that chat more than I've contributed to it. I'm good with group workouts. Or talk about the game. But I don't need to be involved in anyone else's business, and they don't need to be involved in mine.

A memory of my day out with Luke comes to mind and I internally groan. I should have left him alone because now he won't shut up about it. And yet, I can't completely regret it because it seems to have helped him. I can, however, refuse to do it again.

Coach actually blows the whistle for us to line up, and my mind shifts into game mode. Though I do find myself glancing over at Reed. I hate to say it, but Luke's right—Reed's usually sunny persona seems to have disappeared.

Though I have full confidence in Luke and Dylan to help him out.

I throw myself into our practice session, pushing myself to the limits, blocking the world out of my mind. And when I'm done, Paige's dad is waiting on the sidelines, his gaze directed at me, a smile on his face, while I have no doubt mine pales as the blood drains away.

"Easton, hi. Can I have a word?"

"Of course." I force a smile but... *Fuck*. He found out. We haven't even been formally introduced, so why else would he know me by name and want a word with me. I'm about to be fucked...and not in a good way.

"What can I do for you?" I ask when we've moved out of earshot.

He smiles awkwardly and huffs out a breath. *Here it comes.* "I need to get in touch with Keeley and she's not answering her phone."

"What?" I do a double take and he laughs.

"Sorry, I know I'm not supposed to know about the two of you. But she mentioned it, and I wouldn't ask if it wasn't important."

Again, what? A few days ago she hadn't even met him, and now he's desperate to speak to her?

"Ah. She..." *Dammit.* How do I tell him that Keeley's taken the morning off to look after my son because my mom had an appointment? "She usually switches her phone off in meetings," I say instead. "I think she mentioned she had one until around midday today."

"Great." He breathes a sigh of relief. "Perfect. I'll try her again after that. Thank you."

He pats my back before walking away and it's my turn to sigh. We were lucky if we saw the previous owner once a month and that was usually just in passing. I swear Paige's father is everywhere. Or am I just seeing him so much because I don't want to? Kind of like when you buy a new truck that you think is unique and then all of a sudden everyone has one. Fuck, he's just like Paige. Until now. Now she's disappeared. And I should consider that a blessing. Because while I'm certain Salvatore D'Angelo doesn't know about Paige and me, with hundreds of new faces for him to remember, he now knows mine. And that's one step closer to him finding out.

Determined to push Paige from my mind, I detour on my drive home to avoid going past the newsstand. Only I find myself looking for the damn magazine at the gas station when I fill up my truck. And then again at the register of the store when I stop to grab food for the week.

But like Paige, it's nowhere to be found.

It's like that newsstand had the only copy in existence. Or I imagined the whole damn thing. Which is possible with the million things I have running through my head at any given moment.

When I finally make it home, sans magazine, the apartment is unusually quiet. I panic until I see a text from my mom telling me she's taken Isaac to the pool and to use the time to rest.

To rest.

I'm not sure I even know what that feels like anymore. There's always something twisting my body in knots, and today, it's Paige.

After unpacking the groceries and deciding on dinner, I spend twenty minutes flicking through the options on TV, hoping to distract myself from my thoughts but failing miserably until I find a replay of the Giants baseball game from the weekend.

Feet up, I take Mom's advice and it's surprisingly not as difficult as I thought it would be.

I'm partway through the second inning when the door slams open and Isaac comes charging through the house. "Daaadddy."

"In here, Little Buddy." I sit up just in time for him to dive on top of me.

"Can we play the pinning game?"

"The spinning game? Now? It's almost dinnertime."

"Please." He hits me with a huge grin and it's so adorable, I can't say no.

"Okay. Let's play the spinning game."

"Yeah." He jumps up and starts pulling at the coffee table, trying to move it on his own. "Dad." Heave. "I." Heave. "Help, please."

With little effort, I shift the table behind the couch, giving us plenty of room to spin, and then it's on. Arms linked, I spin Isaac around until his legs are flying through the air, his giggles drawing Mom's attention.

"Hi, Mom." I nod in her direction. "All good at your appointment today?" I ask, my vision blurring as the dizziness overwhelms me. "Hang on, Buddy. I need a quick break."

I lower Isaac to the floor and he loses his balance. "Woah." He spins on his own before flopping onto the couch.

Mom laughs as she joins us. "My appointment was fine. How was your day?"

"Uneventful."

"That's nice. Oh...we saw that girl from your work. The big boss's daughter I think you called her."

Paige. Goddammit. And I was doing so well. "Oh yeah? I'm surprised you remembered her."

Mom laughs as she shakes her head. "I know I'm older than you but I'm not losing my memory yet."

"Come on." I roll my eyes. "I didn't mean it like that. I just didn't think you saw her."

"I saw enough. Is she an artist?"

"Huh?"

"An artist. Is your boss's daughter an artist?"

"How the hell would I know?" I only know she's one hell of a model and a goddess with her m—

"No need to get all"—she looks at Isaac still rolling around on the couch—"grumpy about it." I have no doubt that if we'd been alone, she would not have used the term grumpy.

"I'm not grumpy. I just don't know her. At all." That's not a complete lie, so I don't feel that bad about it.

"Next time I see her, I'm going to ask."

"Ask what?"

"If she's an artist. Jeez."

"Come on, Mom. Don't do that. Please leave her in peace."

"Why? Are you worried I'll make you look bad?"

"What?" My eyes widen of their own accord. "Why would I be worried about that?"

"Because of your big boss?" She raises an eyebrow as though she's caught me doing something I shouldn't be doing. But she's fishing. She's got nothing. Because there's nothing to get. Paige and I are over. Done. Finito.

"He doesn't even know who I am, Mom. But I'd prefer you left P— his daughter alone."

"Okay." She smiles to herself. "I will."

Mom thankfully moves on to other topics, and after dinner, Isaac and I walk her to her car before I get him ready for bed.

Despite asking Isaac how his day was several times throughout the night, he only manages to remember after I've switched off the light, having convinced myself he was asleep.

"The girl was nice today," he tells me as I'm closing the door.

"What girl?"

"The one at the pool."

Shit, now he's talking about Paige. "That's good. What did she do?"

"She helped me when I fell over."

"You fell over? Are you okay?"

"Yeah. I was running." He hides his face and I smile.

"You won't do that again, will you?"

"No. Water is lippry."

"It is. I'm happy the girl was there to help."

"Me too. She didn't get mad."

I should hope not. "Did you think she would?"

"Mom did. When I fell over at the zoo."

She what? Jesus, Macy.

"You never told me you hurt yourself at the zoo."

"I didn't mean to."

Shit.

Walking to the bed, I tuck him back in and lie beside him before pressing a kiss to his forehead. "You're not in trouble for falling or for not telling me. I just want to know you're okay. Always. I care about you."

"Okay." I'm not sure my words have sunk in, but when he lets out a loud yawn, I park the conversation for another time.

"Time to sleep."

"Okay, Daddy. Good night."

"Good night, Isaac. I love you."

He immediately rolls over, so I chance leaving the room again, quietly pulling the door shut before switching on the monitor.

As soon as I've cleaned up, I fall into bed, exhausted, purposely bringing Paige to mind so I don't get worked up about Macy.

She got mad at him for falling over? He's three and— No, think of Paige. Paige who I can't find while everyone else does.

Maybe she's avoiding me. God knows I should be doing the same thing. If only I could stop *thinking*.

I allow myself a moment to picture her, to question what she's doing, to imagine my face between her legs, and then my mind drifts to the cover of her magazine.

Again.

Maybe I need to see the pictures to take my mind off it. Once I know, I'll be able to move on. It's a stupid curiosity thing. And it's taking up too much of my headspace.

Decision made, I bring up a search engine and type in her name. At least, I type Paige D'Angelo, assuming she has the same last name as her father.

I get hit after hit of associated links. Some take me to gossip sites with paparazzi shots of Paige out and about in New York, some take me to social media, showing me her personal pages or photos she's tagged in, and *a lot* of links take me to fashion magazines. She's definitely a model and Goddammit...I don't need to see these. The idea was that I'd move on, but fuck, she's stunning. She has an edge to her that differs from the other models in the shots and— who the fuck is that guy? He's draped over her like he owns her and...*not fucking important.* God, what am I doing?

I groan to myself before closing my eyes and searching my mind for the name of the magazine. M...? No. Something about glitter. No... Silver and... *Got it.*

A second later I have the cover image in front of me and a link directing me to the rest of the article. My finger hovers over the link. This is it. The moment.

Cursing myself for being so goddamn crazy over this, I laugh and press on the screen, ready for whatever I see.

But when the first picture loads, my eyes widen as my jaw comically drops. Scrap that. I'm not at all ready because... *Jesus fucking Christ.*

CHAPTER EIGHTEEN

PAIGE

My eyes bounce between my latest sketch and the junk stack of paper on the floor which is getting dangerously close to toppling over. I can't seem to get anything right at the moment. Sometimes the hands look disfigured, sometimes the lips are too thin, sometimes the eyes don't bore into your soul like I want them too. Like they once did.

And I have no idea what I'm doing differently.

Is it my new environment? The fact that I'm not living the same carefree life I was living back in New York. Yes, I helped work on charity events, and used my platforms to raise awareness for the things I was passionate about. But my spare time was mine, and I spent that time living my best life.

Now, it feels like I've been hit in the face with reality. Nothing has really changed, and yet, everything has. I've had a wake-up call but I can't even pinpoint what it was that woke me up.

I trace my finger over the pencil strokes of the face, taking in her smile lines and the evidence of a happy life, and instead of adding it to my rejection pile, I fold it in half and slip it into my top drawer, giving myself another twenty-four hours to mull over it.

Not that I have a deadline for anything. I just don't like to dwell on things for too long.

When I'm done, I pour a glass of wine and pull up the file for the Storm charity event. The board opted for my conservative venture consisting of a cocktail-style dinner with a dance floor and silent auction but allowed me to at least set a theme. What theme, though, is still to be decided.

Setting pen to paper, I try to brainstorm, but my mind drifts to my afternoon by the pool, or more specifically, to meeting Easton's mom and his beautiful little boy. I had planned to leave them alone, because what good could possibly come from getting to know the family of a guy you're not supposed to have anything to do with? But when Isaac fell over in front of me, I couldn't hold back.

Turns out my heart isn't frozen or dead like Christian claimed it to be, because that little boy's expression broke it. It wasn't so much the tears of pain that got me, but the fear in his eyes when I raced over, as if I was going to make it worse. As if I was going to scold him for it. I would have blamed Easton; I've seen his gruff side, so it easily could have been that. But when he asked for his dad to make the pain go away, it was clear he wasn't the issue. But who?

His Nana very obviously worshipped the ground he walked on, but I guess you never know what goes on behind closed doors.

A memory of Easton's and my first conversation comes to mind and I remember what he said about his ex. How she was always breaking shit. Is that Isaac's mom? I'm not even sure she's still in the picture, but if she is... No. *Goddammit.* I can't get involved. It's not good for anyone at this time in my life. There's too much uncertainty. But one thing I know for sure...I don't like her. Even if she's nice.

Getting back to my work, I spend the next hour researching themes, trying to find one that works for a bunch of brawny men and executives, and when my phone rings, I welcome the distraction. Even if it is an unknown number.

"Hello, Paige speaking."

"Paige, it's Austin." The guy I hired to look into the Mikkleson family.

"Austin. Hi. Please tell me you've found something."

"I have, but you're not going to like it."

Shit. "My ex is involved." *Dammit.* I may not care for him anymore, but I was genuinely hoping he wasn't a part of it.

"No," Austin states plainly, making me frown. "At least, I don't think so. Other than his questionable habits with women, namely having a different woman in every country, when it comes to his business, he's squeaky clean. To the point that I have to wonder if he's actually clueless."

My lips quirk into a smile, but I don't let the humor take over because that's not why he called. "What won't I like then?"

"Your mom invested in their company about six months before you called me."

"What the actual fuck? Why would she do that?"

"I don't know. I'm not usually hired to understand people's psyche."

"Sorry." I huff out a laugh. "I know that. But I don't get it. Did you find anything else? Evidence, maybe? Something I can use to ensure it's not just my word against theirs?"

"Not yet. Their systems are tight and they're undoubtedly being careful now that they think you know something. But rest assured, I will. It's only a matter of time."

"Thanks. In the meantime, I'll wait to see what they're going to release about me next."

Austin falls silent for a beat before clearing his throat. "Would you rather know ahead of time, or is that going to make you stress?"

"Oh God, you know?"

"I...ah... got access to a file they weren't too worried about protecting. Photos and..."

"I don't need the details. I wouldn't put it past them to have access to Christian's phone, so I know what exists. I just hope we beat them to it."

"I'm on it."

"Thank you."

I blow out a breath when he hangs up and throw myself back into my work. Funny that barely five minutes ago, I wanted to distract myself from work and now I want the opposite. I need it.

How the hell is my mom involved with Christian's family? What happened to the simpler life?

For the next couple of days, I focus on the work I need to do for the upcoming charity events and not much else. I've always liked to get the bulk of my work out of the way so I can take my time with the details and not stress that I'm going to let the charity down. This time around is no exception. The only issue is that now, I feel like I'm racing the clock.

The Mikkleson leaks may not have bothered me in the past, but if they're sitting tight on photos and videos, like the one Christian sent me a little while back, I'm fucked and it's not going to look good for the charities. Or my dad.

Every time my phone rings, I jump at it, hoping it's Austin with some news, and every time it's a text, I cringe, wondering if it's going to be someone telling me they've seen something about me online.

On Tuesday morning, I'm on my way out for a run, hoping to clear my head, when I come across my dad in the lobby.

"Paige." A beaming smile adorns his face just like it always does when he sees me, and a load of guilt settles in my stomach. What if I fuck this all up for him? He's already having a hard time with his business and the big decisions he has to make with the team. He doesn't need to add a disgraced daughter to the mix. God, maybe the half-naked photo shoot wasn't a good idea. If some of Christian's and my photos leak, it's going to add to my father's embarrassment.

But even with that in mind, I don't regret it. Any of it. No one forced me to do anything. The only injustice would be Christian's family stealing from Christian's phone and choosing to share the photos with the world.

"Why the grim expression?" Dad asks, and I quickly school my features.

"Sorry, I've got a lot on my mind. How are you? It feels like forever since I've seen you," I joke and he laughs. It's only been a few days, but since I moved here, it's the longest we've gone. A huge contrast between the years we spent apart.

"I'm good. Now. Ask me again at the end of the week."

"Why?" I wince as he hits me with an equally grim look.

"I'm making my first big changes to the team structure, and they're not going to like it."

Apparently nobody is going to like anything at the moment. So much going on. "What are you doing? Does it affect the players?"

I hold my breath for Easton, but when Dad laughs, I relax. "For the bigger picture, yes, but I'm trying hard not to mess with a championship team."

"Understandable. I better let you go then."

"Are we still on for dinner tonight? I could use the company."

"Of course. There's something I wanted to talk to you about."

Dad's eyes widen before he steps closer. "Everything okay?"

"Yes." I laugh at his protectiveness. It's strange and I'm not used to it. "I'm fine. I just wanted to talk to you about Mom."

He fakes a shiver. "What did she do this time?"

"That's a good question, Dad. But it's nothing you need to worry about. We'll talk tonight." I'm not sure how I'm going to ask him for advice without telling him how I know about Mom or why I'm worried, but I've got the day to figure it out. Because as much as I'd love to take this all on by myself, I think he knows Mom better than I do.

Blasting my music while I run the streets of San Francisco, I make my way toward the beach, running along the shoreline, taking in the calm. And when I get back, I'm feeling better. More refreshed. Ready to tackle the big questions in my life.

But when I walk through the lobby and find Easton standing in front of the elevator, I pause, and almost consider turning around and heading back in the direction I came from.

Easton is another of life's problems, and one I'd foolishly tried to take off my list.

It's been over a week since I've seen him, and I'd prefer not to be a sweaty and emotional wreck when I do. Because despite us both knowing that what we had was casual and fleeting, I liked the way he made me feel when he looked at me. It was a different kind of wanted. Even if it was just sex.

Slowing my pace, I run through my options—to see him or not to see him—but when the elevator doors open and he steps aside to let people out, glancing in my direction, the decision is made for me. Busted.

Biting back a smile, I lift my fingers in the smallest of waves while he nods expressionless, and after we both enter the elevator, we stand on opposite sides of the space, making way for it to fill.

There's an invisible tension in the air as we coast toward my floor, but I'm unsure if I'm the only one feeling it because Easton's doing a damn good job at keeping his eyes focused anywhere but on me. And just when I think we're going to go another day without speaking, the last person departs the level before mine. And we're alone.

The buzz running through me intensifies and I both love and hate it.

On one hand, the spark he ignites in me is exciting, but on the other hand, it sucks that I can't do anything about it.

Easton remains silent as we travel the additional floor to my stop, and I arm myself, ready to call him out, when he finally speaks.

"I saw your photo spread," he says, holding the button to keep the doors open.

And my stomach sinks. That's all I need right now. For Easton to jump on the Paige-shouldn't-be-naked bandwagon. Because if he's not happy about those photos, it's potentially about to get worse.

"I'm sorry if it affected you in any way," I say though I don't really mean it. "I clearly wasn't thinking about anyone else and—"

"What are you talking about?"

"You said you saw my photos. It's not hard to guess which ones you're referring to. So I was preempting your disappointment."

"Disappointment? The fuck. I've spent the last few days thinking about those damn photos, and I mean, *really* giving them thought. The only disappointment I feel"—he pins me with his stare and my heart pounds in my chest—"is that I wasn't there to bend you over that bathtub, and that I'm no longer allowed to be thinking that way. Because Paige...that fucking body. That photo. It could make a man crazy."

"A man... or?"

"A man. I can't give you any other answer."

He releases the button and steps back, allowing the doors to close, but I throw my hand out to stop them.

"Why did you have to be a football player?" I ask, my heart lodged in my throat.

Easton huffs, a soft smile on his lips. "The same reason you're a D'Angelo. It's in our blood."

"Ugh. That's not something that can easily be changed. Trust me, I've tried."

Easton's smile widens and my chest tightens. I could spend hours trying to elicit that little twitch of his lips. Surly Easton is hot, alpha Easton is even hotter, but happy Easton? That guy could melt a woman's panties right off. Including mine.

"If you ever figure it out," he says, his smile gone, "let me know. Until then, I'll see you around?"

"You will."

I let the doors go but they open again before I've taken a step. "And Paige,"—Easton's eyes lock on mine—"don't take that disappointed crap from anyone. Be proud."

I'm so unprepared for his comment that the doors shut before I've even uttered a thank you. Because while I am proud, and I don't need anyone to tell me I should be, I kind of like that he did.

CHAPTER NINETEEN

PAIGE

Dad stares at me with his eyebrow cocked. "Well, that certainly took my mind off my own issues." He frowns, seemingly lost in thought until he adds, "You're right, that's very odd behavior."

I just told him about Mom's interest in the Mikkleson business, and the face he pulled was priceless.

"So, I'm not missing something?" I've been thinking about this all day, and I can't for the life of me figure out why she would invest in a company she has no interest in. She told me that herself.

"You could be," Dad says, still musing. "I may not know much about your mom's dealings anymore, but if you'd have asked me, I never would have guessed she'd get caught up with your ex's family."

I cringe. "I don't think he was my ex when she invested."

"Shit."

"Yep."

"Could she have done it thinking your families—our families—were going to merge?"

My eyes widen as I quickly shake my head. "If she did, she was completely misguided. I never once gave her any indication that we were end-game. I'm not even sure I believe in all that, so there's no way I spoke to Mom about it."

"*Paige*," Dad lightly scolds, "I hope that's not because of your mom and me."

"It's not. Believe it or not, I can make up my own mind. I'm pretty clever like that."

Dad rolls his eyes. "I know how clever you are. But that doesn't mean your childhood hasn't influenced your decision-making. In your *own* mind."

"You're not that important, Dad. Don't get a big head."

I smile like I'm joking, but we both know I have daddy issues. I've never shied away from that. Doesn't mean I need to discuss them with my father. I'm not closed off to the idea of love or marriage, despite what Christian believes; it's just not high on my priority list. But even if it was, it was never going to be him.

I want someone that sees through my name and my wealth and wants me for who I am. I want someone who is willing to protect me with all that they have but understands that I'm going to want to fly. And I want someone that doesn't need to play games to determine who's more desperate. I want someone just as obsessed with me as I am with them.

I want an equal.

And it wouldn't hurt if he was built like a god, with an expert mouth and fingers that... Anyway, is that too much to ask?

"Have you spoken to your mom?" Dad asks, interrupting my thoughts. "Maybe there's a simple, noncontroversial explanation. You never know." His expression suggests he doesn't necessarily believe that, and it makes me laugh.

"I thought you still loved her? That doesn't sound like a man in love."

"Does it sound like a man scorned? She broke my heart. It would make me feel better to discover she was a bad person."

"Shut up. No, it wouldn't. You'd hate that. For me."

"Uh. Why are you so smart?"

"I don't know, but it certainly doesn't come from my dad."

Dad laughs before a puzzled expression takes over his features. "How did you know about your mom anyway? If not from her?"

"If I tell you, I'm going to have to kill you."

"*Paige.*"

Why doesn't anyone ever accept that as a response? Or laugh? It's funny.

"I can't tell you right now. All you need to know is that I'm fine. And you don't need to worry about me."

"I'll *always* worry about you. Even when you weren't speaking to me, I was worried. But I also trust you. Though, I think you should call your mom."

"I will. If for no other reason than I miss her."

Dad and I keep the conversation light for the rest of dinner. He doesn't mention what's going on with the football team, and I don't ask, knowing he wanted me to take his mind off things. But it's obvious that it's eating away at him, so I make plans to have dinner with him again in a couple of days. My way of checking in because I too worry about him.

When I get back to my apartment, I bring up Mom's number and stare down at the screen. We've been speaking often, with me pretending she's not still a little annoyed that I left New York, but now that I have something to ask her, I can't bring myself to call.

Benching the conversation until tomorrow, I'm about to put my phone away when it rings in my hand.

And it's Mom. As though she sensed I needed to speak with her.

"Mom?" I answer, a little thrown.

"Hi Sweetie." She sighs loudly into the phone before whispering, "I'm sorry."

"What?" My confusion deepens.

"I miss you and I shouldn't be holding that over your head. Plenty of kids fly the coop. I shouldn't have expected you to stay close forever."

Wow. Again... what? "Thank you. I miss you too. But where did this come from?"

Mom sighs again. "I was updating my will, and it made me realize how selfish I've been."

"Did you take me out of it?" I joke. At least, I hope it's a joke. And when Mom laughs, I'm somewhat relieved. Not because I'm desperate for the money, more so because I wouldn't want her to cut me out of her life like that. *And* because my brother should not be left with our family's fortune. The world doesn't need that. And he can't handle that much responsibility.

"I would never take you out of my will," Mom confirms. "Your brother drives me crazy on a daily basis and he's still there."

"Good to know." That confirms that he hasn't changed. I really should call him too. One day. For now... "I was actually about to call you."

"Yeah. Yeah. I already said you're in the will."

I laugh but it lacks enthusiasm. "I know. But I'm not kidding. I... I..." *God, why is this so hard?* "I wanted to ask you about the Mikkleson family."

"Oh." Mom falls silent before she sucks in a breath.

"Do you know why I'm asking?"

"I have an idea."

"So..." I trail off, prompting her to fill in the gap.

"How did you find out?"

"It doesn't matter. I just want you to explain."

Mom's quiet again before she releases a sigh. "Okay. I'd been out drinking and met Gabriel at Rounders Bar. We'd crossed paths many times before, and I always found him a little boring. But when he drinks, that man is a hoot. I wasn't thinking. Neither of us were. And it just happened."

What? My brows furrow as her words roll around in my mind. Gabriel? "Are you saying you slept with my ex-boyfriend's dad?"

"Yes. Isn't that what you were talking about?"

"No. Mom. Ew. When?"

"A year ago."

"A year ago? Then..." This doesn't make sense unless— "Are you still fucking him?"

"Paige. You're talking to your mother."

"Excuse me. Are you still having relations of a sexual nature?"

Mom releases a slow drawn-out breath, giving me my answer. And God, does it complicate things. "He's married," I say in case she needs the reminder.

"I know."

"*And* he's my ex's dad," I add, hoping she'll see the error of her ways. But of course she doesn't.

"I know that too."

"So you invested in his company."

"What? *Jesus.* How do you— Shit. Is that what you were talking about?"

"Yes. And I want to know why."

"Because it's a great company. It was a no-brainer."

What?! "Maybe that would be true if you hadn't rolled your eyes when I first told you about Christian and his family. You've *never* cared about finance stuff."

"People change, Paige. He needed an investor, and on paper it looked too good to pass up."

"That's great. Just be careful, Mom."

"His wife won't find out. And if she does, so be it. I'm not overly invested in the relationship."

No, just his company. And that's what I was referring to. God, what if he's playing her? Or worse? What if she knows?

After a sleepless night, I call Dad around midday, needing more advice. As much as I'd love to handle this myself, I'm out of my depth.

Dad answers seconds before voicemail takes over, and I've never heard him so dejected.

"Hi, Paige," he says softly, his voice flat. "Everything okay?"

"Is everything okay with *you*?" A panic runs through me.

He blows out a sigh and I picture him shaking his head. "I had to let the Storm general manager go today."

"You fired him?" My voice rises and I wince. "Sorry, I didn't mean to yell."

"That's okay. You actually made me smile. It needed to happen. But he's been there for a long time. It wasn't fun, and I pissed off a lot of people."

"Oh, I'm sorry. That sucks."

"It really does."

"Did you have anyone on your side?"

"I did. A majority of the board members were very supportive of my decision and had wanted to get rid of him sooner, only the previous owner loved him. And on top of that, the team's media liaison helped ease my mind."

"Keeley?"

"You know her?"

"Yeah, we ah... I ran into her and she introduced herself."

"Great. Well, she was supportive of the decision too."

"You spoke to her about it?"

"No, it was more of a heads-up in case it caused a media frenzy. But she was happy to offer her opinion." I smile because I can totally see that side of her even after only meeting her once. She's the opposite of her brother.

"I imagine those things are never easy, but I'm happy you've got some support for it. I'm sure it will blow over soon enough. The season's about to start, right? You said that, yeah?"

"Yes, Paige." Dad laughs to himself. "The season's starting soon. Which reminds me, you're coming to the first game, aren't you?"

I smile, but I'm lucky he can't see me because it's completely fake. Attending feels like torture now but... "I wouldn't miss it for the world." I laugh.

I get to spend hours drooling over Easton only to go home alone. Yay for me.

"Great. Good." The relief in Dad's voice makes me smile. I'll suffer the hardship for him. Although, let's be honest, it's not going to be that difficult.

"Anyway," Dad continues, "you called me and I took over. What's up?"

"It's not important." Now is not the time. "We can chat at dinner later in the week."

"Are you sure?"

"Definitely. You have a lot going on." And I need him to have a clear head when I tell him what I know.

"Okay, but you know I'm always here for you, right?"

"I do. Thank you."

I hang up and I've just grabbed my bag to head out for a walk when an old friend texts me a link to a news headline. It's not hard to guess who it's going to feature.

My stomach knots as I click on the link, and when I read it, I feel sick.

So it begins.

Sources at Coastal Media say they've received never before seen intimate photos of Paige D'Angelo and Christian Mikkleson. The two have confirmed they remain friends. But are we about to find out what happened to send Paige running?

❧ ❧ ❧

I'm on edge for the next few days, waiting for my intimate photos to be broadcast to strangers. Ironic, really, considering I did a paid photo shoot full of intimate photos that I love having out in the world.

But this feels icky.

If they're the photos I'm imagining them to be then they're not at all the tasteful images the magazine took. No, these are raw and somewhat dirty. There's nothing pornographic. It's not like we filmed a sex tape. But Christian and I had an interesting sex life. And sending each other photos was just one of the games we played.

And despite what they think, unless it's the photo Christian sent me, then I have no doubt the images Coastal Media claims to have are *not* of me and Christian at all. They're me with other guys and Christian with other girls. Intimate poses, but innocent despite how they look.

At least mine were.

I always assumed his photos were too, but in hindsight, that may have been naive on my part. It was supposed to be a joke. Foreplay. A way to wind each other up to see who got jealous first. It made for incredible sex afterward. And I'm not at all ashamed of it. But now that it could affect the people I love, a little part of me regrets it.

Of course, I have the original photos on my phone and could easily prove what they are, but if no one believes the story behind the images, then I'm the bad guy. Suddenly the world isn't just seeing photos of my life with my ex-boyfriend, but I look like the girl that cheated on her boyfriend multiple times and documented it with photo evidence.

And that's so much worse.

Maybe I should have seen that coming.

Needing a distraction, I head to the gym after avoiding it for the past couple of weeks. For obvious reasons. And when I walk in, the obvious reason is lifting weights off the rack, his muscles bulging beneath his tee, his signature cap pulled low on his brow, confusing me until I realize we're not alone.

Forcing my gaze away from Easton, I dump my bag in the corner of the gym and smile at the stranger on the treadmill.

I keep my eyes on my mat as I get ready for my warm-up stretches and try to ignore the way my heart races just thinking about the possibility of Easton watching me.

As my pulse spikes, I work through a few yoga moves on the floor, slowly stretching my body, pushing through the tightness and pain.

But while my eyes focus on the task at hand, my mind runs wild, replaying our previous encounters, imagining the things Easton would do to me if we were alone, and in another life.

When I'm done on the mat, I internally laugh at myself for acting so crazy, but when I stand up to stretch my arms, my eyes lock on Easton's in the mirror, his gaze feral beneath his cap.

He feels the same.

For the next painful hour, we work out in silence, but our lingering looks speak volumes. Another two gym goers arrive, while the first one leaves, but it's like neither of us wants to break the spell, because no matter how tired I am, I can't leave.

I lift weights—tiny ones compared to Easton's—and jog on the treadmill. I work my arms, my legs, even my goddamn pelvic floor, only that's not intentional. No, that's getting a workout from how much I'm clenching, trying to dull the ache pulsing between my legs.

I want him. He wants me. But we've made our bed and now we have to lie in it.

It was only casual, for God's sake. There are other men for me, other women for him.

We have to move on.

And yet, neither of us leaves.

Until I'm finally at my breaking point.

Slowing down the treadmill, I begin my cooldown, prepared to concede until Easton's phone rings and he quickly packs up, disappearing without a backward glance.

The tension snaps as the door clicks shut and I'm finally able to breathe again.

No words were spoken, there was no touching, no feeling, and yet, I don't think I've ever been that turned on in my life.

What is this man doing to me? And more to the point, how long can we keep this up?

CHAPTER TWENTY

EASTON

I swear my cock has been half-mast since I spent that torturous hour in the gym with Paige. From the outside looking in, we were two strangers —or more if you count the other people there with us—innocently sharing a gym. But my thoughts were anything but innocent. I'm almost thankful that others were there. At least it stopped me acting on the graphic visuals I had running through my mind.

I wanted to fuck her. Plain and simple. I wanted to strip her naked, lay her flat on the weight bench, and spread her legs. Then I wanted to feast on her. Work her clit until she was screaming my name, begging me to stop. And fuck—goddammit, I'm going to get hard again.

Today is going to suck.

"East—"

"Nope," I cut Zane off before he's even said whatever the fuck he wanted to say because today is not the day. "Unless you're about to tell me that you're a fucking idiot and want to worship me at my feet, then no. I'm not interested."

"The fuck. I didn't do anything wrong. How many times—"

"Not today."

"I was just going to tell you that Coach wants us to run drills and—"

"Again. No. Not today."

Zane's jaw drops, but he walks away in the direction of our offensive coach, and a little part of me is glad it's not Coach Pierce. I'm not at all worried about what I said, but I'd rather not get in an argument with the head coach when I can already feel a weird tension surrounding the staff.

I'm not sure what Zane says—whether he complained like a whiny little schoolboy or took the blame. But either way, when the coach calls us for drills, he teams me up with our second wide receiver instead of Zane, and God am I happy about that development. Michaels is great. He keeps to himself and like me, he doesn't get involved in other people's business. He also doesn't fuck his teammates' girlfriends, so he's got that going for him.

With the season opener this weekend, Coach pushes us to the limit, but there's not one person on the team that doesn't welcome it. We're out to win. To show the world we're still a force and that we're gunning for that back-to-back championship. To prove the drama surrounding us hasn't affected our game. The TV show and our previous owner's departure are a thing of the past. A blip on our radar. Nothing anyone has to worry about. We are the team to beat. I can feel it.

Has some of Luke's cockiness rubbed off on me? Maybe. But he was right. He told us from day one last season that it was going to be our year, and his confidence never wavered. It makes sense for us to follow his lead. Even if it pains me.

I'm wrecked by the end of practice but feeling good about the team, and it's clear to see I'm not the only one. There's a high around the locker room, and it's difficult not to get caught up in it. Until the door opens and Paige is standing at the threshold, chatting closely with my dearly beloved sister. The one I'm about to disown.

Sure, she knows nothing about my situation with Paige, but isn't she supposed to have some kind of built-in sibling intuition? Shouldn't she just know to stay the fuck away?

As I stare at her, my mind conjures up the images from Paige's magazine shoot, and I have to bite my cheek to shift my focus.

Paige's hands move around animatedly, like they often do when she's invested in a conversation, and my sister's hooked on her every word, making me wonder what the hell they're talking about.

After a few seconds, Paige glances up and her eyes lock on mine as she pauses midconversation, holding my stare until the door closes again, cutting off our connection. I shake my head and continue getting ready, but my thoughts remain on the scene in the hallway.

Trying to figure out what's being said.

No, trying to work out *Paige*.

Although I have a feeling I could spend a lifetime doing that.

There's just something about her. Something that draws me in. Intrigues me. And it's a shame I can't explore that further.

When I'm dressed, I grab my bag, ready to head to the meeting room, but pause when Keeley enters the room, her expression serious.

One of the guys tries to get her attention, but she shakes him off and continues on her path, stepping up onto her usual bench and yelling to get our attention. "Hey! Quiet. Now. Eyes on me. I'm not messing around today."

The room hushes immediately. Keeley often calls for attention, but she's never that aggressive about it. *What the hell is going on?*

"Coach Pierce will be back in a minute along with Tray McGuire, and I need you all to be on your best behavior. For once. Can you do that?"

One of the guys says something about being a good boy for Keeley, and I have to stop myself from decking him. Other than that, the room stills as Coach and our general manager, Tray, arrive. We don't need convincing to hush. The fact that Coach didn't tell us all to shut the fuck up is a little unnerving.

"Thank you all," he says once again out of character. "I know this time would usually be spent on me telling you all to get your heads out of your asses, but let's face it, they wouldn't fit right now with how big they've grown. While I don't want you to get ahead of yourselves, I can agree that you are killing it out there. So if you keep that up, we've got another shot."

Now I definitely know something's up. He's being too nice.

"That aside. I'm not here to compliment you. Or tell you what you did wrong. That will come later. I'm here for Tray. But I'll let him fill you in."

Our GM steps up and the already quiet room stills. "There's no easy way to say this, but I'm moving on. This place has been my life for the past decade, but I've neglected my family and they want me back. It's time for me to take on a new venture and let another sucker take the reins. It's been a pleasure manning this ship, and while I might be gone, I'll still be cheering you on from the sidelines. I'm a Storm boy for life, and I expect you to be the number one team again this year. Make me proud."

He steps down and walks away without any further interaction, and you could hear a pin drop. *Because what the actual fuck?*

Coach jumps up again and thanks Tray for his years of service, talking about his achievements as a GM, crediting him for getting the team to where it is today. And when he's done, the shock finally wears off. But he too doesn't give us a chance to question him before they're both gone.

I expect an uproar, for questions to be flying around, or at least for there to be whispers of speculation. But after they've left the room, no one says a thing. Almost like it never happened.

People resume their conversations but the energy is off. The tension is palpable. Whatever just happened was not what they made it out to be. There's no way he left of his own accord. He would have demanded a proper send-off.

There's definitely more to it.

I try to catch Keeley's eye before she slips out of the locker room, but when I raise an eyebrow, she subtly shakes her head. Either she doesn't know anything, or she has no plans to tell me. Either way, I'm going to ask. Because while I normally wouldn't care or get involved in matters I'm not a part of, the last thing I need is for the team to fall to pieces. Not when my personal life is a mess.

Word spreads that our meetings are canceled for the day, and the locker room clears out not long after that announcement.

I follow suit, heading home early, and I've just pulled into my parking space, ready to switch into dad mode when the messages begin.

> Luke: What the fuck was that?

I curse under my breath because I should have seen this coming and switched off my phone. But once I start reading, I can't stop.

> Reed: I don't know, but I don't like it

> Dylan: What did I miss?

> Luke: Tray got the axe

> Dylan: What? Why?

> Reed: He didn't get the axe. He resigned

> Luke: Bullshit. My money's on D'Angelo

Dylan: I thought you said he was cool

Luke: I thought he was

Reed: He is. We don't know he's behind this

Luke: East. Care to weigh in? I can see you've read our messages

Fucking technology. While I agree with Luke that he didn't resign, I know better than to entertain him and his wild ideas. But it's strange. And the timing couldn't be worse. It's our first game this weekend. The start of a new season and now all the media will be talking about is McGuire's resignation. If he really loved the team as much as he claims he does, he would have made this announcement during the offseason. So no, I don't think he resigned. He was definitely forced to leave.

The question is why? And the answer is none of my business. I'm staying the hell out of this. But I fucking hate the fact that we'll garner more negative media attention. I just want to play the goddamn sport that I love, kick ass, and get on with my life. Why can't it be that simple?

Easton: I don't know what happened. And I agree with Reed. We shouldn't be speculating

Luke: I bet you could find out

What the hell?

Reed: Who?

Luke: Easton

Jesus. Fuck. What does he know?

Easton: What makes you think I'm in the know? Why don't you ask your brother-in-law?

Luke: Good idea. BRB.

Fucking Luke.

I throw my phone onto the passenger seat beside me and move to open the door. But my phone vibrates again, and I can't stop myself from checking it. Why the fuck would he think I could find out?

> Luke: Thomas knows nothing. Or at least, he's not telling me over the phone. I'm going to head to his place, but in the meantime. East...

I don't give Luke the satisfaction of responding to his little tension builder. Instead I wait as the three little dots appear. My chest tightens as I prepare to be outed for messing with the owner's daughter.

> Luke: Ask Keeley

Jesus. The relief I feel over something I've worked hard to keep quiet is immeasurable. Thank God he said Keeley. I had planned to ask her after she finishes work anyway, knowing she's probably still at the stadium managing the news. The guys discovering Keeley is my sister is painful, and I expect magnitudes of ribbing coming my way, but at least he didn't say Paige. That's a secret I'd prefer to keep hidden. For both our sakes.

But if I can't stop thinking about her naked, and if she's going to be hanging around the stadium, it's going to be a hell of a lot harder to hide it.

Chapter Twenty-One

PAIGE

I barely sleep the night before Storm's season opener with a nervous energy coursing through me as though I'm one of the guys about to run onto the field. When in reality, I'm nervous for my dad. The news of the GM's departure hit the media yesterday with full force, and the accusations flying around are devastating with most aimed at my dad. Blaming him for the demise of the team. Calling him egotistical. Speculating that he'd cleared the position for himself so that he'd have a more hands-on role.

All the while, he stayed quiet. I'm sure he had lawyers telling him what to do, but it kills me to think that the fans hate him when they don't know what's really going on.

Hell, I'm his daughter and I didn't really know what was going on until I spoke to Keeley. I obviously knew the business side of things. The GM and the previous owner had pretty much run the team into the ground when it came to the finances, but it turns out there was more.

Both the GM and the previous owner received a paycheck from the Storm TV show, but the team itself received little to nothing. He'd also come on to Keeley and other women who work for the team on multiple occasions, despite being married and regardless of their complaints.

Keeley claims he never touched her, but made her feel uncomfortable several times, even insinuating that he could help her rise to the top if she stopped refusing his advances.

Not that she told my dad that. In her mind, Tray was gone so there was no point in her dredging up her issues with him to help the case. It was done.

I'm not entirely sure why she told *me*, but I promised to keep it quiet. What's another secret to add to the list?

After a quick shower, I throw on the unnumbered jersey that Dad gave me and head to the stadium. Dad said I could work on the fundraiser in his office, and I'd rather be there if he needs me than home worrying about him.

Oh how things have changed between us.

I never stopped caring about him. I never once stopped loving him. But when he left my mom, I stopped *worrying* about him with my focus solely on her. If he could leave her knowing how much it affected her, then he didn't need me. At least, that's what I thought at the time. Now I'm full of regrets. It's amazing what a little maturity and perspective will teach you.

God, I was a brat.

Keeley's in the hall outside my dad's office when I arrive, and her warm smile brings on my own.

"You're here early. Are you staying for the game?" she asks, her expression hopeful.

"I am. I have no idea where Dad's got me sitting, but I'll be there. I just have to get some of the charity event planning out of the way before it starts."

"You are a godsend, you know that. I know how expensive event companies can be, so the team and the board are lucky to have you."

"I don't know about that. I'm no event organizer, but I'm trying. Also, my dad didn't give me much choice."

Keeley laughs. "Then we should be thanking him too. Let me know if there's anything I can help with."

"You've already done enough. Your contacts have been amazing."

When Dad first reintroduced me to Keeley, in a professional capacity, he thought she'd be able to help me with the event, but didn't mention the fact that I wasn't the event planner he'd pitched me to be. He failed to mention that I'm only helping because the team is struggling financially but still needs to save face. I was the one that shared that news with Keeley, feeling like a fraud. I've helped out with events, come up with ideas, used my influence to get support, but I've never taken the lead. And I'm a little terrified, if I'm honest.

But Dad wanted to make sure the focus was on the team's chance of back-to-back wins, not the fact that they had money issues. And since I'm the doting daughter that owes him for treating him badly, here I am.

"Well, I'm here if you need an extra pair of hands," Keeley adds, waving said hands in the air. "*Or* if you want a laugh, I could volunteer my brother. He's *never* up for a good time, so it would be fun to watch him try to either get himself out of it, or to pretend he cared to impress his new boss."

I laugh out loud, though I do agree—it would be fun to watch him squirm. "That's okay. At the moment, I'm on top of things. But I'll let you know when that changes. And I still have four weeks, right?"

"Yes. I can't believe your dad asked for such a short turnaround. He clearly doesn't know the work that goes into big events like that."

"I think he just wanted it to be on a bye weekend, so the team had no excuses when they were asked to attend. And we're up first when it comes to byes."

"We?" Keeley smirks and I roll my eyes.

"That was a line I'm repeating directly from my dad. I will admit, I enjoyed watching practice. But I don't think I'm a full-blown football fan yet."

"But you could be swayed?" She grins excitedly, baring her teeth comically.

"Yeah, I think I could be," I admit, with one player on my mind.

"Good to know."

I lose track of time working, and before I know it, Dad's texting me to tell me he'll be by in ten minutes to show me to my seat.

I've just started packing up when Keeley pops in again.

"So... I've decided you're coming with me."

"What?" I laugh.

"I know your dad said he has a seat for you, but would you rather ogle the hot guys while sitting with your dad and other official men? *Or* come and watch the game from a suite with some like-minded and amazing women...and a really cute baby?"

"Again, what? Who?"

Keeley laughs. "I was chatting with Luke's wife about you, and we decided you need to be watching the game with her and some of the other wives and girlfriends."

"But I'm not a wife or girlfriend."

"I know that. But neither is Amelia's bestie, Hayley, so you're not the only one. Plus you're still connected to the team. In fact, you're like the team's daughter, since your dad owns them. Oh my God. It just occurred to me that one day *you* could own the team. You might inherit it."

"Oh no. That's not for me." But if it was, I definitely scrap the "no seeing the players" rule. In fact, I'd encourage it. "Also... are you killing off my father?"

"God, no. He's still so young. I mean *way way* in the future."

"It would still be a no. He better either live forever or find himself another heir. One that is *not* my brother. He couldn't handle that kind of pressure. I guess I could sell the team and make billions. Does it work that way?"

Keeley laughs as though I'm joking and she'd be right. But lucky for me, Dad knows I am not cut out for the sports world. But if he wanted to leave me an art studio in his will or a modeling agency, I wouldn't mind owning those.

"Regardless, can I take you up to my friends?"

"I don't know." I scrunch my nose as I think about disappointing my dad. "Dad's about to be here and—"

"I'm here."

"And here he is."

"Hi Keeley." Dad nods. "Sweetheart,"—he kisses my head—"are you ready?"

"I was just asking Paige if she wanted to watch from the suite with some of the wives and girlfriends," Keeley cuts in before I can answer, a comfortable air between them, and there goes lying to keep Dad happy.

"I said no." I shake my head. "Where are we sitting?"

"Actually, I think that's a great idea," Dad says, shocking me. "Maybe with new friends, I might be able to convince you to come to more games."

Keeley smiles, while I study Dad's expression. "Are you sure?"

"Yes." He smiles wide and points to his mouth to make sure I saw it. "I'm sure."

"But—"

"I'm old enough to look after myself, Paige. How about we meet up after the game for a drink?"

"Okay." I hesitate. I wanted to be here to support him, but how can I do that if I'm not with him?

"Go." Dad laughs as though reading my mind. "I'm good. See you after we win." He presses another kiss to my head and smiles at Keeley. "Go, Storm."

I shake my jersey to show my support and then Keeley drags me away. "You're going to have so much fun."

By halftime, my cheeks hurt from smiling. Keeley was right. These women are awesome. Luke's wife is a riot—the way she teases her husband when he celebrates a touchdown has me laughing out loud. It's easy to see that she loves him, but it's refreshing to note that they keep things light between them. The world is dark enough.

And their daughter. My God, is she adorable in her tiny little Bennett jersey and pink bow. I bet she melts hearts everywhere she goes.

Then there's Hayley, who I recognized the second I saw her. She's starring in a huge movie they're making based on a book I *love* and I'm in awe of her. She's not only stunning and exactly as I pictured the main character, but she's also incredibly down-to-earth and fun, unlike the character she'll be playing. On top of that, she's Australian and I could listen to that accent all day. What's even cooler is that she recognized me. Said she's been following me on social media for years, and I'm not ashamed to admit that I pretty much fell in love with her at first sight.

Actually, it's safe to say I fell in love with this entire group on sight.

Lainey, Thomas's wife—I discovered they're newly married—is also an amazing woman. And someone I could see myself hanging out with. It took no time at all to discover she's great with advice which I'm told is what led her to become a dance therapist, mixing her passion for dance with her ability to know what to say in any given situation.

I almost asked her if she could help fix my life. Or at the very least, tell me what the hell I should be doing because I have no idea. But that's a lot to load on someone I just met.

Along with having fun like Keeley promised, being here with these beautiful women made me really miss my female friends back home.

In New York, I was constantly surrounded by friends and then they just disappeared when I moved. Ghosted me as though I'd never existed.

I've never had trouble making friends, yet I've been here for months and haven't even tried. Until now.

I bet Lainey would have something to say about *that* revelation. Am I holding back because somewhere deep in my mind this is all temporary? I'm here because I was running away. If Christian's family is caught, like I'm hoping, am I going to go home? I always thought I would, but now I'm not so sure.

Then there's the other possible reason for my hesitation. My friends broke me and I lost all trust in females. Or maybe I'm just lazy. Who knows.

Whatever the reason, I like this group of women, so maybe things are about to change.

"Okay, ladies," Keeley calls out as she enters the suite when the second half of the game begins. "I've got fifteen minutes. Do you have any gossip for me?"

"I do." Hayley raises her hand enthusiastically and rushes over to pull Keeley in close. "I need to thank you because Paige is my girl crush. Has been for so long and I can't believe she's standing in front of me."

All eyes flit my way and I laugh out loud. "Says the woman who is set to become Hollywood's IT girl."

"Maybe so, but I will never be Paige D'Angelo. I will say I'm happy you ended things with Christian. I always thought he was a bit of a dick."

"He was. Still is. But the sex was amazing. I'm only twenty-five; that's all I needed from a relationship."

"Yes," Hayley and Keeley both cheer. "Get it, girl. What about now?"

"What?" *Dammit*, I walked right into that.

"What's your status now?" Hayley asks again. "Met any San Fran men that you fancy? Having any hot sex?"

"Hayley," Amelia cuts in, shaking her head with a smile. "You can't ask her that on day one. At least let her settle in."

"Why? She knows we're about to become besties. All of us."

I laugh while my mind drifts where it shouldn't. To Keeley's brother, their husband's teammate, my dad's player. And no matter how forbidden it is, I still want it.

Dammit.

I give a coy smile and shrug my shoulders, making the girls burst out laughing.

"Oh, you have a story to tell. I can feel it." Hayley taps her fingers together like she's some cartoon villain. "But don't worry, I'm patient. I'll wait until you're ready to share."

"Since when?" Amelia's jaw drops and I laugh at the banter between them all.

"I've got to say, I'm with Amelia on this one, Hayley," Lainey adds with her hands in the air for surrender. "When I mentioned I'd bought a *special* gift for my wedding night, you wouldn't stop until I told you what it was. And I'd only really known you for a month."

"Very true. But it's day one for Paige. She gets twenty-four hours grace."

"Run," Keeley jokes. "Run before it's too late and you find yourself telling these ladies *everything*."

I once again laugh along with them until another reason for not having friends pops into my mind. I have secrets. Secrets I can't tell anyone right now. And I've always been known as an oversharer. Am I walking into fire if I get to know these girls? Is it easier to keep to myself?

I think on that for a second as they all stare at me in anticipation, but it doesn't take much for me to make my decision.

"I can handle that. But be prepared; I've lived a good life."

"Yes."

Cheers ring out from the crowd and my new friends all cringe before racing back to the glass. At least, Lainey and Amelia do. Hayley shrugs like she could take it or leave it, but when she glances down at the field, it's easy to see she's just as obsessed as they are.

Keeley takes that as her cue to leave again, and we watch the rest of the game without her.

The girls chat about the plays, cursing the referees or umpires or whatever they're called, bouncing excitedly when one of the players does something impressive—I think—while I try hard not to spend all my time watching Easton.

Though that task is next to impossible.

He's a goddamn machine. An incredibly sexy machine who even looks good with a helmet and gear on. Which is really freaking annoying. I have no idea what position he plays, or if he's even a good player—though that should be assumed since he's playing in the top team—but what I do know is that I wish I had number 11 painted on my back. I wish this was a Wilder jersey.

At some point during the second half, someone mentions Zane, and I have to fight to quell the rage inside me after reading about what he did to Easton. Yet another reason to dislike Isaac's mom. No matter what the circumstances are, you don't cheat. Period. Maybe I should introduce her to Christian—they'd get along well with their similar lack of values.

Ignoring the new protective vibe I have coursing through my veins, I watch the rest of the game with my heart racing and my body tense, praying for a good result. When the Storm takes the win, the relief I feel is surprising. I wanted them to win for Dad; I didn't realize I'd want them to win for me too. Maybe Dad was right and football is in my blood. He said he always tried to get me interested at a young age and I'm finally there.

The crowd goes absolutely wild for the team's success, and it's impossible not to get caught up in the celebrations. The energy buzzing around the room is like a drug, giving me a high I never expected. So while I still have no idea what happened—I never really took the time to learn the game—I know they won and I still had fun. I'm glad I listened to my dad and Keeley. Maybe this place is going to grow on me.

And I think I just might attend a few more games.

CHAPTER TWENTY-TWO

PAIGE

The next few weeks fly by in a heartbeat with my time spent between preparations for the event and two modeling jobs I'd completely forgotten about. One last week for a swimwear magazine, and the other yesterday and today—a campaign for an up-and-coming designer brand. And God, has this one been fun. There's a group of us involved, and so far the shoot has taken us to various landmarks around San Francisco. All places I'd planned to visit but never found the time. We've already danced on Alcatraz Island, brooded on the tiled steps of 16th Avenue, and casually strolled past the Painted Ladies. Next up, we're staging a fake runway on the Golden Gate Bridge—which I'm told is going to be wild and windy—and then we'll end the shoot in a secret location. It's like a dream. And something I almost turned down.

While we're waiting for them to set up the bridge runway, I bounce up and down on the spot, trying to keep warm in my skimpy dress. I'm just about to ask for something to cover myself when a warm coat wraps around my shoulders.

"Whoever you are," I say, assuming it's someone from the crew, "I love you."

I turn to find one of my fellow models—a guy from Germany with boyish charm—and smile at his thoughtfulness.

"Thank you, Ben. You're a godsend. I wish they'd set up before we got here."

"I don't think they were allowed. They're limited with how much time they get here."

"That makes sense. It would be fine if it wasn't so windy." *But I guess I was warned.*

Ben nods before stepping in beside me as we watch the traffic driving by. "Want to get a drink after the shoot?" he asks, and while he's super cute and looks amazing in designer clothes, he's not really my type. "I think we're finishing up near the Wharf," he adds when I turn to face him. "It's touristy but I know a place."

"I've only been here a few months which I think makes me still half tourist, so I'm game. Who else is coming?" I spin in anticipation to find we're alone, and when I turn back to face him, he's gesturing between the two of us.

"Just us," he confirms.

"Like a date?" A lump forms in my throat and I wish I'd paid more attention to where the other models had gone because when I glance back, I find them huddled under a tent I didn't even realize they'd erected. *Smart.*

"It doesn't have to be a date," Ben's quick to say, perhaps sensing my hesitation. "It can be whatever you want it to be. A drink or two...or something else entirely."

I smile while an uncomfortable feeling settles low in my stomach. "I'm kind of seeing someone, but a drink would be nice. To new friends."

His face pulls into the smallest frown before he schools his features and smiles. "Yes. Yes. To new friends."

"Perfect."

The runway shoot is even more fun than I thought it would be, despite the wind, and when we're done, I'm full of giddy excitement for our final destination.

"Okay, everyone, listen up." The campaign assistant gets our attention while we're waiting for our transportation to arrive. "We've got a short drive and then we're ending our day with a photo shoot on one of San Francisco's famous cable cars en route to Fisherman's Wharf."

Ben was right.

The fashion designer heading up this new brand was born in San Francisco and wanted to showcase the beauty this city has to offer, while also "pitching it to an international market," their words not mine. It makes sense that they'd keep the locations iconic, and now I get to cross a lot of tourist attractions off my list, so I can focus on exploring the *real* San Francisco, when I have the time.

After we wrap for the day, my new friend Ben is waiting for me, ready to go as planned, and I can't shake the strange energy coursing through me —as though I'm doing something wrong. But it doesn't take long for that feeling to dissipate when it's apparent that he took my friendship offer seriously, never even offering to pull out my chair.

Thanks, Dad, for setting that as the standard for how a man should treat a girl.

We've been in this cute eclectic bar for a couple of hours now and I've got to say, I'm having fun. It's been a while since I had a drinking session like this and I miss it. I miss letting go.

"So you snuck out in the middle of the night?" I burst out laughing as Ben regales me with stories of his time backpacking around the world before he was discovered in London a couple of years ago, signing with one of the country's top agencies.

"I did." He chuckles. "But did you really expect me to stay? The guy talked about eating slugs and worms in his sleep. Descriptively." He pulls a face and I gag.

"Eww. You told me you weren't going to mention the disgusting things he was dreaming about."

Ben shrugs. "I lied."

"Yeah, you did. And ew." I hide my face as I cringe.

"You said that already."

The drinks keep flowing and we keep talking until I can't hide my yawns anymore. "I have to call it a night." I scrunch my nose, because I've actually had a great time.

"I can tell." Ben grins and I frown apologetically. "Am I boring you?"

"No, not at all. This has been fun."

"I agree. I like drinking with new friends."

"Me too. I like it *way* better than drinking with old friends." Ben raises a brow and I giggle. "Don't mind me. That's a long story for another time."

"Well, you've got my number if you want to talk."

"I do?" I stare at him confused, squinting my eyes as I try to recall that moment, but I don't remember getting his number. *Am I that drunk?*

Ben laughs before standing up and offering me his hand for support.

Which I happily take. "My number was on the information sheet from today. If you want to do this again. As friends."

"Oh, that's right. The sheet. That means you have my number too. And look how easy that was. We talked about numbers without giving it a second thought."

"Another story for another time?" Ben questions and I replay my words in my head before laughing.

"Yep. Another story for another time."

How is it possible that Easton and I never exchanged numbers? I'd really like to text him and ask right now. But I can't. Because I don't have his number.

"Which way are you headed?" Ben asks, concern etched in his features when I stumble slightly. "Can I help with an Uber?"

"I'm south of here. But I've got someone I can call."

"The guy you're seeing?"

I picture my ride and giggle hysterically. "No. Not this time. It's my dad's driver."

"Okay, good. Would you like me to wait? I'm going to walk home. I live a few blocks from here."

"Uphill?" My face scrunches and Ben laughs.

"Yes, most of it's uphill, but I don't mind. It keeps me fit."

"I don't think I could walk straight right now, let alone *up*. But good for you."

I text my dad's driver as we walk toward the street, and when he tells me he's fifteen minutes away, Ben waits, both of us people watching in a comfortable silence.

I wave when my ride arrives, and the second I'm settled in my seat, my eyes drift closed, my mind immediately bombarding me with images of Easton. As though I cheated on him. When it's not even close to the truth. Because my night was innocent, and even if I'd kissed him good night, it wouldn't be cheating because we're not together. We're barely even talking at the moment. In fact, I think I've had more conversations with his son recently. Like Easton, we keep running into each other, and he's so freaking cute. *Unlike* Easton who's ridiculously hot and so deliciously tempting.

I hate to admit that this mess with Easton is driving me crazy. He's driving me crazy, and I'm not sure I like this feeling.

It's after midnight by the time I get home, and as I enter the lobby, I find myself holding my breath, hoping I'll run into him again. That he'll be in the elevator when I get there. Waiting for me. Desperate to see me. Feral for it. Like he was in the gym.

But he's a dad. And it's late. I may as well be dreaming because it's the only way I'm going to see him.

The doors to the elevator open and my jaw drops until an old man exits, walking his giant dog as he sleepily rubs his eyes.

I laugh to myself as I get in, and I'm so lost in thought that I press Easton's floor number instead of my own, feigning shock when it opens on his level.

I hold the doors ajar and search the space for any sign of Easton, but of course there's nothing. Even if I was crazy enough to forget all our reasons and knock on his door in the middle of the night, I don't know his apartment number and I can't freaking call him. Nope, we relied on the fact that we kept running into each other and never worried about a time when that may not happen. Like now. But it's probably good that it doesn't.

Laughing again, I stumble back inside and press twelve, closing my eyes as the elevator starts to move. My head falls forward, snapping me out of my microsleep when the doors open and my dad steps in, his expression filled with relief.

"You're here."

"Dad?" I startle. "What are you doing up so late?" I slur slightly and he frowns.

"I work later than this, Paige. It's not that late."

"It's not?" I stare confused. Wasn't it after midnight?

"No. Are you okay?"

"Of course. Why do you ask?"

"Because my driver called. He wasn't sure you'd make it to your apartment by yourself."

"Your driver called you?"

"Yes."

I stare at him for a second before my eyes widen and I pout, stomping my foot with my hands on my hips. "Isn't that a gross invasion of my privacy?"

"You called *my* driver to pick you up."

"Yes, but I didn't know he was a tattletale."

"Wow. And I didn't know you reverted back to your childish self when you drank. It's fun getting to know you again."

"Shut up, Dad."

"I was worried, Paige. And so was he."

"As you can see, I'm fine. So I want you to get out and let me prove that I can get home all by myself."

"This is your floor."

"Ugh." I throw my hands in the air. "Well, let's go up to your floor and then I'll come back down *alone*."

Dad bites back a smile and it makes me frown.

"Okay, fine," he says, giving in, knowing I have some stubborn tendencies. "But you're being ridiculous. How will I know that you got home safe?"

"I'll text you."

Dad pushes the button for his floor and we travel in silence, only speaking as he gets out, wishing each other good night. And then I'm alone again.

I've lived by myself since I was eighteen. I don't need help getting home, and I don't need Dad checking up on me.

I rock as the elevator takes me back down to my floor, but when the doors open, I'm shocked awake. Or maybe I passed out and didn't realize. Because this is a dream.

"Easton Wilder, is that you?" My heart races as a heat consumes me.

Easton—or my imagination—frowns as he steps inside, turning my way when the doors close. I sway when we start moving again and he catches me, his strong grip curling around my arms. "Are you okay?"

"Never better." I fan myself. "Though I had no idea there was a gentleman under all that gruff hotness." Since he's holding my arm, I figure it's only fair that I do the same and reach out to squeeze his bicep before letting my hand fall to his fingers. "I miss these fingers," I say, lifting his hand for closer examination. "You really have talent."

"Football?"

What? Ooh. "Yes. Of course, football." That's totally what I was thinking.

Easton smiles, and the sight of it makes me dizzy as the elevator comes to a stop.

"We're here," he says, making me frown as I fight to remember where we were going.

"At your floor," he adds, pointing into the hallway, his eyes on my door.

"Oooh. Are you coming in?"

"No, Paige." He smiles. "Not tonight."

"Shame." I pout and he shakes his head.

"It really fucking is. But how about I walk you to your door?"

"I like what happened last time you did that."

Easton chuckles and it lights up his face, making me giddy. "You should laugh more. It suits you."

"Thanks. Do you have your key?"

"Yep." I pull out my key and unlock the door, but I can't bring myself to step inside. "You're really not coming in?"

"Paige," he warns, his deep, strained voice making me shiver. "I—"

"You can't. I get it. I do. But just so you know, I really want you to. Actually, I want you in general." I step forward and walk my fingers up his chest as I whisper, "All the damn time."

"Fuuck, Paige." Easton steps back and runs his hand through his hair, his expression pained.

"Sorry. I—" My phone rings, cutting me off, and I groan. "Shit, that's my dad. I better answer."

"You better. I have to go anyway."

He takes another step back but doesn't press the button until I walk inside, waiting. I hold the door open and wave, my longing gaze lingering as I sigh.

"Night, Paige." Easton shakes his head and spins around.

"Night, Window-Seat Guy," I say to his back, smiling when his shoulders lift in another laugh.

"I'm home, Dad," I answer when the doors shut. "Safe and sound." And very much alone, just like I wanted.

Only I no longer wish that were true.

CHAPTER TWENTY-THREE

EASTON

It's a short week for me with the bye this weekend, so I make the most of my time with Isaac, packing as much into my days off as physically possible.

This morning—the movies. Which I'm still uncertain about, but he's been desperate to go, so I figured it was worth a shot, and I'm hoping the early screening will be less busy.

On our way down to the parking garage, we stop off at the lobby to check for mail, and I instantly regret it when I find Paige walking through the glass doors at the front of the building, heading in our direction.

I smile, but my expression remains cool and definitely doesn't reflect the fact that I am still cursing myself for walking away the other night. Isaac was at my mom's ahead of a game against our biggest rivals—which we won —so I had no reason to go home, and fuck... I wanted her. But I would never take advantage of the situation when she was obviously drunk.

Our eyes lock, and I can tell instantly that she remembers as her nose crinkles adorably. As though she's embarrassed. But she has nothing to be embarrassed about. I'm the dick that rejected her. I should be embarrassed.

Each step brings us closer together, and I'm grappling with what to do or say when she turns toward the building's restaurant seconds before we've reached her, making the decision for me.

I've barely taken a step toward the front desk when Isaac tugs on my hand, pulling me in Paige's direction.

"That's my friend, Dad."

"Your friend?" I scan the lobby looking for other kids but there's no one around. "Who?"

"Paige."

"Paige?" My voice is louder than I planned for it to be, and Paige pauses before spinning around to face us. And when she spots Isaac waving her way, a warm smile lights up her features, gutting me in the chest. With her smile still locked in place, her eyes lift to mine before she slowly walks over, perhaps giving me the chance to escape the situation. We haven't directly spoken about Isaac, but I'm sure she knows he's the reason I'm holding back from us. And while I should be mad about the fact that they clearly know each other—and on a first-name basis—I'm not.

It feels oddly comforting to know there's someone else in this building that cares about him.

Isaac tugs on my arm until I walk with him, but when we reach Paige, he shies away, trying to hide behind my leg. Unsurprisingly though, Paige doesn't let him. It seems to be her thing.

"Hi Isaac. How are you?" She squats down to his level, peeping around my legs to see him.

Isaac nods his head, but otherwise remains silent.

"I like your sneakers," she says as she keeps trying. "Are you going out with your dad?"

At that, Isaac's confidence returns. His mom bought him new shoes—with my credit card—and it's like he's never been given a present before.

"They're red and Mom says that will make me go faster. Like this. Zoom. Zoom." He runs to the door of the restaurant and back again like he has super speed, and Paige laughs, but not before giving me a sympathetic smile.

"I think she's right," Paige says, her face scrunching when Isaac glances away. "You were so fast I couldn't see you at one point."

"Really?" He smiles so wide it's infectious. "Was I, Dad?"

"You sure were, Buddy. I thought we'd lost you."

Isaac shakes his head and reaches out to grab my hand. "Don't worry, Dad. I wouldn't go away. Never."

My smile internally drops but on the outside it remains strong, hiding my true feelings. And the truth is that I'm breaking for him. His mind shouldn't "worry" like that. At his age he shouldn't even know the feeling of someone disappearing. But he does. All too well. And I hate that for him.

And I hate that she keeps sucking him back in. Buying his love when he's too young to know better. I want Macy to fuck up, but at the same time, I don't. I know what it's like to grow up in a broken home. Especially one where the party that walks out never fully gives their kids the love and attention they deserve. Like my dear ole dad. Keeley may have forgiven our father, but I haven't. I was only a year older than Isaac when Mom had to go it alone. Raising us with barely any help except the rare pop-in visits and minimum child support. Keeley and my older sister Addison accepted it easily, claiming they loved the second birthdays and Christmases—the only time he ever showed up. But I just wanted my dad.

They were at school when he left. And Mom never cried around them. I was home. And whether she thought I was too young to remember or too busy playing with my toys, she was wrong on both counts. I heard it. And I've never forgotten.

I will never put Isaac through that.

Over the last month, Macy's only visited once and called twice. It's not enough. I'm giving her another couple of months to get her shit together and then I'm seeking legal advice. I'm not naive; I know the courts usually side with the mother. But a little part of me hopes it will be too much effort for her and she'll give up the fight. She's never been big on commitment.

Paige asks Isaac if he thinks her red-soled stilettos are as fast as his new ones, changing the subject, and I smile when he laughs out loud. "No." He covers his face with his hand. "They're not like mine."

"You're right. I think I need to get some red sneakers."

"Dad can take you." Isaac straightens on the spot, the excitement obvious in his stance. "He said he knows where Mom got them."

"Oh, really?" Paige stands tall, hitting me with a mischievous grin. "Do you think you can help me?"

I don't have to look to know Isaac's expectant eyes are gazing up at me, waiting for a response. I can feel it. But what the hell do I say to that? And why is Paige playing with fire?

"I think they only sell kids' shoes," I say as a buffer, knowing neither Isaac nor Paige will let me get away with that response, but at least it gives me a second to come up with another excuse.

Deep down, I know Paige is joking. But even so, I'm not ready to joke about us yet. Even now we shouldn't really be talking to each other. Her dad lives in this building, and I know some of the guys frequent the restaurant here. We're on dangerous ground.

"That's too bad," Paige says, instead of calling me out like I expected her to do. "I'll have to keep an eye out when I'm shopping. In the meantime, I don't mind you beating me in a race."

"Do you want to race?" Isaac asks, arms locked, ready to take off.

Paige bursts out laughing at the same time Isaac does, and the sound is so beautiful it warms me. My heart bleeds for how badly I want Isaac to be *this* happy all the time.

My phone buzzes in my hands and I realize the time. "We have to get going, Buddy," I say reluctantly. "We'll miss the movie if we don't leave now."

Isaac pouts until I remind him what we're going to see and then he's tugging on my arm again, ready to go in the opposite direction.

"Let's go." He takes a few steps before pausing and turning back around. "Want to come, Paige?"

"Oh." A strange expression washes over her but in an instant it's gone, replaced by her warm grin. "I would love to, but I have a meeting." She glances down at her phone and cringes. "Which I am running late for. Maybe another time?"

"Yes. Okay. Bye."

Isaac moves on, making Paige laugh again, but it doesn't surprise me. When he's a man on a mission, nothing will slow him down. Kind of like Paige.

And I like that.

When the charity event rolls around, Mom insists on adjusting my tie like I'm heading off to my junior prom, while I stare at her deadpan. "You know this isn't my first rodeo, right? I've done this before."

"I know that. But I want you to humor me. I miss these moments."

"What moments? I never let you do up my tie."

"Exactly, that's why I missed it."

"You're so funny that I have stitches from my internal laughter."

Mom rolls her eyes and pulls my tie a little tighter. "I love you, son. How does *that* feel?"

"Perfect," I lie, stepping away without further response.

"I lub you, Nana," Isaac says when I don't return her sentiment out loud. She knows I love her; I'm just not one to say it all the time. Except with Isaac.

Mom gives me a friendly shove before turning to Isaac and dropping to her knees to get to his level, like Paige did, only Mom's legs are shaking as she does it.

"Mom, sit on the couch, would you? You're not getting any younger, and you don't have to get on the floor with Isaac. He understands."

"I tell her to get up, Dad," Isaac says proudly, as though we are a team trying to help my mom.

Mom, on the other hand, scoffs. "I'm fine and if I want to sit on the floor with my grandson, I will."

"Okay. Okay. I've got to go. Can I have a hug, Little Buddy?"

I do exactly what Mom just did and lower myself to his level, waiting for him to run into my arms. And he does. Right on cue. "You'll be good for Nana, won't you?" I ask, knowing the answer.

"Yes."

"And go to sleep when she asks you to."

"Yes," he repeats but his eyes flash to Mom conspiratorially, making me shake my head.

"And you'll ask him to go to sleep on time?" I turn to Mom, sensing they've made some kind of late-night deal since I won't be home until the early hours of the morning.

Stupid charity events. Why can't I just hand over a bag full of cash or my credit card and be done with it? I'm all for raising funds as long as I'm not expected to do anything.

Mom nods with thin lips, and I can practically see the lie forming in her mind. "Just not too late, please."

"He'll be asleep before you get home. That's a promise."

Uh. I know she's joking but still... "It better be *well* before that."

After saying my goodbyes again, I head down to my truck, releasing a slow breath.

I know it will be an unpopular opinion, but I decided to drive. I've got a big morning planned with Isaac tomorrow and I don't want to be hungover for it. Plus, I think it's better to keep my head clear around Paige. If I drink, I'm likely to do something I'll regret. Or don't regret but still shouldn't do.

Paige leaves my mind for barely a second before an image of her and Isaac pops up. I spent most of the movie with Isaac replaying their little interaction, and I still don't know how to feel. On one hand, fuck, it was amazing to watch, seeing the way his eyes lit up when Paige smiled. And the shared affection they had for each other. But on the other hand, it makes me nervous because if she disappears, I'm not sure how much more heartbreak he can take.

He's never that happy when he's talking about his mom but wouldn't shut up about Paige on our entire drive, and when the movie ended, he asked if I thought she would have liked it. Paige, not his mom.

After two goddamn interactions.

I know Paige is great, I get it, but it makes me sad to think that it takes so little to make his heart soar and Macy still can't do it.

She barely even tries.

The sun's setting as I pull into the circular drive on the venue, and I have to admit, it's pretty fucking epic with its grand structure and incredible view. Even if it does look like I'm arriving for a wedding.

It seems I'm not the only one with the idea to drive, because there's a line for the valet so the journey to the front entry is a slow one, giving me the chance to really take in the scenery. And I know where I'll be spending my time. Outside. Away from the crowd. I must remember to thank Paige for giving us a venue with space. There's nothing worse than being cooped up inside with everyone drinking and dancing and acting like they've never had more fun in their lives.

When I'm second in line, a sleek black car with dark windows drives past me, coming to a stop in the drop-off zone closer to the door. It's the type of car you'd expect to be hosting someone famous, obscenely wealthy, or private. Or someone in love with themselves. So it's likely to be either Luke, Zane, or—

A female alights from the backseat and my internal questions stop, knowing immediately that it's Paige, her long legs giving her away. I've pictured them wrapped around my shoulders on more than one occasion since we were last together. And it's been awhile.

Other than our little interactions over the past week, we've been like ships passing in the night, seeing each other regularly but never getting the chance to speak. Which is probably a good thing.

As fun as it was, being with Paige was never going to work. We were keeping things casual before we found out about her dad, and with the season starting, I don't have time to be sneaking around. If I didn't have Isaac, things might have been different, but then I wouldn't have Isaac and that's not a reality I would ever entertain.

While I wait for my turn in line, I take advantage of the view, my gaze gliding from Paige's sky-high stilettos to the split in her dress, the fall of the material showing off way more skin than I'd like, and my cock twitches.

What I wouldn't give to be slipping my hand beneath that dress, to feel her wet for me. Desperate for my touch. Aching for it.

Fuuck. I need a distraction. We agreed to cut ties. It makes sense to cut ties. But after the other night... God, why am I still thinking about her a month later? Why is she always on my mind?

Paige is slow to get out of the car, so I've reached the valet stand by the time she finally steps out and—*god-fucking-dammit*. She looks like sin. Pure sin. Deliciously hot sin that I'm supposed to avoid at all costs.

I cannot let Paige get under my skin. I can't. I won't. It can't happen. I've established that. And yet, she's already fucking there. Buried deep like my co—

Fuck this. I groan, my mind replaying our conversation from the night she was drunk. She wants me. I want her. And now she's here. Looking like that. Fuck it. I can't hold back any longer.

Jumping out of my truck, I toss my keys to the kid and jog to catch up with her, throwing a glance over my shoulder before grabbing her hand and pulling her around the corner, out of sight of the driveway and away from any windows.

Paige gasps at my attack, throwing her free hand out to stop me until she registers who I am and gives up the fight, a soft sigh passing from her lips.

"What are you doing?" She half laughs, shaking her head, and her gaze bounces around.

Grabbing her chin, I still her, turning her face toward mine, locking her with my stare. "You expect me to spend the next five hours pretending I haven't been inside you? And dreaming about doing it again? After the way you were aching for me the other night."

Paige's eyes widen but she quickly recovers, hitting me with a coy smile. "Yes." She shoves me back and takes a step away, her hands raised to stop me from moving closer. "That's exactly what I expect you to do. How else could this possibly play out? We're at a work function."

"I know. I fucking know. But I can't get you out of my head, and if I don't do anything, tonight will be torture. Well worse than I thought it would be."

Paige blinks and I can tell she's warming to the idea.

"The way I see it, you have two choices. Let me fuck you now, against this wall as the party guests arrive. *Or* be ready for me to steal you away sometime during the night. And it's likely to be when you *least* expect it."

Her breath hitches before she licks her lips absentmindedly, and I have to admit it's good to know I affect her as much as she affects me.

"Well, D'Angelo." I make a point of enunciating her name and she rolls her eyes. "What's it going to be?"

Headlights illuminate our path as another car pulls into the driveway, but it's so far away, there's no chance they saw us. And judging by Paige's thoughtful expression, she didn't notice.

"Decisions, decisions," she sasses, making me chuckle.

"You have ten seconds before I make the decision for you." And I'm going with option C—All of the above.

"I thought we agreed this was a bad idea?"

"We did. But that was before you decided to put yourself in my path, looking like the personification of a goddess, after offering me the world the other night. I know why we made our agreement and I'm not saying we break it. Think of it as an addendum. One night. We have a bye this weekend. We could pretend I don't even play football."

"And tomorrow?"

"Back to normal but a little more satisfied."

Paige glances away so I step forward, looking to seal the deal. There's no fucking way I can walk away from this right now. I want her too much. And

I'm desperate to escape. "I know you want me, Paige. Even if you hadn't told me, I can feel it every time we share a space. The tension. The need. I have never wanted to sink inside another woman like I do with you. Right now."

"In that case, I'm choosing option B. Inside."

Fuuck. "Are you sure about that?"

"Yes. But only because the anticipation will kill you and it'll make it all the more fun for me."

Jesus Christ. I groan, my proposal backfiring. *How the fuck am I going to walk away?* "As you wish," I say reluctantly. "Be ready. It could be any given moment."

With my teeth clenched, I turn to leave but Paige stops me, her fingers curling around my bicep. "Wait. Before you go."

She drags me backward until she hits the wall behind her, not letting go until only a breath of space divides us. Lifting to her toes, her lips meet my ear as she moves my hand to her waist and glides my palm down her silk dress, stopping when we reach the slit.

She lets go and I take over, my hands snaking under her dress, lifting the material as I skate my fingers across her skin. I've just reached her ass when she whispers, "If I have to suffer, so do you." Her timing lines up with the moment I find her skin bare, and I can't hide my groan.

"Miss *D'Angelo*..." I grate as I pull away, my eyes locking with hers. "Are you missing something?"

"Nope." She shakes her head, batting her eyelashes innocently. "This dress fits me like a glove and highlights my curves to perfection." I'm not going to argue *yet*—I happen to agree with her—but it's coming. "I have a motto when it comes to gala events like this. Never let a pair of panties get in the way of a good dress."

"Noted." A brief wave of jealousy floods my chest, but I bite my cheek to stave off another guttural groan. Since it's working to my advantage tonight, I shouldn't be mad about it, but I am really fucking livid. "Here's the thing." I squeeze her ass, letting my hand fall until my fingers settle between her legs from behind. "I'm going to reap the benefits of your outfit choice tonight, but the next time you go sans panties, you better be sure I'm going to be there." As if anticipating my next move, Paige spreads her legs and I plunge a finger inside her, then a second, and a third, completely filling her as I step closer, crowding her in. "I want this pussy to be mine, even if I can't use it."

Paige melts against my hand before her body jolts and her eyes fall shut. Her head drops back to the brick wall as I slowly work her with my fingers, careful not to give her too much before the main course later. Her breath picks up and I want more. But before I get the chance to do anything, she wraps her fingers around my wrist and stills me, her eyes opening to pin me with her stare.

"I'm sure you can feel how much your assertiveness turns me on. But I draw the line at fashion. Don't tell me what to wear and I'm yours."

My cock twitches. Every time she pushes back, I want her even more, and maybe she knows that. "Fine, but don't expect me to be happy about it."

CHAPTER TWENTY-FOUR

PAIGE

I take a moment to compose myself when I get inside the venue, making sure to fix my dress and check my hair, and then I'm on—albeit a little flustered—greeting guests and thanking donors.

After spending the day setting up for the Storm event, I rushed home to get ready, planning to be back before the majority of guests arrived. And I was. But I didn't count on Easton accosting me before I got to the door.

Though I wouldn't say it was unwelcome.

I haven't been able to stop thinking about him since the night of my photo shoot. I may have been drunk, but I can still remember every bit of our encounter. Of my advances and his restraint. I was frustrated when he didn't want to come in, but I also understood his view on things. It should have been my view too.

Now, something seems to have shifted between us, and the pull is impossible to ignore.

I have never wanted anyone more than I want him, but God is it complicated.

Thirty minutes later, when most of the guests have arrived, I take to the stage, gaining attention to run through the schedule for the night.

After a lot of negotiating, the board finally agreed for me to set a golden age theme. I had the era of cinema in mind, but I didn't specifically say that to avoid setting a dress code. I was happy to accept the golden age of fashion or even sport. It was left up to the guests themselves and they did not disappoint.

There are top hats and ball gowns, but also attire a little more casual, and I am loving the mix.

If the effort is anything to go by, it's shaping up to be a successful night.

After welcoming everyone and explaining the details of the auction, I pause to check my notes, making sure I've covered everything. And when I'm certain that I have, I glance up and catch Easton's stare.

"From the bottom of my heart, thank you," I say, ready for my moment to be over. "And that's all from me. Hopefully we're all on the same page and excited to—" Easton subtly raises an eyebrow and I stumble over my parting words. "Excited to donate. I'll... ah... hand the floor back to... to... the band."

Dammit, Easton. I don't get nervous like that. I'm not the girl that struggles when a guy gives me attention. That's not me.

When I get off the stage, I make my way through the crowd, head down, only looking up when a hand gently squeezes my waist.

Easton.

Without drawing attention, he subtly leans in, his palm scorching my skin, while I school my features, anticipating his words. "Your guests sure as hell better be on a *different page* than mine or there will be hell to pay."

Jesus Christ.

He keeps moving as though the exchange never happened, while my entire body melts. And for the next two hours, I'm on edge. Twitchy. Hot with anticipation even though Easton doesn't so much as glance in my direction.

Why the hell would I choose option two? I'm clearly crazy. He's much better at keeping his cool than I am.

When the crowd gets loud and tipsy, I seek Easton out, finding him talking to a beautiful woman, and the sting of jealousy bites me. I laugh to myself as I shake off my thoughts. Christian and I used to play those games —purposely making each other jealous, increasing the tension until one of us got mad—then making up for it the second we were alone.

Easton and I don't need the tension from jealousy. He has me wound so tightly I could snap at any moment just from thinking about what he's going to do. Or when. How... God, what is he doing to me?

I glance his way again, and it's obvious from his bored expression that there's nothing between them. He's not talking to her as a message to me. They probably work together. Nothing more.

It's me he wants.

And it's me he's going to get, because as tense as I am right now, I'm his for the taking, his for whatever he wants to do to me. And he knows it.

I'm actually surprised by this side of him. I never would have expected it from my private football man. He's always so guarded and— *Wait... My man? Jesus.* He tells me I'm his—no, he tells me my *pussy* is his and suddenly I'm calling him mine. *Bad idea, Paige.* Tonight is about an addendum to our agreement. Nothing more.

Our lives haven't changed. Easton still has his son. His sweet-natured little boy who I simply adore. And I still have my own issues. One day the veil of my perfect life is going to be ripped away and the truth will come out. I'd never let my mess affect Easton, and more than that, I'd never let my mess lead back to Isaac.

Another hour passes and I'm talking to Amelia about the Storm TV show when one of the stars himself, Zane, swaggers over, a cheesy smile on his face, while I struggle to force one myself. I'm not going to pretend I've learned the names of all my father's players yet, because I'm lucky if I know a handful of them, but I know him.

How could I not? On top of the fact that I've had three people warn me away from him, he's also the cause of some of Easton's pain. And I don't like him.

"Ladies." Zane bows his head as though he's about to tip his hat and I roll my eyes. "How are you both?" he continues. "Amelia, it's been too long."

"What can we do for you, Zane?" Amelia keeps a smile on her face and her expression calm, not giving any of her thoughts or feelings away.

"I thought I'd come over and introduce myself to the woman of the hour. Amelia, do you know you're in the presence of social royalty?"

Amelia shakes her head but laughs. "Speaking of royalty, if Paige is a princess, does that make her father the king? If so, it's time for you to fall to your knees." She points over Zane's shoulder, drawing our gazes to the stage as my father, the king as she called him, takes his position, demanding attention with his presence alone. The lights dim as a spotlight bathes him in a glow, drawing the guests forward like sheep.

I follow, of course, but move to the side of the room, out of his line of sight, behind the masses. The last thing I want is for him to see me in the crowd and call me to the stage.

While I obviously don't mind the spotlight, I've done my bit, and I'm currently too worked up to be coherent.

"Good evening, everyone," Dad begins, and I hold my breath, nervous for the reception he'll receive. It's been four weeks since the general manager "resigned" on Dad's request, and while the stories have died down in the media, he's still receiving some pushback.

The room falls quiet and I sigh in relief, my shoulders physically dropping as some of the tension leaves my body. Some. Not all of it. Because the rest is attributed to Easton and it's not going away until I discover his plans.

For all I know, he was joking, and he's going to disappear after the speeches are done without a word. *Wouldn't that be torture?*

"Thank you," Dad continues. "We appreciate you all for coming tonight and raising money and awareness for this special cause. As Paige mentioned, Parkinson's disease is a condition close to our heart and affects many families across the world." I smile as I think about my grandfather, and send out a silent prayer that we can help others going through what he did. "We may not be able to work miracles, but we can do our bit through donations, and I'm blown away to announce that we've raised over a million dollars tonight."

I clap along with the crowd while a sense of pride washes over me. I'm never going to move mountains, but if I can do my bit with the small luxuries I've been afforded then I'm happy.

"Before I get down to the specifics, I'm going to hand the mic over to Victoria Kate of The Wiser World Foundation to announce the winners of the door prize and big-ticket auction items."

Knowing this is going to take a while, I close my eyes and sigh, letting my head fall back before rolling it from side to side, stretching out my neck.

Strong hands grip my waist from behind and I startle until a warmth hits my neck and Easton's husky voice penetrates my senses. "You look tense. Let me fix that."

I try to turn but he holds me in place, my strength no match for his own. "Keep your eyes forward, D'Angelo. No matter what happens. Trust me."

I barely know him, and yet I don't have to think to decide that I trust him completely and I don't award that faith to many.

Nodding by way of answer, I keep my eyes on the stage, butterflies swarming my chest as he subtly drags me back, only stopping when I'm pressed against him.

Then his hands disappear.

He's so still that if I couldn't feel him against my back, I'd assume he was gone. But on top of his touch, there's a heat radiating between us. A spark. The signal that our moment has come.

My mind whirls with possibilities during the excruciatingly long minute before the tips of his fingers scrape the back of my legs through my dress, making me jump.

I recover quickly and cough to hide the sudden movement while at the same moment Easton glides his leg between mine, forcing them apart. "We can do this here, discreetly, with my fingers inside your pussy, or I can take you behind this wall and fuck you with a little more abandon, both while we listen to your dad's grand speech."

Oh God. The venue we booked has been partitioned off to allow space for the auction. And since the auction is now closed, I'm certain that section is clear. But the idea of getting caught has my pulse spiking and arousal pooling at my center.

I rock my hips, brushing my ass against Easton, and he grows hard behind me, the bulge in his pants pressing into me, making me more desperate to touch him.

I want his fingers, but more than that, I *need* his cock. I need him to lose control just as much as I do.

Without a word, I walk away, keeping close to the wall on my way to the auction area, my heart beating so fast, it's hurting my chest.

When I round the corner, out of sight, I heave in a relieved breath. But it's short-lived. Within a heartbeat, Easton's there, pushing me against the wall as his hand slips beneath my dress.

"You were right about the torture of anticipation," he growls, his voice deliciously deep. "But it's going to be that much more satisfying when I finally sink inside you."

Jesus. My legs clench and I want to tell him to do it now. I'm ready. I've been ready since he had his fingers inside me hours ago, but I'm also greedy and want it all.

"Fuck me with your fingers first; you owe me that. And then, I want your cock."

"Fuck, Paige. You're really something else, you know that?" His fingers drift through my center as he speaks, back and forth before he applies a little pressure and my breath hitches, stopping me from answering.

My head falls back as Easton continues to tease me, but when I finally allow myself to relax and enjoy his slow movements, he pumps a finger inside me, immediately curling it to rub against my walls.

My hips buck as I gasp. "Oh *God*," I rush out, clenching my teeth as he rolls my clit with his thumb, working my heat, his fingers like magic.

"You're always so ready for me," he whispers, leaning into me, his free hand gliding along my silk dress until he reaches my breasts, squeezing me through the material.

He groans when he finds me braless too, but he shouldn't be surprised. As if I'd let straps or outlines ruin my glamour.

As if for punishment, he pinches my nipples, and a shot of electricity sparks to my core. But when he gently rubs the pain away, the sensation of the soft material and his warm touch has my body aching for more.

And I've changed my mind. "I need you inside me. Now."

"Not yet, D'Angelo. You can take a little more."

One of his fingers plays with my ass while the other works my pussy, forcing me to bite my lip to stop myself from screaming.

"Now, Wilder," I demand somewhat quietly, wrapping my fingers around his tie, pulling him down until we're face-to-face. "I need you *now*."

Reaching for his waistband, I frantically unbutton his pants and lower the zipper before slipping my hands inside, cupping his hard length. He growls as he bucks against me and then he's spinning me around, pushing my upper body against the wall as he lifts my dress, flashing my ass to whoever may come in.

He waits a few torturous seconds before stepping into me, his fingers spreading my lips before he glides his cock through my slick heat.

"Fuck, I've missed this," he whispers and I push back as I moan, more desperate for him than I've ever been before.

He thankfully doesn't make me wait, sinking into me in one quick movement, groaning as he does.

I haven't been with anyone since we first started seeing each other, and his thickness burns, but I welcome it, holding my breath until he's buried to the hilt.

I'd love to stop and enjoy the feeling of him filling me up, but we both know we don't have the time for that and immediately start moving, him grabbing my hips and guiding my movements, me gripping the wall so I can push back, meeting his fervor.

With his movements frantic, I rock my hips hard as I straighten up, reaching back to curl my arm around his neck, the new position squeezing his cock before he's ready.

"Fuck," he groans, and his breath on my ear, mixed with the feel of him inside me, has me melting for him.

I buck in the new position and Easton clears his throat in warning seconds before a guttural groan rips from within him, my movements making it harder for him to stay quiet.

A smile pulls at my lips, but Easton wipes it off my face by pinching my clit while he pumps into me, forcing me to cover my mouth as a cry escapes my lips and my orgasm consumes me.

My hips buck uncontrollably, and I'm high on the ecstasy of Easton until I hear my name and freeze.

"Before I call her up here, I want to tell you a bit about the work she's done to make tonight possible."

Fuck. I squirm, trying to wriggle out of Easton's grasp but he doesn't move. He's not done. Instead, he pumps harder while his thumb runs circles over my clit, sending my body into a fit of spasms, with him following me over the edge, grunting through his release.

My body collapses against the wall but Easton grips tighter, holding me against him until my breathing slows and the pulse of his cock makes me shiver.

I don't get a chance to enjoy the moment before I'm being spun around and guided down a darkened hall, confusing me until the exit sign shines a light on the bathroom door.

"I thought you'd want to clean up before Daddy called you onto the stage," Easton rasps in my ear. "You can't have him knowing you're not the dutiful daughter he thinks you are."

This *man. Fuck.* I shiver at his gravelly voice, but by the time I'm focused enough to turn around, he's gone.

Snapping out of my daze, I run in and freshen up before making a dash to the side of the stage, hearing my dad call my name as I reach him. "Paige, honey. Where are you?"

"I'm here." I rush up the steps, settling myself under his outstretched arm. "Sorry, I was near the back because this is unnecessary. You don't have to praise me."

Dad smiles, shaking off my concern as he whispers, "Of course, I do. This is all *you*." He lifts the mic to his mouth and sets about embarrassing me. "If you haven't met my beautiful daughter, this is Paige."

As he speaks, I think about Easton, imagining him watching me, smiling at our close call, my body heating at what we just did.

I thank the heavens for the sheer number of auction items and my dad's over-the-top speeches because without that, we never would have made it to the end.

Speaking of over-the-top, "As well as being a model and artist," Dad continues and my eyes flash to his, my smile locked in place, when I'd rather scold him. "...she's also the founder of the D'Angelo Foundation, and I think we can all agree, she's one heck of an event planner."

He's embellishing the truth, but I let that slide. I'm not an event planner. I've only really *planned* this one event on my own, and technically he and Mom founded the charity, putting it in my name before handing it over to me.

I love the D'Angelo Foundation and wouldn't change a thing, but it's a step I probably wouldn't have taken on my own.

"Paige and I will be hosting multiple events over the next few years, in partnership with The San Francisco Storm, and hope to see you all here again, doing your bit for these amazing charity foundations. I understand a lot of you have charities you regularly support or charities of your own, therefore we appreciate anything you can do as we as a team give back.

"For our next event, we're teaming up with Thomas Kelly's mental health project, a cause I wholeheartedly believe in. It's important to raise awareness of mental health in athletes, specifically men, and I can't wait to see what we can do to support Thomas's wonderful foundation. We know the spotlight's on us as a team this year for a number of reasons—the Super Bowl for one, and the other little prime-time moment that we won't be talking about—and with the help of Paige and her foundation, we're planning to step up and shine."

The crowd laughs at the mention of the TV show, but it's still a sore point with the team. I've been told the players and officials are divided in their opinions of the show. My dad sits firmly in the *"not a fan"* club, as does Keeley. And I'm sure Easton would feel the same. Understandable considering how he was portrayed on top of Zane's tell-all about his ex.

"Our team may be a mix of the young and the older, but at the heart of it, we're a family. A family that cares. A family that supports each other. A family that enjoys a good celebration when one of their own achieves greatness. So, cheer us on as we achieve greatness this year both on and off the field. And let's get this party started. I'm sure you're all sick of my voice. It's time to get back to the festivities. Thank you all for coming. And here's to back-to-back wins."

He raises a glass, the base of it almost hitting my ear, and I smile while the crowd cheers.

I've got to admit, he's good. I just hope it's enough to win over those still on the fence when it comes to his choices.

Dad and I walk offstage and the second we're out of earshot, he releases a deep sigh. "That never gets easier. Put me in a negotiating situation and I'm on fire. Need me to do a speech about a hot topic, I'm your man. Ask me to speak about something that's personal to me and I clam up. Just calling your name had me sweating."

My shoulders drop. I was all set to tell him off for mentioning my artwork, but now I feel bad for him. He probably doesn't even realize he did it. "Who knew under that tough, bulldog exterior there was a sensitive soul."

"You did," he scoffs, rolling his eyes. "I've always been real with you."

"I think I might be the only person."

"Shame it's not mutual." His brow raises but I know better than to take the bait.

"I'm real with you, Dad. This is who I am," I lie. Yes, I love my public persona. But there's so much more to me. No one is that happy all the time.

No matter what they project to the world. Thomas and his charity is a good example of that. He announced he had depression a few years ago, and he's been fighting to reduce the stigma around it ever since. I admire him for that.

I have a feeling this team is going to grow on me. But there's one player in particular that I want to see right now.

CHAPTER TWENTY-FIVE

EASTON

I watch Paige standing proudly next to her dad, and the reality of what we did sinks in. We could have been caught, but for the life of me, I can't bring myself to care. Not for me anyway. If getting caught affected Paige's relationship with her dad then I'd put a stop to it.

But if she's holding back because she thinks I'll be dropped from the team, I'm willing to take the risk.

The problem is... this thing between us is complicated by more than just Paige's dad. And if it really was *casual sex*, I'd be all for it.

But we moved past that when Isaac decided to get attached to her. He's only met her twice and thinks the sun shines out of her ass.

And while he's not wrong, it makes life difficult.

What if we continue on this casual path and it ends badly? Will Paige ignore him when he walks past, his smile wide as he waves to her?

Deep down I can't imagine she will, but can I really risk that?

As she walks off the stage, Paige's eyes scan the crowd, and I know she's looking for me. But I don't know what the fuck I'm going to say when she finds me.

Since having Isaac, my world has consisted of two things—football and him. I was an ass to Macy. I've had time to reflect on our relationship and I know she's not the only one that changed after Isaac was born. I don't know if I have room in my life for more than that. My headspace is jam-packed with enough of Macy's drama, meaning I struggle to think more than a few days ahead.

And yet, I keep making space for Paige.

Because when I'm with her, a little part of the pain and drama melts away.

I'm not sure I can give that up, but at the same time, I'm worried we're playing with fire and there are more than two people that could get burned.

"East." Reed nods as he joins me, a warm smile on his face. He's a nice guy, one of the good ones, and if I had the capacity to let someone else into my life as a friend, it would likely be him. But the most I can afford is teammates. "Are you having a good night? I saw you got stuck with Pierce for a while. Any chance he decided to spill his thoughts on the new GM?"

The new GM. A sore point that I have no intention of touching, not even with a ten-foot pole. They're still looking for someone. And while we've heard many names thrown around, the one everyone seems to be excited about is Wes Johnson. Former player turned coach, turned college football GM. He's the perfect candidate. But the word is that he's reluctant.

And I don't blame him.

In the weeks since Tray left, there's been a strong divide between management and coaches. Some are openly pissed off about his departure, while others seem relieved.

When I finally asked Keeley about it, she didn't give me much—she never does—but she did say that the team was better off, even if we couldn't see it. She can be annoyingly cryptic sometimes, but I believe her. Not only because she's my sister, but also because of Paige. I can see parts of her in her dad, and I can't fathom him firing Tray for weak reasons—or as some people have said, so he can claim the role for himself.

But if the team *is* better off without him, it begs the question, what's the new GM walking in to? What mess is he going to be left with?

Reed raises a brow in anticipation and I actually smile. It seems everyone's jumped on the gossip train since this mess began.

"He didn't say a word. We didn't even talk about football."

"You didn't?"

"No, he was asking about Isaac and that led to us talking about schools in the area." Yet another thing that's going to be made harder thanks to Macy's need to weigh in on every decision when she doesn't even live here anymore.

"Oh yeah?" Reed nods, seemingly interested though I have no clue why. "Did he offer any good advice?"

"Got a kid coming, Reed?"

He laughs before his eyes dart to someone behind me, and I don't have to turn to guess it's his friend. I don't remember her name but I saw them together earlier, and the way he looks at her is possessive.

"No secret babies for me." He gives a firm shake of his head. "That's Luke's thing."

"Ah, Luke. Who would have thought he'd ever grow up? Not me, that's for sure." Although I'm still not entirely convinced that he has.

"I saw it," Reed confirms, and I don't doubt his words—he's one of those optimistic types that sees the good in everyone. "The mature side of him was buried deep, but I knew it was there."

"You're a good guy, Reed. Better than most."

"And you're not always an asshole yourself," he adds and I groan.

"I take back my compliment. You're a dick. I'm out."

Reed laughs like I'm joking, and he'd be right, but this side of me only comes out for those that deserve it. And in reality...most people don't.

As if hearing us talking about him, Luke joins the conversation, along with Dylan, and I reluctantly hang around, listening in until Luke opens his mouth.

"Look at us, the support gang hanging out together."

I groan—out loud—making sure he can hear me over the music, and the guys laugh.

"Easton, my man," Luke continues, draining the life out of me, "you need to embrace it. We're here for *you*. What do you need?"

"I need for you to shut the fuck up."

He pretends to zip his lips, put a lock on it, and throw away the key, while I roll my eyes. But it lasts all of two seconds before he's speaking again. "See, I'm here for you."

"You just spoke."

"To tell you that. It doesn't count."

I stare at him deadpan and he smirks.

"Okay, you caught me. I assumed you meant that I couldn't talk about your issues with Zane and your ex. Or the fact that you've been hiding your relationship with Keeley. How the fuck didn't we know she was your sister?"

"Reed, did you hear something?"

"You're hilarious for an asshole. I hate to break it to you, but Reed and Dylan want to know too."

Dylan raises his hands in the air. "Don't bring me into this. I've retired."

"And yet, you're still in the group chat," Luke quips back and he has a point. "Reed then?" he asks.

We all turn to Reed as he curls his lips into a very un-Reed-like smirk. "Not going to lie, I'm curious."

For fuck's sake. "Why don't you ask Keeley then?"

"We did. She said to ask you."

"Uh. If you must know, it was easier that way. I didn't want anyone to think she got the job because of me."

The guys fall quiet, their expressions comical as Thomas joins us. "Wow. What did I miss?"

"Easton just admitted he has a heart," Luke fake gushes and I almost deck him.

"Why the fuck were you even questioning that, Luke?" Thomas shakes his head as his gaze bounces between me and Luke. "East almost beat the shit out of that dick for harassing Amelia last season. If the security guard hadn't stepped in—"

"Enough," I cut in. "I'm out."

I walk away, leaving them undoubtedly talking about me, but I don't need to listen. I know what happened. I was there. And I didn't almost beat the shit out of him. I had him up against a brick wall with my fist clenched, ready to strike. We'll never know if I would have hit him or not. But God was he a fucker.

He got what he deserved in the end. No one will work with him. And I heard he got a year's community service for what he did.

The only thing *I* did was remove him from the situation. I couldn't stand by and watch him attack Amelia. I may not have been happy about her or the TV show, but she didn't deserve that. And I've come to realize, she's one of the good ones too.

Truthfully, she's probably the only reason I haven't shut down the group chat entirely. If she thinks Luke's a good guy, then maybe deep down he is.

Aftter walking away from the guys, I force myself to endure another twenty minutes of mingling, then I'm ready to leave.

I look for Paige, not wanting her to think that I disappeared without seeing her, and find her on the dance floor, smiling and laughing with Amelia, her friend Hayley, and of course, my goddamn sister.

I bite back a groan—Paige being friends with my sister couldn't possibly be a good idea—yet my lips pull into a smile completely of their own accord.

As if sensing my stare, Paige glances my way and her own smile widens. She's breathtaking when she's like this—happy and carefree—and it makes it that much harder to leave.

I nod subtly before walking toward the door, hoping she gets the hint that I'm leaving. I have no doubt we'll see each other soon, and if we don't, maybe that's not such a bad thing.

Beelining for the valet stand, I pray that he'll let me take my truck since I never bothered to collect my ticket when I handed over the keys. But before I can ask, a loud whistle sounds from behind me, drawing my attention to Paige disappearing around the corner, back to the scene of our first little moment.

After checking my surroundings, I spin on a dime, then stalk toward the side of the building, only stopping when I've found her.

I open my mouth to speak but she stops me in my tracks, throwing her arms around me before slamming her lips to mine, her tongue immediately seeking entry.

It takes me a second to catch up before my stiff body relaxes and I wrap my arms around her waist, my hands splayed on her back, forcing her closer.

Her breath hitches as we kiss and a soft mewl escapes her throat, her sounds alone making my cock harden.

Moving a hand to her neck, I curl my palm beneath her styled hair, careful not to mess it up, while tilting her head back and deepening our kiss. Our tongues clash at first, fighting for control, but after a beat, we settle into a smooth rhythm, my heart pounding like I've never kissed this way before—slow yet possessive and...*Jesus*. Maybe I haven't.

But fuck if I'm going to get caught up in that now.

We kiss for another minute until Paige pulls away, stepping out of my hold. "Sorry about that," she says, wiping her lips with a grin that suggests she's not sorry at all. "You didn't kiss me earlier. So"—she shrugs, not a care in the world—"I hope it's okay that I did that."

I wish I could answer her but I'm not entirely sure how I feel, except that I don't want this to end.

"Yeah, it was okay." I smile. "Maybe we need a few more addenda."

"I think I can get behind that. But for now, I better get back." She points toward the building behind her and I nod.

"You better. This isn't going to last long if we get caught."

"Definitely not. My dad's likely to riot." Outwardly she's joking, but how much truth is there to that statement?

"Who would take the brunt of that?" I ask, my hand cupping the back of my neck. "You or me?"

Paige laughs, and like always it's infectious. "Definitely you."

"And you're not worried about your relationship with him? If he found out?"

"No, I'm not. We've been through some stuff and we've only recently repaired our relationship. I don't think he'd let something like this set us back. I can't say the same for you. He seems serious about the 'no dating my daughter' rule, but the question is—how far will he go if someone breaks it? And trust me, you don't want to find out."

Paige smiles as she makes her way inside, but I don't let her get far before calling out in a loud whisper. "What if I do?"

"What?" Paige spins, confusion marring her features.

"What if I don't mind finding out? The last thing I'd want is for this"— I gesture between the two of us—"to affect your relationship with your dad. But if it's just about me, I don't care."

"What if he drops you for a game?"

I shrug.

"What if he drops you for a month?"

I shrug again, though in reality that would be his loss as much as mine. The team needs me.

"Okay, what if he gives you that look of disappointment that makes you squirm every time you see him? I bet you know the one. I think they hand it out when you have your first child."

I know the look she's referring to. I've seen it many times. But I'm willing to take that risk.

"Bring it."

Paige laughs before running back over and pressing a kiss to my cheek. "I'm almost afraid to ask, but even if my dad's not a concern...what about Isaac? And all the other complications we had before we realized my dad connected us?" She frowns and I feel it in my chest even before she adds, "Has anything really changed? Think about it, okay?"

Chapter Twenty-Six

EASTON

Paige's parting words linger in my mind long after she's gone. "Think about it, okay?"

It's been over twenty-four hours. In fact, we're pushing thirty-six, and I'm still doing as she asked—*thinking about it*—and it's driving me fucking crazy. It makes sense to walk away. It's casual sex, and we don't need it fucking up our lives, but at the same time, walking away doesn't feel like an option anymore.

Yes, I have Isaac to think about. And I've been thinking about him 24-7. He's usually *all* I think about. But I've got to believe that as long as it doesn't affect my time with him, and Paige doesn't disappear, then it's not hurting him. Right?

Or wrong?

Fuck, I don't know. But what I do know is that it shouldn't be this complicated for a casual fling. Maybe we're putting too much stock into it. Maybe it's best to just see what happens. We just fuck if we find a moment that presents itself, and don't if we don't.

It worked with us in the beginning. It could work again.

When I pull into the parking lot at the stadium Monday morning, it's suspiciously empty. But who am I to complain? I'd much rather work out alone than listen to the guys go on and on about the event Saturday night —we were all there; we know how it went.

Taking my time, I've just made it to the door when my phone rings. *Mom.*

"Is everything okay?" I ask as I answer. I only left them thirty minutes ago.

"We're fine but Isaac wants to wear his Halloween T-shirt and I can't find it."

"His what?"

"His Halloween T-shirt. He said he's got one with a truck on it."

I rack my brain, but for the life of me, I can't picture what he's talking about. "I don't think-"

"Mom said she got it for me," Isaac calls out in the background, his voice shaky. I pause, my eyes falling shut as I try to remain calm. It's not them I'm angry at.

"Can you please put Isaac on the phone?" I ask before taking a deep breath.

"Of course. I'm sorry, he didn't say that before."

"You haven't done anything wrong, Mom."

Isaac comes on the phone but stays quiet.

"Are you okay, Buddy?"

"No."

"Can I help?"

A few cars pull into the parking lot, so I duck around the side of the building, out of the way as Isaac sniffs. "Do you know where my Halloween shirt is?"

"Your Halloween shirt?"

"Yeah."

I pause and my shoulders drop. The way I see it, I have two options, and as much as it pains me, I have to be the bigger person here. "It might be in the washer. Can you wear something else today and I'll have it ready for you tomorrow? The one with the truck, right?" I ask, going along with what Mom said.

"I want it today." Isaac begins to cry and it breaks me.

"I know you do, Buddy. I'm sorry. I wanted to make sure it was clean for Halloween." *God, now I'm taking the blame.*

He's silent again before he sniffs. "Okay. I'll wear it tomorrow."

"Thank you." I bite back a relieved sigh. "I love you."

"Lub you." He hangs up before letting me speak to my mom, and I groan as I note the time. I *was* early and now I'm going to be late because I have to find a goddamn Halloween T-shirt. Thank God, it's the right time of year.

I shouldn't have lied about washing it, but I'm sick of seeing his disappointed little face or hearing his broken voice whenever Macy fucks up. It's not his fault she's unreliable.

Taking a deep breath, I dial Macy, the last person I want to speak to, and release a slow drawn-out breath before she answers.

"Hey, Baby," she says in a childish voice.

"It's not Isaac."

"Oh. It's been a while since you've called me."

"I'm not calling for a friendly chat. Isaac said you promised him a Halloween T-shirt."

Macy laughs. "I didn't think he'd remember that."

"You didn't—" I stop myself from attacking her because it's not going to get me the information I need. "Do you remember what it looked like or where it was from?"

"It was from Macy's." She laughs like she always does when either one of us mentions the department store with her name. I used to laugh, or at least smile, but now I've got nothing.

"Can you send me a photo?"

"It was Halloween with a truck."

"I know that, but there could be more than one."

"Ugh, fine. I'll send it when I finish at the nail salon. I've got you on speaker, by the way. Say hello to Easton Wilder, everyone."

Fuuck. My fist clenches as I grit my teeth. "Send me the photo, Macy. It's for Isaac." I hang up and slam open the door, not even checking if anyone's nearby before beelining for the locker room, keeping my head down.

But apparently that's not a clear enough indicator that I want to be left alone because Luke's in my face the second I step inside.

"I don't want to hear it," I preempt whatever he's about to say, continuing on my path.

But of course, he follows. "You know what, East? I don't give a fuck what you want because I'm not walking away until you listen."

Jesus. I groan before dropping onto the chair in front of my locker and raising my hands. "Have at it then."

"Great. I wanted to say thank you," he begins softly and my frustration wavers. "I had no idea you did that for Amelia. You told me you watched him leave. You never mentioned..." He trails off but I don't need him to continue.

"I didn't—"

"I know you didn't do it for me. You made that clear last year. I'm thanking you for Amelia."

"Don't. It didn't really stop him, did it?"

My mind flashes back to that day and I tense, swapping one awful person for another. The dick we're referring to had an issue with Luke's wife. Though she wasn't his wife at the time, I don't think... I never asked about their timeline. But she was pregnant with his baby and this guy—I can't remember his name—was a piece of shit. I didn't do what I did for Luke or Amelia specifically. I didn't give it much thought at all. I just reacted.

And I think it has a lot to do with growing up surrounded by women. If that had been one of my sisters or my mom, I would have done the same thing. So I did.

"You don't have to thank me," I add genuinely. "I'm sure you'd do the same for me." Luke's face lights up and I immediately regret my words. "Don't," I warn.

"What?" He lifts his hands in surrender but hits me with his thoughts anyway. "I was only going to ask if there was someone special you needed me to keep an eye on?"

"I can take care of myself and my family."

"I know you can but—"

"But nothing, Luke. It was a throwaway comment."

"East."

"I want you to stay out of my business."

I grab my phone from my pocket and make a show of bringing up our chat, leaving the group.

EASTON LEFT THE GROUP

Barely a second passes before both our phones chime with a notification.

REED ADDED EASTON TO THE GROUP

Motherfucker. I can't escape this.

My gaze shoots to Reed's and the guy smirks. There's not even a hint of apology in his expression.

I offer them both a glare before turning away and aggressively shoving my bag into my locker, ensuring my phone is out of sight and hopefully out of mind. For the sake of this and Macy.

Luke's still standing behind me when I'm ready for the group workout, so as I walk away we bump shoulders.

"See you in the gym." He smiles as though all is good. "Let me know if you need someone to spot you."

My fists clench but I keep walking. I can work out my frustrations during our weight session.

As soon as I'm back at my locker, I check my phone, holding my breath for an image from Macy. Stupid idea. I'm likely to die before she does something helpful.

Bringing up my search engine, I look for options and find two Halloween tees with trucks on them, so I call in a favor—another favor— with Keeley.

> Easton: Any chance you can go to Macy's (the store) for me on your lunch break?

I'm thankful when she responds right away.

> Keeley: What lunch break? What are those?

Typical Keeley. I'd snap back if I wasn't desperate.

> Easton: It's for Isaac

> Keeley: What do you need?

I audibly sigh in relief because if she'd said no, I might have had to actually ask one of the guys for a favor, and that's the last thing I want to do. But Mom needs me as soon as I'm finished here and I don't have time to shop.

After sending Keeley the two images and asking her to buy both, I finally relax. Macy owes me big time. And I owe Keeley.

My body aches as I slump into the mirrored wall of my building's elevator, two Halloween truck tees in hand. My need to forget about Macy, Luke, and the goddamn group chat meant that I pushed myself to my limits today and I'm feeling it.

But at least I was smart enough not to go *over* my limit—even while stressed—so recovery shouldn't take long.

The elevator doors open again, and I look up to find that I'm still in the goddamn lobby. I've been so caught up in my head that I never even pushed the button for my floor.

Good one, East.

I curse myself for being so mentally fucked until Paige steps in, immediately changing my mood.

With her nose in her phone, she's completely oblivious to her surroundings, smiling at something she sees as she brushes a hair off her face. I watch her, my eyes grazing over her skin tight black pants and loose-fitting top until she looks up, her eyes widening when she sees me.

"Oh," she gasps, reaching out to press the button for her floor, the happy surprise in her expression matching my own.

If I wasn't so busy, this could have been one of those moments I was thinking about. After all, if the opportunity presents itself, who am I to say no? In fact, my cock twitches just thinking about it.

But now is not the time.

I raise an eyebrow and open my mouth to speak when another person rushes in before the doors close.

"Paige. I'm so glad I caught you," our elevator companion grins as she reaches out to pat Paige's arm. "I forgot to get you to sign."

To sign? While their conversation intrigues me, I'm more pissed that I've lost my alone time with Paige. I've only got a few minutes before I need to be home, and it would have been nice to spend that time talking with her.

Paige throws a smile my way before the two of them exit on the next level and my good mood fades.

At least it does until I walk inside to find Isaac's expectant gaze staring back at me, and I know that unlike his mom, I didn't let him down.

"Hey, Buddy. How was your day?"

"Good. We played monster trucks."

My eyes flash to Mom's to find her rubbing the base of her spine. "Did Nana get on the floor again?"

Isaac's nose scrunches. "The trucks don't fly, Daddy."

"Very true. So—"

"Can we get my Halloween shirt, *please*?"

Luckily, *I* didn't bank on him forgetting about it like Macy did. If she bothered to get to know him, she'd quickly discover he never lets things go. "Of course, we can, but I want you to remind me what color it is."

"Black." *Shit.* This is going to be tricky. "And green." *Yes.* Got it.

"Thanks, I'll go and check. You wait here."

I make a show of going into the laundry room and opening the dryer door before producing the green-and-black Halloween top and hiding the purple-and-black one back in the bag.

"Here you go," I say, holding it up as I re-enter the room.

"That's it." Isaac runs forward and launches himself into my arms. "You found it."

"I did. How about you go and put it on your bed for the morning?"

He runs off again and Mom raises a brow. "What's in the bag?" She grins knowingly.

"Another top." I shrug.

"Just the one? You did well."

"I had to call her." Mom's nose scrunches before she opens her mouth to speak. "Don't say it. I know. I shouldn't have let her get away with that, but what was I going to do, break his heart?"

"I wasn't going to say that."

"Then what were you going to say?"

"You're a great dad, Easton. I'm proud of you."

Her smile widens while I grimace. "I'm really not, but thank you."

Isaac comes running back into the room, talking animatedly about Halloween, cutting off whatever Mom was going to say in response to my proclamation. But I wouldn't have listened regardless. Yes, I do all that I can, but I don't see him enough. And that's what's important.

Why can't life be simpler? Why can't he have a mom that wants to spend time with him so we can balance the time between us and ensure he's never without?

My mom is amazing. But it's taking a toll on her. And I'm not sure how much longer she's going to cope.

After a quick goodbye, Mom heads home, and I get Isaac off to sleep before eating dinner and crashing on the couch. I don't sleep well as my mind runs wild processing everything I've got going on, and by Tuesday afternoon I'm a little on edge and desperate to relieve some tension.

And I don't think the gym will do.

Thoughts of Paige run rampant, and I find myself wanting to call her.

Only we never exchanged goddamn numbers.

I grapple with my conscience trying to decide between right and wrong when it comes to Paige, but there's one argument that reigns supreme. *I'm a fucking adult and I don't play games.*

I know what I want. I know my limits and I know how to protect my family. I would never let things with Paige affect that.

So...it's time to make it happen.

Chapter Twenty-Seven

PAIGE

I'm still reeling after signing on as one of the models for a huge runway event when my phone rings the next day. I pause my walk and smile when Hayley's name pops up.

She kept the party going beyond the time I thought the charity event would be over on Saturday night, and I'll forever be in her debt. People kept donating to the website we'd set up long into the early hours of the morning, and I'm certain that's because they were still drinking and having fun. I know a little part of me should feel guilty that they donated under the influence of alcohol, but I don't. They're adults; they can make their own decisions.

But I am grateful that Hayley was there.

"Hayley, my angel. I'm so glad you called."

"Hi Babe. I wanted to call Sunday but I wasn't feeling that great. And yesterday I was at the studio for a meeting."

"Ahh, the *studio*. I've had a lot of famous friends but none that have starred as my favorite character before."

"Ugh. Stop with the pressure."

"You love it."

"I do. It keeps me honest." There's a smile in her voice and I'm about to laugh when she continues. "*But*"—she trails off for dramatic effect—"I didn't call to talk about *me*. I called to talk about *you*. Who was that guy following you around all night? He was dreamy."

"Which guy?"

"Sorry, of course," she says exaggeratedly, "there were *so* many." Sarcasm oozes through the phone and I burst out laughing.

"I didn't mean it like that. I just can't remember anyone."

"I thought you might say that considering you never once acknowledged him. And he was gorgeous."

"I was busy."

"I would have accepted that excuse for the first half of the night. But after the speeches, you were on the dance floor like the rest of us. And you iced him out."

"What?" I huff out a laugh. "I don't ice people out."

"Okay, you didn't do that, but you gave him nothing. Which left me wondering... Who's the guy?"

"What?" I try my hardest to remember, but for the life of me, I'm drawing a blank. "I honestly have no idea who you're talking about." *Was I really that oblivious to someone following me around?*

"I meant... Who's the guy occupying your mind?"

Oh. *Dammit.* "No one." *That I can tell you about.* "I guess that because I haven't been looking for anyone since my breakup with Christian, I didn't realize anyone was there."

"Hmm, okay. I'll believe you for now. But we need to change that thought process. You can look for something that isn't serious. Have some fun. But I will warn you, sometimes that leads to something more serious. Like when I told Amelia to sleep with the hot football player and she ended up pregnant and married."

"That's not going to be me. Moving on."

Hayley laughs. "Okay. Were you serious about me being your date to your next charity event?"

"I was." I almost squeal. "Are you saying yes?" Hayley and I got to talking after the ball finished the other night, and I mentioned I needed a plus-one for the event I'm hosting in a few weeks. It's the same foundation I helped back in New York, so I wanted to continue supporting them.

Hayley had said she'd check dates when she got home, and I'd completely forgotten about it. I would have loved to invite Easton. But for one, it's public, and two, it's definitely *not* his thing. I'm actually surprised he came to the team event—grateful and satisfied—but surprised.

"You bet your ass I'm saying yes," Hayley cuts into my thoughts. "You, Paigey, know how to put on an event."

"I wasn't as involved in the one coming up, but I think it will still be fun."

"We'll make it fun."

I know she will—that's why I invited her. I can't imagine she'd ever let things get boring, and we get along well. She doesn't take life too seriously and I like that.

"Just tell me the details and I'll be there."

"Thanks, Hayley."

"Don't thank me. I should be thanking you. Open bar, hot men, a night of dancing. I can't wait."

We chat for a few more minutes and then she's called away by one of the production assistants.

I'm in my head, imagining what life would be like as an actress when an alert goes off on my phone, making me freeze as I reach the front of my building. That annoying little chime means my name has been mentioned in the media, and while I'd love to think it has something to do with the Storm event, I have a feeling I'm not going to be that lucky.

Reluctantly, I check my phone, my breath caught in my throat.

New details have emerged surrounding billionaire Christian Mikkleson's relationship with socialite and new heir to the San Francisco Storm football team, Paige D'Angelo.

Goddammit.

Sources say the two shared a sordid relationship of games and blackmail that often included other people. A friend close to the pair said the games started off as a bit of fun but Christian was left heartbroken after Paige took things too far. The ex-couple are yet to comment.

Yet to comment? No one fucking asked me.

I want to throw my phone but clench it tightly in my hand knowing my whole life is on this damn thing. And I know better than to shoot the messenger, even if it is a device.

Who the hell is my so-called "friend" and if he or she *was* a friend, why throw me under the bus like that? I never hurt Christian. He's engaged, for God's sake. He's *fine.*

Needing to get to the bottom of this, I call the man himself, and he answers immediately, groaning by way of a hello.

It's safe to say he saw it too.

"I know why you're calling," he snaps. "It wasn't me."

"It was your goddamn parents, wasn't it?"

"Most likely. Which means it's actually your fault."

"How—"

"Tell me what you know, Paige. Or what they think you know, or they're never going to stop, and I can't help you."

"I'm not the only one that looks bad in this scenario."

"Really? Did we read the same headline? *You* took things too far, according to a source. My offer still stands. Meet me for lunch. Let's show the world we're united and that the rumors are just that—rumors."

"No."

"You're being ridiculous."

"You need to control your parents, Christian. Because like I said, I have plenty to say and I'm not afraid to say it."

"You're just as bad as they are with the threats. I wish you'd both keep me out of it."

And *I* wish you weren't a naive piece of shit and that you actually paid attention to the crap going on in your own fucking organization... but here we are.

"Tell them to stop or I'll release a tell-all. On them and *you.*"

I hang up before he finds out that my threat's empty. I can't say anything yet because it would just push his parents to hide evidence before I get any. At the moment, I'm a light threat to them. They know I overheard something, but Christian's mom spilled a lot during that chat with her sister so they don't know the full extent of what I heard. If I tell anyone before getting evidence, I become a bigger threat and I'll admit, I'm worried about what they'll do.

Between Christian and the article, I'm livid by the time I get in the elevator to my apartment. I need to vent, but I have no one I can talk to about any of this. Because no one will understand.

I still haven't told my dad, even though I said I would. He's got too much going on with his business back in New York and the team. I can't add another layer to his stress. Not when I know he'll put me first when he can't afford to do that right now.

I pace the small space on the way to my floor, mumbling to myself as though that will solve all my problems, knowing without a doubt that it won't.

I could call Austin, but all that would do is piss him off. He's looking, and I need to give him time.

When the elevator stops on my level, I throw my head back and sigh. This is all I need. If they release the images along with that article, I'll never live it down. Or worse, I could—

"Easton?"

I stop halfway out of the elevator, my eyes wide, to find Easton pacing the hall near my door, his cap pulled low on his brow, his muscles tense under his fitted tee.

He spins at the sound of my voice and pauses. "You're home."

"I am. And you're *here*."

"I am. I..." He trails off as I step out, motioning for me to walk to my door. And God, I hope that means he wants to come in.

"Do you..." I gesture inside when I've opened up. "I—"

"I can't fucking do this," he cuts in before I can ask my question, but makes his way into my apartment. "I know we have to be careful, for both our sakes, but this pretending bullshit is not for me. I don't usually give a fuck what other people think, and if our situation was different, even if we were casual, I wouldn't be worried about hiding it. Only it's not just me anymore so we have to hide it. But I refuse to pretend I don't want you. Not anymore. So here."

He holds out a key and I still, my puzzled gaze lifting to his. "What's this?"

"What does it look like?"

"A key, smartass. But what's it for?"

"My apartment."

"Your what?" My brows shoot up toward my hairline as I stare down at the key.

"My apartment," he repeats. "I'm sick of leaving it to chance to see you."

"Ah...we could start with phone numbers. This is—"

"I'm not asking you to move in. I just figured we needed another option instead of sex in a goddamn gym bathroom."

Sucking my lips into my mouth, I picture said bathroom and giggle until another location comes to mind. "We also have a very public event full of almost everyone you know."

Easton smirks and it hits me in the chest. Don't get me wrong, I like my grumpy asshole, but when he smiles... God, he could melt the most impenetrable heart.

"Very funny. You know what I mean."

"I do." I smile until I think his offer through. "What about Isaac? What if he comes in one night or hears me?"

"Isaac spends Wednesday nights at my mom's. I have a late meeting, but I want you there when I get home. *Waiting* for me."

Jesus. Why is that so hot?

"How late is late?" I challenge him while my chest burns with excitement.

"I'm usually home by nine."

"Oh, shame. I'm usually asleep by nine."

"That's fine by me, but I'll be waking you with my tongue."

My God, I love this man's mouth. "Are you going to dictate what I'm wearing too?"

"If you're wearing *anything*, I'll be disappointed."

I smile though I don't think he's joking. At all. And I kind of like that. Plus, it's Wednesday today and I could definitely use some time together.

"So you trust me with the key to your family home?"

"Is that your way of saying that I shouldn't?" He bites back another smile and I laugh. At least, I do until the gossip article reminds me that I shouldn't.

"The media have been saying some things about me," I say, deciding to give him a reason to trust me, by being open.

"I don't care for gossip."

"Some of it's true."

His eyes briefly widen before he schools his features. "Will it hurt Isaac?"

"No, I don't think so. They're just words. About me. And I'd never let that happen. But it's not very nice and—"

Easton steps forward, his fists clenched. "Did it hurt *you*?"

My heart slams in my chest at his protective stance, his penetrating gaze a force against my need to put him at ease. But I win.

"I'm fine," I lie. "It's nothing I can't handle." So what if it ruins my reputation and makes me look like the bad guy. There are more important things in life, right?

Easton continues his visual standoff, trying to catch me in a lie, and I stare right back before raising an eyebrow as I smirk. "I promise."

I should be used to this by now, but I've worked hard to give myself a good name. I grew up in the public eye. Everything I do, say, or wear has been curated to portray the life I want people to see. Or the life my mom wanted people to see.

What they're saying now may not align with that version of me, but it's also not exactly a lie, apart from the reports that I hurt Christian.

"Do you want to know what's being said?" I ask hesitantly, not entirely sure what to say.

"Do I need to?" Easton's response catches me off guard, and I open my mouth to question him but he cuts me off. "I mean, if you want to talk about it, I'm here to listen, but if you don't want me to know..."

He trails off and I suddenly want him to know everything, but I can't because something tells me he'll fight for me and that's not going to end well. So instead I give him what I can.

"My ex and I used to play games in our relationship. We'd make each other jealous, use people to get the other excited. I'm not ashamed that it happened, but I'm not thrilled it came out. It's my personal business and shouldn't have been shared with the masses."

"*Jesus*. Was it your ex?" His expression turns dark, and I almost say yes to see what he'd do to Christian. I've never had someone in my life that wants to hurt someone else on my behalf, and Easton's face is screaming "let me at him."

"It wasn't him. He didn't want that part of our lives to come out any more than I did. He's engaged and trying to move on."

"Do you know who?"

I shake my head to stop myself from verbally lying to him. It's better if he doesn't know the answer to that question. I need to keep him as far away from this as possible.

Easton nods, but the tension remains in his shoulders. "Is that something you like? The games."

"No." I'm quick to cut him off, the thought of him flirting with someone else making me ragey. "That was the way my ex and I worked. It's not something I've ever sought out with anyone else, and I definitely don't want that with you."

"Okay."

"Wait. I'm not explaining myself properly."

"I didn't say anything."

"I know, but I think that came out wrong. It's not that I don't *want* that with you. I don't *need* it. Christian and I made each other jealous to increase the desire. That's not a problem that you and I have."

"I see." Easton's blank expression gives nothing away, and my heart lodges in my throat. *Was I an idiot for being honest with him?*

"Easton, I—"

The smallest of smirks tugs at his lips and I'm dead. Someone needs to pick me up from the floor because my *God*, this man. "You're messing with me, aren't you?"

"I'm not." He shakes his head. "*Entirely*. I just like seeing you a little flustered for me. But don't get me wrong. I'm happy you said no, because I don't want to play games. I just want to fuck you whenever I want to. And if that fails, I want Wednesday nights."

God, I want that too. "Do you think one night a week will be enough?" I tease. It's certainly more than I've been getting lately.

Easton growls in the back of his throat and my legs clench. "It will never be enough, but it's all I've got."

"I'll take it. But I'm not at your beck and call. If I'm there, I'm there. If

I'm not, I'm not." I stand firm, but as if I'm not going to be there, knowing this incredible man is coming home to me.

"I wouldn't want it any other way, Paige. Take the key. Do with it what you will."

He turns to walk away and a little part of me panics. "You're going?"

"I told you; I have a late meeting Wednesday night."

"That's right, you did. I guess I'll see you around."

"You will." He opens my apartment door while I put the key down on my kitchen counter, contemplating what to do with it.

"Oh, and Paige..."

"Yes." I glance up to find Easton standing on the threshold, his arms crossed as he leans casually against the door, holding it open, watching me.

"You're not fooling anyone, and if I ever find out who shared your private life with the media, I'm going to destroy them."

My breath hitches at the intensity in his gaze. "But Isaac," I whisper, stunned. I don't know why I said that, but I needed to take the focus off me.

"I never said I'd use my bare hands. There are other ways of destroying a person."

He turns again but I stop him this time, suddenly needing a way to connect with him.

"Can I have your number?" I ask in a rush, holding out my phone. "You know, in case I'm in your apartment and need to reach you."

"Sure." He frowns, his brows creasing. "You didn't have to justify it."

"Good." I hand over my cell and he enters his number before calling himself so that he has mine. And while that's generally not a big deal, something shifts inside me as I watch him walk away, my heart pounding in my chest.

I think I like him more than I should.

CHAPTER TWENTY-EIGHT

EASTON

Thomas launches the ball toward Zane, and after beautifully flying through the air, it hits the mark, landing in his hands as Luke slams into a player trying to get to him. Zane takes off running, unopposed, and makes it to the end zone, spinning around for a victory dance.

My heart pounds in my chest but I refuse to celebrate. Not yet. Not until we know the final score.

We may be up by six points in our away game against Chicago, but we came from behind, so we could easily end up back there. It's still anyone's game.

Our kicker, Blake, moves into position and I hold my breath. We need this, but he's been off all day. We all have. We're lucky Chicago isn't playing their best game either.

Something in the air maybe.

Blake lines up, running through his pre-kick rituals—bouncing his shoulders before shaking his body out—then he goes for it. The perfect kick. The ball soars through the air and I have no doubt it's going the distance. We just need it to—

"Yes." The crowd erupts with cheers as Blake gets the extra point while I breathe a little easier.

We've got this. I hope. I could use some of Luke's confidence right now. He's once again convinced we're winning the Super Bowl this year and has been since preseason.

Blake kicks off from the thirty-five yard line, sending the ball flying toward Chicago, and they attempt to advance, running forward with speed.

They get close, but our defense is finally on their game, quickly forcing a fumble to give us the ball back with less than a minute left on the clock.

With our offense back in possession, our center snaps the ball to Thomas and I race ahead, ready to end this. Thomas's throw is perfect as always, and the ball soars through the air, landing with precision in my outstretched hands. Tucking the ball in my arm, I take off in a run toward the end zone. My eyes on the prize. The world around me no longer there. This is it.

We need this.

Adrenaline courses through my veins as players charge my way, propelling me to dodge and weave until I see Zane open and ready. As much as I hate him day-to-day, when we're on the field, he's my teammate and I know he'll get us what we need.

He slows and I launch the ball backward toward him just as I'm flattened to the ground, and I miss seeing if he secured it in his grasp. But I know he did. I'm sure of it. And when I finally look up, Zane's dancing his victory dance as the guys go wild and the whistle blows. That's it. We won. We fucking did it.

Thomas helps me to my feet and I finally smile.

As a team we're always out to win, but today I *needed* it. I don't think I could have handled a loss right now.

Every day that we move closer to Thanksgiving and Christmas has me more on edge, wondering what the hell Macy's going to expect. Is she going to be here? Is she going to want to take Isaac there? And if she does...can I stop her?

She may not think about him *that* often, but one thing about Macy is that she loves the holidays, and I'm terrified of what that means. Especially since Isaac hasn't heard from her since before I asked about the Halloween T-shirt.

Celebrations are loud and obnoxious when we get back to the locker room, and I find myself accepting praise from my teammates. That was a fucking close call, but we did it. We're still undefeated almost halfway through the season, and fuck, does that feel good.

"Easton, my man," Reed says as he hesitantly wraps his arm around my shoulder, excited but still wary about my asshole ways. I shake him off but smile.

"Good game today," I say in acknowledgment.

"Right back at you. Please tell me you're coming out to celebrate."

"I—"

"Isaac's at home. You deserve some time to yourself."

Reed means well, but his words are like a knife to the chest. I barely see Isaac; what right do I have to my own time? "Reed—"

"Please. You don't have to enjoy it. Just come." He bites back a smirk, but at the last second it shines through.

"Okay. Fine. But I am hating every moment."

"That's the spirit." He slaps me on the back before heading over to Thomas next. Though from the look of euphoria on Thomas's face, I don't think he'll need much convincing.

We crowd into a local bar, taking the booths in the back, spreading out like the cocky assholes most of us are, our obnoxious celebrations never wavering.

Luke buys the first round of drinks for our table, announcing that he's leaving soon to talk to his wife and I'm not mad about it. Though I do note that's a huge change for him. He was always the guy leading the party charge. It's nice to see him putting his family first.

I check the time when he heads to the bar, wondering what Isaac's doing now.

Since we had a day game, with the time difference it's midafternoon back home, meaning I have another two hours before I promised I'd call. Like Luke, I have my priorities. On the field I'm dedicated to my team, but even then, Isaac is number one.

After we've been drinking for the better part of an hour, talk turns to the GM position and I catch Luke glancing in Thomas's direction before Thomas subtly shakes his head. He knows something. He'd have to. It's no secret that Wes and Thomas are good friends.

It shouldn't be a big deal—the interim GM is doing a fine job—but I'm not convinced it's the GM position that has the team rattled. I think it's the fear that there's more to come. That we're about to see a wave of firings camouflaged as "resignations"—and the team is going to suffer.

I want to ask Paige about it. But I also don't. Because what if it's true? What if Coach Pierce is next? He can be a pain in the ass, but he's good. He got us to where we are today, and we respect the hell out of him.

"I think it will be the guy from Tampa," offensive tackle Wyatt says, raising a brow in challenge, "and none of you will convince me otherwise."

"I bet Thomas could," Luke chimes in, and I choke on a sip of my beer as I actually laugh. If you can rely on anything from Luke, it's that he doesn't play favorites. He'll gladly throw a friend or brother-in-law under a bus.

Thomas groans. "How many times do I have to tell you? I haven't spoken to Wes. I'm staying out of it."

"Really? So it never came up when you watched the game with him the other week?"

"Nope. Because I *never asked*. And you know he's not a big sharer."

"Yeah, yeah. Good excuse. Are you curious?"

"Of course I am. Just like the rest of you. But I don't have any insider information."

"Okay. I believe you. This time."

"Thanks. Next time you want to call me out, asshole, do it in private." He sounds pissed but since he's smiling, I'd say he's used to Luke's shit.

Luke laughs before gesturing in my direction and I frown. "If I did it in private, it wouldn't have made Easton laugh. You're all welcome, by the way. It's a nice sound, isn't it?"

I almost laugh again, but refuse to give him that satisfaction, scowling instead so the others laugh for me.

Luke heads back to the hotel after that and the conversation moves on. When I next check the time, I have twenty minutes left before I need to be in my room. But since talk just entered more personal territory, I'm done.

I give a quick wave to anyone paying attention and opt for the short walk back to the hotel over taking a cab. I've just reached the door to my room when my phone rings.

"Hi, Mom. I was just about to call you."

"Hi, Honey. Good game today. Isaac and I caught the end while we were breaking for lunch."

"Breaking for lunch? That late? Sounds like you had a busy day."

"We did. But I'll let Isaac tell you all about it. I just put on an episode of that Halloween cartoon so we could talk first."

"What's going on?"

"Macy called about thirty minutes ago." She pauses and whether she meant it as dramatic effect or not, it worked, because I am already fuming. I've asked her time and time again to call me first. Or to call on days she knows I'm there. That if she needed to speak to Isaac, I had to know. But of course she'd wait until I was at an away game.

"What did she say? Please tell me you kept the phone on speaker."

"Oh, definitely, and she asked him if he wanted to spend Christmas with her in Florida."

"Florida? What's in Florida?"

"She is. Apparently."

Fuck. I can't keep up.

My heart lodges in my throat as I ask the next question. I'd rather not know the answer, but I have to. "What did Isaac say?"

"He said yes. He asked if she could take him to Disney World. She mumbled a half-assed noncommittal response, but he was still pretty excited."

I put Mom on speaker and drop my head into my hands, groaning. "What the hell do I do? Can I stop it?"

"I don't know. We can try. Your father knows a great lawyer and—"

"No."

"No?"

"I don't want him involved, Mom. He'll use it as a favor, so that I owe him one, and I don't want to owe him."

"When are you going to forgive him?"

"When I forgive Macy."

Mom sighs. She knows the answer to both is never.

I can handle a lot of shit being thrown my way. I can forgive a lot of things. Hell, I have no doubt that I'll one day forgive Zane. But I draw the line at walking out on a child. I get that there are extenuating circumstances at times, but neither Macy nor my dad had a solid excuse.

"Find another lawyer then," Mom says, a little annoyed. "But do it quickly. That woman doesn't want to spend time with Isaac when she's here, so why would she want him there?"

That's a great question and one I'm afraid to have answered.

Isaac's sweet voice filters in from the living room before we get the chance to say more, so I talk to him instead. I doubt we would have come up with any brilliant ideas anyway.

Isaac tells me about his day at the park and seeing the seals at the pier—one of his favorite things to do—and then we say good night and hang up. With no mention of his mom. At all.

He didn't even mention Disney.

Since it's still early, I change into sweats and a tee and crash on the couch, massaging my temples as I watch the last half of LA's game against Philadelphia.

My phone rings again just as the game goes into overtime, and I almost throw it against the wall in frustration, until I realize it might be Mom calling me back now that Isaac's likely asleep.

Taking a deep breath, I lift the phone to my face and a smile pulls at my lips. Paige. It's been two weeks since I gave her my key and she's yet to use it. I'd be demanding answers if my life wasn't as crazy as hers. And on top of that, we've been texting and she admitted she's got some stuff going on with her dad.

Yet another reason I should ask her what she knows.

"It's not a Wednesday, Paige," I answer, my lips curled into a smirk. "Are you calling to tell me you got your days wrong and you're finally in my apartment?"

"No." She giggles and the sound vibrates through my chest. "I actually have no idea why I'm calling. Is that okay?"

Her response catches me off guard and I pause. There's a hint of vulnerability in her tone that I'm not used to from Paige. But I saw it when she was telling me about that damn gossip magazine, even if she said she was fine.

"It is. But is something wrong?"

"No, of course not." Her voice rises leaving me unconvinced, but I let her off the hook. For now.

"Okay, so—"

"I was worried it wouldn't be okay to call since we've only ever texted." She cuts me off, further proving my theory. Paige talks a lot when she's nervous. I discovered that the first day I met her. But still, I let it go. "Anyway, how was your day?"

"Honestly, my day was great but my night turned to shit." The words are out of my mouth before I've thought about it and I freeze, backtracking. "Sorry, you don't need to worry about that. How was *your* day?"

"What happened?"

"Nothing I can't handle. I want to know about you."

"My day was okay. I booked another photo shoot and got my nails done. Did I tell you I'm going to be working the runway soon for that new San Francisco designer? I've only walked the runway once, so I'm a little excited. And the clothes are beautiful. They're high quality and the colors are to die for. I can't wait."

"I can hear it in your voice. Sounds like you had a good day." But there's that rushed talking again.

"I guess."

"Why are you calling, Paige?"

"What?"

"I'm happy to hear from you, always, but like you said, we've never spoken on the phone and I'm—" *worried.*

"Ugh. I know," she cuts me off again. "I was thinking about you and —" She cuts herself off this time and laughs. "Are you alone?"

"Huh? Of course I'm alone." I get defensive. "Who do you think is here?"

"I don't know. A teammate." I picture Paige shrugging her shoulders, and I smile before cursing myself for being a dick.

"Sorry, no. I have my own room."

"Why are you sorry? That's good."

"Good?"

"Yeah. I lied about my day."

"You lied?" *I mean, I could tell but still...*

"Yes, I told you my day was okay. But it sucked. I got some bad news and while I'd usually just go to the gym or for a run, I can't do those things now without thinking about you and... I'm not great at holding back when I want something."

An image of Paige naked in the gym comes to mind, and I swallow a lump in my throat. "What is it you want, Paige? Do you want to talk about it?" *I'm not great with advice but I can listen.* "What are you holding back from?"

"You?" she whispers before sucking in a breath. "I want you to get me off, Easton. Help make my day better. Who knows, maybe it will improve yours too."

"Fuck, Paige. You know I'm in Chicago, right?"

"I do. But I don't need you here."

"You don't?"

"Nope. I just need you to tell me what to do."

Jesus Christ.

CHAPTER TWENTY-NINE

EASTON

"What would you like to do first?" Paige asks, her voice flirty while I'm still processing.

"Honestly?"

"Please." She giggles.

"I'd like you to get on your dad's private jet or helicopter or whatever he has and fly yourself here so I can show you the sights of Chicago while fucking you against the window."

"Oh," she rushes out. "That's a good visual to start with." She pauses and I chuckle. "But... what if Dad's private jet or helicopter or whatever aren't available?"

"I'd say too bad and tell you to get naked. Then I'd want you to get on your knees and spread your legs wide, opening yourself up for me."

"God, that sounds good."

"Do it, D'Angelo, and let me know when you're back."

Her breath hitches before there's a thud, and I imagine the phone just dropped to the bed. Silence follows until the bed creaks again.

I wait patiently, my cock swelling as I picture her slowly removing her clothes and getting into position, exactly as I asked.

"I'm back," she says breathlessly. "And now it's my turn. I want you naked and lying down. I'm going to picture you with one arm behind your head and the other wrapped around your cock, ready for me."

Jesus. This woman. "You sure you don't want me to stay in my sweats? I know chicks dig that."

Paige laughs but she doesn't say no.

"You're contemplating it, aren't you?"

"I am. And I think you're right. Leave the sweats but the rest has to go."

"As you wish." I smile and do as she asked, and when I'm on the bed, I put the phone on speaker and tuck my arm behind my head, exactly as she wanted. "I'm ready."

"Me too."

"Good. Next I want you to skate your hands down your body and picture my face between your legs, staring up at you, my fingers spreading your lips, getting you ready for my tongue."

Paige sighs as she whispers my name, and the sound has my cock jolting. "That's it. When you reach your pussy, I want you to slowly run your finger around the edge of your clit, but don't touch it. Not yet."

"God, East."

"Keep going. Circle your clit a few more times and then I want you to do the same with that perfect hole, never touching, but getting as close as physically possible."

Paige moans as she curses under her breath, and I picture her head dropping back as her pussy weeps for me.

"How long?" she rasps, her breathing picking up pace. I give my cock a squeeze but don't pump it. I'll move when she finally gets what she wants.

"Keep going. I want you to tease yourself until you can't take it anymore. I want you begging me to let you touch yourself."

"Oh God."

She falls silent, with only her rapid breaths and soft mewls filling the air, and while she could be doing anything right now, I know that she's not. I know that she's doing what I've asked of her. Obediently.

My cock throbs in my hand, begging me for attention, but I hold strong.

"That's it, Paige. Keep going. Good girl."

"Fuck. East. Please. Please. I need it. I need your finger or tongue. I need you to touch me. I need you inside me. Now."

Fuuck. My balls tighten and I involuntarily buck against my hand. I've never heard her so desperate and I want more.

"Keep going until I say." My voice comes out rushed but I don't mind her knowing I'm just as desperate as she is.

"East. Please. God. I can't."

"Fuck, Paige. I need to see you."

"What?" she rushes out breathlessly.

"I need to see you. I want to see what you're doing."

"Oh God. Yes. I can do that. But I need to be honest."

"Okay."

"I'm not naked."

"You're not?"

"I'm not."

The phone buzzes for a video call and when I press connect, Paige's body fills the screen, making me groan out loud. She's wearing a matching pink lace bra and panties, but the bra barely covers her nipples. *Jesus Christ.*

"Are you going to punish me for lying? More than you already are."

God, this woman. She's the perfect mix of light and dark and I can't see myself ever getting over her. "I think I have to. Because how could you possibly have been doing what I asked when your pussy's covered."

"It's not."

"What?"

The phone moves until it's positioned between her legs, giving me a clear view of her bare pussy, lace on either side. "Holy shit, Paige." My cock jolts again, and this time I can't ignore it, slowly pumping, taking the edge off.

The phone moves again and Paige's flushed face comes on the screen. "I need to see you too. What are you doing?"

I flip the screen until she has an image of my chest and then slowly lower it to reveal my hand beneath my sweats, letting her watch as I pump a little harder.

"Your turn. Hold the phone out while you work your clit."

"Yes. Actually, I could do one better."

She momentarily drops the phone and I groan at the loss. I listen as she moves and then the phone visual bounces around, making me dizzy, until it stops with the camera aimed at the bed. Paige crawls back on and returns to the same position, giving me a wave.

"Fuck. Do you have a tripod?"

"I do," she says, bending down so I can see her smile.

"What fo—" I cut myself off, shaking my head. "You know what? I don't want to know."

At that she fucking laughs. "I use it for social media content and video calls to book modeling gigs. I'm not over here filming amateur porn clips if that's where your mind went."

"What?" I choke on air. "That's not what I was thinking." But now that she's said it, I want her to make one for me.

"Good. Now are you going to punish me or can I touch myself?"

"I want you to move closer to the camera, lie down, and spread your legs for me."

"Okay." She begins to move but I stop her.

"And Paige."

"Yeah."

"I'm not going to record this. You don't ever have to worry about that."

She falls silent and I'm worried the phone disconnected until her face appears on the screen. "Thank you. But I trust you. I always have."

I can't help but smile even though her words hit me in the chest. "Good to know."

After getting into position, Paige spreads her legs, angling her body toward the camera, and the view has me almost coming in my sweats. "God, I miss that pussy. It's been too long."

"I miss you too, I mean your hands, your... I'm sorry. You're making me crazy."

I smile as she shakes her head, and when she opens her mouth to undoubtedly apologize again, I cut her off. "Shhh. No more talking." She zips her lips, and it makes me wish I was there to kiss her to silence. "Thank you. Now don't move."

"What?" Her jaw drops and I'm happy she changed positions so I could see her reaction.

"You asked me to punish you. So that's what I'm doing. You're going to watch while I finish fucking my hand. And you're not allowed to move. At all. Not until I say."

"Fuck, Wilder. I don't think I can do that."

"You will." I stare at her pointedly, and she moans as her head drops back.

"God. Hurry up."

I laugh until my eyes lock on her pussy again and my cock twitches.

Without another word, I lower my sweats, letting my length spring free before positioning my phone so that she can see what I'm doing while I watch her. The angle's uncomfortable for my arm but it's worth it when I get to see her gasp, her eyes full of need as she stares at my cock in my hand.

I pump slowly at first, teasing her as much as I'm teasing myself, but while she doesn't touch herself, she does start rocking her hips like she's fucking the air, and the visual has my cock weeping for her. What I wouldn't give to be sinking inside her. To have her tight walls sucking me in. Squeezing the cum out of me.

I pump harder, my eyes falling closed as I squeeze, picturing my cock between her legs, moving inside her.

She moans and my eyes flash open to see her legs fall shut as she squirms on the bed, visibly struggling.

"Fuuck." A groan rips from the back of my throat. "Legs open, Paige."

Her knees drop to the bed and she reaches forward, palming her legs near the apex of her thighs.

"Can I speak? Please."

"Yes." I give in. The way she whimpers when she begs sends a current to my balls, but I fight it, needing a little more time.

"Thank *God*. I need you, Easton. Please let me touch myself. Let me sink my fingers into my pussy while I pretend that it's you. I need to fuck my hand so I can fuck you. *Please*."

Jesus fucking Christ. "Yes. But keep talking."

She sits up suddenly, then locks eyes with the camera before biting her lip and finally sinking her fingers inside herself, groaning as her hips buck.

"God, you feel so good, East. Tell me what you want me to do."

"I'm close. I need you to rub your clit while you curl a finger against your wall. Can you do that?

"Yes. Oh God. Oh God. I'm going to come."

"Imagine it's my mouth. Sucking your clit, working your pussy."

"East. Jesus."

She works her core while I pump so hard I'm seeing stars, and just when I think I'm going to explode without her, she screams out my name as her body convulses, sending me flying as I spill onto the bed, my body shaking as I groan.

"Fuck, Paige."

I move the camera to my face and find her staring back at me as she floats down to earth, her breathing frantic. After shaking herself out, she crawls to the phone and pulls it off the tripod before her eyes lock with mine once more. I expect her expression to be feral or wanton, but her gaze is soft, her eyes full of a warmth that has my heart racing and a new fear taking over me.

I think I'm falling for her.

CHAPTER THIRTY

PAIGE

I hadn't meant to call Easton while he was at an away game. I got his phone number so I could tease him when I was in his apartment, but after my shitty day, I realized he was the only person I wanted to talk to. Whether I told him about my day or not, I knew he'd make it better, simply by hearing his voice. Only this was *way* better.

"How do you do that?" I ask as my breathing slows, an incredulous smile on my face. "How do you make me feel *everything* from a million miles away?"

"I don't think I'm that far." He shrugs and I laugh.

"Thousands, whatever. The point is that you're not *here,* and yet, I have never felt so close to a person." My cheeks heat and I glance away. I've never been one to get embarrassed like that. But while I'm not directly saying I have feelings for Easton, I'm not exactly being subtle. And that's crazy. Because I've never felt like this before. Never wanted to call a guy when I was down, never hoped that the sound of his voice could improve my day. I'm a strong, independent woman. I can look after myself. But God, it's nice to think about having someone to share that with.

After hearing that Austin still hadn't found any information on the Mikkleson family, I'd hung up to find a text from Christian, reminding me that he'd be in town soon, offering me another chance to go out with him and his fiancée. But like every other time he's asked, I told him to fuck off—in nicer terms—and he once again got angry.

I should just tell him what's going on, but while I may not be any closer to finding evidence, I'm not giving up. I had planned to keep quiet to protect him—so he wouldn't know anything if he was questioned, but the more he pushes for this stupid meeting, the more I change my mind. And now I have another worry taking over—what if I tell Christian what I know and he freaks out. I can't have him ruining it for me by running to his dad. And I have no doubt that he would. He'd tell them what I know. Whether because he was angry that they were keeping things from him or he already knew himself, there is no way he'd keep that quiet.

Easton runs a hand down his face and I bite my tongue. God, what am I doing speaking so openly? This is a casual fling. We both know that. We made it clear from the start.

"I know that's not part of the deal, but I'm saying it because—"

"You're one in a million, Paige," Easton cuts into my admission. "And since you are *thousands* of miles away, I'm going to use this screen as a shield and admit..." He trails off and my heart stops while I wait for his confession. "You're getting under my skin too. I think about you all the time, but I don't know what to do with that information." His voice drops to barely above a whisper as he takes the phone off video. My heart slams against my rib cage and I have to fight not to say anything, in case he has more to add. And he does. "You're a fucking goddess, D'Angelo. I wish I'd met you in another time. But I didn't. What if this is all I can give you?" His voice breaks and I shiver.

"Then I'd say, you and I are alike. I can't give you any more than you can," I whisper the unfortunate truth, staring at the phone even though his face is no longer staring back at me. "But is it okay if I tell you I want to?"

If it was another time, I think I'd be all-in and that's goddamn terrifying.

"Yeah." Easton's quick with his response. "You can tell me anything."

Butterflies flood my chest and I smile through my words. "Thank you. I better let you go. It's getting late there, right?"

"It's not too late, but I do have to be on an early flight."

"Talk tomorrow, maybe?"

"Sounds good. And maybe I'll see you Wednesday? You know, if you ever decide to use my gift."

"Your gift?" I laugh and my chest warms. Even after the heavy conversation, he still wants to see me. "I would have thought that me being naked in your apartment when you got home would be a gift to *you*."

Easton chuckles. "Has anyone ever called you a brat?"

"All the time."

"Well, Brat, I want you there. Wednesday. No excuses."

"Or what? Would you have to punish me?"

Easton groans and I laugh. "Goddammit, Paige, now I'm hard again."

"Well, if you turn the video back on, I'm still practically naked."

"Even if you weren't, I could easily picture it. But the next time you're screaming my name, I'm going to be inside you. That's a promise. And it better be Wednesday."

"Do you mean this one or will any Wednesday do?"

"Paige," he warns.

"Okay, I'm hanging up. I'll see you Wednesday." I can't help but giggle as a feeling of contentment takes over. I wanted him to make me feel better and mission accomplished.

"Bye, Paige. Sleep well."

He hangs up but I don't move. I just stare into the ether. "Sleep well." It was a throwaway line, but do you think my heart took it that way? No, the little romantic fucker just skipped a beat because his tone was softer than usual. It doesn't mean anything, but the feelings I *should not* be feeling keep getting stronger. It's not just about sex anymore. And like him, I don't know what to do with that.

I'm busy Monday and Tuesday, meeting with the youth foundation to run through the charity event. We've got two weeks to go, meaning we've had almost double the time I had to organize the Storm event, and yet, we're still behind on things. The women running the charity are lovely, and I'm also working with a San Francisco news presenter who volunteers her time with youth services around the state. But while we all get along well, I wonder if it's a case of too many hands in the pies. I think that's the saying. All I know is that whatever we're doing, it's not working and it's driving me crazy.

On Wednesday, I wake in a good mood and I'm not ashamed to admit that I'm giddy at the prospect of waiting for Easton in his bed. Only, I still have to get through the day and it's currently out to mess with me.

I've just hung up from talking to my agent, when one of my so-called friends calls me from New York.

"Hi Janie," I answer nicely. "It's been a while."

"Too long. But honestly, we all thought you'd be back by now. It's been months."

"Well, I thought you didn't want to be friends anymore since you ghosted me after I left. I've called a few times and—"

"No. My God. I'd never. Life has been crazy. I had to take over running the Youth Voices annual event and I stepped up to help your mom with a few of her events too. You left quite a few people in the lurch."

Bullshit. If she stepped in or up to help out with anything I had previously worked on then she did that all on her own. I made sure my positions were covered. I'd never leave them with no one. Especially my mom.

"Why are you calling, Janie?"

"I'm calling for two reasons. One, because a little birdy told me you were running the Youth Voices event in San Francisco, and I wanted to attend so I could see you. Do you think you could put me on the list?"

"You can come any time. You don't need to use the event as an excuse."

"I know, but this is a two birds, one stone situation. I get to see you and mingle with the who's who of California."

Ugh, she doesn't want to see me at all.

"I'm so sorry," I say with a sadness in my tone. "I think we've sold all our tickets." I'm lying. The event space is huge; we'd gladly accept more guests.

"I'm sure you can get me in. We've done it for each other in the past."

"That was the past. This is now. I don't see how it's possible."

"Ugh, fine. Can you at least tell me where it is? I know the date because Evelyn's going."

Evelyn's the director of the overarching charity. She works out of the New York office but oversees all the US branches. If she didn't give Janie any details, it's because she didn't want her there.

"It's at the Belford Studios," I offer reluctantly because it wouldn't take much for her to find out online.

"Thank you. You're definitely going to be there, right?"

"I am."

"Good. That will be fun for you."

"What was the second thing?"

"Huh?"

"You called for two things?"

"Oh, yes." Janie's voice bounces with excitement and I internally groan. "I can't believe you never told me about your games with Christian. It's all everyone's been talking about over here. What a thrill it must have been. Shame the media found out."

I roll my eyes despite her not being able to see me and plaster a smile on my face. "That was another life, Janie. It is what it is."

"You're not annoyed that people know?"

She's fishing for gossip, but it won't matter what I say—she'll still spin it however she pleases. "Nope. I've moved on. It's time everyone else did the same."

Janie moves on to tell me about the guy she's been seeing, and by the time she hangs up, I feel a little brain dead. Is that what I used to be like? I didn't think I'd changed that much, but I no longer have any interest in what she has to say. In fact, I couldn't think of anything worse.

Since I don't have much going on in the early evening, I don't have anything to distract me from our conversation, and by the time I'm due to go to Easton's, I'm pissed off. How dare she call me after all this time. As though nothing has changed. What is wrong with people?

I'm still worked up when I arrive at Easton's door, but when I step inside, a wave of calm flows through me.

It's strange being in his space for the first time without him. But there's also something exciting about it. Still, I'm not ready to pry into his private life, so I go in search of his bedroom, finding it easily with the layout similar to my own.

With Easton mentioning he'd be home by nine, I arrived at eight thirty, giving myself enough time to get naked, but not enough time to actually get too comfortable. Because I wasn't kidding about my early bedtime. It's a new development. I used to be able to stay up all night, but I've been keeping so busy that I'm usually exhausted by this time.

While I wait, I find myself doomscrolling through my social media accounts and instantly regret it. This used to be my life. Social media was my world. If I missed a few hours, I thought my life was falling apart. And now it's been days. Mostly because I haven't had the time, but also because I was afraid of what I'd find.

What if I see something about me? More people spreading rumors. Or worse, what if I see picture after picture of the life I had and I miss it? I like the woman I've become, but I was a different person not too long ago and that life was somewhat simpler.

A mental picture of Easton comes to mind, and I shake off my thoughts. I don't think I could leave right now, even if I wanted to. I'm invested. And while I have no idea where this is going, or even if it can go anywhere, I'm not too worried about finding out. What we have is working, and I'm not ready to give it up.

At 9:05, the distinct sound of a key in a lock alerts me to Easton's arrival, and I throw my phone onto the other side of the bed before lying down, pretending to be asleep. My lips twitch as he walks through the apartment, but when his footsteps get louder, I school my features. I can't remember a time I've been this excited.

My chest flutters as I lie in wait, and when the door opens, I fight not to open my eyes.

"Fuuuck." A feral groan releases from the back of Easton's throat as he enters the room, dropping something to the floor. "God, you look good in my bed, Paige."

I want to respond, but I also want him to wake me with his tongue like he said he would so I hold strong, keeping my eyes closed, thankful that I was clever enough to face away from the door.

"I know you're awake, Paige," he continues, his voice gravelly, turning me on. "But a promise is a promise."

He rummages around in his bedroom for a bit, teasing me until I hear what I assume is his clothes dropping to the bed. A drawer opens and closes and then the bed dips behind me as my pulse spikes and need pools at my center.

My heart races in anticipation, but instead of using his tongue, like I expected, I startle when he brushes a finger across my cheek before gently gliding the tip along my skin, both of us pretending I'm asleep. When he gets to my shoulder, he rolls me onto my back, then continues his path, circling one nipple and then the other, adding a second finger as he moves with gentle strokes toward my center, spreading my legs when he's close.

"I'm not sure what I like best," he rasps, his voice making my body heat. "I can't choose between fiery Paige, the version of you that gives as much as you get, or this version—open, trusting, at my mercy."

My breath hitches and I'm sure he will have seen it in my chest even if he didn't hear it, but he doesn't draw attention to it.

"Are you ready for me, Paige?" he asks as his fingers brush back and forth across my inner thigh. So close, but not close enough. "It's about time you woke up." Easton doesn't wait for me to answer before he spreads my lips and licks a path through my center, circling my clit before biting down on the bud. I cry out as my body bucks off the bed, the tension wound so tight that it instantly snaps.

I perch on my elbows and stare down at him nestled between my legs, watching with rapt attention until he pauses, smiling up at me.

"D'Angelo." He nods. "Nice of you to join the party."

Jesus. Who is this man? He's a walking contradiction. That's for sure.

"I could get used to being woken like that."

"Good. Because I have never wanted anyone more than I want you right now. Roll over and hold on to the headboard. I'm going to make you come while you ride my face, and then I'm going to flip you onto your back and fuck you until you're screaming my name."

Oh God.

"Does that work for you?"

"God, yes." I moan, unable to hide my desperation. "Please. I need you to start now."

Chapter Thirty-One

EASTON

I wake to Paige's naked body wrapped around me while the events of last night play on repeat in my mind. Like Paige, I could get used to this, and that's a dangerous notion.

I've spent so long concerned about Isaac getting attached to someone else and losing them, like he did with Macy, that I never stopped to think about what would happen if *I* got attached to Paige... and lost her.

Reaching for my phone, I switch off my alarm before it wakes Paige and allow myself another minute to bask in her warmth.

The situation we've created for ourselves is so delicate it could break at any given moment. If it's a crack, I'm sure one of us could fix it. But what if it shatters beyond repair, and we're all destroyed in the process?

When the sun peeks through the gap in the curtain, I reluctantly get up. Paige stirs when I move but thankfully doesn't wake, mewling as she rolls over. It's so adorable, I can't stop myself from pressing a kiss to her cheek, wishing I could stay longer.

She's still asleep when I have to leave, so I write a note and sneak out, closing the door softly behind me.

Other than Macy, I have never had another woman in my bed. I've never wanted to. But with Paige, I could happily spend every night lying next to her. It's so easy between us. Which is a comfort considering God knows both our lives are complicated as fuck.

Not that we've ever really spoken about the details.

She doesn't need to hear about Macy. I'm not stupid; I know no one wants to know about their partner's ex. The problem is that Macy's not going away, and at some point, I'm going to have to face that.

I'm early for practice, as usual, and as I pull into the parking lot, Coach Pierce pulls in behind me.

"East. Any luck with the school situation?" he asks, waiting until now to bring up our conversation from the event, somehow knowing that I'd never want to talk about my business if any of my teammates were around.

"Honestly, I haven't given it much more thought, because when I do, it's closer to being real."

"Ahh, I know that feeling. It's hard when they grow up."

"It is. But at the same time, I love the little man he's growing into."

"How's things with your mom? Is she still looking after him?" I spoke to Coach about my situation as soon as Macy left. He's the only one I opened up to, other than my mom. And that was because I had to. I wasn't sure if I'd have to miss practices or bring him to away games, but Mom's been an angel and I haven't missed a thing.

"She's a godsend. And I have no idea how she does it."

"She's a mom. They have superpowers." He laughs until he realizes what he said. "At least, most do. Fucking Zane."

I laugh at his attempt to correct what he said and shake my head. "At some point I have to stop blaming him. Macy fucked up long before that, and I just refused to see it. Or maybe I was the problem."

"Either way, that kid needs to grow up. Zane, I mean. He's a hell of a player, but he's too cocky for his own good."

"Kind of like Luke was?"

"Still is. But at least he doesn't get himself into trouble with the other players."

"True, but if things had worked out differently with Amelia and she'd ended up with one of our teammates, that may have changed."

Pierce laughs. "Always so much drama. Here's hoping that D'Angelo really does improve things for the team. I may have been against the change in the beginning, but the guy is growing on me."

"Really?" That's interesting. Maybe he's not worried about his job like some of the other coaches are. "You think he's going to help the team?"

"I fucking hope so, or we're doomed."

"Something tells me we'll be okay. It's just going to take a bit to get used to the change."

❧ ❧ ❧

Practice runs smoothly, so I'm on time to pick Isaac up from Mom's, and when I arrive, she has dinner on the table and a smile on her face.

"We've had another busy day; this little man should sleep well tonight." She kisses me hello and ruffles Isaac's hair. "Any news?"

I know what she's asking but it's been radio silence. Macy's yet to ask *me* if she can take Isaac for the holidays. "Not yet, but I'm looking into my options."

"Good to hear. And remember, I can get you a contact."

"I know." But I have a feeling I could get one too if I asked Paige about it. I bet her father has friends in high places.

After a somewhat quiet dinner, Isaac and I head home with him regaling me with stories of his day. Since Mom bathed him before dinner, we're able to start our bedtime routine as soon as we get inside. And it's only then that he finally mentions Macy. *Four days later.*

I'd almost wondered if I'd imagined the whole thing since he's usually excited about everything that relates to his mom.

"Will you come to Flowida, Dad?"

I wish I could pretend I didn't know what he was talking about, but I can't lie. "Did your mom invite you?"

"Yeah. And you."

"I don't think she meant me. I think she wants to spend some time with you. Alone."

His nose scrunches before he curls his body into mine and shakes his head. "I want to go with you."

"I can't go, Buddy. What about Nana? If we all go to Florida, she'll be alone."

"She can come with us. And Auntie Keeley too."

"Auntie Keeley is going to see her dad for Christmas." I internally cringe while I smile.

"Where's your dad?" *Dammit.* I should have seen that coming.

"I don't see him anymore." Isaac pouts so I'm quick to ease his mind. "I'm okay." I smile again, ruffling his hair. "Do you know why?"

"Why?" He shakes his head.

"Because I'm lucky enough to have you and Nana and Keeley and Auntie Addison who we'll see again soon."

"I have those people too!" His voice raises excitedly, and a beautiful smile lights up his face.

"You do. And no matter what, they love you."

"Then can I stay with you and Nana for Christymas?"

My world stops for a second before my heart starts beating at double time. "You don't have to do that. The choice is yours. You know I'd love to spend Christmas with you. But if you want to go with your mom, it's okay. I won't be alone."

He shakes his head almost violently. "I want to see Nana."

"How about we think about it." I pull him into a hug. "You don't have to decide right now. Right now your big job is to go to sleep."

"Daad." He playfully pushes me away. "That's not a job."

"Maybe not. But it's time to turn off the light and say good night."

"Will you leep next to me?" he asks, his hand clenched at his heart.

"Yeah, Buddy. I can stay for a little while. At least until you're asleep."

After getting less sleep than usual last night with Paige, I fall asleep next to Isaac, and when I wake around ten, my neck aches from curling up in a small space.

Feeling out of it, I beeline straight to my bedroom, stretching out my body before getting changed and switching off the light. The glow from the city shines a spotlight on the empty side of my bed until I close the drapes and block it all out.

I never put much thought into how I felt in the past waking up next to someone, because while Macy and I shared a bed for years, our feelings had gone long before she did. But with Paige, everything feels different and I wish I had more to give her.

Tucking my arms behind my head, I stare up at the ceiling and try to drift off while my mind spins. And when I'm finally a little drowsy, my phone rings, making me jump.

I usually silence it at night, so I'm clearly not thinking properly.

"It's ten thirty, Keeley. Why are you calling so late?" I whisper to keep from waking Isaac as I walk into the kitchen, closing the door between the living area and the bedrooms.

"Late?" Keeley scoffs. "I just got home."

"Good for you. It's late for me. You know I'm up at five tomorrow? Anyway, what's up?"

"I called to ask if I could take Isaac out for a couple of hours tomorrow afternoon?"

"What, why?" I shouldn't be suspicious but I am. Keeley's great with Isaac, but I usually have to ask her to help out—she doesn't volunteer.

"I want to impress a single dad, to show him that I'm marriage material."

"*What*? Fuck, no. You can't—"

"I'm joking, dickwad. I promised him I'd take him to that new animal exhibition at the wharf and I got free tickets, but they're only for today or tomorrow."

I bite back a groan. It's after ten p.m. I can't deal with humor right now.

"That's nice. He's been talking about that. What time were you thinking? I'll need to let Mom know."

"I already did. I told her I'd take her shift. Give her the day off."

"Her shift? You make it sound like I'm forcing her to work." Guilt swirls around my middle as tension works its way into my chest. I know she's tired, and she definitely deserves time off. But she won't let me seek an alternative.

"I know it's not you, East. She argued with me too when I offered. But I think she needs it. She looks tired."

"I know. God, I know. If only it had been someone more responsible that offered to help out."

"Uh. Shut it. I'm responsible. I pretty much manage an entire team of children. Children that are far less mature than Isaac is."

I huff out a laugh. Can't deny that she has a point. "Okay. I'll put my life in your hands."

"Aww, that's the sweetest thing you've ever said. You are getting soft, Bro."

"Want me to change my mind?"

"Nope. You're the greatest. I'll be there at six. Mom usually comes then, right?"

"She does."

"And she stays until..." She trails off so I can fill in the blanks.

"I'm usually home by late afternoon on Friday. You know this."

"I do. But how was I to know you'd be going straight home? Maybe you have a date."

"Ha ha. You're hilarious."

"Well, date or no date, we'll be at the exhibition until around four, and I want to take him to Mom's for dinner so she still gets to see him. I'll bring him home after that. I can stay at your place later if you want to..."

"I'm not going on a date, Keeley. I'll see you in the morning."

She hangs up and my thoughts drift to Paige. *Again.* I can't see this getting any easier. But at the same time, I don't want it to end.

What the hell do I do?

CHAPTER THIRTY-TWO

PAIGE

Until next time. I'll be thinking of you.

It's been over twenty-four hours and I'm still smiling about Easton's note. So much so that Dad gives me a strange look when he arrives at the bar to meet me, pressing a kiss to my cheek.

"Sorry I'm late. We finally appointed a new GM, and I got the fun job of announcing it to the team management. But that's not important. What or *who* made you smile like that?"

"What? No idea. And that *is* important," I change the subject back to him. "What happened?"

"We appointed a guy from Tampa and not everyone is happy about it. Apparently, it's my fault that Wes Johnson, a past player on the team, didn't accept my offer, even after I begged."

"God, I'm sorry. Want me to talk to—" *Shit.* I cut myself off and smile. "Keeley?"

"Keeley?" Dad frowns and his brows furrow. "She knows."

"I just mean that maybe I can ask if she'll talk to the guys and tell them you tried."

"Thanks, but it's okay. I'm a big boy. I can handle it. I just wish they'd realize I'm doing all that I can for the team. I'm working *with* them. Not against them."

"They will. It just takes time. The old GM had been there for most of the guys' careers."

Dad's eyes widen before he laughs. "Who are you and what have you done with my daughter?"

"What?"

"Since when do you know about the team?" Oh. *Shit*.

"Since I started hanging out with Keeley and the wives. They seem to know a lot about the game."

"Not everyone despises sports like you do." Dad laughs at his own joke.

"I don't think I do anymore." I shrug. "It's growing on me."

Dad eyes me curiously and I internally tense. "Just the sport? Or... is there something else?"

"Just the sport." *For now.*

Dad nods before waving for a server and ordering our drinks. As I take my first sip, I decide it's my turn to share now that his stress has lifted a little. And because I'm so far out of my depth that I'm drowning.

"I need to talk to you about something."

Dad's gaze shifts to mine, and he nods before leaning back in his chair.

"Remember when I told you about Mom and Christian's dad?"

"Unfortunately, yes." He groans, making me laugh.

"It gets worse."

"Jesus, she's not having a baby, is she?"

"What. Ew. Dad. No." Dad smiles and I laugh. "Funny. But I'm being serious."

"Sorry. Go ahead."

I look around to make sure no one is listening and lean in, waiting for Dad to do the same. "I think the Mikklesons are extorting money from clients, and I'm worried she's involved."

"What?"

"I—"

"Wait. Should we be having this conversation in my apartment?"

Jesus. Should we? I've been so careful up until now, never talking about it, except with Austin. "Good idea."

We finish our drinks, and Dad pays the check before guiding me to the exit. We're both quiet in the elevator, but the second we get inside and the door closes, Dad turns my way. "Tell me what you know."

After forcing him to sit down at the dining table, I fill him in on the conversation I overheard between Jill Mikkleson and her sister. I tell him about Christian's apparent naivety and about hiring Austin. When I get to the threats, I pause. He's going to lose his mind and that won't be helpful for anyone, but I promised him the truth. I'll just have to sugarcoat a little.

"They know I know something. But they don't know what. So they've kind of been threatening to out me in the media."

"Out you?" He stands up, his fists clenched by his sides. "For what? What are they doing?"

I open my mouth to answer but he cuts me off. "Wait. Does this have anything to do with that article about your games with Christian?"

Ugh. I cringe, since I was really hoping he hadn't seen that headline. "Yes. That was a message to me. To get me to tell them what I know."

"And did you?"

"Hell, no. I'm not giving in before I've found what I need to destroy them."

Dad wants to be angry, but he can't hide the proud expression lighting up his face. "I always knew you were tough, but this is next-level, Paige."

"Thank you."

"Does Austin have anything? And how did you manage to convince him not to tell me about it?"

"What? You know Austin?"

"Well, I assume you found him through your lawyer who is also my lawyer."

"Right. Of course. Well, *I* assumed you found a different lawyer after divorcing Mom."

"Nope. One and the same."

"I guess Austin's a professional. He never even mentioned you."

"Good. I like that he's treating you like he'd treat everyone else. So what's he got?"

"Nothing yet." I drop my head to the table, defeated.

"I see." Dad sits down again and taps his fingers against the wood. "Has he tried posing as a potential client?"

"What?" My eyes flash to his. I never would have thought of that.

"We could give him some funds to play with, and I'm sure he'd know how to get some fake accreditations drawn up so that he looks legit. Then he approaches them and we see what happens."

"That seems risky."

"It is. But it's worth a try. If anything, it might get him a meeting and he can check them out."

"Okay. Yes. I'll ask Austin what he thinks."

I reach for my phone to text him but Dad grabs my wrist. "Mind if I do it? If it all goes wrong, I'd rather you weren't involved."

"I'm already involved, Dad."

"I know. But now that I have the details, I can't let you continue. It's my job to protect you."

"It's not. I..." I trail off as I think about Easton and Isaac. I know without a doubt that Easton would do anything to protect Isaac, so how can I deny my dad the same? "Okay. But you have to keep me in the loop. If you don't, I can't be held responsible if I do something stupid."

Dad groans before his lips purse. "You are going to be the death of me, Paige."

I smile. "Thank you. I love you too, Dad."

He shakes his head but curls his lips into a warm smile and I'm not sure I've said that allowed to him for a while, even in jest. "On another note," he changes the subject. "You're not going home for Thanksgiving, are you?"

I cringe because I hadn't decided yet, but Mom's been asking. "I...ah..."

"Your mom called me."

"What?" My jaw drops. "Is that the first time you've spoken since..." I trail off because he knows what I mean.

He laughs out loud. "No. We used to talk all the time. But only about you kids."

"Oh. Okay. And?"

"She asked if I'd convince you to go home for a few days. In return for her letting me have Christmas."

"Letting you? Like I'm a kid that has no say in the matter?"

"Pretty much." He shrugs. "I get that she misses you. A lot. And I was going to help her. But given the new information I have..."

All I hear is the part about Mom missing me and I feel guilty again. "Maybe I should go. Can I take your jet?"

"My what?" His brows furrow, making me laugh as I think about my call with Easton last week.

"Never mind. You convinced me. I'm going to go home."

"What? No. I said I didn't want you to go."

"I know, but you also made me feel guilty about Mom missing me. I'll tell her you helped and you'll get brownie points."

Dad rolls his eyes as he groans. "You're killing me, Paige. It better be a short visit."

I spend an hour with Dad, and when I get home in the early evening, I change into more comfortable attire before dropping to the couch, ready for a night of TV. I've just found the remote when Easton texts.

> Easton: Isaac's not getting home for another hour

I bark out a laugh as my body heats.

> Paige: Are you booty-texting me, East? Is that how this is going to go now?

> Easton: So what if I am? Got a problem with that?

> Paige: Definitely not. I'm impressed. What time will you be here?

I assume that he's coming to me since it's not a Wednesday, but when the three dots appear and disappear a few times, I second-guess myself before he finally responds.

> Easton: Five minutes

Five minutes? Jesus. I stare down at my yoga pants and oversized hoodie. In the past, I would have spent that five minutes racing around the house, putting something sexy on, freshening up, ensuring I look my best. I would have taken the time to be perfect. But with Easton, I pause. He's not like the other guys I've been with. He doesn't expect perfection. We've been together after a sweaty workout. And I don't want to be someone I'm not when around him. Instead, I remove my yoga pants and use the rest of the time to rehydrate instead. I've just finished a glass of water when he knocks on the door, and my chest tightens with a new kind of euphoria. Not that I allow myself to process it.

"I'm coming," I call out as I make my way to the door, picturing Easton's smile at my choice of words.

"Hi," I say as I open up, my next words getting caught in my throat. "You—"

Easton's leaning against the wall opposite my door, his ankles and arms crossed, his hat pulled low and a wicked smirk plastered on his face. When he sees me, he stands tall and strides toward me in two quick moves, pinning me to the door as his lips crash to mine.

He wraps a hand around my neck before running his finger across my cheek, slipping it between our lips, breaking the kiss.

"I've got an hour, and I've got plans for you, but I need to know... bedroom or kitchen?" He raises an eyebrow and I laugh.

"Bedroom. I've got a full-length mirror and I want to watch while you worship me."

"Christ, Paige. You really are everything and more."

"Only for you." I push him away and slap his ass as I walk past, loving his growl as he stills.

"Are you coming?" I ask, walking backward as I slip the hoodie over my head, revealing that I'm completely naked underneath.

"Fuuck, you drive me crazy, Paige."

"Maybe so, but you love it."

For the next week, Easton and I see each other any chance we get, stealing moments, borrowing time. And while it's fun, it's also making things more complicated than I would have liked.

I haven't heard from Dad yet, but I have a feeling his plan is going to work. It's a great plan. It has to. But that means I'm one step closer to my world being blown apart. Because make no mistake, the Mikklesons are not going to go down without a fight, with me being the target of their firing line.

And that's not going to be good for Easton and me.

Chapter Thirty-Three

EASTON

"Come on, Isaac, Nana will be here soon," I call out and laugh when Isaac mumbles in return. My early riser has suddenly decided he's a threenager and prefers to sleep in, which makes things difficult when I have to be at the stadium by eight fifteen.

"I've got your favorite juice this morning." I switch to bribery since it's not often that I give him juice. It's what we call a "sometimes drink." But in reality, it's rare. I know Mom could get him ready after I leave, but then I'll barely see him and I'm already going to be late getting home tonight. "Should I count down?"

"I'm coming," Isaac calls out as he races down the hall, running through the kitchen before sliding to a halt at his chair, his eyes on the empty cup in front of him. "Where is it?" He frowns, making me laugh.

"I had to make sure you were going to eat with me first. I'll get it now. You can start on your breakfast."

"Oatmeal again?"

"Yep. It's good for you. Eat up. I'm on my way."

My phone rings as I'm pouring the juice, so I grab it without checking the screen, wedging it between my shoulder and ear.

"Hello," I say, noting the smile in my voice. That's been happening a lot more lately.

"East. It's me, Keeley."

"Hey Keels." I laugh at her tone. "Why are you speaking so formally?"

"Mom's in the hospital."

"What?" I drop the juice and it hits the edge of the sink before falling in, the contents emptying while I watch, unmoving. "What do you mean she's..." I trail off so Isaac doesn't know what we're talking about.

"I got a call about five minutes ago. All they said was that she'd had a fall and a neighbor called for an ambulance. She's at San Francisco General. I'm on my way there now, so I'll fill you in as soon as I know anything."

"I'm coming." I snap back into action, taking Isaac's juice over to the table before grabbing my breakfast to start clearing up until Keeley stops me.

"You can't. What about Isaac?"

Dammit. I pace the kitchen, thankful that Isaac has his back turned. I can't stay home. What if this is my fault? I've been asking so much of her. Pushing her too far. She's always telling me she's not getting any younger. Of course, she says it jokingly but she's not wrong.

"I'll... um..." Paige's smiling face comes to mind as I watch Isaac eating, and a sudden wave of relief rolls over me. "I know someone that can help. Can you pick me up on the way?"

"Of course. I'll be there soon."

She hangs up and I immediately walk into another room to call Paige, my heart seizing in my chest, struggling to function.

Paige answers right away and I take a quiet breath while she speaks. "Hey you," she says sleepily and I cringe. "I didn't think I'd hear from you at this early hour, especially after yesterday. Did you miss me?" The smile in her voice makes me momentarily pause, wishing I was calling at a happier time.

"East?" She breaks through the silence.

"Sorry, yes, I'm here. I...ah...I need a favor. I know I shouldn't put this on you but—"

"Hey, it's okay. What's going on?" I can hear her moving around, and I'll put all my money on the fact that she was still in bed, but I have to ask.

"It's my mom. She's in the hospital and—"

"What can I do? How can I help?"

I knew she'd be there for me and yet hearing it out loud makes me sigh in relief.

"Is there any chance you could be here for Isaac? It's a lot to ask since he doesn't know you that well, but he at least *knows* you, and I don't want to call a babysitting service or—"

"Of course I'll do it. I'd be happy to. Just let me get changed and I'll be on my way." The phone rustles as though she's moving around but she keeps talking. "Do you need anything? Is she okay?"

"I don't know, Paige. I don't know anything and I'm going crazy."

"It's going to be okay. That's why you're going to the hospital. To find out. Are you going by yourself?"

"With Keeley. She's coming to pick me up."

"Okay, good. Is she all right to drive?"

"Keeley? Yeah. She works best under pressure."

Paige laughs softly and it makes me smile. "Good. Well, I'm heading to the elevator now, so it might cut off. I'll be there in a minute."

Paige arrives, and without me having to say a word, she doesn't make a big deal out of it. She just knows. And God, am I grateful for her.

I hold the door as she walks past, and she subtly squeezes my hand before Isaac runs to meet us.

"Nana," he calls out as he rounds the corner, coming to a stop when he sees Paige.

"Actually, it's me." She smiles, dropping her bag to the floor. "I came over to ask if you wanted to spend the day with me."

Isaac's face lights up before his wide eyes bounce to mine. "Can I?"

"Of course you can." I force a smile of my own.

"What about Nana?"

"I'll let Nana know."

"Yes!" There's a moment of quiet before Isaac runs forward and grabs Paige's hand, dragging her away. "Let's go to my room. Want to see my trucks?"

"You have to finish breakfast," I call out and they both wave as they disappear.

I watch until they're gone before I completely shatter, my body deflating as I fall into the wall, covering my face in my hands.

Mom has to be okay. She has to.

Because I don't know what the hell I'll do without her.

CHAPTER THIRTY-FOUR

EASTON

The ER is crowded when we arrive, and we're asked to sit in the waiting room until they've seen Mom.

A couple of hours pass without so much as a wave and I'm getting anxious. There's only so much pacing a man can do. "What the hell is taking them so long? I'm going to ask."

Keeley grabs my arm to stop me. "You've already asked three times. We were told to wait."

"How are you so calm?" I frown, crossing my arms over my chest, huffing when Keeley rolls her eyes.

"I'm calm because we don't know anything and I refuse to jump to the worst conclusion—like you clearly have."

"I haven't. I just want some goddamn answers."

Her phone buzzes in her hand, and when she sees who it is, she hides it.

"Who's that?" I snap, not in the mood for bullshit if she's holding something back.

"No one."

"No one? Why'd you hide it?"

"Why do you care?"

Her words hit me and I shake my head. *Jesus.* "I don't. Whatever. I just want to know what the hell is going on."

Blowing out a breath, I pace as I try to ignore the stares directed my way from around the room. In my rush, I forgot my damn hat and I'm regretting it. Short of putting a sign on my chest to tell them to stay away, I think I've made it clear that I'm not to be approached right now, but I still hate people knowing my business. I've barely shared any of my life with Paige and I should have. I really fucking should have.

It's another thirty minutes before a nurse finally calls for Keeley since she's Mom's emergency contact, and when she does, I'm the first to head over, not even pretending to be nice.

"About time."

"Your mom has been taken to a room." The nurse ignores me. "She's okay, but we had to stitch up her leg, and she received a nasty bump on her head that we'd like to monitor for a few days."

Shit. "Can we see her?"

"She's resting at the moment. We'll call you when she wakes up, but you can head to the waiting room closer to her ward if you'd like. I think it will be more comfortable. And private." Her gaze subtly shifts to mine when she says the word private and I internally grimace. Why can't I play football and not be recognized everywhere I go?

Keeley's phone rings as we're walking, and she lowers her voice as she answers. "We still don't know much but she's okay," she says, walking ahead. Or at least trying to, while I walk faster to keep up. "I'll call you later, maybe when I get home."

Her short conversation pisses me off and I don't hold back. "That better not have been who I think it was."

Keeley's eyes widen as she winces. "Who?"

"Dad." Her shoulders drop and she curses under her breath.

"It was."

"*Keeley.*"

"What? I called him to ask if he knew her blood type in case we needed it."

"*Jesus.* Did he remember?"

"No."

I huff out a laugh. "Typical. And now he's calling to pretend he cares."

"He cares, Easton. They were together for years. They share three kids."

"Fine. Believe his bullshit. It doesn't matter. We're here."

I've just sat down when *my* phone rings and I groan. Out loud. Showing Keeley my screen.

"Don't answer."

"She'll just keep calling. Trust me."

I turn around and accept Macy's call, even though I'm not happy about it. "Yup."

"Hello to you too."

"What's up? You know I'm not with Isaac on Fridays."

"So sue me for forgetting. I called your place and a woman answered. Paige."

Shit. "Macy, I can't deal with this right now. And what do you mean you called my place? We don't have a phone."

Was she at my apartment? Does she mean the intercom?

"I want answers, Easton," she says, ignoring my question. "Are you leaving Isaac with anyone now? Or is she one of your girls? Let me guess… she sucked your cock and that was enough of a reason to let her babysit our child."

"One of my girls?" I come to a halt and slowly drag a hand down my face. "God, you're full of it. But you know what? If pretending I'm an asshole makes you sleep better at night, then do what you have to do. I'm hanging up."

"Wait," she calls out and I pause. I shouldn't, but I fucking pause. "I'm in town. Can I see Isaac?"

Shit… she is in San Francisco.

"No."

"No? You can't stop me, Easton."

"Maybe not, but I'm going to. I need Isaac at home right now. I don't have the headspace to be worried about him while he's out with you."

"Oh, but a stranger is fine."

"Paige would be a better mother than you have *ever* been and she barely knows Isaac. I'd even wager that if I asked Isaac who he wanted to spend time with, you wouldn't like the answer."

"Easton, you can't—"

"Whatever you have to say, save it. I've got to go. I'll call you when I'm ready."

Hanging up, I turn around to find Keeley behind me, her jaw on the floor as her wide eyes lock with mine. "Two things," she says, holding up two fingers, her gaze laced with confusion.

I turn away, but it's no use. I'm not going to escape this. But also, I'm sure she could use the distraction. "Okay, go ahead."

"One. You are my hero. Way to put Macy in her place. Now if you could take that attitude all the way to a lawyer's office, that would be great—for everyone involved." I stare at her without comment or emotion and she continues on. "Two... Busted." She smiles and while it doesn't completely reach her eyes, it's better than nothing considering we're still waiting to see Mom. I know that she's trying to stay positive, but there are only so many lies you can tell yourself before everything starts to feel dirty.

"You caught me." I raise my hands in mock surrender. "I know Paige and she's looking after Isaac."

"Oh, that's not what I'm referring to and you know it." Keeley stares at me knowingly. "How long have you loved her?"

The fuck. "I don't—"

"Ms. Wilder's family?" A nurse interrupts and whatever we were saying goes out of my mind as I spin to face her, nodding. "Your mom's awake and she's asking for you."

"Thank you," we answer in unison before following the nurse back to Mom's room, rushing to her side when we find her sitting up.

"Jesus, Mom. What are you doing?" Keeley says as she reaches her, helping her get comfortable. "You scared the hell out of us."

Mom scoffs with a laugh. "I'm sorry. But I didn't fall on purpose."

"What happened?" I ask, wishing the doctors had given us more information.

Mom sighs and a hint of embarrassment flashes across her face. "I fell on my way out of the house this morning. Of course I was on my front steps so I did a small amount of damage. But as you can see, I'm okay. Luckily, Phil was on his way to work and saw it happen."

"Phil?" I ask stupidly, as though that's the important part of her story.

"Phil is Mom's neighbor. You'd know if you ever asked."

"Asked what? For Mom to name all the residents on her street?"

Keeley snorts, crossing her arms over her chest. "She's also been on a date with him. So—"

"What?"

"*Keeley*," Mom scolds, and it would bring me joy if we weren't currently in the hospital.

"Sorry, it slipped out." Keeley shrugs and Mom actually smiles.

"Thank you both for acting normal around me. The last thing I need is for you to panic."

"Are you joking?" I grab her hand and give it a gentle squeeze. "This is me *panicked*. This is Keeley panicked. She defaults to humor and I default to normal. So what, you just fell? Did you trip over something?"

"No, not exactly."

"What does that mean?"

"It means that my legs gave way and I went ass over tits."

"What?" Keeley and I both grimace while Mom laughs.

"It's a term I heard on an English TV show I've been watching. I never thought I'd get the chance to use it."

"Mom, this isn't funny. You could have broken something. Like your hip."

"I didn't break anything. It's just a few cuts and bruises; otherwise I'm okay. Practically perfect in every way, like Mary Poppins."

Keeley smiles while the blood drains from my head. Keeley's not the only one that defaults to humor when she's emotional. She learned it from Mom. "What's wrong, Mom? What aren't you telling us?"

Keeley's eyes meet mine, and I see the moment she catches up, her face falling while Mom's shoulders drop and she sighs. "I have ALS."

"ALS?" I choke on my words.

"Yes. I found out last month."

"After your appointment? The one where you told me you were fine?"

"Yes."

Keeley's eyes water but I stay strong. For Mom.

"What does that mean?" Keeley asks through her tears, her voice audibly shaking.

"It means I have a motor neuron disease that messes with my nerve cells and my spine, and it's slowly getting worse."

"Jesus, Mom." I run a shaky hand through my hair as my world crumbles. "Why didn't you tell us? You've been doing so much. And I've been pushing you."

"You haven't pushed anything. *I've* been pushing it. If my life has an expiration date, then I'm going to spend as much time as I can with my kids and my grandchild. You can't stop me."

"But—"

"I won't let you ruin the time I have left. That's why I never told you."

"Fuuck," I curse under my breath and run my hands down my face, letting my fingers drag, pulling at my skin. "What if you're speeding things up? What if—"

"How long?" Keeley cuts me off and my gaze flashes to hers.

"How long, what? How long have I known?" Mom questions, but I know exactly what Keeley's asking.

"How long do you have left?"

Mom sighs, holding her hands out for both of us to take. "No one knows exactly. Could be a year, could be ten."

"Christ."

"Only He can help me now."

"*Mom.*" God, she can be so frustrating but I get it. I'd probably act the same way if I knew death was coming for me.

"What are—"

"Now that we have that out of the way," Mom cuts me off, "I need you to distract me with something."

"Have you told Addison?" I ask, switching into pragmatic mode, needing to get things organized. "Is she on her way here?"

Mom groans. "How is *that* a distraction?"

"She's the dramatic one of the three of us," I say even though that's not at all what I meant. "I'm sure she's got some issue she'll need help with."

"I'm sure you're right, but I haven't told her yet. She doesn't need to rush here. I'm not dying tomorrow."

"*Mom,*" Keeley complains and this time, I agree with her response.

"Stop. Both of you. The best way to help me is to let me live. So either distract me or go home."

"Fine. Isaac had—"

"Easton's in love," Keeley blurts, making me choke.

"The fuck, Keeley?"

Mom's face lights up and I both love and hate it. "That worked. Thank you. Now I need all the details."

"I'm not in love."

Mom frowns before it morphs into a smile again. "Maybe not. But I'm guessing there is a girl. A special someone. Whether you love her or not."

"There's no one."

"It's Paige," Keeley answers for me and I groan, throwing my hands in the air.

"Paige. As in your big boss's daughter, Paige? Isaac's bestie, Paige?"

"Isaac's what?"

Mom laughs to herself, muttering something about how much fun this is going to be. "Isaac talks about her all the time. I thought that was just from the few times we'd seen her. I didn't realize he knew her better than that."

"He doesn't. He doesn't see her that often."

"But she *is* with him now." Keeley continues to stir the pot and I want to snap.

"*Keeley.*"

"What? It's not a lie."

"Paige and I... It's complicated," I reluctantly admit, hoping it will shut them up.

But of course, it doesn't.

"Ooh." Mom claps excitedly. "That's code for it *was* purely sexual but *now* you're falling for her?"

"What the hell, Mom? No." *Yes.* Fuck. "It's *complicated*," I repeat. "And she's doing me a favor by looking after Isaac. That's all you need to know."

"I bet that's not the only favor she's doing for—"

"Fuck, Keeley. Don't talk about her like that. Isn't there some kind of girl code where you don't say that shit?"

"You know Paige and I are friends, right?"

"Unfortunately, I guessed. But I pushed it out of my mind because it was easier that way."

"Well, too bad. You can't escape it. If I have to come to terms with the fact that the 'hot guy' she's seeing is my brother, then you have to deal with my torment."

"What did she say?"

"Nothing really. At first, she wouldn't give us any details. But when pushed, she said you were the best she's ever had. And now that I've said that out loud I'm going to go and rinse my mouth out and maybe throw up."

"Everyone has sex, Keeley." Mom shakes her head as her eyes bounce between us like a tennis match.

"It's okay, Mom. I don't need you to defend me. I'm happy to drop it."

"I'm not," Mom says. "I'll never understand why it's so forbidden to talk about sex. People talk about their bodily functions, for God's sake. I don't want to hear about the texture of your shit. I'd much rather hear about the partner that blew your mind last night."

I groan so loud I expect a nurse to come in. "When it comes to you or Keeley, Mom, I don't want to hear about either."

"That's a shame because Phil—"

"La-la-la." I cover my ears and start singing like I used to as a kid, and it shuts Mom up completely. Only she doesn't laugh like I expected her to. "What happened?"

"I found you doing that once when I was fighting with your father. I didn't think you could hear us."

"Oh. Shit. I didn't mean to dampen the mood; I just wanted you to stop talking."

"That's okay. Memories have been hitting me harder lately."

God, I feel like a dick. We were supposed to be distracting her and now we've done a full 360, but I still have questions, so I'm asking them. "What can we do to help you? To..." *Delay.* I trail off because I don't even know if that's possible. We raised funds for ALS at our annual charity event during my rookie year, but I was young and stupid. I was happy to help out, but I didn't pay much attention to what I was supporting. Now I wish I had. And I wish I'd done more.

"Please just be yourselves," Mom begs, her eyes full of emotion. "And Easton, please go home. Isaac needs you more than I do."

I freeze, caught on her words, but while she may be right, I know that he's in safe hands. "Let me call him and check if Paige is okay. I want to stay a bit longer."

Keeley and Mom both smile but I ignore them. Today isn't about my feelings for Paige. It's about my mom.

CHAPTER THIRTY-FIVE

PAIGE

After spending the morning playing at the park, Isaac falls asleep on the couch while I'm making his lunch, leaving me alone with my thoughts. Other than a short "is Isaac okay" text, I haven't heard from Easton in hours and I'm worried for him. For his mom. For Keeley. I can't imagine what they're going through, being told your mom's in the hospital and having no idea what's going on.

I wander aimlessly around the apartment, smiling at the little things that no one would believe were Easton's—the fluffy toys, the photo of Isaac and him dressed as superheroes, even the mess. Sure people know that he's a dad, but no one ever sees the real him. Hell, I've only seen pieces of it and I'm hooked. Imagine what would happen if I ever saw it all. I've just picked up a photo of Isaac and a young woman that I'm assuming is his mom when a phone rings near my ear, making me jump until I realize it's the intercom. I have the exact same one in my apartment but it's never rung before.

"Hello?" I answer hesitantly just in case Easton forgot his keys.

"Hello, I have Macy here for Mr. Wilder."

Macy? My eyes widen as I stare at the photo of Isaac and the woman beside him. Is it her? Or someone else. Another sister? A girlfriend? No. I smile to myself. He wouldn't have time for that. It doesn't matter who it is. Mr. Wilder is not here. "Thank you, Rex," I say, recognizing his voice. "I'm sorry, but Mr. Wilder isn't here at the moment, so please tell her to come back tomorrow."

"Of course."

He hangs up, but the phone rings again seconds later.

"Hello?"

"I'm sorry, miss, but she would like to speak to you."

"Me? Ah. Okay. Sure."

"Who is this?" Macy barks into the phone, not even bothering with pleasantries.

"It doesn't matter who I am. Easton's not here. He should be home late tonight or tomorrow. Please come back then."

"I don't *want* Easton. I'm here to see my son." *Shit*. The attitude. Guess I was right not to like her. "I'm visiting from Florida," she continues, like I care. "I'm not leaving until I see him."

"I'm sorry. As I said, Easton is not here. And we've never met. You'll have to come back tomorrow."

"Tell me the apartment number. I'm coming up so we can talk in person."

"No."

"No?"

"I'm not giving you any of their information; it's not my place to say."

"Then bring him down."

"I can't do that." *Thank God, he's asleep.*

"I'm his mother. I have the right to see him."

"That may be so, but Easton asked me to look after him, and he never mentioned that you'd be coming by. I'm not letting you see Isaac unless Easton tells me otherwise." God, I hope I'm doing the right thing. What if Easton just forgot and this messes things up for him?

"Call him."

"I can't. I'm sorry." I stare at her picture and my dislike grows.

"Put Isaac on the phone. Now."

"I can't do that either. He's napping."

"He's napping? Why?"

"Well, since you're his *mother*, I'm sure you remember that he still naps a couple of times a week."

"Who do you think you are?"

"I'm nobody." I almost raise my voice but hold back. I need to keep my cool.

"Damn straight you're nobody. You—"

"I'm nobody but I'm here to protect Isaac, and that means I'm not letting a stranger in. Come back tomorrow. Goodbye."

I release a rushed sigh and move to hang up but she calls out.

"Wait. You're Paige, aren't you?"

Dammit. "I am."

"So what? You're trying to take my ex and my son."

"I'm not trying to *take* anything." Did Easton tell her about me? Or Isaac? "I care about them both and I'm doing what I feel is right. Goodbye."

I hang up quickly this time and take a deep breath as my mind whirs. God, I hope I didn't fuck things up for Easton. Why don't we ever talk? I should know more about his life. Shouldn't I?

Isaac wakes up twenty minutes after Macy called and when he finds me, still in the hallway next to the photo with his mom, he smiles.

"That's my mom," he says, resting his head against my leg. "She lives at Disney."

"At Disney? Wow. She's pretty lucky. Do you get to see her much?"

"No. But she got me my red shoes, remember?"

"Yeah." My heart breaks for him, but I smile and ruffle his messy brown hair. "I remember. They make you super-fast."

"Yeah." He smiles back at me but there's a sadness in his expression. I'm about to change the subject when he keeps talking. "Daddy has to stay here for Christmas with Nana, so I'm staying too. I can go to Disney another day."

"That's nice of you. Your dad and Nana will love that." A tightness pulls at my chest, but I ignore it. No matter what happens today, I know Easton will make sure he has a good Christmas and if not, I will.

"What's your favorite thing about Christmas?"

He shrugs his shoulders and I let out a little laugh. What a stupid question to ask. I don't think I could narrow it down to one thing either.

"What about an easier question? Should we make cookies today?"

Isaac's face brightens and he bounces on the spot. "Yes. Can we?"

"Of course. We just have to go down to my apartment to get the ingredients. Are you up for that?"

"Yes. Can we go now?"

"Let's do it."

✎ ✎ ✎

We spend the afternoon baking, and while we're eating our creations, I get another text from Easton, asking if it's an okay time to speak to Isaac. As though it's up to me. I respond with a yes and he calls right away.

"Hey you," I answer the same way I did this morning, somewhat wishing we could rewind and have the day play out differently... and for his mom to be okay. "Any news?"

"She's okay. Sort of. If that makes sense."

"I think so. What about you?"

"Me?"

"Yeah." I walk around the corner out of earshot but keep my eyes on Isaac. "Are *you* okay?"

"Sort of."

He laughs and I smile as my eyes threaten to water. "We had a great day," I say, changing the subject. "Isaac's amazing, Easton. You should be very proud."

"I'm pretty lucky."

"Nah, I don't believe that. He's got an amazing dad. I think he gets it from him."

"Thanks, Paige."

"Want me to put him on?"

"I do, but first, is it okay if I stay here a little longer? I can come home if you need me to, but—"

"No, I'm fine here. Isaac already asked if I could read to him at bedtime, and I saw you had some chicken and veggies in the fridge. Can I cook that?"

Easton audibly sighs. "Paige, you could give him ice cream for dinner and I'd be grateful."

"I'll cook the chicken." I huff out a laugh.

He sighs again and I wish I was there until I realize being here would mean more to him.

"Thank you, Paige. I don't know what I'd do without you." Once again, it's one of those throwaway lines, but the thing is, I'm not sure what I'd do without him either. Not that I tell him that. Now is not the time.

"Don't thank me yet, because in all honesty, I don't know what I'm doing and I'm freaking out."

Easton laughs and I can picture him shaking his head. "Welcome to my world, every day."

"Panic aside, it's not such a bad world. I kind of like it." Easton falls silent and I curse myself for speaking so openly. "Anyway, I'll get Isaac. One sec. Isaac," I call out. "It's your dad."

He runs in from the kitchen, abandoning his cookie, and grabs the phone from my outstretched hand. "Hi, Dad. Did you have a good day?"

I walk away, giving them some space, but my heart stays in the room with them. I may not know much about kids, but I've been one, and I have younger cousins. I don't remember any of them being this sweet.

When they've been talking for a couple of minutes, I walk past to see if they're wrapping things up and hear Isaac say three little words that completely shatter me.

"I lub Paige, Dad." He hangs up and I barely get a chance to process it when he comes running toward me with my phone. "Here." He hands it over. "Can we play now?"

"Of course." I smile while my heart pounds in my chest. "What do you want to do next?"

"One more book. Please." Isaac smiles up at me and I laugh. "I'm worried that if you keep saying 'one more,' it's going to be morning and you won't have gone to sleep yet. I can't say no to you."

His eyes widen before he sucks his lips into his mouth and shakes. "Can I stay up *all* night?" he asks excitedly. "Dad never lets me do that."

"No, you *definitely* can't do that. Your dad will never let me look after you again. And I like getting to play with you."

"Me too. I like that too."

"Good, so you agree. One more book and then sleep."

"One more." He nods before curling into me, and a short burst of pain hits deep in my chest. I can't say for sure, but I'm almost certain it was my heart breaking so I could give a piece of it to Isaac, while another piece already belongs to his dad.

God, what am I doing?

I can't fall for Easton. He doesn't want that and my life is already so complicated. And likely to get worse.

Isaac jumps off the bed while I'm lost in my head and searches his bookshelf for another book, throwing the rejects onto the floor until he's found one he wants.

It's on the longer side, but I don't mind. I like his company, and if I'm being honest, the second he's asleep I'm going to have to face my feelings, and I'm not ready to do that.

"One day, in the magic forest of Esterold, a little boy..."

As I read, Isaac starts off staring at the pages, but it's not long before he rests his head on my shoulder, and then when I'm only halfway through, his breathing slows as his head lolls to the side. I smile as I readjust him on the bed, making him comfortable before tucking him in.

Today may have been completely out of my comfort zone, but I enjoyed every second of it, and I don't want to leave him alone. But I do.

Tiptoeing out of the room, I gently close the door and switch on the monitor before cleaning up. When I'm done, I curl up on the couch and close my eyes, needing a moment to rest.

The door rattles sometime later, snapping me awake as I jump up. I hadn't even realized I'd fallen asleep, but judging by the crick in my neck, I've been out for a while.

I check the time on my phone and find a text from Keeley, my heart breaking.

"You're home?" I say as I greet Easton in the entry. "I was waiting for you to call and—"

Without a word, he strides forward and throws his arms around me, pulling me into his hold as he buries his face in my neck. His body shakes as I curl my arms around his waist, emotion clogging my throat while I comfort him. "I'm here, Easton. I'm here."

He shakes his head before pulling away. "My life is falling apart, Paige. I don't know what the fuck I'm doing anymore."

"Tell me what you need. I'm here to help. Put me in, Coach."

The smallest of smiles tugs at his lips before he grabs my face in his hands and kisses the life out of me. Or maybe he's hoping to kiss away the pain. He walks me backward until I hit the wall and then sinks a hand under the waistband of my leggings, immediately running a finger through my heat.

My body melts for him, just like it always does, but I fight to keep a clear head. Despite what he may think, this isn't what he needs right now, and he'd never usually risk Isaac walking in on us.

"East."

"I just need to forget."

"Easton, you—" I gasp as one of his fingers slips inside me, and my traitorous body bucks against him.

"Fuck, Paige. You're always so ready for me."

"Stop," I rush out, ignoring the heat taking over me. "You're not thinking clearly. Isaac's home and you've got a lot going on. Let me help in another way. *Please.*"

I prepare myself to push him off me, but I don't have to, because the second I say please, he stops and takes a step back.

He stares at me for a moment, unmoving, until emotion wells in his eyes and he breaks down, falling into me once more.

"She's sick, Paige. Really sick. And I'm so fucking scared."

Chapter Thirty-Six

EASTON

I was sure the reality of Mom's condition and her future had sunk in while I was at the hospital. But the second I saw Paige, it hit me like a freight train and my entire world came crashing down.

"What if it doesn't stop there, Paige?" I ask, as if she'll have all the answers. "What if Isaac gets sick...or you? Meanwhile, I'm here playing a game that takes me away from my family all the fucking time."

Paige shakes her head as she walks me to the couch and pushes me to sit before making herself comfortable beside me, grabbing my hands, the warmth of her touch bringing me a moment of comfort.

"It's your job, Easton," she says, squeezing my hands when I try to rebut. "Lots of people have jobs that take up their time," she continues, not allowing me to speak. "Some do night shifts and sleep all day, some travel. Some people don't have a choice."

"But I do." I pull my hands away and point to my chest. "I chose this. I'm *still* choosing it despite having more than enough money to support Isaac for the rest of his life."

"You're hurting. Emotions are high. Now is not the time to make life-changing decisions. We'll get through this."

"We?" I ask, my heart pounding in my chest.

"Yes, we." Paige smiles and I wish more than anything that our life was simpler. "I'm here to help with whatever you need." She grabs my hands again and stares into my eyes, making sure I believe her.

"Even if that means letting me in?"

"Yes," she answers barely above a whisper.

"And me letting you in?"

"Yes."

"Fuck, Paige. Are you sure? Because I don't know what I'm doing anymore, with anything in my life. I'm failing Isaac, my mom. You. I'm a mess and you deserve better than that. I can't give you what you want. No matter how much I wish I could."

"What do you think I want?"

"The world, Paige." My chest tightens as I note the sadness in her eyes, and while I'd love to do anything to make her happy all the time, I don't think it's possible. "You want the world. And God knows you deserve it."

"I—"

"You deserve someone who'll stand by your side at your incredible charity events, someone that can follow you to Paris and Italy to watch you walk the runways of fashion week. You deserve someone who can give you one hundred percent of themselves without a second thought. You deserve it all."

"You're wrong." She holds my gaze, her expression defiant. "I don't want any of that. I want someone to come home to. Someone to talk to about my day. Someone who looks at me like you do even when they can't give me a hundred percent of themselves. I want you, Easton. That's all I've wanted since the moment we first kissed, but I'm terrified of what that will do to you. My life is a mess—I told you that—and I'd never forgive myself if any of it came back to haunt you." She pauses and her face drops before she shakes her head. "Only, I don't think I can let you go. I don't think I'm strong enough. Not now."

I stare into her beautiful dark eyes and process her words. She wants me. And while I'm equally messed-up, I want her too. "I don't think I'm strong enough either, but..." I trail off. I've never felt this way about anyone before, but I have this feeling I'm setting us up for failure when we haven't even started. "There are some things about me that I need to tell you. Some things I'm not proud of."

"East—"

"No, please. You need to hear it."

"Okay." She moves to get comfortable while I face forward, unsure I'll get through it all if I'm looking at her.

"I've never been easy to live with. The asshole version of me isn't the result of my current situation. It's me. All my life I've only cared about a few things, and everything else fell into the *too hard* basket—something I had to do or someone I had to talk to but didn't want to. I know it stems from my dad walking out on us. I've always struggled with that, and I don't need a shrink to tell me he's a big part of the way I am. But it's been years and I haven't changed."

"You're not like that with me," Paige cuts in, her warm palm cupping my leg.

My shoulders drop as I sag back into the cushions. "I know, Paige. And that scares the hell out of me because I care. I really fucking care and I could easily fuck it up. It's like I'm programmed differently. I cared about Macy too. At one point. And look how that ended."

Paige squirms beside me, and when I look her way she grimaces. "Before you say any more, I need to tell you that she was here today. Macy, I mean. She called and I wouldn't let her see Isaac. I'm sorry if that was the wrong decision but I didn't know and—"

"She told me," I cut her off to ease her mind. "You made the right decision and I'm thankful you were here. Things between me and Macy are complicated to say the least. I should have told you about it before asking you to help with Isaac, but I didn't think. In fact, I don't *think* enough when I'm caught in any situation I'm not prepared for."

"Like your mom being rushed to the hospital? No one would think clearly if that happened."

"Maybe not, but there have been other opportunities to talk to you. I just—"

"Don't like letting people in. Like me."

"Yeah."

"We're talking now." She shrugs softly. "I'm here to listen. To help."

"You are now. We'll see how you feel after I tell you what I did."

Paige offers me a slight nod, but I can tell she wants to argue. To defend me when she doesn't even know what she's trying to defend. I wish I could pretend to be the guy she thinks I am, but I can't hide anymore. Not from her.

"I was an asshole to Macy after Isaac was born. I basically trapped her and then blamed *her* for it. She never wanted kids. Hell, neither did I. It's why we worked. But then she became pregnant and I promised to support her. I convinced her it would be a good thing. That when our baby was born, something would change in both of us and we'd love our new life. And I was right. The second I saw Isaac, my entire world fell into place. It was like nothing I had done before that moment mattered. He instantly became my everything. But it wasn't like that for Macy. Nothing changed, and she begged me to put him up for adoption. She loved our life the way it was before she was pregnant. She didn't want the responsibility and thought I'd come to resent it too."

I chance a look at Paige and find her eyes glassy but wide. I'm sure she's wondering how anyone could possibly think that about Isaac, but Macy barely knew him then. Some people aren't meant to be parents, and I should have acknowledged that. But I didn't.

"I made so many promises to get Macy to stay and play happy family. I was convinced she just needed time. And that Isaac needed us both. For over two years, I bribed her to stay. Adoption was never an option, but I also never considered going it alone. And I should have. I was wrong. Kids see and feel *everything*... On some level, Isaac knew she didn't want to be there. I can see it in their interactions together now. I hate the way Macy is treating him, and I want her out of his life. But more than that, I hate that it's my fault we're in this situation to begin with. And I know she's hanging around to spite me. I've fucked up so much that I no longer know what the right thing is."

"Oh, Easton. You haven't fucked up. You're doing what's right for Isaac."

"Is it right, though? Was it right to force someone to be a mother? Is it right to keep threatening her now when she doesn't spend time with him? And is it right to be thinking about hiring a lawyer to take *her* rights away when I'm the reason she ran? If I'd let her go when he was first born, she may have realized she wanted to be part of his life on her own. I hate her for what she's doing to him, but I hate myself more."

I rub my eyes to hide the tears threatening to fall, and when I drop my hands, Paige throws her arms around me, smothering me in a hug. "Did you love her?"

"I don't even know anymore. At one point I thought I did, but..." That was nothing compared to how I feel now.

"But then you felt real love with Isaac?"

"Yes." And maybe even *you*.

"You can't blame yourself for everything, East. Macy made her own choices. Did you lock her up?"

"No, but—"

"Did you threaten her physically? Tell her you'd hurt her if she left?"

"Fuck, no. I'd never do that and she never thought I would. Is that what *you* think?" My heart seizes and I can't bear to look at her face.

"No. God, no." She grabs my chin and forces me to face her. "I'm trying to make you see that you didn't do this. You tried to hold your family together but the glue wasn't sticking. And maybe it was never meant to. Have you talked to anyone else about this? Your mom or your sister? A professional?"

"No."

"Why?"

"Because I never wanted them to look at me like you're looking at me now."

"How?"

"With pity."

Paige raises an eyebrow and leans back. "Please don't hate me for this but...you need to suck it up." She pauses to gauge my reaction and I laugh. Trust Paige to put me in my place.

"Go on."

"I really am sorry, but if anyone is looking at you with pity, it's because they feel bad about the situation you've been forced into. It's not a reflection on you. This would be an awful situation for *anyone*. And while I'm not saying others would have made the same choices you did, there's also no guarantee someone else would have achieved a better outcome. But no matter what, you need help. You can't do this alone."

"I've got help, Paige. At least I had it until I pushed my mom so far she ended up in the hospital."

"That wasn't you."

"How do you know?"

"Because Keeley texted me about a minute before you got home."

"She what?"

"She was worried that you'd keep everything bottled up. I guess she was wrong." Paige shrugs and I force a smile, thinking about what Keeley did.

I'm pissed off until I realize she's right. I'd normally keep it all bottled up. But with Paige, I no longer want to.

"What if—"

"No," she cuts me off. "There are no what-ifs..."

"But—"

"No. Your mom has ALS, Easton. She didn't get it because she was helping you with Isaac and—"

"I—"

"You didn't *make it worse*." Paige's gaze softens, and I finally let some of what she's saying sink in.

"Okay."

"Okay?"

"I believe you, but I still need to look after her moving forward. She can't be doing as much as she was."

"My guess is that she wants to. I'll bet she'll do anything to keep her life as normal as possible."

I huff out a laugh. "That's exactly what she said."

"Great minds." Paige smiles and a feeling of comfort takes over me.

"Thank you for being here today. And all the other times you've appeared out of nowhere when I needed someone."

"Funny. I thought you were the one always showing up."

"Maybe it's both of us."

"Either way, I'm glad I could help. I had a lot of fun with Isaac."

"And he had a lot of fun with you. I heard all about the cookies."

"Hope you don't mind him being high on sugar for the next few days. There are plenty left, and I'm not taking them because then I'll eat them all."

"As I said, I would have been good with you giving him ice cream for dinner."

"Thank you." Paige smiles to herself and it's a little infectious.

"What are you smiling about?"

"You. Isaac."

"Yeah?"

"Sometimes you're so alike, and other times you're not. But he's a great kid. And he's so smart. He'll get through this. I know it."

"You're right. At least about him being smart. He told me something on the phone tonight and I laughed it off. Until now." Until I realized how stupid and blind I'd been.

"What did he say?" Paige's smile remains and I find myself drawn to her lips, her face, her eyes. I'm drawn to her. Have been for a while now.

"He told me he loved you," I say with Isaac's voice playing in my mind as if he's saying it again.

Paige swallows and her eyes water. "I heard him," she rasps.

"Do you know what that tells me?"

"No."

"It tells me that he saw something in you that he trusted. That he knows how special you are. And it tells me that he's more observant than I realize. Or maybe observant isn't right; he's more emotionally aware. Because Paige... it took me *months* to realize I was falling in love with you and he's already there."

Paige bites her lip before her eyes lock with mine. "You're falling in love with me?"

"I am. I can't get you out of my head. I want to see you all the time. Touch you. Be with you. But it wasn't until I wanted to let you in that I realized what I was feeling. This is bigger than I meant for it to be."

"I wasn't looking for anything more than sex. Actually, I wasn't even looking for that. But I'm falling in love with you too. With both of you."

My eyes widen as my heart cracks open. That means more to me than anything else. "And I think I just fell a little more."

Paige laughs as I grab her face and press my lips to hers, sealing our confessions with a kiss. I still have no idea where we go from here, but I'm going to do anything I can do to fix my life, because I want Paige to be a part of it. And she deserves better.

Pulling away, I grab one of her hands and press another kiss to her fingers. As much as I'd love to take her to my bedroom right now, she was there for me and it's my turn to be there for her. "Now that I've confessed everything, I want to know about *you*. All of it. The good, the bad, the stuff that makes you want to spend your time with an asshole and his son."

Paige laughs before falling back against the cushions and resting her head on my shoulder. "I'd rather we—"

"Nope." I press a finger to her lips to shush her. "It's time to talk, D'Angelo. And I want to know *everything*."

CHAPTER THIRTY-SEVEN

PAIGE

"You're not going to let me off the hook, are you?" I keep my eyes forward and my head on Easton's shoulder, feeling him move beside me.

"Hell, no." He laughs. "But you're cute for asking." He bops my nose, and I huff out a laugh of my own even though what I'm about to share is anything but funny.

"I don't know where to start."

Easton turns, forcing me to sit up and look at him. "How about you start with the reason you're holding back, since we've established it's not your dad."

I bite back a smile as I shake my head. He's right. I'm not worried about my dad, but I still don't think it's going to be a fun conversation when we decide to tell him. Taking a deep breath, I grab my knees when they start to bounce, then I nod. "I—"

"You don't have to be nervous," Easton cuts in, his gaze moving to my legs as he slowly reaches out to touch me, placing a tentative hand on my knee. "Whatever it is, I'm here."

Our eyes lock as my breath hitches. He's here. With me. But what happens when he finds out about my past?

"I hate to talk exes but—" Easton scoffs, his brow raised. "Okay. I realize we just spoke about your ex, but this is different. And you're not going to like it."

"Try me."

"Christian and I had a purely physical relationship. His family business takes him around the world regularly, so he didn't want to commit to anyone and I didn't either, though I had no excuse except that I didn't feel like it. We never had an emotional connection, but the physical side of things was incredible. At the time." I cringe and Easton laughs, though it's easy to see it's a *God, why am I listening to this* chuckle.

"Want me to keep going?"

"Please. But no need for great detail."

This time it's my turn to laugh, and while I'm sure he's not actually joking, it puts my mind at ease.

"In short, I've already told you that we played a lot of games in our relationship, but what I didn't tell you was that his family were the ones that leaked the details to the media."

"What? Why?"

"A month before I moved here, I was at Christian's parents' house because he needed to pick something up. He was taking too long in the attic, so I decided to help myself to a drink. Only I didn't realize his mom was home and when I approached the kitchen, she was talking to his aunt. They were discussing some ah...illegal practices that Christian's dad was partaking in. I turned to walk away, not wanting them to catch me, but Christian chose that moment to call my name. So of course, his mom rushed into the hallway and found me."

"Shit. That's not what I was expecting you to say. What happened?"

"She asked if I'd been listening in on their conversation, and while I told her I just got there, she didn't believe me. Rightly so, because I heard a lot. Too much. But since she's not aware how long I was listening, so she has no idea what I know."

Easton stiffens, his eyes narrowing. "So she leaked information to the media?"

"Yes. And I think she's kind of blackmailing me."

"She's what?" His voice raises as he stands, his fists clenched. "She's blackmailing you?"

"Yes."

"Fuck, Paige. Why didn't you lead with that? Why didn't you tell me and—"

"Shhh. You'll wake Isaac. I didn't tell you because I thought I could handle it and I didn't want you involved. I still don't."

"Well, it's too late for that."

"No, it's not. I told my dad. He's helping so that you don't have to."

Easton shakes his head. "What if I want to?"

"Then I'll say thanks but no thanks. My biggest fear in all of this is that you or Isaac will get caught up in it. I don't want to hurt you. I couldn't care less what happens to me anymore."

"The problem with that statement is that *I* care what happens to you. And if something happens, you better believe it will hurt me. And Isaac."

My stomach drops but I refuse to acknowledge it. That's a different kind of hurt. They could survive that. It would be harder to survive something directly aimed their way.

"Dad's handling it. I promise."

"Fuck." Easton runs a hand through his already mussed hair and sits down again, his expression pained as he turns my way. "So you expect me to sit back and trust that nothing's going to happen to you?"

"Yes." I climb into his lap, cupping his face in my hands. "But I will say I'm loving this protective side of you."

Easton releases a grunt low in his throat. "I know what you're doing and it won't work."

"What am I doing?" I raise my hands in surrender.

"You're trying to distract me so I'll relent."

"Never. I just thought you should know that I like it. A lot."

"How is she blackmailing you?" he asks, moving us back on topic. "What is she doing exactly?"

Dammit. My shoulders drop and I move to climb off him but he doesn't let me, gripping my waist to pin me in place.

"You can tell me from here."

I nod as my nose scrunches. "On top of releasing the stories about my past and making me out to be someone I'm not, they have photos of me and Christian. And me with other people—innocent photos that look bad. And possibly some X-rated ones."

"X-rated? What the fuck does that mean?"

"Photos of me and Christian having sex." I cringe but only because I'm anticipating Easton's reaction. And he doesn't disappoint.

"*Fuck.*" He squeezes my waist. "How?"

"My guess is that they went through Christian's phone."

"Why the fuck does he have them?"

"Because we were in a relationship for years. Because I was young and stupid and I did things without thinking about my future. When Christian first took a photo of us, I considered the fact that he could share the images, but honestly, I didn't think he had it in him. I never once considered that someone else might find them and use them against me."

Easton opens his mouth to speak but I cut him off.

"And before you ask, I don't regret that part of my life. I'd just prefer it stayed private."

"I wasn't going to say that. I was going to ask if there's any chance Christian gave his parents the photos."

"I don't think so. He doesn't seem to know what's going on. He's a smart guy when it comes to business, but he's pretty clueless about everything else. Actually, self-centered is a better word."

Easton closes his eyes as he releases a breath. "That actually makes it worse. I wish he knew what was happening so he could stop it."

"Me too."

"And you don't want to tell him?"

"I've thought about it, but no. I think it's best if I don't. And Dad agreed. For now."

"What's your dad doing? I mean, to stop them from releasing more information."

"Um, well, he's not really dealing with that side of things because I didn't give him all the details. He's looking into finding proof about what I overheard."

"What? *Jesus.* Isn't that going to make things worse for you?"

"Possibly. But I couldn't let them get away with it. I know their clients are wealthy, but that doesn't mean they deserve to be ripped off."

Easton stares up at me for a beat before he smiles. "You have a good heart, Paige. I just wish it didn't have the potential to get you into trouble."

"Me too. And thanks."

"For what?"

"For not telling me I'm crazy."

"Why the hell would I do that?"

"I don't know. But it wouldn't be completely off base. I tried to go it alone. I hired someone to look for evidence, and if he'd found some, I was going to take them down. But he didn't. So now my dad's taking over."

"And you think he'll have better luck?"

"He's taking a different approach. Christian's family owns a few hedge funds, so my dad and Austin, the guy I hired, are going to try and invest their money. See what they do with it."

Easton glances away thoughtfully, before looking back at me. "I think that's a good plan."

"I know. But it's also risky."

"I'm glad you're here then." He squeezes my waist again. "In San Francisco."

"Me too. And I have no plans of going back...except for Thanksgiving."

"Thanksgiving?"

"Yeah, I'm going to spend it with my mom's family."

"I'm not sure I like that plan." Easton frowns. "You'll be careful, right?"

"I promise." As I say it, my first thought is that my mom wouldn't let anything happen to me, but then I remember she's involved with Christian's dad and suddenly I'm not so sure. "I'll look after myself."

"What if that's not enough?"

"Are you really worried?"

"Nope," he lies. I can see the concern etched in his features. "I barely know you."

"Barely know me, huh?"

"Yep."

I grab his hands and place them on my breasts. "You know these."

"I do," he confirms with no emotion.

Lifting to my knees, I glide one of his hands between my legs and rub his finger against my core, trying hard not to moan. "You know this."

"Yep."

Next I lift his other hand to my mouth, holding his fingers against my lips as I speak. "And this."

"I know your body, Paige. But I want to know this." He drops his hand to my heart and holds it there, his eyes locked on mine. I can't do anything but suck in a breath. "I don't know where we go from here," he adds, "but I want more."

"I want that too. But I'm so scared."

"Nothing needs to change from the outside looking in, but I want you to be mine, Paige. Even if I'm the only one that knows about it."

"Funny thing is...I've been yours since we met, and I've never felt like this before."

Easton's hands move to my face before sinking into my hair. "I've never felt like this either," he whispers, his eyes bouncing between mine. "And while there's a chance I'll fuck it up, I can't stand being casual anymore. In fact, we've been way beyond casual for a while."

He pulls my face toward him and I press my lips to his, instantly opening my mouth to let him in. The kiss is soft and explorative. Different. We're different. It's not about a release anymore. It's so much more than that.

Grabbing Easton's face, I lean closer and deepen the kiss as I gently rock my hips. His cock hardens as he lets out a soft groan, but nothing changes, both of us keeping things slow, taking our time, feeling the moment.

My heart beats frantically as we kiss, and after another minute, Easton pulls back, his crystal-blue eyes staring into my soul. "I never saw you coming, Paige. But fuck, I'm glad that you're here."

CHAPTER THIRTY-EIGHT

EASTON

I stand up with Paige still in my arms and walk her to my bedroom before laying her down on my bed.

The intensity of her gaze as she stares up at me has my pulse racing, and I feel it too. Something has shifted between us. My feelings were already big, and I told her as much...but now, I want to show her.

Sitting her up, I slowly drag the tee over her head before kissing her shoulder while I undo her bra, letting my lips linger as I kiss a path toward her neck, sucking the flesh into my mouth as we both fall back to the bed.

Paige mewls as her arms tighten around me, but I don't stay like that for long, brushing my lips across her skin, making my way toward her navel.

Slipping my fingers under the waistband of her leggings, I drag them down her legs and leave her panties in place, my gaze locked on the see-through material as I fight to keep things slow.

When I reach her pussy, I blow on the fabric covering her clit, loving the way her body lifts to get closer to me and the soft moans that escape her.

"God, East," she whispers, her voice shaky. "You haven't even touched me."

I kiss her clit through her panties, once, twice, squeezing her thighs as she jolts, and just when I think she's going to beg me for more, I guide the material to the side and lick a path through her folds, needing her tonight just as much as she needs me. I'm past the teasing; I just want to be with her.

As I switch between licking and sucking, Paige squirms beneath my touch, fighting for the control she's used to. She grabs the sheets before lifting her hands to her pert breasts, squeezing her nipples while I pleasure her.

Her orgasm builds while I work her pussy with my tongue, and I'm about to add my fingers to the mix when she calls out breathlessly. "Stop," she rasps. "I'm close but I want you inside me. I want to finish together."

I pause, glancing up at her through her open legs, my brow raised in question. "Please, East," she giggles as she pleads again.

As if I could say no. "Done."

I strip in record time, sheathing myself before I crawl onto the bed, hovering above her. Paige sits up, her face flushed, her hair a mess, and I've never seen her more beautiful. "How do you want me?" she asks, a hint of nerves in her tone.

"I want you like this. I want to watch as I slide into you, and then I want to see you, all of you, as you come apart."

Eyes wide, she nods as she spreads her legs farther, welcoming me between them, watching our connection while I line up with her entrance. There's already tension in the air, but when I push inside her, we both pause, our eyes meeting as all the emotion comes to the surface.

I groan as I fill her, my eyes never leaving hers, catching her throat bob as she swallows. And a sad reality hits me. I have never made love before now, because this is so much more intense than anything I've ever experienced. This connection with Paige is beyond anything I've ever felt. And that's as terrifying as it is thrilling.

When we finally move, it doesn't take long to find our rhythm.

With my arms braced on either side of her head, I cage her in as I rock, meeting her thrust for thrust as the pressure builds inside me.

"God, East..." she trails off but...

"I know. Fuck. I know."

Her walls tighten around me and I pick up speed, pounding into her as she bucks her hips, chasing the high, ready to fly over the edge.

She cries out and my balls tighten, the sound of her moans sending a spark through me as my release hits.

"Oh God," Paige gasps and her body spasms, her orgasm hitting as my cock jerks inside her.

I grunt as my arms shake, slowing my movements until her body stops convulsing, dropping to the bed beside her.

We're both silent for a beat until Paige lifts to her elbow and runs a finger down my cheek, her gaze soft. "You were quiet," she whispers as her breathing slows.

"I was taking it all in." *Processing my feelings.*

"I like you telling me what to do...but I also loved that."

"Me too. I'll take both."

Paige giggles before tucking herself into my arms and laying her head on my chest. "We'll have to do it again sometime."

I smile but don't respond, not that I have to. With the way I feel about her and her about me, I think this might just become a regular thing for us. And God am I happy she's with me.

"Thank you for today, Paige. For everything."

"You don't need to keep thanking me, but you're welcome. Though, I am about to say something that might piss you off."

"Oh, yeah?"

"Yeah. I think you should talk to Macy."

"I—"

"*Without* yelling at her. Have a proper conversation. You said you think she might be doing things to spite you. Be nice and maybe she'll stop."

"Goddammit." Paige giggles because she knows she's right. "It's not a bad idea."

"Of course it's not." She smiles triumphantly. "It's a good one."

"Fine, but if I'm talking to Macy, then I want you to do something for me."

"Oh-kay?" she tentatively agrees.

"Stay out of your dad's plans with Austin. Let them handle it. And before you say anything, I know you're more than capable, but I can't protect you and—"

"Okay."

"Yeah?"

"Yes. I'll let them handle it."

"Thank you."

"I don't want to make your life harder, East. At least not on purpose." Her voice is soft, and maybe a little saddened, so I twist in bed until I can see her.

"Paige, I—"

She laughs, cutting into my panic. "I get it. I do. You've got a lot going on and while we have to keep this thing to ourselves, I know you care. Thank you."

"You really are going to be the death of me."

"I hope so. But let's make it a billion years from now."

I open my mouth to respond when Paige sits up and shuffles to the edge of the bed. "I'm going to go." She stands next and searches for her clothes, her eyes flashing to the door. "I shouldn't be here when Isaac wakes up."

I cringe because she's right but at the same time... "I really want you to stay the night. You know that, right? This is—"

"Different? I know. But we have to take things slowly for Isaac's sake."

My chest fills at her concern for my son. She's always thinking of him. Almost as much as me. "You're an amazing human, Paige D'Angelo."

"I know." She winks and I laugh. "Which is why I really have to go. I'll be back in the morning to look after Isaac again."

"You don't have to do that." I smile, watching her move around the room. "I'll call Coach and—"

"I'm coming. Believe it or not, I like spending time with him. I'm looking forward to it."

She turns her back to me and I get up, taking two strides to reach her, wrapping her up in my hold. "Thank you. That means a lot to me."

"I know." She spins in my arms, taking my lips in a chaste kiss. "I'm happy to help. Anytime."

"Again. Thank you. But I'll have to figure out what I'm doing long-term. I'm close to retirement anyway and—"

"No." She pulls back, staring up at me.

"What?" I raise an eyebrow as a small laugh escapes me.

"You're not retiring yet. I need to see you win one of those Super Bowl things."

"Super Bowl things," I repeat and Paige laughs.

"My dad needs you. And so does the team. I think. You're good, right?"

"Yeah, I'm good."

"Then you can't retire. Please. Let me help."

"*Paige...*"

"I'm not taking no for an answer. So don't even bother."

"Why are you so good to me?"

"I'm not doing it for you." She wriggles out of my arms and slips her tee over her head braless, before stepping into her leggings. "I'm doing it for that gorgeous son of yours. This is just a bonus."

"Ah, so you want a kid. Is that it?" I laugh, but Paige pauses, her brows furrowed.

"Actually, I haven't really thought about having kids." She shrugs like that's no big deal and resumes getting dressed. "I just happen to like Isaac."

She giggles to herself, probably thinking her words were meaningless, when in reality, they mean everything. That's all I ever wanted for him. For someone to love him for him. I thought he needed Macy for that. But all this time, I've been wrong. He just had to wait for Paige.

"Have a good sleep." Paige kisses my cheek when she's dressed. "I'll see you in the morning." She opens the bedroom door and tiptoes down the hall before disappearing out of sight, and I don't move until I hear the front door click shut.

What a fucking day.

I think I've felt more emotion today than I have in my lifetime. And I don't exactly hate it.

As promised, Paige knocks at seven the next morning while I'm on the phone with the hospital, asking if I can visit on my way to the stadium. The answer being no. I'm still frowning as I open the door.

"Everything okay? Is it your *mom*?" She whispers the word "mom" and I'm grateful for that.

"The nurse said she had a good night, but they won't let me see her until later today. I thought I could sneak in early."

"Ugh. I'm sorry. Want me to ask the team owner if he can cut you some slack today?" She raises a brow and I laugh.

"Thanks, but that's okay. Keeley's heading to the hospital when visiting hours begin, so if I go on my way home, at least she'll have more company that way. And Keeley can take over from you later on today so you get some time to yourself."

"I don't need time. I can stay until you get home."

"You're not working at all?"

"Nope. My next modeling job isn't for a few weeks, and I'm not needed for the charity event this week."

"Okay. But honestly, you don't have to."

"What? Really? I thought you had a gun to my head."

"Okay. Okay. I'm being a D. I. C. K," I say as I hear movement from Isaac's room. "Thank you."

"You're welcome. Now where's my little buddy?" Paige raises her voice and Isaac hears her, calling her name as he runs down the hall, the nice moment breaking my heart. This is how he should be greeting his mom.

And while I'm thinking of Macy, I better call her before she turns up at the apartment again. I think it's time we had a proper conversation. But first, I need to find a lawyer.

Chapter Thirty-Nine

EASTON

When I'm on my way to the stadium, Macy calls, saving me from calling her, and I take a deep breath, ready to be civil. Only she doesn't make it easy.

"Since you won't let me see him while I'm here, I need you to book a flight for me and Isaac for Christmas. I assume you don't want him flying alone, so you'll need to fly me to San Francisco first and then I'll take him home. Maybe you can come and get him."

Dammit. "He changed his mind."

"Excuse me?"

"He said he wants to spend Christmas with my mom. Don't worry, he's not choosing me over you."

"Bullshit. What did she say to him? I bet she forced him."

I huff out a sigh, rubbing my temple as I drive. "He may only be three, Macy, but he knows what he wants."

"No. I don't accept that. He said yes, so he's coming. He has to come."

"What does that mean?" I bite back a groan. I knew this wasn't going to be easy, but I didn't think she'd argue this much.

"I need him. It's Christmas. I need my family during Christmas."

"Then come to San Francisco. You can take him for lunch and I'll—"

"No."

"No?"

"He's coming to Florida."

"He's not going."

"He said he wanted to come until you brainwashed him."

"Kids change their minds. All the time. He told me he liked broccoli but that only lasted a day."

"You're comparing my situation to *broccoli*?"

Fuck, she's impossible. I pull into the parking garage at the stadium and park, wishing the call would have cut out when I drove underground. "He's not going, Macy. If you want to spend time with him, it will have to be here. And that's his choice. It didn't come from me."

"He's coming. He has to."

"Why?"

"Because you don't get to have everything you want. All the damn time."

"What? Macy, I—"

She hangs up, cutting me off midargument and I panic. So much for being civil. I'm not sure that's even possible anymore.

Coach Pierce is waiting for me outside the locker room when I arrive. He nods his head toward the stairwell and I follow him out of sight.

"I was expecting you to call this morning. How's your mom?"

My shoulders drop as emotion clogs my throat. I knew I'd have to talk about this today, but I thought I'd have some time before it happened. "She's not great. She...ah...she has ALS."

"Fuck." Pierce's eyes widen as his face pales. "I thought you were going to say she broke her hip."

"That would have been a better alternative."

"Jesus. I'm sorry."

"It's not your fault."

"I know, but—"

"Wilder," someone calls my name and I turn to find Paige's dad walking toward me, his expression somber. Did Paige tell him? "Hi Jonathan," he acknowledges Coach before turning his attention to me. "How are you holding up?"

"Ah. I'm okay. Thanks." I hesitate, unsure how I'm supposed to respond, and Coach notices. "I'm ready to get back into it. I won't miss any more practice."

"We wouldn't fault you if you did," Salvatore says, and surprisingly Coach nods in agreement, confusing the hell out of me. I didn't think they got along.

"All good. I just want things to proceed as normal. But I appreciate the support." I want to tell them both to fuck off, but somehow I don't think that's a good idea when I just promised Paige I wouldn't do anything rash. And one of the guys is her dad. But it was hard enough talking to Paige about everything and now the world knows my business? What the hell is going on?

"Totally understandable," Sal continues on. "Keeley said you'd say that."

"Keeley?"

"Yeah. She missed a marketing meeting yesterday and emailed to apologize. She didn't say much, only that your mom was in the hospital."

So it wasn't Paige? I can't decide if I'm relieved or not. Maybe it would be better if it was out in the open.

"Thank you both. But I'm good."

I give them a nod before walking away, frowning when I reach the locker room to find them still chatting. Are they friends now? Actually, not my problem.

Taking a deep breath, I walk in and beeline straight to my locker, ignoring the looks aimed my way. Since having Isaac, I've only missed a few practice sessions, and it's been a while so they all know something's up. I just hope they don't know wha—

"East, how are you, man?" Thomas asks, coming over to pat me on the back, Luke and Reed trailing behind him. "I hope you don't mind us intruding, but we wanted to offer some help."

Fuck. "I'm good."

"I'm sure you're great," Luke cuts in, having to have his say. "But you're still going to listen."

"Fine. Get your 'condolences' off your chest."

"We're not here to say sorry about your mom," Luke snaps back, his expression a mix between annoyance and sympathy. "We're here to help. Amelia and Lainey both offered to look after Isaac if you want to bring him to the game tomorrow. Lainey used to be a nanny for Dylan so she knows what she's doing."

Goddammit, I didn't think about the game.

"And I'm sure I could ask— ah... Bria to help," Reed adds with an awkward smile while I bite back a groan. "She loves kids."

"So everyone knows my business now?"

"No," he says, putting my mind at ease before adding, "only the people that care about you."

"I don't even know Bria; why do you think she would care?"

"*I care*," Reed snaps. "Luke cares, Thomas cares. No matter how hard you try to push us away, we'll still care."

"I appreciate the offers but I'm fine and—" *Paige already offered.*

"You know your sister is friends with Amelia, right?" Luke cuts in, ready to push the issue.

Fucking Keeley. "So that's how you found out she was my sister?"

"Yep. But that's not the point. The point is that we know you're going to need help and we're all here for you—whether you like it or not."

My shoulders drop, and for the first time I look past the surface level of the guys in front of me, seeing the decent men that they really are. "Thank you. I'll keep all your offers in mind."

"Honestly," Reed says with a smile, "that's the best response we could ask for."

I'm tired as I walk through the hospital corridors, but I couldn't go home without seeing Mom, and when I get to her room, I'm happy I did.

"Easton." Her face lights up with a smile. " I wasn't expecting you."

"Why?"

"Because you've got Isaac to worry about...and the devil."

"*Mom.*"

"What? Keeley told me she turned up at your apartment yesterday. Have you seen her?"

"No. Not yet." My body tenses but I try not to outwardly show my anger toward Keeley. She really needs to keep her mouth shut. "I'm also guessing Keeley told you Paige wouldn't let her in."

Mom's smile widens. "She did."

"I, ah...I think I'm going to take another approach with Macy." *Thanks to Paige.*

"Ooh. Are you finally going the lawyer route?"

"Yes and no. I'm going to seek advice but I'm also going to talk to Macy —civilly."

Mom frowns. "Do you think that will work?"

"I have no idea. But I have to try."

"And where did this idea come from? I admit, it's not a bad one."

"It came from Paige," I admit, sheepishly.

"Paige, huh?"

"There's nothing—" Mom stares at me deadpan, cutting me off. "Okay, fine. I like her. A lot, but life is crazy at the moment so we're taking it slowly."

I expect Mom to gloat, but she hits me with a warm smile as tears well in her eyes. "I've only met her a couple of times, but I like her too, and by the sounds of it, she'll be good for you. Is she with Isaac now?"

"She is."

"Then I like her even more."

I do too, but I don't admit that out loud. I've already given Mom enough tonight. Though she didn't give me shit about it like I thought she would.

"You should go and be with them. I'm not going anywhere."

"That's the precise reason I want to stay—to keep you company."

"I'm fine. They're sending me home tomorrow. If I'm home early enough, I can watch Isaac."

"Not a chance, Mom." I laugh incredulously. "You need to rest. But I'll bring him over for a visit on Monday. I just didn't want to bring him here and worry him."

Mom reaches out and squeezes my hand. "I wouldn't have let you if you tried."

"Okay." I nod a few times. "Good to hear."

"Go home."

"Jeez, okay. I can take a hint. I'll call you tomorrow. Is Keeley picking you up?"

"Nope. Phil's coming."

My face contorts but I smile through it. "That's great, Mom."

"Don't worry, I'm not going to tell you about my sex life. But you need to get used to him being around. One day he'll be your new dad."

"What?"

Mom bursts out laughing, and while she's being annoying, I love that she's happy. "Oh, Easton. You're too easy. Now go. Say hi to my beautiful grandson."

"I will. And I'll call you tomorrow."

"Good."

I turn to walk away, but she calls out when I'm halfway through the doorway. "Oh, and Easton. Don't mess it up with Paige. You and Isaac deserve someone good in your life."

And there it is. I knew she'd have something to say. "Bye, Mom."

Paige and Isaac are playing when I get home, and I'm greeted with a bout of laughter making my heart full. This is how I always thought my life would be after Isaac was born...coming home to a house full of warmth. True that I get it with Mom and Isaac, but this feels different. And I like it.

Making my way quietly down the hall, I find them playing with action figures and bite back a laugh.

"Come with me," Paige says in her best superhero voice. "I'm here to protect you."

My smile widens until I note what she's wearing and pause, my chest tightening. It shouldn't be a big deal to see her in my hoodie, but it is and it makes me want to replace her entire wardrobe with mine, claiming her.

Despite the fact that my clothes swim on her, I like seeing her comfortable in my world. In my home. In my clothes. With my son.

I take a step back, leaving them alone to gather my thoughts, but Isaac sees me and immediately jumps up, running over to throw himself into my arms.

"I've had the best day, Dad. Did you know that Paige knows about Spiderman?"

"No, I didn't know that."

"Well, she does and we played *all* day."

He runs off to his room for God knows what and I grimace at Paige. "Sounds like you had a busy one."

"It was great. I don't mind playing superheroes. I've seen a few of the movies so I can pretend to know what I'm talking about."

"Well, Isaac enjoyed it."

"He did. And I know I sound like a broken record, but he's an amazing kid."

"He is. And he has an amazing woman looking after him."

"Thanks." Paige smiles and I note there's something shy about it when she's usually so confident. "On that note, I've been thinking... You have an away game next weekend, right? I want to look after Isaac, whether I stay here with him or we come with you. Either way, just let me know."

Her offer catches me off guard and I pause. "I can't ask you to do that."

"You didn't. I've cleared my weekend, so it would be rude of you to say no." I laugh until a thought hits me.

"You cleared your weekend?"

"Yes, from Friday to Monday."

"But it's your charity event?"

"So." Her brows furrow as she shakes her head. "I've already done the groundwork. They don't need me on the day."

"Call them back and tell them you'll be there."

"No."

"I'm not making you look after Isaac all weekend, and even if I did, we're playing Monday night. So you can still go to your event on Saturday."

"Monday night? I thought football was on Sunday."

I bite back a smile, my gaze drawn to the adorable crease in her nose. "You really don't follow the game, do you?"

"Not previously, no. But it's growing on me. And since you're playing Monday night, you can't use my event to say no. I'll go to the gala and be ready to help on Sunday."

"Paige—"

"I'm helping. Don't make me ask my dad for the details."

My heart swells as I nod. It's going to take time to get used to having a team player with me again. Macy stayed with Isaac when I needed her to, but she never offered and she was never this eager.

"Okay. Thank you. If you don't mind looking after him here, I think he'll be more comfortable. If that's okay."

"It's perfect. Now enough of the 'thank yous.' I better go. Let you two have some time to yourself."

"You don't have to rush off."

"Yes, I do. You need family time."

The words *you are family* pop into my head but I don't voice them, mainly because the idea of that shocks me.

Unaware of my crazy thoughts, Paige calls out to Isaac, and he runs back into the room holding something black in his hands. "Here's your top, Paige."

"Oh, yes." Paige glances down at my hoodie and laughs. "Hope you don't mind that I borrowed this. My top got a little wet when we were playing in the sink."

"Of course not. Anytime." I hold back what I really want to say and nod. But after Paige says goodbye to Isaac, I walk her to the door, waiting until I'm certain Isaac's out of earshot before I lean in. "I think you should live in my clothes." I slip my hand under the hoodie and give her waist a squeeze. "That's one way to get everyone to back off. To show them you're mine."

Her breath hitches, but she doesn't respond, making me smile. "I'll see you tomorrow."

CHAPTER FORTY

PAIGE

I spend the next week bouncing between my apartment and Easton's, watching Isaac whenever Keeley can't, and I have to admit, I'm way beyond falling for that kid. I'm there. And it blows my mind to think that I love someone else's child when I don't even know if I want my own.

Spending time with Isaac isn't helping my cause with Easton either. We're supposed to be taking things slowly, but every time I see them together or Isaac tells me a story about something they've done—showing me a different side of Easton—I fall even harder. And I barely get to see him.

When Saturday arrives, I'm leaving Easton's midafternoon when Hayley texts me about the event.

> Hayley: You better be ready for a HUGE night.
> We both deserve some fun

We've been talking a lot this week and while I held back from telling her about Easton and Isaac in the beginning, when she invited me to go dress hunting—her words not mine—I had to tell her why I couldn't go. Though I didn't mention my relationship with Easton, she assumed my dad had asked me to help and I didn't correct her.

Another text comes through before I've responded to the first and I laugh.

> Hayley: You better not be lying about the hot
> guys either. I'm ready to get my flirting on

"What's got you smiling?" Easton asks as he walks me to the door, the only time we're able to sneak a moment to ourselves.

"My date." I shrug with a laugh, watching his eyes widen.

"Your date?"

"Yep. I'm taking a gorgeous, blonde Australian and—"

"You're taking Hayley?"

"Dammit. Couldn't you just pretend to be jealous for a second?"

"You want to make me jealous?"

"No. I don't." I laugh. "I was joking. But I wouldn't say no to seeing you all feral for me."

Easton glances down the hall before stepping closer and wrapping his hand around my throat, pushing me against the open door, his lips hovering an inch from mine. "I'm not jealous because I like the thought of you out there without me, looking hot while guys ogle what's mine, thinking they have a chance. But trust me when I say I *am* feral for you. All the fucking time. And when we're finally alone, I'm going to worship every inch of your body until I'm all that you think about, ruining you for any man that dares to try and take my place."

"Jesus." I fan myself as my legs clench. "You're brave, sending me off when I'm feeling like this."

"I trust you."

"Good."

"But if you're really struggling with the pressure between your legs, find a room and call me. I'll help ease the pain."

"Dammit, Wilder." I shove him backward and glance down the hall like he did, making sure Isaac's nowhere in sight. "That's mean."

"I seem to remember you love the anticipation."

"I do. When you're *there*." I shake my head and turn to leave, but Easton catches me by the wrist and pulls me into him.

"Maybe you should come back here." The playfulness in his voice is gone, and I freeze.

"What?"

"When you're done, don't go home. Come here. You've got a key."

"But what about Isaac?"

"He'll love seeing you in the morning. As will I."

My pulse spikes as I stare into his eyes, looking for clues to his true feelings. "Are you sure?"

"One hundred percent. Now go before I change my mind and make you cancel the event again."

Easton lightly slaps my ass as I walk out the door and I instantly melt. Who is this man and what has he done with my Easton?

I planned to walk away without looking back, but a thought hits me and I turn to call out before he shuts the door.

"I almost forgot...I hope it goes well with the lawyer tonight. Let me know, yeah?"

"Thanks. I will." Easton smiles but it's impossible to miss the stress behind his expression. He's at a loss with what to do at this point, and it's taking a toll on him. We've got to hope something changes moving forward or he's only going to get worse.

After rushing to the venue to double-check that everything is set up, I race home to get ready. When I'm dressed, I stare at myself in the mirror and curse. Dammit, East. The dress is perfect without panty lines and yet I can't bring myself to walk out the door without panties—his words from the last event running through my mind. *The next time you go sans panties, you better be sure that I'm going to be there.*

He's not going to be there. And even if he wanted to, he can't be.

With a groan, I slip on a barely there pair before crossing my fingers and glancing up at my reflection, squinting in the hope that makes it better. But to my relief, it's fine. The panties really are barely there, because even I'm struggling to notice them under the shine of the burgundy material.

Letting out a sigh, I grab my bag and shoes and run to the elevator, putting my stilettos on while I travel to the lobby. After a short cab ride, I'm back at the venue again, arriving just as Hayley steps out of a cab in front of me, looking stunning as always.

A wave of flashes announces her entry, and I smile from behind her as she drinks in her moment, posing for the cameras. I try to sneak in, hoping to go unnoticed, but of course, that doesn't happen, and I offer the photographers a smile and a wave.

I knew they'd be here; I arranged them in the hope that the photos would bring exposure to the youth charity. Exposure equals money, and we need every cent we can get.

When I catch up to Hayley, she's smiling wide. "I always wanted to be an actress, but I don't think I'll ever get used to that."

"You will. And you'll probably come to resent it."

"I hope not. I chose this life knowing what I was getting myself into, but I guess who knows what the future will bring. Are you ready?"

"I sure am. Let's do this."

We're barely inside for a minute when I hear my name and a shiver makes its way down my spine. Not the good kind. I turn slowly, hoping I imagined it, but no such luck. Christian is here in San Francisco and he's walking my way.

"Holy shit," Hayley says beside me while I glare in his direction, not even bothering to hide my disdain. "Did you know he'd be here?"

"I did *not*." If I had, I wouldn't have come.

When he reaches me—a beautiful blonde attached to his arm—he winks as he smiles. "Paige. Nice to see you."

"I wish I could say the same."

He rolls his eyes and turns to Hayley, offering her his hand. "Hi, I'm Christian and this is my fiancée, Nicola. Nicola, this is Paige and..." He trails off for Hayley to answer but his fiancée cuts in.

"You're Hayley Jackman," she says with a squeal of delight. "Oh my God." She covers her mouth with her hand and gasps. "You're starring as Riley in *Jaded Beginnings*." Her voice lowers to a whisper as though it's some big secret, and she leans in with anticipation.

But Hayley gives her nothing. "I am?" she questions and a laugh bursts out of me.

Nicola's jaw drops until Hayley laughs. "I'm kidding. That's me. It's lovely to meet you."

"Oh." Nicola pauses before she giggles. "Is that Australian humor?"

I don't think it's Australian humor so much as Hayley sticking up for me, but still I wait for her response. "Sure." She shrugs and I laugh again. *Thank you, Hayley.*

"I'm going to get a drink," Hayley says before turning my way. "Are you coming, Paige?"

"I am. It was nice seeing you both. And nice to meet you, Nicola."

"You too." She waves as we both turn away, but I don't get far before Christian calls out again.

"Paige, wait." I ignore him, following Hayley toward the bar as she laughs beside me.

"So...that was fun." I perch onto a bar stool and drop my head to my arms, resting on the counter.

"Is it bad that I don't even know her but a little part of me wanted to slap some sense into her?" I look up to see Hayley's nose crinkle, making me laugh out loud. "For you," she adds, but I guessed as much.

"You won't hear me judging because I feel the same. I'm sure she's nice but—"

"It doesn't matter. She's dating your ex; we don't like her on principle."

"Do we still do that if we don't really care about the ex?" I ask, my brow raised in question.

"Absolutely." Hayley laughs. "Now, what are we drinking?"

I sip on the same drink for the next hour, holding it in my hand as I flit around the room, chatting with guests and people in high places, including Evelyn, the director of the foundation.

Despite knowing that Christian's lurking somewhere, I actually have a good time. Hayley and I even dance for a few songs. But as the night goes on, I wish I was home, curled up on the couch, watching the latest superhero cartoon with Isaac or the latest action movie with Easton.

Not that I've ever done either of those. But I want to.

I have always loved my life. Always loved the spotlight. But lately, it's different.

That girl—the socialite that shared her life with the world—isn't me. I'd much rather be home. At Easton's. Where I finally feel like my true self.

Hayley waves to me as I head to the bar for a rest, but of course, Christian's there to stop me once more. And like earlier, I ignore it.

"Paige, stop." He grabs my hand, pulling me to a halt, and I force a smile, spinning around, shaking myself free.

"I'm working, Christian. How can I help you?"

Christian's fake smile matches my own as he steps closer, lowering his voice. "We've been over this. I just need a goddamn photo with you and Nicola." To the outside world, I'm sure we look like old friends catching up, but on the inside...a completely different story is playing out. This is me and Christian at our finest. This is what we do. We fake it for appearances. Always have.

"I'm not letting you look like Mr. Perfect while your parents splash intimate photos of me all over the Internet. If you wanted my cooperation, you should have helped me first."

"I told you I couldn't. Not unless you tell me why they're doing it."

"Have you ever thought that maybe I'm trying to protect you? I cared about you once."

"That thought never crossed my mind, Paige. Like I said, you're heartless. You cared for me about as much as you cared for your hamster in fifth grade."

"I never forced it to run outside and— No. You know what? You're a dick. I'm not helping you, so fuck off."

"Oh, Paige. That's where you're wrong. You *are* going to help me. And I'm going to tell you why. Very soon."

My anger boils but I keep the smile locked on my face. "What the hell does—"

Christian presses his finger to my lips, silencing me while he laughs. "Don't go far. I'll be back."

He walks away but makes sure to glance back over his shoulder, smirking my way, and I huff out a laugh. He's trying to rattle me. Just like his goddamn parents. And all this time I've been trying to keep him away from their business. Well, fuck this. If he tries to mess with me again, I won't bother keeping his name out of the mud. In fact, I'll grab a stick and write it myself.

Servers circle with sweets, and I only then realize the time, going in search of my bag so I can text Easton. I hope it will distract me from whatever it is Christian thinks is going to change my mind.

But when Easton responds, telling me he's fine when I'll bet he's anything but, my night gets worse. I should have stayed home. Even if I didn't have to help with Isaac, I should have stayed home for them both.

CHAPTER FORTY-ONE

EASTON

R unning my hand down my face, I sit back and internally sigh. "I understand. I appreciate your help."

I've been on the late call with my new lawyer for thirty-five minutes, and ninety-five percent of the call has been negative. Short of Macy signing over her parental rights, there's not a lot I can do. If she fights me for custody, a judge is likely to side in her favor, no matter how much I bring to the table.

Other than being a shitty mother, Macy's a law-abiding citizen, and with the amount I'd have to pay her for child support, she could easily provide for Isaac. There's no real reason not to give her custody, except that she doesn't want it. But if she's standing in court, pleading her case, they're not going to listen to that argument.

"I'll get the paperwork drawn up and sent out by the end of the day Monday. But if you're right in saying she doesn't want the responsibility, then I suggest you talk to her, maybe arrange some kind of mediation to see if you can come up with an amicable plan. And if that fails, that's at least more evidence that you tried to come to an agreement but that she wasn't willing to be civil. At this point, our best option is for her to sign those papers. Anything else will take a miracle."

"Thank you. I'll try."

"I'm sorry I don't have better news, Easton. But I promise that if it comes to a court case, I'll do my best to win."

"I know. Thank you again."

"Talk soon."

I hang up dejected and fall into a heap. Deep down I knew I'd be faced with that response, and a little part of me wonders if that's why I never made the call. I'm no closer to creating a better life for Isaac. In fact, I'd say I'm going backward, and I can't keep going along like this.

Staring down at the phone in my hand, I consider calling Macy when someone knocks on my door.

My stupid chest tightens, picturing Paige on the other side despite knowing she's not there, but God knows I could use her company.

Taking a deep breath, I open the door to Keeley and sigh. "What are you doing here?"

"I was visiting Mom and she mentioned you were talking to a lawyer tonight. Thought I'd stop by since she can't."

I internally groan and immediately change the subject. "Can we talk about Christmas?" I say instead, catching her off guard.

"Ah. Sure." She frowns as she steps inside, hitting me with an expression that screams "what the fuck?"

"Good." I fake a smile and gesture toward the kitchen, following behind her. "Instead of a present this year, I want you and Mom to stay out of my business and to stop talking about me behind my back."

"Ha ha," Keeley deadpans. "You're so funny."

"I wasn't trying to be funny. I mean it."

"Whatever." She shrugs. "How did it go?"

"Keeley. Please. Do you want me to beg?"

"No. I want you to grow up and understand that we are here for you and we only talk about you because we care."

Fuck. That's exactly what my teammates said. "Okay. Okay. I'm sorry. I'm juggling a lot of balls, and they're all going to drop any minute."

"So let me catch some. Let Paige catch them. But maybe not Mom; she needs a break."

I let out a long sigh and scratch the back of my neck. "I don't know what I'm doing, Keeley. And Paige will yell at me for saying this, but I think I need to retire."

"No," she snaps.

"God, you sound just like her."

"Because she's right. You're grumpy enough these days. Isaac doesn't need a dad that's given up on his career and moping around all the time."

"I wouldn't mope."

"Sure, you wouldn't." She rolls her eyes as sarcasm oozes from her pores. "But either way, before you do anything rash, sit down and make a plan. I can help, or I'm sure Paige will. Hell, we're friends; we can do it together. Just don't give up yet."

"I'm not really the type to do something rash, Keeley. I've been thinking about this for a while."

"Well, keep thinking. Paige deserves to be able to say she has a football player boyfriend."

"We're not—"

My phone buzzes on the counter in front of us, cutting off whatever bullshit I was about to say. Keeley glances down at the same time I do, so there's no hiding the name on the screen. But I'm at least able to hide the message, much to Keeley's annoyance.

> Paige: I'm just checking in. How did it go with the lawyer?

> Easton: All was fine. Let's talk about it tomorrow. Enjoy tonight

> Paige: Um no. Saying it's "fine" is the worst response you can give if you don't want me to panic

I smile and of course Keeley notices since she's watching my every move. "Oooh. What did Paige say?"

I shoot her a death stare before responding. "She's asking about the talk with my lawyer. Just like you. Her dad was the one that suggested them."

"Sal did? Did you tell him?"

"Tell him what? About Macy?"

"No, about Paige."

"Not yet. There's nothing to tell. She told him she was helping out a friend. Which in this case is true."

I feel a little bad lying to everyone, including Keeley and Paige's dad. But until things settle down for both of us, we're keeping our relationship quiet. Mom's the only one I've told. Everyone else can wait.

Keeley eyes me suspiciously just as Paige texts again.

Paige: Easton? Please

Easton: I promise. It went as well as I expected and I'd love to talk to you about it. Tomorrow

Paige: Why do I feel like you're being cryptic?

I laugh again. *Probably because I am.* It's time for a subject change.

Easton: How's the event?

Paige: It's fine. Or it would be if Christian wasn't here

The fuck? He's there?

Easton: Doesn't he live in NY? What's he doing there?

Paige: He wanted to see me

My body tenses as anger courses through me. I know she can handle herself, but I'm pissed off about the little fucker's parents and what they're doing to Paige when he's too blind to see it. He doesn't deserve a second of her time. And I'm choosing not to think about the fact that he has intimate photos of her on his phone. Because that's likely to lead to me driving over there and kicking his ass. Paige doesn't want that.

Easton: ...

Paige: Before you ask why... He wants a damn photo with me so that we look amicable. He doesn't want people to think he cheated on me

Easton: Tell him to fuck off

Easton: Better yet. Get him on the phone and I'll tell him myself

Paige calls and my eyes flash to Keeley before I answer. "Hello."

"You'd risk him telling everyone that we're dating just so you can tell him to fuck off?"

"I wasn't going to tell him who I was. Is he there?"

Paige pauses and the background music fills my ears. "Paige?"

"He's not with me now. He's talking to anyone that wants to listen about boring finance stuff."

I huff out a laugh because I bet she'd think that about me and football. "I guess that's a good thing. Is Hayley still there?"

"She is but she's off chatting with... Dammit, he's coming back."

"Put him on." My fists clench by my sides.

"I'm not putting him on. I can handle it. I just thought you should know that he's here. In case someone decides to mention it in the media. Or you see a photo."

"I'm sure that will happen. But I trust you, if that's what you mean,"

"It is. Sorry. I guess I always assume people will think the worst of me."

"Paige—"

"I'm on the phone," she says abruptly, her voice a little distant like she's no longer talking to me. "I get that you want to talk, but you can wait."

"Paige?"

"I'll meet you at the bar."

She's silent for a second before she groans and her voice becomes clear again. "God, I'm sorry. He just started talking to me, ignoring the fact that I'm on the phone."

"Is he still there?"

"No, I'm meeting him at the bar. You said you trust me, right?"

"I did."

"Good. Because I need to go. Can I call you back? I'm going to drink myself stupid so I can deal with the rest of tonight."

"I don't think that's a good idea."

"I'm joking. Sort of. I think."

"Paige?"

"I promise, I'll call you when I'm on my way home...I mean, to your place." My pulse spikes when she says the word home but I try to ignore it —that's not what's important right now.

"How about you call me when you're done with your conversation?"

"I can try."

"Please."

"Okay. I better go. Bye."

She hangs up, and the second I turn back to Keeley, she demands answers. "So there's nothing going on between you two?"

"Nope."

"So why do you sound like a jealous boyfriend?"

"I don't...and why are you listening to my private conversation?"

"Bit hard not to when we're in the same room."

"You could have walked away."

"So could *you*."

Fuck. I drop onto the stool beside her and run my hands down my face, groaning. "Paige is having trouble with her ex, and he turned up at her event tonight."

"Shit. He's there for her?"

"Yep."

"Asshole."

"My thoughts exactly."

"She's with Hayley, right?"

"She is."

"Good, because that woman will defend her friends with everything she's got. Paige is in safe hands."

"*If* she asks Hayley for help."

"My God." Keeley groans. "Don't tell me she's as bad as you. How's that relationship going to go? You'll never talk. All you'll be able to do is have sex and—" She cuts herself off before laughing. "Never mind. There's nothing wrong with that. Who needs communication?"

"Keeley. *Enough.*"

I shake my head as Keeley continues to ask question after unanswered question before finally giving in and changing the subject. We've been chatting about the team for the better part of an hour, and I'm welcoming the distraction, when my phone rings again.

Keeley raises a brow and I suck in a breath before answering, hoping she's okay. "Hello."

"Hey Baby. I miss you." *Dammit. She's been drinking.*

"Are you okay?"

"I'm good. Now. I had a few shots and I feel better."

"Good. I'm glad. Are you with Hayley?"

"Nope. I wish you were here. But I'll have to wait until I get home to you later. You're waiting up for me, right?"

Shit. Something's wrong. "Is that fucker standing nearby?"

"Yep. And you know how much I love that."

"Is he threatening you?"

Keeley's eyes widen before she covers her mouth with her hand.

"No. Nothing like that. I just wanted to say hi. I miss you."

I know she's saying everything for his benefit, but the words "I miss you too," escape my mouth without thought. "Are you sure you're okay?"

"Definitely. You know me." She releases a soft giggle before thanking me with her bubbly persona and then she rushes out two little words that I was not prepared for. "Love you, bye."

And I see red. *What the hell is going on?*

The line cuts off and I couldn't say if it was Paige hanging up or something else, but before I get the chance to question it, she sends me a text.

> Paige: Thank you for going along with that. I needed him to believe that I'd moved on. But it wasn't all for show. It felt nice to say it out loud

My heart thumps in my chest as I turn to Keeley, unsure if she meant mentioning our relationship in general or her admission of love, but either way, I'm worried.

Keeley frowns, her eyes still wide. "Is everything okay?"

I let out a sigh as I consider my options, but it takes all of three seconds before I turn to Keeley for help. "I need you to watch Isaac without asking questions. You know I hate having to ask but—"

"Go. I'll stay until you get back." She gives me a gentle shove and I release a held breath.

"Thank you." I turn to walk away but she stops me.

"I'm not going to hold you up for too long, but I expect answers when you get home. And I need to know... Is Paige okay?"

"Yes," I lie. I'm not so sure that's true. "And I wouldn't expect anything less."

"Good. Go. I've got this."

"Thank you. He shouldn't wake up, but if he does, tell him I'll be home soon."

I'm tense on my drive to the venue. I don't have a plan. I haven't thought this through. I only know that I have to find Paige. Something deep in my gut is telling me to go to her, and for once, I'm doing something for me.

After pulling up at the venue, I park in the parking lot rather than using the valet and sneak inside, hoping they're no longer worried about the guest list. And thankfully no one's on the door.

I spot Paige as soon as I walk in, her burgundy dress and high stiletto heels standing out against the more conservative attendees. And even from a distance, she's breathtaking.

Since she hasn't seen me, I move through the crowd, trying to get a glimpse of who she's standing with before I approach, but they're just out of sight.

I continue to walk closer, and I've just pushed past a couple mauling each other on the dance floor when Paige looks up, her gaze meeting mine.

A million thoughts run through my mind—what I'm going to do, what I'm going to say—but the second she smiles, all rational thought escapes me as I stride toward her, the world around me ceasing to exist.

Paige's eyes widen in question as she meets me halfway, but I don't explain—I can't. I'm not running on logic; I'm running on pure impulse and that impulse is telling me to claim what's mine.

"What—"

I grab her face in my hands, angling her toward me until she's staring into my eyes. Her breath hitches, but I don't let her speak as I slam my lips to hers, pouring everything I have into our kiss.

Paige stiffens before melting into me, her arms wrapping around my waist as she meets my intensity.

My heart hammers in my chest as I caress her soft lips, my hand cupping her neck, brushing my thumb across her cheek.

Everything in this moment feels right, and yet in the back of my mind I know we still have a lot to work through.

Before I'm ready to let her go, my thoughts take over and I break away, my eyes locking on Paige as she stares at me breathlessly. "You're here?"

"I'm here." I smile, tucking a loose strand of hair behind her ear.

"And you kissed me? In public?"

"Well, what the fuck did you expect me to do after that call?"

Paige giggles and the sound sends a shiver down my spine. "You could have waited until I got home?"

"Are you kidding me? That was never going to happen. And I'm sick of pretending."

"But what about—"

"But nothing. Our lives are always going to be complicated, Paige. But together, it will be a hell of a lot easier to get through."

"You like me?" she asks with a smile, already knowing the answer.

"I do." I huff out a laugh. "I like you a lot. And when we get home, I'm going to show you exactly how much. But first... where is that fucker, and what did he do? I think it's time we had a chat."

CHAPTER FORTY-TWO

PAIGE

E aston glances around the room and my chest flutters. As much as I'd love to see him beat the shit out of Christian after the little stunt he pulled... "I think it's best if we leave."

"Fuck, no." Easton stands tall and for the first time I have absolutely no doubt that I'm in love with him. And I'd rather talk about that than confront my ex.

"He's harmless." Grabbing Easton's hand, I turn to drag him away. "Let's—"

"Who's your friend?" Christian calls out and I cringe. We were so close.

I try to keep walking, but Easton stands firm and there is no way I'm moving him.

"Paigey baby, wait." *And...Christian's drunk now. Great.*

"Paigey baby?" Easton grates from beside me, and I squeeze his hand to calm him.

"He's drunk, East. Can we please go?"

"Why did you call me? What did he do?"

"Let's talk about it somewhere else."

"Paige."

"He sent an intimate photo of us to his friend, who happens to have a contact at the modeling agency I work for."

"The fuck?" Easton pulls his hand from my grasp and steps forward as Christian greets us.

"You must be the new man Paige was talking about. If you need any tips on how to handle her, I've got plenty."

Easton's fists clench as he steps forward, but before he can open his mouth, I step between them. "What the hell, Christian?"

Hayley rushes forward, but I shake my head to stop her before turning to face Easton, securing my palms on his chest as I glance up at him.

"Please, Easton. He's not worth it. I promise he didn't hurt me—they're just threats. I need to keep you out of it. Please let me do that."

"Fuck, Paige." His strained voice makes me even more determined to remove him from the situation. He's not thinking clearly. Because if he was, he'd realize I'm right.

I push him back a few steps, and he reluctantly lets me guide him, but his eyes remain locked on Christian behind me. "Don't make me drop to my knees and beg you," I whisper, drawing his gaze. "Because I will. Right here in front of everyone. I'll beg."

A strangled groan releases from his throat, but his eyes alight with fire. "You're playing dirty, Paige."

"Take me home and I'll show you how dirty I can be."

"Why won't you let me talk to him?"

"Because I'm worried about you. Please think about it."

Easton sucks in a breath and I copy him, waiting to see what he does next. His eyes bounce between Christian's and mine before he finally unclenches his fists and turns, wrapping an arm around my shoulder. "Let's go."

Thank God. I sigh in relief, my gaze bouncing around the room to find we haven't drawn as much attention as I thought. Hayley catches my eye and waves, motioning for me to leave as her gaze flits to Christian. I glance back his way, ready for a triumphant smirk, but he's frowning as he watches us, completely ignoring his fiancée beside him.

When we reach the door, a wave of air rushes into my lungs as though I'm finally able to breathe, and it's only then that it hits me how badly that could have gone. Easton could have lost Isaac. Macy doesn't need much ammunition to take him away. And I'll bet she's ready to pounce the second Easton files for custody.

Easton's silent on the way to his truck, so I keep my mouth shut, but the second we reach it, he pushes me against the door, his hand curling around my throat as he forces me to look at him. "I have never wanted to hurt someone as much as I wanted to hurt that poor excuse of a man. Thank you."

"Thank you?" My eyes widen as I stare up at him, at the same moment his hold on me softens.

"You were right. I couldn't see past my rage. Don't get me wrong. I would have hurt him for you, but it would have come at a cost."

"Whether you hurt him or not, you're still my hero."

The smallest of smiles pulls at Easton's lips. "You don't need a hero. I can't imagine you ever have."

"Don't be so sure. We all have our moments. Plus, heroes are sexy." I waggle my eyebrows and laugh.

"Okay, fine. I'll be your hero." He chuckles and the sound arouses me, especially when he adds, "What would you like me to do?"

"Kiss the girl," I blurt without giving it much thought. "I want you to kiss me again exactly like you did inside. Show me how much you want me. Let me feel the tension you felt back there when you were trying to protect me."

Easton's brows lift and he stares at me in challenge, waiting for me to back down. But I don't. I want to share every emotion with him. The good, the bad, the tense. I want it all.

"Show m—"

He slams his lips to mine, stealing my breath along with my words, and a soft mewl escapes me. His kisses a path down my neck, driving me wild as his hands roam.

"God, I want you so badly," he rasps against my skin, the vibrations making me shiver as I moan once more.

"Me too. Let's go home."

"What if I can't wait?" He pulls back to stare at me, his bright blue eyes darkening. "What if I need you now?"

"Not here," I rush out, my voice breathy as his hand makes its way under my dress. My breath hitches in anticipation, but while we're hidden in our current position, that doesn't mean someone isn't going to leave the venue soon and walk right past us.

I try to find my voice, but I'm enjoying his touch too much to pull away. His warm palm wraps around my thigh before his hand glides up my leg, moving toward my center. I hold my breath and my legs clench, waiting for his reaction, and when he finds my panties, he pauses.

"Fuck, Paige. You wore these for me, didn't you?"

"I did," I admit, biting my lip as he brushes a finger across my heat, setting my body on fire. "I did it for you."

"*Christ*." His fingers wrap around my hair and he pulls my head back, the intensity of his gaze making me shiver as he stares down at me. "Get in the back seat and lie down. You deserve a reward."

"Oh God." Arousal pools at my center, and despite my earlier reservations, the second he steps back, I do as he asked, opening the back door and crawling inside, slowly, my ass wriggling in the air.

"Actually, no. Stay like that." I freeze before glancing over my shoulder, catching the intensity in his gaze. "I'm going to slide underneath you and you're going to ride my face while you suck my cock. Right here in the parking lot. While your guests are inside. And that asshole is wondering why the fuck he ever let you go."

I 'm still panting when we pull into our building parking garage, and I can't wipe the smile off my face. I'm learning new things about Easton every day and God, is he full of surprises. I love his gruff exterior, the man he presents to the world. But then he hits me with this protective alpha vibe along with his sweet tender moments, and I am head over heels for this man.

He's everything I didn't think I wanted, and I can't believe how lucky I am to have found him. "I think I'm past the falling stage, I think I'm in love with you." I pause with my confession out in the air and wait for the anxious buzzing in my chest, only it doesn't come, making me more determined to tell him how I feel. "Actually, no. I am one hundred percent in love with you."

Easton laughs as he comes to a stop and puts the truck in park, spinning in his seat to face me. "What did you say to me once? Don't make any life-changing decisions while emotions are high. It's been a big night and—"

"No." I reach out and grab his hand. "That's not it at all. You're an amazing man. There are so many layers to you that I'm not even sure anyone has ever seen them, but I want to. I want to see them all, experience them all. I want all of you. If you'll give it to me."

"Paige, you already have all of me. You've had it for longer than I realized. And you're the only woman I've ever wanted to give it to."

My breath hitches as he reaches out and brushes his thumb across my lips before dropping his hand to cup my neck. "This is fucking terrifying," he whispers, his eyes on my mouth as though it's too big to say into my eyes. "But it's more real than anything I've ever felt. I *know* I'm in love with you. Without a doubt."

He leans forward and kisses me softly, his lips gently caressing mine, while my heart pounds so hard I'm almost certain he can hear it. This feeling of love is something I've never experienced before. It's a feeling I never even knew I was chasing. But now that I've felt it, I'll never settle for anything less. Because this euphoria is everything and more.

Easton's phone buzzes and he groans against my lips before pulling away. "Sorry, it could be Keeley."

He checks the screen and scoffs. "It's not. It's Luke telling the group that he can't sleep. He's too revved up for our away game on Monday." Easton rolls his eyes, but I don't miss the slight lift of his lips as though he wants to smile but thinks better of it. Like he doesn't deserve too much happiness.

"Now, where were we?" he asks, leaning in to kiss me again until I raise my hand to stop him.

"We were going inside. You go and relieve Keeley. I need to change the panties you destroyed."

Easton chuckles again before his expression turns serious. "Pack a bag; you're staying at my place."

"I—"

"No arguments."

"I wasn't going to argue. I was going to say I know. I won't be long."

"Good." He smirks.

We're quiet again as we get into an occupied elevator, but when we stop at my level, Easton squeezes my ass before I move toward the door, raising an eyebrow when I glance back. *Tease.* There's another Easton to add to the list—playful.

Despite saying I'd be quick, I'm slow to get changed, and by the time I'm back at Easton's, I'm relieved to find Keeley gone. I've texted her about her mom, but I'm not ready to talk about my relationship with her brother. Not yet, anyway.

It's after midnight, but I find Easton on the couch, a beer in hand as he stares at a blank TV screen, lost in thought.

"Are you okay?" I ask, no longer holding back when I have something to say.

He glances up at me and smiles, lifting his arm for me to join him. "I am now." He winks. "You're back."

"But something's bothering you?" I drop down next to him, curling my legs under me as I turn his way, waiting for a response. "Now that I know you better, I can read the signs," I joke to ease his stress, and he huffs out a laugh.

"You've always been able to read my signs, and you're right again. I'm thinking about everything that's going on. The future."

"Sheesh. The future. That's heavy." I smile before lifting his arm and tucking myself into his hold. "Anything I can help with?"

"You just did. Being here helps. I feel stronger. Like this is all going to work out. Is that crazy?"

"No, not at all. Because I feel the same." A yawn escapes me and I try to hide it, but Easton notices.

"We should go to bed." He moves to stand up but I stop him.

"Can we just sit for a while? This feels nice. Just being."

I curl myself farther into him and he welcomes me, making himself comfortable. "That sounds good. Actually no, just *being* sounds perfect."

Easton turns on the TV but I don't really watch it. Instead, my mind drifts to the future, just like his was, only instead of panicking like I thought I would, a sense of calm takes over me.

I must fall asleep right there on the couch, because when I wake up suddenly, I'm in Easton's bed with him breathing softly beside me. I smile to myself until my eyes focus and I realize what woke me.

Spotting Isaac, I gasp and sit up, thankful that I'm still fully clothed. "Isaac, are you okay?"

"I had a bad dream. Can you take me back to bed?"

"Ah, sure. I'll wake your dad."

He shakes his head no and reaches for my hand, curling his warm fingers through my own. "I want you to cuddle me."

My heart fills with a new kind of love, one different to what I share with Easton. And I know with absolute certainty that I'm going to protect this little boy with all that I have. I love his Dad, more than I've ever loved anyone before, but Isaac just became my number one priority. And together, I feel whole for the very first time.

CHAPTER FORTY-THREE

PAIGE

I wake to a chaos that I'm not at all used to. Easton's running around packing his bag, Isaac's chasing after him, asking questions at a rate of a million miles per hour. "What day are you getting back? Does Paige like toast with jelly? Will I see Nana? Are you going on a plane or a bus?"

To Easton's credit, he's doing a damn good job at answering every question with a smile on his face, because even I'm overwhelmed.

"Can I help?" I interrupt and they both freeze. "I'm sorry I slept in. You should have woken me."

"Paige." Isaac rushes over and wraps his arms around my leg. "Daddy told me to let you leep."

"You didn't have to do that." I smile as Easton walks over, pressing a kiss to my forehead.

"You needed it. I know you were with Isaac for at least an hour last night and you can't have slept."

"I lept," Isaac announces, making me laugh.

"I dozed off here and there. It's not a problem. It was actually nice. He doesn't snore as much as you do." The joke's out of my mouth before I've thought about it and I gasp, mouthing a sorry as Isaac darts away to grab something.

"Why are you sorry? For teasing me?"

"No, because I shouldn't really be talking about you and me in bed."

"Isn't that where Isaac found you?"

"Yes but...shouldn't we be hiding it from him?"

"Nope."

"Nope?"

"I had a good talk with him the other day. I told him that you might start sleeping over and that you wouldn't be replacing his mom but that you were important to me."

"The other day? As in *before* you asked me to stay over?"

"Yes." Easton chuckles. "It was inevitable, so I wanted to make sure Isaac was okay with it."

"And was he?"

"No, Paige. He told me he didn't want you here but I invited you anyway." He stares at me deadpan and I laugh.

"Okay. Geez. What did he really say?"

"He said that you're important to him too."

Jesus. My eyes well with tears, forcing me to frantically wipe them away. "God, sorry. I don't know where that came from."

Easton reaches forward and pulls my hands from my face, pressing a kiss to my fingers. "You care. That's what that is."

"I do. I care so much."

Isaac chooses that moment to run back in and then metaphorically attaches himself to me for the rest of the morning, happily waving goodbye when his dad departs.

We spend the next two days together, playing at the park, swimming, and watching Easton's game on Monday night, which is conveniently late afternoon for us. Isaac keeps me so busy that by the time he goes to bed on day two, I'm exhausted, but also feeling more alive than ever before.

I thought I'd be nervous having to take care of another human for a few days, but he makes it easy. It feels natural.

After switching on the monitor, I text Easton to let him know Isaac's asleep and grab my sketchbook from my bag, stretching out on the couch. I've just started working on the outline of a new drawing when my dad calls.

"You didn't tell me that Christian was at the event Saturday night," he says as soon as I answer.

"Hello to you too, Dad."

Dad ignores my teasing and launches straight into his questioning. "Did he do anything? Say anything?"

"He was his usual annoying self, but nothing I can't handle."

"Okay, good." He sighs in relief. "Sorry, I panicked. The Mikklesons have our money. The first part of the plan worked. Now we have to wait. I'm a little on edge because of it."

"You and me both. But I'm fine." I don't tell him that Easton came to my rescue. It's better to leave that part out. "How did you find out anyway?"

"There's a photo of the two of you doing the rounds on social media. I'm surprised you haven't seen it."

My heart spikes thinking it's the photo he sent his friend, but I quickly realize he's talking about the event. "Ah. I've been trying to cut back on social media. I haven't had a lot of time for it lately."

"About that. I haven't seen you around much. Where have you been hiding?"

"I've been here, in the building. Guess we've just been on different schedules."

"Possibly. So, what you're saying is that you don't have any news for me." He's fishing, meaning he knows something, but I'm not giving in that easily.

"Nope. Not really."

"Okay. Well, if you're all good and you've got nothing to say, I'll let you go."

Goddammit. Now I feel guilty. He definitely knows something, and I'll put all my life savings on that something being Easton. "Spit it out, Dad."

"What?"

"Why did you really call?"

"I called to ask if you were okay after spending time with Christian."

"Okay." I breathe a sigh of relief.

"And to ask how long you've been seeing one of my players." *Fuck*. This would have been so much easier if I'd told him myself rather than letting him find out by some other means.

"Social media?"

"Nope. A friend who was at the event."

Shit. My nose scrunches and I cringe, picturing his reaction. "Are you mad?"

"No. But I'm a little hurt that you felt you couldn't tell me."

"It's complicated."

"Aren't all relationships?"

"Yes, but—"

"He's about to be locked in a custody battle with his ex and you're caught up in a scandal with yours. I get it."

The sadness in his voice makes me hurt for us both. I should have told him. Neither Easton nor I were worried about his reaction, but we haven't told anybody. Although, after the other night, I guess people know. Thank God Easton told Isaac.

"I'm sorry I didn't talk to you about it."

"Look, he gets bonus points because he was there for you, and from what I've been told, he's not a social guy. But is he good to you?"

"He is. Almost too good."

"Paige, you—"

"I know, Dad. I deserve the world. The thing is, I'm pretty sure that if I asked for it, Easton would give it to me."

"Good. I'll allow it then."

I laugh, while my chest tightens. Because while I'm generally confident when it comes to relationships, with Easton, there's so much more at risk. And for the first time, that includes my heart.

When Easton gets home from his away game after another win, we settle into a very un-Paige-like routine. I spend my days with Isaac, out and about or playing in their apartment, and then the two of us prepare some kind of random dinner before Easton comes home. I guess some people would call that normal. But for me, it's the polar opposite of how I spent my days, and I think I prefer this life.

On the eve of his next game, Easton's mom calls and it's obvious from her tone that she's happier today.

"I'm ready to look after Isaac," she announces as soon as Easton says hi. "I'm feeling much better and I've been given a clean bill of health. Sort of. You know what I mean."

"Are you sure?" Easton asks, hesitantly. "We have help and—"

"Help? Is that what you're calling your girlfriend now?"

Easton's jaw drops while I laugh. I knew his mom was something special when I first saw her with Isaac, but now I'm even more fond of her.

"She's not—"

"The next words out of your mouth better not be that she's *not* your girlfriend, especially if she's there. Hi, Paige."

Easton glances my way as he shakes his head.

"Hi, Rochelle. I—"

"I wasn't going to say that," Easton cuts in. "I was going to say that she's not the help."

"So she is your girlfriend?"

"What are you doing, Mom?"

"Embarrassing you. So you'll say yes to me looking after Isaac just to get me off the phone."

"Oh, you're good," I say, smiling at Easton. "I'm going to need some lessons."

"I'm here any time."

"She doesn't need lessons." Easton rolls his eyes as he frowns, and I bite back my grin. "She's already just like you in that sense."

"Good. Don't ever change, Paige. Easton needs to be challenged."

Just like Rochelle expected, Easton gives in and agrees to drop Isaac at her house the next day to get her off the phone, but it's obvious he's worried.

"Do you think she's lying?" I ask when he hangs up, watching closely for his reaction.

"Lying? No. But there's a possibility she believes she's more capable than she is. Having said that, it will be good to have her help around Thanksgiving."

When I'm away.

An aching pit forms low in my stomach as I think about leaving Easton and Isaac. On one hand, Easton won't be happy if I stay—he already thinks I'm doing too much for them—but on the other, he needs me, and I can always go home for Christmas.

I lie awake for most of the night, trying not to toss and turn to avoid waking Easton, and come morning, my mind's made up. I'm staying. It's settled.

Now if only I could work out how to keep everyone happy.

After an easier than expected conversation with my mom, she accepted my decision to help Easton and even got excited when I called him my boyfriend.

"You know you never once called Christian your boyfriend out loud," she tells me, her voice lifting. "You mentioned it on social media, but never voiced it. I'm guessing this is bigger than that."

"It is," I admit. "So much bigger. And I'm freaking out."

"Because he has a son?"

"No, Isaac's amazing. I'm scared I'll mess up."

"Not possible. I don't think you've ever messed up in your life."

I almost laugh thinking about how wrong she is, but since I never told her about Christian's family, I hold back.

"I hope you're right."

"I usually am."

With Mom somehow on board with my decision, I just had to convince Easton, which was proving as difficult as I thought it would be.

"I can't let you stay. You're already doing so much for me and Isaac."

"I want to stay. Have you thought about that?"

"What about your mom?"

"She's fine with it. She understands. This is where I need to be right now—with you and Isaac. And honestly, I don't care what you say. I'm staying."

"You don't care what I say?"

"Nope. I already canceled my flights."

"I'm sure I could convince your dad to give you his private jet."

"Oh, you're going to talk to my dad?" I bite back a smile. "Please do. I'd love to witness *that* conversation."

Despite my dad being good with our relationship, he and Easton have yet to talk about it. And it's hard to say who's avoiding whom. I'd love to put them in a room together and watch it play out. Dad can be all "don't mess with my daughter" while Easton gets his back up with "why would I do that? Maybe you should make sure *you* don't mess with your daughter."

Since Easton and I started talking more, rather than just focusing on the sex, I've filled him in on my relationship with my dad. And he told me about his. Which, in hindsight, wasn't a great idea since it stressed him out about being away from Isaac.

But their circumstances are different. Easton's there for Isaac any chance he gets. Dad, on the other hand, liked to fill his spare time with more work. We barely saw him when we were younger, but he's making up for it now.

"I'm not afraid of your dad, Paige. We've just been busy."

"Of course." I bite back a smile.

"If it will get you on that plane, I'll talk to him."

"I'm staying. So you'll be wasting your time."

Easton groans and I can't help but laugh. "Are you going to be this stubborn for the rest of our lives?"

"Probably." I shrug. "You may as well accept it."

"Fine. You can stay." Easton huffs out a laugh as he pulls me into a hug, pressing his lips to my temple. "But you're coming to Thanksgiving dinner then."

I try to hide my beaming smile, but it shines through, making Easton laugh again. "I'd love to," I say, bouncing on my toes. "Thank you for asking." I wink and he rolls his eyes.

For the next few days, Easton's mom looks after Isaac while I'm on standby, and I find myself twiddling my fingers with nothing to do. I'd become so used to spending my days with a three-year-old that I'm now bored with my own company. And I've always loved my own time.

Realizing I need to talk to Keeley before showing up at her mom's for Thanksgiving, I pick up my phone to call her and find a message I hadn't noticed from earlier.

> The A-hole: I swear this wasn't me. I would
> never go this far. Please tell me what's going on

My heart stops and my stomach churns as I click on the link to a popular gossip columnist.

We've got the exclusive pictures of Paige D'Angelo's new beau and we have to ask... Does Daddy D'Angelo know she's fooling around with his star wide receiver? In public

---

The article goes on to mention Easton by name, along with the controversy surrounding his split from Macy, and it's accompanied by grainy photos of the two of us in the parking lot after my charity event. One photo taken seconds before he wrapped his hand around my neck, and the other of his hand up my dress. Both relatively PG unless the photographer has more images ready for release.

With my heart lodged in my throat, I keep reading and my world completely shatters.

With the recent reports of Paige's history with Christian Mikkleson coming to light, Easton should be considering if she's really the best role model for his young son.

Stay tuned, as sources say there's more to come.

I stare down at my phone, my eyes welling with tears as my heart breaks. *What have I done?*

CHAPTER FORTY-FOUR

EASTON

I smile as I jump into my truck after practice, excited for some alone time with Paige. Since Mom got sick, we've been spending a lot of time together, but our focus has been on Isaac, and we've barely had time to talk. While I'm still hesitant to let Mom watch Isaac every day, like she wants to, she's been very persuasive in keeping him for as long as possible when she does have him, and tonight, he's staying at her house for the first time, ahead of Thanksgiving tomorrow, giving Paige and me some time to ourselves.

Switching on the ignition, I've just changed gears when Macy finally calls me back after ignoring me since my mom was in the hospital. My body tenses when I answer, ready for her wrath, but it doesn't come. At least not at first.

"I'm calling to talk to Isaac. I trust it's okay for me to speak to him since it's almost Thanksgiving."

Her tone is light, friendly even, despite the underlying sarcasm, and it softens my anger. Which is probably a good thing considering the conversation I'm about to have. "You can talk to him anytime, Macy, but today he's with my mom."

"Of course he is. Will you be together tomorrow?"

"We will—"

"Okay, tell him I'll call then."

"Wait. I wanted to talk to you."

"I have plans soon and—"

"It's important. I've been calling you for a couple of weeks."

"I've been busy. What do you need?" There's some bite to her tone now, and I want to snap back, but my conversation with Paige runs through my mind. Macy and I need to talk. Properly. The constant arguments are getting us nowhere.

"I want to talk about Isaac and more specifically, a permanent custody arrangement. By now you should have received—"

"They won't take him away from me. You know that, right?"

I bite back a frustrated sigh and rub my hands down my face. "Did I say I was trying to do that?"

"No, and I haven't read what you sent, but you are, right?"

"I'd rather come to an agreement. Something that works for all of us, but something that's best for Isaac."

"What if I like the way it's working now?"

"Come on, Macy. We can't keep doing this. You never wanted a kid. And you may not realize it, but you're stringing him along."

"Kind of like what you did to me?"

"What?" My stomach sinks and I pause.

"You heard me and you know exactly what I'm referring to."

Is she fucking kidding me? She's hurting Isaac because I hurt her. I was right? Anger swirls in my stomach, but I fight hard to quell the rage. I have to tread lightly.

"Please tell me you're not messing with him as payback to me." It's what I always feared, but it's the first time I've actually said this to her.

"I was never your priority, Easton. *Never.* I gave you years of my life and yet you were always just out of reach. When it was the two of us, you never hid the fact that football was your first love. You always put me second. No matter what. And when Isaac was born, I dropped lower on your scale. He came first, then football, then me. How did you think I was going to react to that? Did you think I was going to lie down and accept it?!"

Jesus Christ. "Football aside, Isaac's your son. You should have been prioritizing him too."

"But I didn't want him!" Her voice raises and I flinch like she slapped me. But instead of getting defensive, for the first time, I really put myself in her shoes and sigh.

"I'm sorry."

"What?"

"I'm sorry. I should have let you go when Isaac was born. I should have listened to what you were saying and let you walk away."

"That's the problem though—you never listened."

"You didn't exactly fight me."

"I *loved* you."

"Macy. I—" A message comes through while Macy's on speaker, and I pause when I see it's from Keeley.

Keeley: SOS. Please call me back. It's Mom

My hair stands on end as I stare down at the screen, Macy's words merely background noise. *Mom's got Isaac.*

"Macy, I have to go. It's my mom. She's sick and—"

"Go, it's fine."

"It's not *fine*. We should have had this conversation a long time ago. Can you do me a favor?"

"Maybe."

"Can you think seriously about whether or not you want Isaac in your life? And read the documents. I want us to put together a formal custody arrangement, and I want him with me."

Macy's quiet for a beat while my heart stills, waiting. "I'll think about it."

"Thank you." I sigh in relief. That's got to be better than nothing. "I'll speak to you tomorrow."

I hang up and immediately dial Keeley's number as I reverse out of my parking space, but when she doesn't answer, I try Paige next, cursing when her phone goes to voicemail too.

Fuck. What is happening?

My chest burns as I drive, heading in the direction of my mom's place, praying they're okay.

Keeley finally calls me back when I'm five minutes away, and I'm tense when I answer. "What's going on, Keels?"

"Mom had another fall. Isaac's okay but a little shaken at not being able to help her. She didn't tell me, but she got one of those alert necklaces and set it up to contact Phil. Thankfully, he was home and raced over."

Jesus. *What was I thinking?* I've pushed her again.

"Are they on the way to the hospital? I'm almost at Mom's."

"No, they're still at home. She's refusing to go."

"God, she's impossible sometimes."

"Yep. But aren't we all?"

She's not wrong, but I wish Mom would put herself first for once. Though I guess it's my fault for giving in too easily.

"Where are you?" I ask, getting out of my head.

"I just pulled up behind you. I was already heading home when Phil called. I texted you while I was on the phone with him."

"Thank you. I appreciate that. But what are we going to do?"

"I wish I knew."

We hang up as we both pull into the driveway, and I'm running toward the house the second I exit the car.

Isaac's on the couch when I make it inside, his arms wrapped around his legs while my Mom tries to comfort him.

"I'm okay, Isaac. I promise."

"Isaac?" I call out, and his gaze flashes to mine before his eyes fill with water.

"Dad." He runs over and I bite my cheek to stave off my tears as his little voice trembles. "Nana got hurt."

I drop to my knees and engulf him in my arms, gently rocking him back and forth. "She's okay, Buddy. Are you okay?"

"I didn't fall." His face scrunches and I almost laugh.

"You're right. You didn't."

Lifting him as I stand, I walk over to Mom and sit down beside her. I'm about to ask her how she is when Keeley walks in, and Isaac jumps out of my arms to meet her.

Her puzzled expression meets mine and I nod toward the kitchen.

"Hey Isaac, want to come and get something to eat with me?" Keeley asks, taking my hint.

"Yes." He runs ahead and the second they're gone, I turn to Mom.

"How—"

"I'm so sorry, Easton. I thought I was okay. I—"

"What? No, Mom. This isn't your fault. I just want to know that you're all right."

"I feel fine. I don't even know what happened. I just fell and couldn't get up for a minute."

God. "Maybe you're doing too much? Maybe you need more time."

"I hate this. I'm too young for this."

"You're old, Mom. What are you saying?" Mom laughs and I pull her into a hug. "Are you sure you don't need to go to the hospital?"

"I'm sure."

"Then what are we going to do with you? Put you out to pasture?"

"Oh, stop it." She shoves me away, but smiles. "Thank you. I really am sorry I upset Isaac."

"Don't be." I shake my head. "He cares. But he'll be okay."

Phil pops his head in, so I hug Mom and go in search of Isaac and Keeley, thanking Phil on my way past, shelving my concern until later.

When I find them in the kitchen, they're making dinner with Isaac smiling brightly. I sneak past and make my way outside, calling Paige and once again getting her voicemail.

With a groan, I allow myself to break, falling onto the outdoor lounge chair, burying my face in my hands, and trying hard not to scream. *Why does life have to be so goddamn complicated?*

Lying down, I rest my head against the backrest and sigh. I've never *needed* a woman in my life, never relied on anyone to lift my mood, at least not for *me*. But right now, I *need* Paige...more than anything. I'm at a loss for what to do.

> Easton: Call me when you can. Please. I'm not going to make it home tonight and I need to hear your voice

CHAPTER FORTY-FIVE

PAIGE

I reread Easton's text and feel nauseous. He's not a vulnerable guy. Ever. And he's reaching out for me while I'm here, fucking up his life.

I hover on his name, ready to call him when my phone starts ringing, giving me an excuse to wait. Though, I'm not sure what I'm waiting for because I have no idea how to fix this.

"Dad?" The second I answer, emotion wells in my throat. Covering the speaker, I move the phone away from my mouth as I sniff, but it's no use. The pain is obvious in my voice.

"Are you crying?"

"No," I lie, wiping my eyes, thankful he can't see me.

"What happened?"

"Nothing, I'm—"

"*Paige*," he warns and I finally give in.

"They know about Easton and Isaac."

"Who? The Mikklesons?"

"*Everyone*. It was in a goddamn gossip column."

"What was? What did it say?"

"They know we're together, which is fine; that was bound to come out. But then it mentioned Easton's issues with Macy, probably thanks to that goddamn TV show, and that I'm not a good role model for Isaac. I don't know what to do, Dad."

"Have you spoken to Easton?"

"No. Not yet. This is going to kill him. This is why I held back. Why... God, why didn't I stay away? They have photos and—"

"What photos?"

Shit. I never specifically mentioned the photos because until now they'd never been released. But...this is bad. "The Mikklesons have been threatening me with photos of me and Christian, but I never expected them to release any because it would hurt him too much. Only now they have photos of me and Easton and... I messed up."

"No, you didn't. I'm going to handle this. Just—"

"You can't. You need to stick to the plan."

"Paige—" Someone knocks on my door and I ask Dad to wait before falling silent, not wanting to talk to anyone else. The knock comes again, louder this time, and I hold my breath until...

"Sweetie, it's Mom. Are you there?"

Mom?

"It's Mom," I whisper to Dad, almost crumbling with relief.

"I know."

"You know?"

"Yeah, she called me before she booked her flight, asking if I thought it was a good idea. We've been talking ever since then. I was calling to let you know she was on her way up."

Mom knocks again and I jump up. "I've got to go, Dad. I'll call you soon."

"Please let me help. I need to."

"I'll think about it."

"At least call Easton. Don't cut him off like you did with me."

Jesus. I can't deal with that guilt right now. I hang up and rush to the door, my heart seizing as I call out.

"Mom?" I open the door, barely holding myself together. "You're here?"

She takes one look at me and springs forward, grabbing my face to wipe the tears from my cheeks. "What happened? Are you okay?"

"No." I shake my head as more tears threaten to fall. "I'm not okay. I messed up."

"I'm sure it's not as bad as you think."

"I—"

My phone buzzes with a message, and when I see that it's Christian's mom, I freeze, a tension knotting my stomach. I can't look at it, but I also can't let it go.

"Paige, what's going on?"

I open the message and gasp. It's a photo of me and Isaac playing in the park. It's innocent enough—you can barely see Isaac's face—but the words accompanying it are anything but.

Jill Mikkleson: Drop your little investigation and the images go away

She knows.

Another image comes through and I struggle to breathe. This one's not at all grainy like the rest and shows Easton and me fucking during my dad's fundraiser speech.

They've been following me.

And I've been so goddamn stupid.

"I've really messed up," I cry, letting my phone drop to the floor. The photos may not show Easton's face, but it wouldn't take much to figure out that it's him. There are plenty of photos from the official photographer during the night. "I've ruined Easton's life."

"Oh, Paige. Come here." Mom links our fingers and walks me through the apartment until she finds the couch, sitting down to pull me into her lap, like she did when I was a kid. After wiping more tears from my face and brushing the hair behind my ears, she strokes my back while I fall apart, finally letting years of bottled-up emotion flood me.

"It's going to be okay. You're going to be okay. I promise."

"How? I've ruined everything for him. He's going to lose his son. His ex is going to use this—"

"You don't know that. Whatever it is, I'm sure we can fix it. Tell me what's going on. We want to help."

"Who?" I hold my breath, half expecting her to mention Christian's dad.

"Your dad and me."

I release a sigh and shake my head. "I don't think this is fixable." My words come out in a whisper as I think about what Dad said. *Don't cut him out like you did with me.*

I don't want to do that. I love him. But that might be why I have to.

"Please, tell me what happened. Let us try."

Spinning around, I sit up straight and stare at my mom. And I mean, really stare at her, focusing on the warmth and sincerity in her eyes as she whispers, "Please, Paige."

"Okay."

With a shaky breath, I fill her in on everything that happened with Christian and the Mikklesons, including my complicated sex life and the photos they have of me and Easton. I tell her about Macy and Isaac. And while she smiles at the obvious love I have for them both, for the most part, she doesn't give her feelings away.

When I'm done, I jump up, unsure if I can handle her response. "I need to call Easton," I say to change the subject, wiping my eyes as I go in search of my phone. "He needs to hear it from me before the other images hit the media."

"Why don't you go and see him? I can wait. You said he lives in the building."

"He's not here," I cry out. *And he needs me.*

My chest aches as I grab my phone and bring up his number, a pit of dread forming deep in my stomach. I'm just about to call him when Mom appears beside me.

"I'm going to give you some privacy, but I won't be far away. Call me when you're done. I'm here for you, Paige."

"Where will you go?"

"I might pay a visit to your father. I need to make sure he's treating you right." Mom's lips thin into a wicked smile and I actually laugh.

"Thanks, Mom. I'll call you soon."

After squeezing my arm, she lets herself out, and I call Easton as soon as the door clicks shut, needing to hear his voice just like he needed to hear mine.

"God, Paige," he answers, dejected, and I hate that I'm about to break him.

"I'm so sorry, Easton." I choke on his name, trying to swallow the emotion clogging my throat.

"Paige? What's going on? Why haven't you been answering my calls?"

Sucking in a breath, I stand tall and own my mistake. I did this. I need to make it right. "I messed up, Easton," I say calmly, my voice clear. "I said I'd never bring you into my chaos and I did."

"Where are you? I'm at Mom's. Why don't you come here and we can talk about it? We're in this together, remember?"

"You don't even know what it is."

"It doesn't matter."

"It *does* matter. It matters more than anything ever mattered in my life."

"Paige—"

"I pushed them too far. I should have gone to the police sooner."

"Paige—"

"They've got photos of me and Isaac, Easton. They've got photos of me and *you*."

"Then we go public. We tell the world we're together. No big deal."

My heart shatters at the absolute certainty in his voice. He loves me. Truly loves me. But he doesn't get it.

"They're intimate photos, East. Photos no one would ever want leaked. Photos from our moment together at the Storm charity event. And I don't think they're going away."

CHAPTER FORTY-SIX

EASTON

uck. Mother-fucking-fuck.

My eyes close as I fall silent. Paige didn't mess up. I did. That was all me. And it's broken her. She's working hard to keep her cool, but she's falling apart. I can hear it in her voice. The way it cracks. The little waver.

"Paige, you didn't—"

"You deserve better, Easton. So much better. Maybe we weren't meant to fall in love. We set those boundaries for a reason. And we—"

"To hell with the boundaries. We're well past that now. We're together, Paige. It happened and it's not something you can take back."

"I have to. If I agree to drop my investigation, they said they'll destroy the photos. But I know them, and they're lying. They won't stop until they destroy *me,* and with those photos they have all the ammunition they need. If they hurt you or Isaac, I'll never recover."

My teeth clench as I groan. I'm caught between telling her she's crazy and panicking if she's not. But I can't give up. "We can fight this. We—"

"No, Easton. I need you to be the guy I first met. The asshole that only cares about two things in his life. Football and his family. I need you to think about Isaac."

Is she kidding me? "You are my family, Paige. And how dare you say I'm not thinking about Isaac right now. He fucking loves you. If you walk away, you'll break him. Worse than Macy ever did. Because she never showed him the kind of love you have."

"East—" Her voice breaks and she falls silent, her soft sniffles the only sound filling the air, and my heart fucking disintegrates.

"God, Paige. I can't lose you. We can't—"

"I love you too much to fuck with your life, Easton. Both of you. Think about it. Macy will use this. She'll use those photos to take Isaac, and you'll never get a say. She's his mom. You know it won't take much for the courts to side with her, and this is a huge red flag."

Goddammit. She's right but I'm not about to walk away from her when I'm part of the problem. "Do I get a say in this?"

Paige sighs and I can guess what's coming before she says it. "Honestly, no. You can't fix this. You need to focus on Isaac."

"Paige—"

"Bye, Easton."

"Don't you dare hang up—" The line goes dead and I scream, "*Fuck!*"

"Jesus, Easton." Keeley runs outside and pulls the door closed behind her, her voice in a loud whisper. "What's going on? You're lucky you didn't wake Isaac."

"Paige is in trouble, and she's shutting me out because she doesn't want me and Isaac involved."

Keeley's eyes widen before she pulls her phone out of her back pocket. "What kind of trouble? Is she okay?"

"Are you planning on recording this? What's with your phone?"

"In case I need to help." She shrugs.

"You can't help. She has some stuff going on with her ex and his family. They're threatening to release photos of her and me... ah... doing stuff."

"What do you mean, doing stu— Oh." Her face scrunches. "Doing *stuff*. How?"

"We weren't exactly doing it in private, but that's not the point. The point is that it could affect my custody case with Macy."

"God, I ha—dislike her. A lot. What is wrong with you? You're a great guy. You could have had any woman and you chose her. This isn't on Paige. It's on you and Macy."

"Jesus. Thanks for the support, Keeley."

"Shut up. You know it's true. You've made some shitty decisions to get you to this point. And now Paige—"

"Why does it feel like you know more about Paige than what I just told you?"

Keeley pauses and her brows furrow as she folds her arms over her chest. "We're friends, Easton. You seem to forget that. And while neither of you bothered to admit you're together, it didn't take much to figure it out."

"Fuck, we should have—"

"Don't worry about that. I told you. I knew. And that was before Isaac told me she's been having sleepovers at your place. But none of that's important. What are you going to do?"

"I have no fucking idea because I share the same fear she does... What if this is all Macy needs to take Isaac away?"

Keeley stays with Mom and Isaac while I head off to my early practice. Since it's Thanksgiving, we're only required for a half day, but it's a half of a day more than I can handle right now, and I'm a fucking mess by the time I run out onto the field.

"Are you okay?" Reed asks when he catches me massaging my temples, and for the first time, I shake my head.

"I'm far from it. But we have a game to win, so I'm here."

He steps forward, undoubtedly to ask me more, but Pierce blows his whistle, saving me from having to elaborate.

Then I attempt to be a football player. I say *attempt*, because if anyone that didn't know me was watching, I'd barely pass as an amateur.

And I have no one to blame but myself.

The one time I let my guard down, letting someone else in, and she's not here when I want her. Somehow, I've managed to fuck up another relationship and, in turn, potentially shatter Isaac's heart. Again.

Zane throws me the ball and I fumble, dropping it to the ground. I expect him to laugh or gloat, but when he frowns almost sympathetically, I shake my head and turn away. I can't think straight for long enough to catch a ball, let alone care about what Zane thinks. That doesn't mean I haven't noticed that the coaches are pissed.

"Get out of your head, Easton. When you're here, you leave all your other shit at the door."

I nod, like I always do when he uses this line on the team, but today, I don't agree with him. It's not that simple. And I doubt I'm going to contribute anything useful to this practice or this team until I've figured my shit out. "I've gotta go, Coach."

"What? We've barely started."

"I know. But if I don't go now, my game's only going to get worse."

He stares me down, his brows raised in disdain, waiting for me to cave, but I hold strong. I'm leaving with or without his permission.

"Tell me what's more important than being here with your team. If this is because it's Thanksgiving—"

"Let him go, Coach." My gaze snaps to Reed's as he steps forward, confusing me. "It doesn't matter why. Easton doesn't fuck around. If he says he has to go, he has to go."

Ah, shit. I cringe. "Thanks, Reed, but I don't—"

"Go," Coach cuts in. "Just go. But you better get your ass back here tomorrow with a clear head or I'll drop you from the game. Got it?"

"Got it. Thanks."

I reluctantly turn to thank Reed again, but he waves me off, turning away before I open my mouth.

And then I run... For all I know, Paige is gearing up to disappear on me, and I can't fucking handle that. Not anymore.

I'm through the tunnel and on my way to the locker room when I hear my name and cringe. "Wilder!" Paige's dad calls out, halting me in place, and it's the last thing I need right now.

"I know we need to talk," I say as I turn to face him. "But now is *not* the time."

"Of course it's not." Sal shakes his head. "You're supposed to be at practice."

Fuck. He's worried about that?

"I—"

"I don't give a fuck about practice. Not today. Did Paige tell you what's going on?"

My head drops back as I sigh. "She did."

"And—"

"And what?" I throw my hands out in question despite being acutely aware that I should be nice. "Sorry, I—"

"What are you going to do about it?" Sal cuts in, waving off my comment. "Are you letting her walk away?"

"What? Fuck, no. Why do you think I'm skipping practice?"

"Good. Cause she's going to need you. I have to head back to New York for a few days and—"

"Now? Today?" My jaw drops because, *fuck*, this is going to shatter her. Just like she always feared, he's leaving when she needs him the most. "With all due respect, D'Angelo,"—I use his last name like he did mine—"your timing *fucking* sucks. She needs you here. How do you think she's going to feel when she finds out you're gone?"

"She doesn't need me anymore. She needs *you*. And I'm trusting you to protect her. She's going to make it hard for you but—"

"At least I'm going to try." *Unlike you.*

"Don't fucking *try*, Wilder," he snaps and my anger simmers. "Get it done. She doesn't give her heart away often. Actually, *ever*. But you're holding it in your goddamn hands, and I need you to look after it. No matter what she says, she's wrong. Walking away from you is not going to solve anything. It's likely to destroy her."

My rage dissipates as Paige's words run through my head. *"They won't end until they destroy me."* How the fuck do I fix things when she's likely to be destroyed either way?

"I've got to go."

"Good. Go find Paige. We'll have a better chat when I get back." He smiles but it's clearly forced, and I don't know if that's because he doesn't trust me or he's worried about Paige. Either way, I can't dwell on it. I have to find her. I can't let her go.

When I get in my truck, I bang my hands against the steering wheel before turning the ignition. *What's the right move here?* Paige needs me. Isaac needs me. Mom needs me. I'm getting pulled in every direction, but there's only so much I can do.

But if I really think about it, Mom's okay, and if Paige is putting Isaac first instead of herself, and her dad's gone, who the hell is looking out for her?

CHAPTER FORTY-SEVEN

PAIGE

Mom and I share a Thanksgiving breakfast at the restaurant in my building, and then she's hugging me goodbye. All too soon.

I want to argue. I want to beg her to stay, but she told me this was a fly-by visit. I knew. Her leaving didn't come as a surprise. She never usually strays far from New York, so I should be grateful she came at all.

"Are you sure you don't want to come?" She squeezes my hand and motions toward the door. "I'm not saying you should run away, but if you need to disappear for a few weeks, you're always welcome home."

"I am home. This is my home. I just have no idea what I'm doing at the moment." My voice wavers and Mom squeezes my hand again, pulling me back into a hug. I may have made a mess of things with Isaac and Easton, but I still can't bring myself to leave. I need to be close to them. Just the thought of going away has me anxious and struggling for air.

"I don't know what to do," I whisper against Mom's shoulder before shaking myself off and stepping back.

"I'm going to come back." She grabs my arms, determination set in her gaze. "Next week, I'll come back. I just have to go home today. It's important."

"I get it, it's fine. You don't have to come back. I'm a D'Angelo and a Bianci. I can handle anything." I smile but it doesn't transfer to Mom. She sees through my attempt to be brave.

"We're not all strong. Trust me. Don't forget I fell apart when your dad left."

"Well, I got the strong parts of both of you. I've got this."

"Paige—"

"No, Mom. You better go. You have a flight to catch."

Mom opens her mouth to speak again, but I turn away and collect her bags. All three of them for one night. If it was anyone else, I'd assume she was staying longer, but this is minimal for Mom.

"I'll call you when I get home. And tomorrow."

"I'm fine." I laugh to hide the sharp pain in my chest. "Go. Before you get stuck here."

Mom frowns and I can tell she has more to say, but she knows me well enough to stay quiet. So, without another word, she presses a kiss to my head, then she's gone.

Leaving me alone.

And I crumble.

I'm not sure how much time passes before I pick myself up and stare at my tear-soaked face in the mirror. What am I doing? I need to pull myself together. This is on me. I can't wallow. I need to do something to get out of my head.

After changing into workout gear, I wash my face and reapply my minimal makeup even though I plan to get sweaty, hoping to convince myself that if I look put together, I might actually feel it.

When I'm done, I dance around my apartment, working to increase my serotonin, shaking the darkness out of my mind until I'm ready to face the world. I need fresh air and a run to clear my head.

I am a strong, beautiful, confident woman. I made a mistake but I will get through it. It's only a matter of time before it all blows over. I asked Dad to pause his investigation, for now, and I told Christian's mom that I would keep my mouth shut and begged her not to release those specific images. I just have to hope she believes me. For Easton's sake.

I'm not giving up on it, because they deserve to be punished, but I need to wait until things have settled down for Easton and Isaac, until they know what their future holds.

Taking a deep breath, I ride the elevator with a smile on my face and alight with a bounce in my step. It's all fake but if I look the part, people will believe it.

Shaking my shoulders one more time, I walk through the doors to the street and come face-to-face with a sea of cameras, seconds before the flashing begins. I lift my hands to shield my eyes, but pause. That's what they want. They want to capture a photo of me falling apart. But I refuse to let them.

Standing tall, I pop my hip and smile, waving to the cameras, not a care in the world. On the outside anyway. Inside, I'm drowning. Mom's gone. Dad sent me some bullshit message about a team meeting today. On Thanksgiving. And I can't go to Easton, no matter how much I want to.

I'm a positive person. Always have been. And yet, on a day that's supposed to celebrate what we're thankful for, I've got nothing. I'm empty.

The gossip-seekers bark random questions my way, all of which I ignore. And when I've given them all I can give, I wave again, tears threatening to overcome me as I turn around, seconds from falling apart.

I've just reached the doors when one of them calls out, and I foolishly glance back.

"I've heard about the unreleased photos, Paige. Are they all Easton? Or have you been doing the rounds?"

My body trembles as I struggle to hold back the floodgates, forcing another smile until a second voice calls out, telling me they love my work.

"Don't listen to the haters," she says and I swallow a lump in my throat, mouthing a thank you as I spin around and trip, or perhaps shatter, crashing into a familiar embrace right as the first tear falls.

Easton wraps me in his hold as he buries my face in his neck and drags me away from the spotlight.

"I've got you, Paige." His grip on me tightens, perhaps aware I'm about to crack, knowing he's the only thing keeping me together. "Just keep walking," he repeats, his voice easing my pain, coursing through me like a shot of morphine. Even though it shouldn't. "I've got you."

I let him hold me until we're in the elevator and then I spring back as though his touch burns, panic taking over. "What are you doing?" I whisper-yell despite being alone. "I told you we can't be together. You have to stay away."

"No. I don't accept that."

"It's not a resignation. It doesn't work that way."

"Like *hell* it doesn't." He steps closer, forcing me backward until I hit the mirrored wall behind me.

"What happened to 'I can't drag Isaac into the spotlight.' You've always said that."

"That doesn't mean I want to break up. Did I ever say I wanted you to run back to New York and out of my life?"

"No. But we knew our situation was delicate. That's why we kept things casual."

"Enough with the casual talk, Paige." His voice rises as the doors open to my level. "This hasn't been casual for a long time." He holds the door and motions for me to step through, following me to my apartment. "These feelings I have are way beyond casual. So what? You expect me to switch them off and pretend I don't love you more than I've ever loved anyone other than Isaac?"

"No. I feel the same. What I expect you to do is focus on that love for Isaac. You need to get custody. You need to do what's right for him."

I unlock the door so I don't have to look at his face, and walk inside, holding it open this time, knowing he's going to follow me.

"I *am* doing all of those things," he snaps, walking through to the living room before spinning around to face me. "I am," he repeats. "But I'm doing them with you by my side. I'm in those photos, Paige. It's not just you."

"But it's not your fault they're getting released."

"It's not yours, either."

He stands tall, defiant, and I change tack. "Okay, you want to be together? What happens if I mess up again? What if we fight our way out of this but then something else comes along? Maybe I'm not cut out for this life. What if we want different things? What if you come to resent me? Or worse...what if you lose Isaac?"

Easton sighs before running a hand down his face. "Is this your out, Paige? Do you *want* to run? To leave us? I pushed Macy into staying when she didn't want to, and I've learned my lesson. I'll never do that again. But I'm not ready to let you go. I want to fight, Paige. But only if there's something to fight for."

His ocean-blue eyes bore pleadingly into mine, and it momentarily renders me speechless, my words caught in my throat. "Please," he says, begging me to stay.

"I'm not leaving, Easton, and I'm not Macy. I want to be with you, more than anything. But I can't be the reason you lose him."

"So you care about Isaac?"

"Of course I do. I—"

"And you want to protect him?"

"*Yes*. How could you even ask me that? All of this is for *him*. And you. I'm a mess. You both deserve so much better and—"

"Do you think you could ever love him?" He cuts me off again, stepping closer, staring at me pointedly. "Like your own."

I pause, though I don't have to think about my answer. "I already love him, Easton. I don't think I've ever given a bigger piece of my heart to anyone before. And I'm not even sorry that it's him and not *you*. I love you, Easton. I'm more in love with you than I ever thought possible. But Isaac... I'd choose him over you. Any day of the week. I love you both."

Easton sucks in a breath, his eyes glistening with tears before he wipes them away and clears his throat. "How can you walk away if you feel all that? How can you break both our hearts when that one little statement just erased *years* of pain and fear for me?"

"Because if I don't, those fears could become a reality."

"But they might not. We could be happy. We could be a family."

"Easton—"

"Don't run. Please. Let's fight this together."

My breath hitches, and all my resolve disintegrates as his words penetrate my heart, the fight leaving me. "I wasn't going to run," I whisper, certain that if I spoke out loud my voice would crack. "I had the chance to go this morning. But I stayed. I can't be away from you. Even if I am ruining your life."

"You're not ruining our lives, Paige. I may not know what the future will bring, and God knows it feels like the world is against us, but our lives are significantly better with you in them. And I don't want to find out what it would be like without you."

My eyes water again, and this time I allow the tears to fall. With Easton it feels easier to show my emotion. "Okay," I whisper through the tears. "Okay."

"Thank God." Easton sighs as he reaches forward and pulls me into his arms, holding me close before releasing me. "A little part of me wants to tie you up and punish you for even *thinking* about running. But I also want to lock you in my arms and tell you it's all going to be okay. Because it is. I won't let this end any differently. I can't. We both need you too much."

"I'm so scared, Easton."

"I know. But I'm not going to let anything happen to you or Isaac." He grabs my chin and tilts my head up until I'm looking at him. "Ever. You got that?"

"Yes." I nod softly, a genuine smile finally gracing my lips. "I love you."

"I love you too." He takes my lips in a gentle kiss before pulling back and resting his forehead to mine. "Can we go and celebrate Thanksgiving now? I know a little boy that will be over the moon to see you."

Just like that. He's ready to begin our lives together. And so should I be. "Of course." I press another chaste kiss to his lips, my mind still reeling. "Just let me get changed."

While my fears haven't lessened, I couldn't say no. I love them both too much. We still have a long road ahead of us with Macy and the Mikklesons. I just have to pray it all goes our way.

With my heart full, but my stomach still in knots, I quickly get ready, already guilty enough without adding the fact that Easton's currently away from his family on this special day.

After cursing to myself, I put on a smile and lighten the mood. "If only I had a quiet life," I call out as I'm walking down the hallway. "Then no one would care. There'd be no articles about me, no photographers wanting to cash in on me falling apart. No threats from asshole billionaires. But who am I if I'm not socialite Paige D'Angelo?"

I laugh, stepping into the living room to find Easton, his brows furrowed, running his finger along a sketch I did of Isaac. "You're an artist," he whispers in awe and I cringe.

"Shit. You weren't supposed to see that." I rush over to take the sketch from his hands, but he stands up and holds it out of reach.

"This is amazing, Paige. If I wasn't looking at it closely, I'd swear it was a photo. The details. The likeness. The shading. It's...no, *you're* incredible."

"It's nothing. I was just messing around and—"

"Nothing? Are you kidding me? Why are you hiding these away? Have you done any more?"

My heart races as he hits me with so much wonderment that it makes me squirm. I have done more. So many. But I never planned on anyone seeing them. It's my escape, my solace.

And yet, as I stare up into Easton's penetrating gaze, I realize I don't need those things to protect me anymore. I have him. And Isaac. It's about time I shared that part of myself with someone else.

It's about time I let someone else in. Completely.

CHAPTER FORTY-EIGHT

PAIGE

My eyes bounce between Easton and the sketch in his hand as he waits for me to respond. I'm not even sure he's aware of the complexity of his question, but I have no doubt he'll understand when I tell him. He gets me in a way I never thought anyone could. I always assumed it was me against the world. I never considered the possibility that I'd fully commit to someone else. That I'd ever share that big a piece of myself. I've seen the way relationships crumble, taking down everyone around them. I've experienced it. How could I ever believe in something that's about as strong as a sandcastle?

My parents are divorced, my grandparents are divorced. My Mom's having an affair with my ex's dad, so clearly his relationship—that I always assumed was rock-solid based on their shared disregard for other people's feelings—is a sham.

The thought of splitting my heart in two and giving up half of it used to make me nauseous. It wasn't something I ever wanted to do. Yet now, I've split it in three. And I've never felt more complete.

Easton must see something in my gaze because he lowers my sketch and his face drops with it. "Fuck, I'm sorry. This is clearly personal and—"

"No." I rush forward, placing my hand on his heart. "I want to share everything with you. You momentarily caught me off guard because I'm not used to talking about that part of me. But I want to."

"You don't—"

"I want to," I cut in. "I'm all in, Easton. You're stuck with me now."

Easton smiles before his eyes drift to my sketch once more. "Have you drawn me?"

I grimace but when he raises an eyebrow, I laugh. "I have."

"How? When? The only time I've ever seen you sketch was by the pool when you didn't know I was watching you."

"I kind of sketch from memory."

"You what?" His eyes widen before he raises the sketch in front of me as though I don't know what's on there. "This is Isaac," he whispers in wonderment. "You've captured the cheekiness in his gaze, the dusting of freckles on his nose that are heavier on the left, his crooked smile."

My nose scrunches as my cheeks heat. "That wasn't my first try," I admit. "I'm kind of obsessed with getting him right. I needed something in case this all went wrong."

Easton's gaze softens. "We really made a mess of things, didn't we? If only we'd realized how important this was from the beginning."

"I'm not sure we'd have ended up in the same place. I needed the time, and I think you did too."

"You're right." He puts the sketch down and wraps his arms around my waist. "I'm happy we finally got there."

"Me too." I palm his cheek and lean back to stare into his eyes. "Only we still have a lot to overcome."

"True, but we're going to do it together." Mimicking my move, Easton grabs my face and gently caresses my lips, his mouth perfectly molding to mine. It's a short kiss, but it packs so much emotion that I feel it down to my toes. He smiles as he pulls back, and my heart races. Until his smile morphs into a smirk.

"So, can I see the sketch?"

I exaggeratedly cringe as my racing heart changes to more of a pounding. "You can. But I haven't spent as much time on you as I have on Isaac."

"Doesn't matter."

"Okay."

I rush off to the spare bedroom, otherwise known as my office, and search through my pile of sketches until I find one of Easton that I'd be willing to share.

With his mussed hair and serious expression, he's staring into the eyes of the viewer, his penetrating gaze drawing you in, making you feel like you're the only person that matters, like you're all that he sees. It's my favorite look of his. And one I keep close to my heart.

"Wow. This is... God, who am I staring at with that much intensity?" He laughs a little awkwardly.

"Me." I scrunch my nose again. "That's how you look at me."

His eyes lift to mine, and a moment of understanding passes between us. This is it. We both feel it. And it's time we let ourselves enjoy it. He smiles but doesn't say as much about his own sketch as he did about Isaac's and I don't call him out on it. I get it. I'm as awkward about it as he is. And after he's had a good moment staring down at my vulnerabilities on paper, he places the sketch next to the other one and nods. "These are phenomenal, Paige. *You're* phenomenal."

"Thanks." I smile shyly. "They're like my own form of therapy in a sense."

"I like that. And I'm glad you have something that gives you that."

"Do you have something?"

"I always thought it was football. But honestly, football has been more stressful lately because I'm always thinking about Isaac. Mom had another fall yesterday and—"

"Oh my God. Is she okay?"

"She says she's fine. But she was with Isaac, and he didn't take it too well. I think he's a little scared to be alone with her now. And I don't blame him. I don't know what to do."

"Yet another thing we'll figure out together." I curl my fingers through his and give his hand a squeeze. "And speaking of that, we should go. You promised me a Thanksgiving Day feast."

"I don't think I said feast."

"I'm kidding. But maybe we can feast later. When we're back here?"

Easton groans, running his free hand through his hair. "Thank you for making this day so much longer."

"Any time. You know I love to tease."

"And you know I love you."

"I do. I'm lucky."

"Nah, it's not luck." Easton grabs my chin, tilting my head to face him, and the look in his gaze floors me. "You're my person, Paige. Always have been. We just hadn't met yet."

🏈 🏈 🏈

Easton tells me about his mom on the way to her house, and my heart breaks, making me even more determined to be there for him and Isaac. I'm tense as we pull up in the driveway, but when his mom greets me warmly, most of the tension washes away.

Until Keeley rounds the corner and my guilt returns.

"Well, well, well, fancy seeing you here, Paige." She smirks, her brows raised, hands folded over her chest. I cringe until she laughs. "Relax, I'm joking. I get it. We all keep secrets. My issue is that I'm not sure which one of you I want to protect more. On one hand, East's my brother, but I really like you, Paige. So, how about both of you work hard not to mess this up and we won't have a problem."

Easton chuckles as though not at all surprised by Keeley's comment, while I sigh in relief. Once I've committed to something, I'm usually so open about my life, so it felt strange keeping this from her. But like everything else, I don't regret it. I had my reasons. Though I do owe her an apology.

"I'm sorry I didn't tell you, but at the time, I made the best decision for the situation."

"I'm not sorry," Easton adds before Keeley can respond. "She's my sister; she doesn't need to know every single detail of my life. She's nosy enough."

Keeley rolls her eyes, but her smile widens. "I have no ill will toward you, Paige. But Easton, you're annoying as ever. And now that's out of the way, there's a little boy very eager to see you."

I glance at Easton, and he lifts his shoulders in a shrug before pointing my way and smiling. I'm confused until Isaac calls my name, the excitement in his voice warming my heart as he slides around Easton to get to me, wrapping his arms around my legs.

I drop to my knees to hug him properly, basking in his happiness. "You've been gone," he complains, and I open my mouth to respond but he keeps talking. "Dad said you were with your other family, but you'd be back with us. Who's your other family?" He frowns and I can't help but laugh.

"He was talking about my mom and dad."

"Can I see them?"

"Of course you can."

"Now?"

I bite back a smile while Easton comes to my aid. "Not today, Buddy. I think it's almost time for our dinner."

"Yes! I made it."

"Wow. I bet it's delicious."

"Elisish," he repeats and I laugh. I have never thought about having my own kids... Actually I've never given much thought to kids in general. And now I know why. I was saving my heart for Isaac, because I couldn't imagine not having him in my life.

We spend the afternoon like a family—or at least what I assume a family would act like, because our holidays were always over-the-top and staged. Perfectly curated for a magazine. Yes, we shared a meal. But there wasn't laughter and teasing. People talking over one another. Banter.

I always felt love in my home, but this is different. And I like it.

Easton's more relaxed than I've seen him lately, but he still has an edge to him. He hasn't lost his grumpy nature, and I wouldn't want him to. I fell in love with that part of him, just as much as I fell in love with his serious and sensitive side. And maybe even his alpha bedroom persona. Maybe. Just a little bit.

When dinner's finished, I offer to wash the dishes and Rochelle chuckles. "We are a rinse-and-throw-in-the-dishwasher kind of family. Time is precious and shouldn't be wasted on dishes."

I laugh along with her. I like the way she thinks. We had a dishwasher at home. Two of them, in fact. But mom insisted all dishes were to be hand-washed, so we also had someone for that. "Can I rinse then?" I ask, needing to do something since I basically imposed on them and ate all their delicious food.

"How about we do it together?"

Easton watches me as I follow his mom into the kitchen, and when she notices, she shoots him a wicked smile, making me laugh out loud. "How can that man be so grouchy when you're all so bubbly and kind?" I mean for my comment to be lighthearted, but Rochelle sighs.

"Has he told you about his dad?"

"A little. Yes."

"He left when Easton was young. It hit him hard." She frowns while my mind spins. Here's yet another reason for me to not believe in true love, but with the way I'm feeling right now, it's hard to deny it. "He's happier with you in his life. And that makes me happy. On top of knowing that he's out there panicking about what I'm going to say to you."

I laugh again when I instantly picture his scowl. "What does he think you're going to say?"

"That I'll either give you 'the talk' or embarrass him somehow."

"But you're not?"

"No, I don't think I have anything to stress about when it comes to you. He mentioned that you were worried about him and Isaac. The fact that he voiced his feelings was already a big deal, but when he said you were putting them first, a sense of ease washed through me. Like they'd be okay, even if I…" She trails off and tears prick my eyes. I can't think about her health and not get choked up.

"I'd like you to stay around for a while, please. I think I might need backup in the future." I keep things light and Rochelle laughs, but it's easy to see that the future is playing on her mind. And why wouldn't it be. I couldn't imagine knowing my body was giving up on me and not being able to stop it. "I'm here, Rochelle," I add, needing to put her mind at ease. "I'm here for anything you and your family need."

"That's enough for me, but if you could get rid of Macy before I go, I'll bless you from above. Or maybe below—I'm not sure yet."

She chuckles to herself while an unease settles inside me. I have no idea what to do about Macy. But if we need to share custody, I'm going to be there to make it work. And to make sure Isaac knows that he's loved, even if his mother doesn't show it.

Isaac falls asleep on the couch while watching a movie, so Easton decides to stay at his mom's house, making the assumption that I'll stay too.

"The spare bedroom is at the other end of the house," he says in a whisper and my eyes dart to his. "I still expect my second dinner."

"That's not happening. I was planning to go home."

"Believe it or not, Mom knows we're having sex."

"It's still a no." I cringe, shaking my head.

"Fine," Easton grumbles. "But you're staying. That's nonnegotiable." He raises an eyebrow in challenge, and I immediately give in. I'm done fighting, and if I'm honest, I don't really want to be alone tonight. If I'm here, I can pretend I'm not thinking about my own family problems. Dad called me earlier tonight, letting me know he's still busy, when he promised he'd changed.

"Okay, I'll stay. But only because you asked so nicely."

Easton smirks, and like always, it makes me giddy. I love everything about this man. And I've got to believe that's enough to get us through the next few months. Because with Macy and my crap with the Mikkleson family, life is going to be challenging.

But no matter what happens, I won't let him down again. We're a team.

D ad texts to say he'll be in New York for business on Friday and Saturday, but I refuse to let it get to me. If I'm going to make San Francisco my home, I need to feel that way without my dad, so I'm looking at this as practice.

On Sunday morning, Isaac and I are eating breakfast while Easton gets ready for his game, and a feeling of déjà vu hits me. As though I've been here in another life. Or perhaps, it's the universe telling me I'm where I'm meant to be.

Easton's saying goodbye when my phone buzzes with a text from Christian, and as I read the message, I audibly gasp, drawing his attention.

> The A-hole: Is this what you've been hiding?
> Call me. Now

Breaking News: Billionaire twins and owners of Mikkleson Equity, Gabriel and Angus Mikkleson, were arrested in New York this morning on suspicion of extortion. We'll keep you updated as the story develops.

"What the f—?" My wide eyes lift to Easton's to find him watching me in concern.

"What's wrong?"

"Christian's dad was A.R.R.E.S.T.E.D." I spell out arrested so that Isaac doesn't ask questions, but he does anyway.

"What's that mean?" he says, his eyes bouncing between mine and Easton's.

"It's something for adults, Buddy," Easton says, giving him a smile. "Have you finished breakfast?"

"Yes, can I go and play?"

"Of course."

Easton waits until Isaac's out of the room before turning my way. "How do you know?"

I show him my message and a growl rumbles in the back of his throat. "Want me to stay while you call the dick?"

"No." I laugh, pulling him into a hug. "You have to go. He's harmless."

"He has the power to hurt you, so he's anything but harmless. I've got a few minutes. Call him."

"East—"

"Please."

"Okay. But I don't want you to be late."

"I won't be." He kisses my head and sits down beside me, pulling his phone from his pocket. "Put it on speaker." He opens a message to me and holds his finger over the record button, as though Christian's going to say something incriminating. While I agree that he's not the greatest example of a decent human, when it comes to this, I'm still certain he's innocent.

Easton nods when he's ready, and I smile at his protectiveness as I press call.

I'm lost in thought while it's ringing, until Easton's eyes shoot to mine and he reaches for my hand. "When you're done, you should call your dad."

"Wh—"

"Dammit, Paige," Christian answers, stopping me from questioning Easton. "Was that you? Is that what you knew?"

He's straight to the point and I'm grateful. Now is not the time for small talk.

"Yes."

"Then why the hell didn't you tell me?"

"Uh... Like I said, I was trying to protect you."

"Why?" he snaps and Easton's fists clench.

"Because, A-hole, despite what you believe about me, I do have a heart. I just never wanted to give it to you."

"A-hole. What's that about?"

"This is a little ears warning. I'm around someone who doesn't need to hear your potty mouth."

"Who?"

I sigh and shake my head. "That's none of your concern. We're talking about *your* family."

"Then explain it to me because all I know is that my business could be fu— you know, and my dad's been arrested."

I sigh again, telling him what I overheard and what his mom was trying to do to me, leaving out specific details about Easton and Isaac. And to my surprise, Christian's shocked, clearly having no idea what his parents were capable of.

"Fu— Jesus. I knew she was cold but that's brutal."

"Yep."

"I get that you were scared or whatever. But I had the right to know."

"Scared? I told you—"

"Cut the crap, Paige. You didn't do it for me. Giving me a heads-up would have been helpful. You—"

"Hey. Shut your mouth," Easton interrupts, his anger growing. "She did you a favor. Say thanks and move on."

"Who the fuck are you? Her latest fling? You're that Easton guy, aren't you?" He laughs like he has no idea who Easton is when I'll bet he looked him up. "I've got some advice for you," he continues and I roll my eyes. "Run," he says. "She's heartless. Take this as an example of that. She could have helped me and she didn't. Now the—"

"You know what?" Easton cuts him off again, grabbing the phone from the table. "I have some advice of my own. Lose this number. Because if you ever call Paige again, or speak to her, or *about* her, to anyone, I'm coming for you. Grow the fuck up."

Easton disconnects the call before standing up and pacing. "That little—"

"Little ears warning. You've already cursed once."

"God." He pauses and looks my way, clearly frustrated. "What the hell did you see in that guy?"

"What did you see in Macy?" I raise an eyebrow and Easton laughs.

"Touché."

Dad calls before I can say anything more, and when Easton sees the screen, he laughs quietly.

"What?" I ask, confused.

"Answer and he'll explain."

My brows furrow but I do as he says and answer rather than questioning him again. "Dad?"

"Hey, Kid. How are you doing?"

"I'm..." I trail off, suddenly remembering what Easton said before Christian answered his phone. Telling me to call my dad. *My dad.*

"Was it you?" I ask and Easton smiles, confirming he had the exact same thought.

Dad laughs and his absence over the past few days starts to make sense. He didn't want me involved. "I helped. But your mom should take most of the credit."

"Mom?"

"Turns out, her affair wasn't the bad thing we thought it was. It proved quite helpful."

"Are you saying he told her about it?"

"She'd had suspicions for a while, but she wasn't going to push the issue. Until she found out you were involved. It seems her mama bear instincts kicked in."

"Wow."

"That's what I said when she first called me. Anyway, I'm coming over."

"I'm not home," I rush out before he hangs up. "I'm at Easton's. I'm looking after Isaac today."

"Can I come there? I'd really like to see you and meet the little guy."

I glance at Easton and he nods.

"Okay. That would be good. It's 16A. I'll see you soon."

"Thanks, Paige."

He hangs up, and when I look back at Easton, his eyes are wide. "Jesus Christ."

"Jesus. Indeed."

"How do you feel?"

"I'm happy that they've been caught. But I'm also freaking out." My heart slams in my chest as I admit that out loud. "They only mentioned Christian's dad and uncle. And Christian's mom isn't going to take this lightly."

CHAPTER FORTY-NINE

EASTON

I'm anxious as I leave for my game, and if I'm being honest, it's the last place I want to be. I was already stressed about Isaac, after Macy said she'd call for Thanksgiving and never did, and now I have to worry about Paige too.

It's going to kill her if that douche's parents retaliate, and if Macy uses it to her advantage, I'm concerned for Paige's reaction. I don't think she'll run again. We're past that. But I have no doubt she'll take the brunt of the blame, despite the fact that Macy and I have had issues for years.

I check my phone before our pregame warm-up and sigh when I have no notifications. I'm not sure what's better—for Macy to call or remain MIA. A little part of me hopes she disappears for good. But then we'll always be in limbo, never knowing if she's going to walk back into our lives. I wanted her around so that Isaac had a mother, but I'm starting to think he's better off without one rather than having Macy as a part-time come-and-go-as-she-pleases type.

With a huff, I'm about to put my phone away when it buzzes in my hand, and on seeing that it's Macy, I snort out a laugh.

Of course, as I think of the devil, the devil appears.

> Macy: I'm on the way to your apartment. I'm taking Isaac with me

What the fuck? I rush out into the hall—risking a fine for being late—and hit call on her name, grinding my teeth as the phone rings.

"Hello," she answers innocently and I want to scream.

"What the hell, Macy. I've told you this before; you can't just turn up when it suits you."

"I can now," Macy practically sings, and her tone sends shivers down my spine. "I'll be there in an hour."

"What? What does that even mean?"

"It means that I spoke to *my* lawyer this morning and mentioned that you'd been leaving Isaac alone with a woman attached to a certain criminal case in New York."

"The fuck?"

"Haven't you seen the news? The Mikklesons are huge, and it seems Paige has been caught up in their mess."

"She's a witness, nothing more."

"Doesn't matter. It's all unknown at the moment and doesn't look good for you."

"You don't even want him. You—" I cut myself off when my voice rises. I can't do this here and now. I can't—

Luke rushes past and I've never been more relieved to see him. "Luke," I call out, before telling Macy I have to go, hanging up on her.

Luke turns, armed with a smirk, but he must see something in my expression because his face drops and he abandons whatever he was about to do, jogging over.

"What's going on?" he asks, his tense gaze locked on mine. "What can I do?"

"I need your help," I admit for the first time, and it doesn't feel as awful as I thought it would.

"Anything. Name it."

"Is Amelia coming to the game?"

"She is."

"Can she look after Isaac in the suite? I need him away from my apartment. I can have someone drop him off. I—"

"You don't have to explain." Luke cuts me off from telling him about Paige and I'm grateful for that. I need Isaac here, close to me, and I would have begged but I'm glad I don't have to. Luke reaches out to cup my shoulder but must think better of it because his arm drops and he shrugs. "I'm here for you, man. Just tell me what you need."

By the time I've spoken to Paige, and Luke's made arrangements with

Amelia, we're both late for our warm-up, but no matter how much I apologize, Luke won't hear it.

"Family comes first. Always. And I'm willing to argue that point if any of the coaches say something."

"I agree, but it's my family and your—"

"You're my family too, man. This team is family. Except maybe Zane. He has potential, but he still has a little way to go before I'd go to bat for him. He's yet to understand you protect your family. You don't fuck with them."

We round the corner to the tunnel and come face-to-face with an angry Coach. His glare travels between the two of us until Keeley comes to our defense. "Jonathan. I've got Sal on the phone. It's urgent."

Coach's glare turns to a scowl while he's talking out of earshot, and it doesn't take a genius to figure out that they're talking about me. I can't be too upset about Coach's reaction, he's been understanding when it comes to Isaac and my mom, but I told him I had it all worked out and that I wouldn't let it affect the team. Now I've broken my word, and dragged a teammate into my mess.

He walks over when he hangs up, his scowl deepening. "Well, today's your lucky day, boys." He rolls his eyes as Luke's gaze flashes to mine. "Bennett, it seems Wilder's girlfriend had her dad come to your rescue, but I'm not fucking happy. Get moving. You better play your asses off, today. If we lose, it's on you."

"Thanks, Coach."

"Don't thank me. Thank D'Angelo."

We nod and walk away, not giving him the chance to say any more, and I hold my breath for Luke's reaction.

He waits until we're out of earshot before grabbing my shoulder, pulling me to a stop. "Did he just allude to you and D'Angelo's girl? The Paige looking after Isaac is Paige D'Angelo?"

"Yep. One and the same."

"Huh." He laughs. "How did I not know about that? Does Amelia know?"

"I'm guessing she does now."

"Well, fuck me. Well played. Remind me of that when I next fuck up with Coach. I'll be calling in a favor."

My relieved expression drops as I grimace. I don't want that. I don't want the guys to think I get away with shit because of my girlfriend's dad.

"Relax." Luke laughs again. "I'm kidding. You should see your face."

"Fucker. Come on. We have a game to play." *Unfortunately*. I wish D'Angelo had given me a pass—I wish he'd had Coach excuse me from the game entirely, without penalty. But since that's not the case, I have to hope that my plan works, and on top of that, I have to hope that Sal's there for Paige. Because if Macy turns up before they've gone, she's going to need it.

I'm a fucking embarrassment in the first half of the game. No matter how hard I try, I can't get my head in the zone because I have no fucking idea what's going on with my family.

My gaze has drifted to the wives' suite more often than it's been on the goddamn ball, and I still have no answers.

Coach pulls me off the field after my next fumble, and I flinch at the venom in his voice. "What the fuck is going on with you, Easton?"

"I—"

"Actually, no. Don't answer. I don't have time for your bullshit."

He barely glances my way as he speaks but it's enough to throw daggers. The thing is, I can't even blame him. I'm playing the worst game of my career, and I've never been one to let my personal life get in the way. Though I've never had to worry about Isaac as much as I have in the last six months.

I watch the rest of the half from the sidelines before making empty promises to play better when the guys run off the field.

Coach looks my way but doesn't respond, and I'm not sure what that means.

When I get back to the locker room, I risk checking my phone and find six missed calls from Macy seconds before Sal calls my name, pushing through the players as he makes his way over.

My hackles rise as a shiver runs through me. He's supposed to be with Paige. "Sal, what's—"

"I never put my family before work, and while I'm happy with where I am today, I'll always regret it. Paige and Isaac are here. Isaac needs you.

Paige is doing an amazing job at calming him down, but he needs his father. And I can promise you, the team won't punish you for walking away."

"No." I shake my head.

"No. Easton, I—"

"I want you to take me to them, but I don't want any special treatment. I'll take the fine, and if Coach drops me from the next game, so be it."

Sal's lips pull into the smallest smile. "I knew I liked you. Come on."

I only manage two steps before Coach calls everyone to attention. Ignoring him, I keep walking until he calls out. "Wilder. Where do you think you're going?"

"I have a family emergency."

"You said—"

"I'm sorry," I cut in. "I have to go." I may not know why but it doesn't matter. I have to be there for Isaac.

There's a standoff between us before he nods and turns away, launching into his halftime speech. I can hear it as I walk, but I'm not *listening*. Nothing is penetrating my mind. I'm focused on following Sal, nervous about what I'm going to find.

Sal leads me to his office, and when he opens the door, Paige spins around to face me, Isaac in her arms.

I rush forward. "Paige, what's—" She shakes her head, cutting me off as her gaze subtly shifts to Isaac, and she mouths "not now."

Nodding, I turn my attention his way and smile. "Hey, Buddy. This is a surprise." His eyes water as he reaches out for me, and my heart clenches as I grab him, holding him close.

"I've got you, Little Man. I'm here. I'm here."

He sniffs as he buries his face into my neck, and the expressions on Paige's and Sal's faces gut me. *What the fuck happened?*

After fifteen minutes, he's finally calm, but I still have no idea what's going on, because despite me asking, all he does is shake his head. And it's messing with me. I have to know. How can I protect any of them if I'm in the dark?

When I realize we're not getting anywhere, I try a new tack. "How about we go home? You and me."

Isaac shakes his head more forcefully and I panic. "How can I—"

"Do you want to see Keeley, Isaac?" Sal cuts in. And I'm just about to tell him I've got this when Isaac lifts his head and nods. "She just arrived. Do you want to come with me to meet her?"

To my surprise, Isaac squirms in my arms as he nods again. "Can I go, Dad?"

"Of course," I say reluctantly, forcing a smile. "I'll be waiting right here."

"With Paige?" Isaac panics but Paige is quick to reassure him.

"I'm not going anywhere. We'll be here. Always."

CHAPTER FIFTY

PAIGE

Easton's brows furrow as he watches Isaac grab Dad's hand and walk away, but he doesn't ask me to explain and I have no doubt it's because he trusts me. Still, I feel the need to tell him. "Dad was with me today and he helped Isaac when he was scared. I think he's still a little nervous and feels like Dad will protect him."

Easton hisses as his face drops. "And he thinks I can't? Because I wasn't there?"

"No, not at all. He clung to you like a lifeline the second you walked in. You know him; it's just going to take time."

"Tell me what happened. *Please*. I need to know everything. Isaac hasn't said a word. Is he okay? Is he hurt?"

"He's not hurt and he *will* be okay, I promise. He's just a little shaken."

"From what? I feel sick, Paige. I knew I shouldn't have played. I—"

"You were where you were supposed to be. Sit down and I'll explain everything."

Easton nods before he sits on Dad's couch, his eyes boring into mine. My chest tightens because I have no doubt this is going to hurt, but he needs to know.

"So, after you called..."

My heart races as I hang up from Easton and pack Isaac's bag, ready for the game, making sure to keep a warm smile on my face. Meanwhile, the panic in Easton's voice runs on repeat in my mind, as do his words.

"Macy's on her way to our apartment, and something is off. She's more determined to take Isaac than usual."

"What do you want me to do?"

"I've spoken to Luke. Can you get Isaac to the game? Amelia will look after him."

"Do you want me to stay with him?"

"No, I want you to stay with your dad. You have your own problems to deal with."

"East, you and Isaac are my priority."

"I know. But—" He trails off and I panic.

"But what?"

"But your name has been released to the media in line with Mikkleson's arrest."

Jesus. That was fast. "And you're worried I'll bring unwanted media attention to Isaac?" My stomach knots as I once again let him down.

"No." Easton's conviction cuts into my self-loathing. "I'm worried about you. I'm worried about you and Isaac, and this is the only way I can protect you both."

"God, I'm sorry, Easton. If—"

"No ifs. We'll work this out. I promise, but... Fuck. What am I doing? Isaac needs me. I'm going to talk to Coach. I'll—"

Now it's my turn to say no. "I'm going to hang up and pack Isaac's bag. He's going to love watching you play in the suite. He knows them, right?"

"He does. Mom took him to one of my games and they watched from the same suite."

"Then you have nothing to worry about. I'll have him there as soon as possible. He knows you have a game today. He may only be three but he's so smart, East. I think it's best if we keep things relatively normal. I told him we were going to watch the game. He's just watching it live."

Easton sighs, and I picture him running a hand through his already mussed hair. "You're right. Thank you."

"Don't stress about us. We've got this. Okay?"

"Thanks, Paige. I love you."

"I love you too."

After sneaking inside from the balcony, I find Isaac still playing with his monster trucks and I explain the new plan, loving when his face lights up with excitement.

Dad smiles from his position on the floor next to Isaac, and I thank the stars that he was here when Easton called.

"Do you want to bring your Superman Teddy, Isaac? I think he's in your room." He rushes off without a word, and I explain as much as I can to Dad.

He glances down at his watch and curses. "I better call Pierce. Easton should be warming up by now."

"I don't think he'd want you to get involved."

"Maybe not. But I'm going to be."

He disappears into the kitchen while I finish packing, and when we're all done, we head off. "I'm coming with you. We can discuss work *in my office," he says as we ride the elevator, referring to my Mikkleson situation as work.*

It doesn't take much for me to agree because despite what Easton said, I'd prefer to be closer to Isaac. I'd prefer to be close to them both.

As the elevator doors open to the parking garage, the nervous energy coursing through me finally starts to ease until Isaac calls out for his mom and I freeze.

"Paige, Mom's here." He lets go of my hand and rushes toward her, stopping short of giving her a hug.

"Isaac, I missed you."

Isaac nods but doesn't return the sentiment while I watch on with horror, my gaze zeroing in on a car seat through the window of the car behind her, confirming Easton's suspicions.

"Hi." I walk over, resting a hand on Isaac's shoulder, feeling Dad's presence without having to see him. "Macy?" I say with a smile while inside I panic. "It's nice to finally meet you."

"You must be Paige." She smiles back but there's something sinister about it. "Isaac's told me so much about you."

"Likewise." Dad steps forward, perhaps sensing Macy's disguised animosity, and comes to a stop beside me. "Macy, this is my dad, Sal." I introduce them just as a huge mountain man gets out of what I assumed to be Macy's car, lifting a hand in a wave as he settles behind her.

"This is my friend Rocky," Macy says but she's no longer talking to us— her gaze is locked on Isaac. "Isaac, Rocky and I wanted to take you to Disneyland. How does that sound?"

Before I can think things through, the word no is out of my mouth as I reach for Isaac's hand. "While that's a lovely offer, we're on our way out."

Macy's lips thin, but she forces a smile and drops to her knees, surprising me by getting on Isaac's level. "Isaac, baby. You want to come, don't you? Remember we talked about this."

"I think—" I begin but Macy cuts me off.

"Let Isaac speak. I'm his mother. If he wants to come with me, he can."

"Yes, but—"

"But nothing." She smiles through slightly gritted teeth. "Rocky, get the car ready." To Macy's credit, she manages to get her feelings across without once raising her voice and even Rocky seems to be buying it. But despite keeping things happy for appearance's sake, Isaac peers up at me, and I see a change in his eyes the moment he catches my concern.

"I want to stay with Paige," he whispers, squeezing my hand.

"I'm sure Paige is lovely. But I came all the way from Florida to see you. We both did. So we're going to Disneyland. I bought you new clothes and a car seat. We can stay in Mickey's room and—"

"He said no, Macy. Why don't you call Easton tomorrow and—"

"No!" Macy finally snaps, grabbing Isaac's hand to pull him away from me. "Come on, Isaac. It's Mommy. We always have fun. Let's go." She tugs on his arm, and he visibly shakes as he tries to pull back.

And it's that moment the protective anger takes over me. "Macy, stop."

"Let him go!" Dad yells, and I should have seen it coming but I was so wrapped up in keeping Isaac safe that his booming voice makes me jump.

I expect Isaac to panic from the obvious anger in Dad's tone, but when Dad steps forward, Isaac pulls his hand away from Macy and jumps into his arms.

"Isaac, no," Macy calls out, and it's only then that I see panic—not coming from Isaac, but coming from her. "Don't do this. Come with me."

Isaac's eyes fill with tears as my dad whispers something in his ear, walking away without a backward glance as soon as Isaac nods in return.

Macy moves to run after them, but I call out at the same time Rocky does. "Macy—"

"Stop!" Rocky yells, and at first I think he's talking to my dad, but when my gaze flits to his, he's looking at Macy. "Leave them be and get in the car."

She shakes her head frantically. "He's not himself, Rocky. I just need to talk to him. She's brainwashed him against me, I know it."

Panic courses through me as my gaze bounces between Macy and Rocky. Is this for him? Does he want Isaac?

I grab my phone to call the police but stop when his face drops and he shakes his head. "You're not the mother I thought you were. You lied to me. Get in the car. We're going home."

"Rocky, no. I love him. I swear. We can be a family like I promised. Your girls will love him."

Holy shit. Easton was right. Macy's using Isaac. But not only to get back at Easton. She's also using him for her own gain.

"Please, Macy. Get in the car," Rocky sighs before getting in and turning the ignition. A car that I'm just noticing is worth hundreds of thousands of dollars. And I feel sick.

Macy turns to walk away, but something propels me to rush forward and stop her. "Wait. Please."

She pauses but doesn't turn around, so I blurt out the first thing that comes to mind, barely stopping for air. "You don't have to do this, Macy. You don't have to pretend for him. There are so many men out there. Men that would love you whether you had a child or not. This isn't the life you want. Find someone that loves you for you. Take it from me, your life will be much better for it."

She doesn't respond, but her shoulders drop and I know she heard me. She's still for a beat before walking away, not even glancing back at Isaac.

And it completely shatters my heart.

Easton stares at me, his grief-stricken gaze boring into mine. "Fuck," he whispers under his breath before shaking off his thoughts and jumping up. "Fuuck." He speaks louder this time and it's enough to make me check the hallway for anyone listening in. "I should have been there. I—"

"*I* was there, East. I will always look after him."

Easton sighs, his shoulders dropping. "I know. Thank you. I know." His lips pull into a soft smile but he doesn't let it fully form. "God, she's unhinged. What if she finds another guy that wants kids?"

"No." I shake my head and rush over, stopping him from pacing. "I think she's an awful human. I'm disgusted by her behavior. But I also think she's lost. And probably a little bit broken."

"That doesn't excuse—"

"I'm not excusing her actions. But I think you should call her."

"What?"

"Call her. *Please*. I don't think she wants full custody. Hell, I don't think she wants any custody. Deep down. She's just lost."

Dad, Keeley, and Isaac arrive back at that moment, and I give Easton a pointed look before smiling their way.

Easton nods, forcing a smile, and lifts Isaac into his arms, giving him a squeeze before the two of them chat with Keeley. I watch on for a moment until Dad pulls me away, moving me out of earshot.

"Are you okay?" he asks, subtly grabbing my arm, likely checking to make sure I'm not still shaking. I told Easton everything except for how much that entire exchange affected me. I don't think I've ever been more scared in my life.

The four of us sneak out before the game ends, with Keeley going back to work, and Isaac falls asleep on the way home, which isn't surprising considering the day he's had. When we arrive at Easton's apartment, I give him some space to call Macy and head back to my place, getting a quick shower before grabbing us both a late dinner on my way back to see him.

I've only just put my key in the door when Easton opens it for me and pulls me into his arms as he closes it behind me.

"Thank you," he whispers, his voice choked with emotion. "You failed to mention that you convinced Macy that she didn't want this life. She's considering offering me full custody. I thought you said she walked away."

"She did. I had no idea that I'd done that. But I could see the resolve in her body language."

"Well, she said it was you." The relief in his tone mixes with awe, and I don't quite feel like I deserve it. "She hates you by the way," he adds with a chuckle. "Even though she never wanted to be a mother, she still feels like you stole her life. Despite her fucking it up long before I met you."

"I can understand that. I get the feeling she just wanted *you*. Your attention. Your love. Your money. And I got those things without really trying."

"Oh, you tried. Nobody sucks my—"

"Easton, I'm being serious," I admonish, but can't hide my growing smile as he laughs.

"I know and I'm sorry. I needed to escape from the heavy, even for a moment."

"You should rest. It's been a crazy—"

"Don't bother finishing that sentence, D'Angelo. I know what you're about to say, and you're wrong. You're not leaving. I don't need alone time. I need *you*." He grabs the takeout from my hands and intertwines our fingers, walking me to the bedroom. "I want to eat, shower, and then fall asleep next to you, so we can wake up tomorrow and make plans for a future together. A future without anything else standing in our way."

"That sounds nice. There's only one flaw in your plan."

"Yeah?"

"I didn't bring any pajamas."

"You can sleep in one of my tees tonight. And then tomorrow, we're moving you in here."

"Easton, we can't."

"Why? I love you. Isaac loves you. This is it for me. Why wait?"

I think about it for all of a second before my racing heart convinces me. "Okay. I'll move in. *After* we ask Isaac."

"Deal." Easton heads over to his dresser and grabs me a handful of his T-shirts, throwing them my way. "Try these. One of them should work."

He drags his own tee over his head, drawing my gaze to his abs before falling back onto the bed and making himself comfortable. "I'll get dinner ready; you get changed."

Dragging my eyes away from his mesmerizing body, I do as I'm told, disappearing into the en suite to get changed before washing my face.

When I'm done, I call out, "Sorry, Easton," as I run my fingers through my hair. "I don't think I'll be bringing any of my clothes here. I much prefer yours." I walk out in nothing but his white tee and my black thong, lifting my arms so he gets a good view.

His eyes roam my body as he groans. "Take them all. They're yours. I don't want to see you in anything else. Ever."

He jumps up from the bed and curls his hands under the tee, grabbing my ass before kissing my neck.

"I thought you said you wanted to sleep. And what about dinner?"

"Sleep is overrated. We've got a lifetime to catch up."

"And dinner?"

"I'm still eating. I've just changed what's on the menu."

CHAPTER FIFTY-ONE

PAIGE

Over the next couple of weeks, Easton talks to his lawyer regularly, and it's a beautiful day when he finally gets the official confirmation that Macy's agreed to relinquish her rights to Isaac. All that's left to do is sign the paperwork.

After fighting for so long, Easton's almost free. But more than that, as soon as he has that paperwork in his hands, he'll no longer have to worry about her showing up to take Isaac away again.

My little, or not so little issue is going to take more time. I was reluctant to leave Isaac and Easton after everything that happened, so I made my statement with the San Francisco police department instead of flying to New York, and it took them a day to send it through, giving Christian's mom enough time to threaten me again, assuming I hadn't spoken with them yet.

Fortunately, after Macy's verbal agreement with Easton, the Mikkleson threats no longer concerned me because Isaac was safe. But that didn't mean I wanted the images released. And thankfully, Dad ensured that wouldn't happen.

Unsurprisingly, Christian's dad and uncle were released on bail. But with the evidence stacked against them, I doubt they'll get away with it. It turns out, the initial arrests were made after Mom recorded a conversation between herself and Christian's dad with him alluding to what they were doing, and on top of that, Christian was now cooperating, giving police access to anything they needed. In the end, my statement meant nothing except to prove that Christian's mom and aunt knew what was going on.

Despite Easton telling me I shouldn't care, I do feel bad for Christian, just like I feel a little bad for Macy. But I have more important things to focus on, and neither of them are our problem anymore.

Dad laughs from across the table as he and Easton talk. He's been popping in a lot lately, checking in on us, and I have to admit, it's nice to have him around. He even joked about Isaac calling him "Pops," and when it stuck, his expression told me everything. He loves Isaac just as much as the rest of us do. And he and Easton's mom get along great. We've been seeing her any chance we get.

Mom's been back for another visit too, as promised, and has plans to come back again next week, complaining that she's missing out.

My brother even threatened to visit, but I'm hoping Isaac's a little older when that happens. The last thing we need is for my wayward brother to influence him.

After dinner, Easton and Isaac head off to his room to run through their bedtime routine, and my dad takes that as his cue to leave. "He's a great kid, Paige," he says as I walk him to the door, making me laugh.

"You say that like I had something to do with that."

"You may not have raised him to this point, but something tells me that's going to change in the future."

I swallow a lump in my throat as my nose scrunches. "What do I know about raising a three-year-old?"

"None of us know what we're doing, Paige. If anyone tells you otherwise, they're lying. You just do the best you can. And in your case, don't follow in your father's footsteps. It took me too long to realize my family should come before my career."

"At least you got there eventually. It's been nice having you around. I know I keep saying this, but thank you again for your help with Macy and the Mikklesons. I don't know what we would have done without you."

"You have to stop thanking me, Paige. I did what any dad would do, but at the same time, I know you would have figured it out without me. You're both smart, determined, and protective. But I'm glad I could help. I would have felt worthless if I couldn't. You'll understand as Isaac gets older."

"Actually, Dad, I understand now." My mind flashes back to Easton not being there for Isaac and I get it. I've never seen him so devastated. But he can't be there all the time, and neither can my father. That's why we're a team.

"Good. I'm looking forward to getting to know him better. Honestly, I wasn't sure you'd give me a grandchild. So thank you."

He winks while my jaw drops. If Isaac's his grandson, that would make him my son. And while that's a scary thought, it's also pretty wonderful.

"Love you, Dad."

"Love you too, Kid."

When he's gone, I grab a drink and wait for Easton on the couch, sitting bolt upright so I don't fall asleep. It's been a crazy couple of weeks, and I honestly don't know how Easton's still standing.

It's another thirty minutes before he appears, and it's easy to see he's exhausted—physically and emotionally. We've both been through so much and he's barely slept. Neither of us has. But tonight, we will. And it's going to be peaceful.

Macy's finally signing the papers, I've made my statement and stepped away from the Mikkleson drama, and my dad's threatened more legal action if any images are released. Things are finally settling down for us, giving us a chance to enjoy being a couple. A *family*.

"Is he asleep?" I ask, patting the seat beside me.

Easton sighs, running a hand through his messy brown hair. "I think so. But I guess we'll—"

"Daad," Isaac calls out before Easton can finish his sentence, and I bite back a smile while he groans. But he doesn't get the chance to turn around, when Isaac calls out again. "I want Paige."

Easton smirks as he raises a brow. "You heard him. He wants you."

I roll my eyes jokingly, but the truth is that I love it.

"I'll be right back." I squeeze his shoulder as I stand. "Give me five minutes. I'll get it done." I wink and Easton laughs.

"Good luck with that."

For a few days after our run-in with Macy, Isaac wasn't himself, but we reassured him that he was safe and promised we'd be there for him, and for the past week he's been happy again.

But we're both conscious of how badly it may have affected him, so we're keeping our eyes open and making sure he knows he's allowed to feel any and all emotions. The last thing we want is for him to be masking his feelings, thinking that's what we want.

Despite joking that I was better at bedtime than Easton, it takes me almost an hour to get him off to sleep, though I savor every second of him snuggling against me. "God, I love that kid," I announce, as I finally sit down, patting Easton's leg.

He laughs before pressing a kiss to my head. "God, I love you. And since we're finally alone..." He snakes his hand under my top and squeezes one of my breasts, groaning as he rolls me onto my back. "We've been too busy lately. I've missed these."

"What about me?"

"Sure, I've missed you too."

I laugh, playfully pushing him away as his phone blares with a string of messages.

"Someone's insistent." I gesture toward his cell on the coffee table. "I think you better check that."

Easton groans exasperatedly. "It'll be the fucking group text. They were messaging today too. I really should have shut it down."

"You don't mean that. They've all had your back lately."

"I know, but I'm not in the mood right now. I'm in the mood for you." He buries his face in my neck but I push him back again. "Stop. They're good guys and they care about you. Plus I happen to love the wives, girlfriends, and friends, so don't piss off their guys."

"That ship sailed a long time ago."

"Why doesn't that surprise me? What are they saying?"

Easton checks his phone and actually smiles before showing me his screen.

> LUKE CHANGED THE NAME OF THE GROUP TO "REED'S SUPPORT GROUP."

"*Finally*. Reed's a good guy, but it's about time someone else suffered."

"Because you were suffering so badly."

"Shhh. This is a victory. Let me have it."

"Okay. Go ahead."

> Easton: Hell-fucking-yes but I still think this chat is unnecessary.

EASTON LEFT THE GROUP

LUKE ADDED EASTON

My phone buzzes several times and I burst out laughing. "Ooh, the girls' chat is going off now too."

"The girls' chat?"

"Yep. Hayley started it after the stuff with Macy. Not that they knew what happened, but it was called Paige's support group, so something tells me that they all talk." I grimace and Easton laughs.

"I don't doubt that. Luke loves to gossip."

"That's funny, because Amelia is the least gossipy person I know."

"That's probably why they work. They're so different. Anyway, what does your chat say? Bria's not in the group, is she?"

"No, but look at you remembering her name."

"I know." He smirks. "I'm growing."

I roll my eyes and check my phone.

AMELIA CHANGED THE NAME OF THE GROUP TO "REED'S SUPPORT GROUP."

My hand flies to my mouth as a laugh bursts out of me.

"What happened?" Easton tries to see my phone but I hide it as I keep reading.

> Amelia: So… Luke tells me Reed needs our help. He's fed up with the friend zone

> Lainey: He actually said that? To Luke of all people? No offense, Amelia

> Amelia: None taken. I said the same thing to Luke. I couldn't believe he'd volunteer that information

I'll admit, I don't know Reed that well, but from what Easton's told me about him, I never pictured him as the type to voice his own issues. He's more likely to help others.

> Keeley: Are we sure this didn't come from Luke needing another project now that Easton's good?

> Amelia: I wondered that but I have my ways of getting the truth out of Luke, and it was definitely Reed

I laugh at Amelia's response, and Easton eyes me suspiciously, making me laugh harder.

"I'll show you in a second. I promise."

> Hayley: Well I, for one, think it's great. Bria's lovely and all, but a guy like Reed shouldn't be sidelined. How can we help him?

> Keeley: I've got an idea

> Amelia: Ooh what?

My eyes widen when I see her response, and Easton groans from beside me until I show him my phone. It takes him all of thirty seconds to read through the messages, and when he's done, I've never seen him laugh so hard. A very un-Easton like response.

"I think this is going to be fun."

Epilogue One

PAIGE

SIX MONTHS LATER

Easton drops his bag to the floor as he slumps against our bedroom door, his expression weary. I toss my book onto the bedside table and open my arms for him, welcoming him into my hold when he drags himself over.

Lying down, he rests his head on my chest and sighs. He doesn't need to tell me what happened—my dad called on his way home—so I give him the moment of silence he desperately needs.

The new GM quit at the end of last season, right before their playoff loss, and this time it didn't come from my dad. Apparently, he and Coach Pierce hadn't seen eye to eye, and when he took his concerns to my dad and the board, they all agreed they wanted Pierce to stay. Understandably. With how well the team was playing, they'd be crazy to fire their head coach.

Still, losing another GM so soon didn't look good for the team, but it was barely mentioned in the media. Until now. With the new season starting, it's become the hot topic again. And it's stressing my dad out. And Easton by the looks of things. Although he's stressing for an entirely different reason, and I give him about three minutes before he mentions it. We don't hold back our thoughts and feelings anymore. We're a team. We share everything.

In fact, sometimes I share *too* much and take enjoyment out of his reactions. Especially when it elicits a quiet groan from the back of his throat. Like when I told him I thought his mom was glowing and was ninety-nine percent sure it was due to her great sex life. Whoops.

Speaking of... Easton releases a guttural groan as he buries his face into my chest before rolling onto his back, throwing his hand over his eyes as he speaks. "Another day, another scandal for the Storm." He blows out a breath as he half laughs. "Do you know people are saying they want a second season of that damn show? They want to know all the crazy that's been going on behind the scenes."

He doesn't mention Macy specifically, but I know he doesn't want that brought up again, not now that she's finally out of our life.

"Dad will never sign off on that." I wriggle down the bed until we're face-to-face and grab his chin, forcing him to look at me. "That part of your life is closed. I can promise you that." I don't even have to ask Dad if that's true. He still curses every time someone brings it up.

Easton sighs and looks away. "I know he's got our back in that sense, but just the fact that there's controversy again makes me wonder if I should throw in the towel. Step away before it blows up in all our faces."

And there it is. That's what I've been waiting for.

After their AFC championship loss, Easton mentioned retiring again, and I said then what I'm about to say now. "If that's truly what you want to do, I will support you one hundred percent. But if there's any part of you that still wants to play football, Isaac and I have got this. We're a team that supports you, just as much as you and I are a team looking out for Isaac."

Easton sighs as he reaches out to squeeze my hand.

After his mom's fall at Thanksgiving, I stepped away from my modeling and charity commitments—despite Easton's reservations—only helping my dad, and took over the care of Isaac while Easton was working. And I love it. He's going to be in school soon, so I consider it my time to bond with him. To really get to know him since I'm already behind. I missed out on the first three years of his life, and I refuse to miss any more.

We visit Easton's mom at least once a week too, but I stay and work in her home office, giving her and Isaac a chance to spend time alone together without anyone stressing. I know it upsets her. We've spoken about it often —she'd much rather be able to live her life as though nothing has changed —but she understands that it's not only Easton that worries. Isaac still asks if she'll be okay every time we visit.

And because of that, he's been seeing one of Thomas's friends who's a child psychologist... And he loves him. He's really grown in the last couple of months.

"How are you real?" Easton asks, lifting to his elbow as he looks down at me with awe in his expression. "We've been together for months and I'm still asking myself that."

"You once said that you were just *you* and I'm the same. I'm just me." I shrug, feeling uncomfortable under his intense gaze. I don't think I'm doing anything special—anything different from millions of others—and yet this feels more important than anything I've ever done.

"Well, you're pretty special to me. I—"

Easton's phone rings, cutting him off, but since it's out of his reach he ignores it. He's about to continue whatever he was going to say when my phone rings instead. And it's Keeley.

"I think she wants you." I hand him the phone and sit up, a nervous energy running through me.

"Keels?" he answers on speaker, his face dropping when she responds.

"I'm worried about Mom."

"What happened?"

Keeley sighs. "She said she was fine, but I was just talking to her and I swear she was slurring some of her words. Not all of them but—"

"Enough to worry you?" Easton cuts Keeley off and runs a hand through his hair as he releases a breath through his nose. "She needs to go back to her specialist."

"I know, but try telling her that." Easton's face scrunches. Rochelle is as stubborn as they come where her health is concerned. "Maybe Paige can talk to her? It's harder to argue with someone that isn't a family member."

"Have you met Mom?" Easton counters. "She'll argue with anyone. And Paige *is* a family member. I hope she slaps you for that comment."

He turns my way with wide eyes, and I laugh. Lucky for him, I knew what she meant.

Easton and Keeley fall silent, and I almost take the phone away to speak for them, until I realize they're both lost in thought. They'll never admit how alike they are and deny it when I point it out. "I don't know what to do, Keels," Easton says after the longest pause, "but we can't sit still and do nothing."

"I know. Are you around tomorrow? Family day?"

Easton glances my way, and I nod. "We'll be there."

He hangs up and sinks into the bed, looking more defeated than he did when he first walked in. He's quiet until he reaches out and pulls me into his arms. "I don't want to lose her, Paige. It's going to kill Isaac."

"Just Isaac?"

He hides his face in my neck and shakes his head. "It's going to kill me too."

"Whatever happens, we're going to get through this together. But for now, we need to keep acting like she's well. She deserves that."

Easton groans and I laugh. "I both love and hate when you're right, D'Angelo. Maybe forcing her to see specialists isn't going to help. She knows what it is."

"Exactly."

"So instead, we should, I don't know...take more photos, be more present, try and keep things as normal as possible but also help in any way we can."

"I think she'll like that. And...ah...speaking of photos,"—I grimace—"I did a thing."

Easton sits up and frowns in confusion. "You did a thing?"

"Yeah. And I wasn't sure if I'd ever share it, but I think your mom might like it."

"What is it?"

Instead of explaining, I get up and head out to the living room, grabbing my sketchbook from the drawer in the desk I've taken over. As I walk back to the bedroom, my breath catches, my heart slamming in my chest. I've shown Easton my sketches before, but this one is a little different, and I've been holding on to it for a while.

Forcing out a shaky breath, I climb onto the bed and hand over my book. "Have a look at the back page."

Easton flips it over without saying a word, and when he opens the cover, he freezes, his jaw agape, seemingly lost for words. And while I'm certain that's a positive response, it still freaks me out.

"What do you think?" My legs bounce as I ask, and Easton places his palm on my knee without taking his eyes off the sketch, instantly calming me.

"This... The... I have no words, Paige. Except maybe when? Or how?"

"I started it when I first saw them at the pool. And the rest was done from memory."

Easton shakes his head, his gaze locked on the sketch I drew of his mom and Isaac laughing in the pool. She's holding him and he's staring at her like she hung the moon and personally lit all the stars surrounding it. I have to admit, it's the best piece I've ever created. But it's intimate and raw and maybe a little intrusive. I wasn't sure I'd ever share it.

"You can say no, but... ah... Do you think your mom would want it?"

"Want it? Paige, if my mom knew this existed, she'd be breaking down our door to steal it. Do you realize how incredible this is?"

"I know it's special, yes." I feel myself blush and laugh. "God, I've had my tits out in a magazine, but sharing this makes me feel incredibly vulnerable."

I cover my face with my hands, but Easton pulls them away, his thoughtful eyes locking with mine.

"It's because your heart and soul are here, in this work. It's... I—" His voice wavers and he pauses, shaking his head as his eyes water. "Dammit, Paige." I don't say a word as he wipes at the tears threatening to fall. "They should have had decades together, not years. I hate this. And I'm so fucking scared."

"I know." I curl my arms around him and press a kiss to his temple. "Me too."

I bounce on my toes as Rochelle wordlessly stares at the sketch, completely still. And since I can't see her face, I have no idea what she's feeling until she glances up and her tears summon my own.

"Thhhank you, Paige. This is... in-incredible," her voice cracks and I smile. "Sorry. I'm a little lost for words... but... this means the world to me."

She reaches out and I take her hand, noting the shake in her palm. "I wanted to do a family one too, but I tend to draw people I know or see often. And I haven't met Addison yet."

"That's great and all, but this is more sp-special. I've spent years looking at th-their annoying faces." Her words falter but they're not as slurred as I was worried they'd be, and her spirits are still high. We both laugh, knowing she's joking, but after a few seconds, her face drops.

"I think I could s-spend a lifetime with Isaac and never get over it. No amount of dayss will ever be enough and I-I hate that it'll be cut short. But more than that, I hate that I'm aware of it. I'd rather be kept in the dark and have it happen out of nowhere."

She laughs again and I smile. Easton told me she jokes when she's emotional.

"I can bring him around more often if you'd like. Easton wanted to give you time to yourself, but I'm happy to come around. I don't want you to think I'm monopolizing his time."

"Oh, Paige. I don't think that. I love seeing the two of you together, hearing I-Isaac talk about you. You're the mother he always needed, the mother he deserved."

My stomach knots but I smile through it. "I don't know about that, but I'm trying. And praying I don't fail them."

"You won't. I've never seen those boys so happy and that's all thanks to you." The slower she speaks the clearer it becomes, and I can see her working hard but also willing me to continue. She doesn't want us to act differently around her.

"I love them both so much. All of you. But sometimes I wonder if that's enough." *If I'm doing enough.*

"Easton told me you don't want to get married." Rochelle misunderstands me, or perhaps she knows me better than I know myself because when she says it, I realize it's been playing on my mind.

"Oh. Ah..." God. Maybe I'm being selfish. Dad always said I was a brat. "I'm sorry," I whisper, not knowing what else to say.

"Why are you sorry? I made the same decision. And so did Easton. Why do you think he and Macy never married? He's cynical because of me and his dad. True, we never tied the knot, but it wasn't because we didn't love each other. God, I loved that man more than I've loved anyone else, apart from my kids and Isaac. At least, until I met Phil. Marriage wasn't something I ever wanted. I *still* don't want it. The thought of being locked into something..." She shivers and I panic.

"That's not it. I...I don't mind being locked into something with Easton and Isaac. I have no plans to ever leave, but I—"

"Sorry, that's not what I meant. I completely understand, Paige. I do. That piece of paper doesn't change anything. Nor should it."

A thought hits me, and I gasp out loud, because... "Actually, it does."

"What?"

"It does change something. I've got to find Easton."

"Paige, are you okay?" I pause and spin around, checking on her.

"Sorry, do you need anything before I go and find him?"

Rochelle smiles knowingly before shaking her head. "I have a feeling you're about to give me everything I'll ever need. Go. I'll be okay."

I stare at her in question, puzzled, until she laughs. "Go, Paige. I'll bet wherever Easton is, he's waiting for you. I think he's been waiting his whole life."

I search the house and find Isaac and Keeley, but Easton's nowhere to be seen. I'm about to interrupt their game until I notice him through the back window, stalking across the yard, making his way to the back gate that leads to a park.

I rush through the house, making it outside as he reaches for the lock.

"East, wait." He pauses and spins, his face lighting up when he sees me, though it doesn't hold the same happiness it usually does. He's still worried. Not that he'll admit it too often.

I jog toward him, and he opens his arms as I reach him, pulling me into his hold. "Hey, you. Did she like it? I bet there were tears."

"You're right. But they were mostly mine. Your mom is one tough woman."

Easton laughs as he nods. "You're not wrong. Stubborn as hell too. Kind of like someone else I know."

"Yeah, yeah." I laugh because he tells me that on a daily basis, and now I'm about to shock him. "I want to get married."

"What?" He coughs, seemingly choking on nothing, and I laugh louder.

"I want to get married, and I want to adopt Isaac. Officially. As your wife. As a family."

Easton's jaw drops and he stares at me in shock. "Did Mom threaten you with something?"

"No." I give him a shove and scoff. "She was all for us *never* getting married. Practically encouraged it."

"Sounds like her." He laughs.

"So…" I pause, waiting for him to give me an actual response—maybe tell me it's a good idea or that I'm crazy—but instead he raises a brow with a smirk.

"Are you proposing?"

"What? No." I burst out laughing. This is not a conversation I ever thought I'd have. "I just realized I want it all. I want to marry you."

"Okay. Well, that's great. But there's one little issue." He grimaces and I roll my eyes, knowing what's coming. "I haven't asked."

"I know." I wink. "But you will. And I'll be waiting. It better be good, Wilder." I spin on a dime and walk away, leaving my words hanging between us while he chuckles behind me.

I've made it halfway across the yard when he calls out and I pause.

"I've already got the ring." I turn so fast I get dizzy. Meanwhile, he shrugs like it's no big deal.

"When did you buy that?"

He shrugs again as he walks toward me, but there's a hint of mischief in his expression. "It's something I've had lying around."

"For how long?" My brows furrow. We've never spoken about marriage other than one early conversation to admit that neither of us wanted it. I'm a little confused.

"I got it about five months ago."

What? "Five months? Even though we spoke about *never* getting married."

"Yep."

"Why?"

"For this moment."

"But—" I don't even know what to say.

"You may have told me you never wanted to get married. But you also said that Isaac was your number one priority. And that you'd choose him over me. Any day of the week, right?"

"Right." I bite back a smile when he pretends to be offended.

"Well, I guess I figured that one day, you'd want to make that official. And I wanted to be ready."

"I could adopt him without it."

"You could, but it would be significantly harder."

"What happens if we get divorced?"

"We won't." He crosses his arms over his chest.

"You don't know that."

"Yeah. I do." He stares at me pointedly, telling me there's no room for arguments. "You're not getting rid of me, Paige. Isaac and I are here to stay. Through the good times and bad, sickness and health, till death do us part."

"I think that might be the most romantic thing you've ever said." I bite my lip and Easton shakes his head.

"Don't get used to it."

"Never."

"So, what do you say, D'Angelo? Should we go and talk to Isaac? See what he thinks?"

Tears prick the back of my eyes, and he hasn't proposed yet, but I know without a doubt that this is exactly where I'm meant to be. Forever. Easton and Isaac are already my family. In my eyes, I'm already Isaac's mom. But... "Nothing would make me happier. I love you, East."

"I love you too, future Mrs. Wilder. And here's Isaac, right on cue."

I glance up to see Isaac racing toward us, his face alight with a smile. I quickly wipe my eyes, grinning when he reaches us.

"I helped to make a cake. Come and eat it."

"Mmm, that sounds great, Buddy. But first we have something to ask you."

"What?" He frowns, his gaze darting back to the house as though we're ruining his life by keeping him from the cake.

Easton smiles as he looks my way, silently asking if I want to speak. And I do.

"I wanted to know how you'd feel about me becoming your mom."

His eyes widen before his gaze bounces to Easton, who nods, giving him an encouraging smile. "Yes," he says. "Yes, please be my mom. Please."

He tentatively steps forward as though not knowing what to do next, but I rush toward him, sweeping him into my arms and pressing a kiss to his head. "Thank you, Isaac. You just made me the happiest person alive."

"Why?" He pulls back and glances up at me.

"Because I get to call you my son."

The beaming smile he blesses me with holds the power to light up so much darkness that it melts my heart. Reaching for Easton's hand, I give it a squeeze, smiling when he winks.

And just like that, they've given me everything I'll ever need...and never even knew I wanted.

EPILOGUE TWO

EASTON

TWO YEARS LATER

"Mrs. Wilder, would you stop *pacing?*" I growl, immediately stopping Paige in her tracks.

She didn't hear me come in and she'd promised she wasn't going to stress.

"How long have you been standing there?" she asks, gritting her teeth while she cringes, watching me with wide eyes as I walk over, settling my hands on her shoulders.

"Long enough to see you driving yourself crazy."

For the first time, Paige is sharing her sketches with the world as part of a charity art auction.

She was reluctant in the beginning, but when Keeley heard they were looking for new, up-and-coming artists, she convinced Paige to submit a piece.

I, too, thought it was a great idea, but I know better than to tell Paige what to do—unless it's in the bedroom.

Paige sighs, and I understand what she's feeling because I see it in her expression every time someone mentions her art. She feels like she's been stripped bare and put on display. But the fact that she said yes speaks volumes.

A lot of her sketches were created when she needed a release—an outlet for her feelings. She's always been a strong, confident woman, but even the strongest can fall, and sketching was her way of holding it together. A piece of her that she kept to herself.

Because of that, I look at it like a new level of therapy, almost like by putting the pieces on display, she's releasing those feelings so she can completely move on.

And I, for one, couldn't be happier for her.

But Paige...

She shakes her body until I let go of her. "I can't help it, I—"

"You've put so much of yourself into these sketches, and you're terrified for the world to see *you*. Not them...you. But I'm here to tell you that people are going to love them, and I'm so goddamn proud of you."

For the last two years, the amazing human standing in front of me has all but put her career on hold to look after Isaac. Hell, to look after both of us. And no matter how many times we spoke about it, she always insisted it was *her* choice and exactly what she wanted to be doing.

And since she's Paige, I know that to be true. She's never held back on telling me what she wants.

And now...Isaac's in school and it's her time to follow her dreams. Only she's still trying to work out what her dream is.

But there's no rush. We've got all the time in the world, and she's proud to call herself a mom, which she's been doing often since her adoption of Isaac was finalized last year.

Paige takes a deep breath and does something we usually do with Isaac. She shakes out her sillies. Just like the kids' song suggests. Starting with her head, she bounces around the room shaking out various parts of her body, working hard to calm herself down. But when she stops, she's still frowning.

"How about I take your mind off things? Like you do for me when I'm stressed."

And God, have we had some stress in the past couple of years. On top of Mom's deteriorating health and the ever present and always changing Storm scandal, we also had to sit back and watch while the Mikklesons almost got away with extortion. At least until they were finally found guilty after Christian's fiancée, of all people, miraculously "came across" some crucial evidence after hearing rumors that Christian was cheating on her and she went looking for proof.

Or he had it all along and foolishly shared it with his fiancée then proceeded to fuck around.

Either way, they got what they deserved.

As for Mom, her symptoms haven't worsened in the past six months, so we're hopeful they've stalled for the time being.

Paige stares at me before crossing her arms over her chest. "I'm listening," she says, pretending she's unaffected even though she's already nibbling the flesh of her bottom lip. "What are you thinking?"

"I'm thinking you need to get naked—now."

"That's it?" She raises an eyebrow and mocks offense. "That's all you've got for me?"

I stare at her in challenge before stepping forward and curling my hand into her hair, tugging her into me. "Let's try that again. How about you run along to our room, strip naked, crawl onto the bed, and bend over with your ass in the air."

"Okay." She nods, and I don't miss the way her chest lifts as she sucks in a breath. "And then what?"

"Then I'm going to finger fuck you from behind until you're dripping for me, lick you clean, and worship that pretty pussy until you stop thinking about the show tomorrow. Hell, I might push you until you can't remember your own name."

"Jesus. Yes. I want that."

She bites her lip again, watching me with anticipation as though I haven't already given her all the instructions she needs.

"Well?" I ask and she frowns.

"Well, what?"

"Run."

Her eyes widen but she takes off with a suppressed squeal, her lips pulling into a smile as she rounds the couch.

No matter how tired we are, no matter how busy we get, when we're alone together, it's always like fire. Whether it's a fire that burns uncontrollably, or one that lights us from the inside, making us feel all the love we have for each other. Whether there's push and pull or one of us telling the other what to do...we are always in sync. That's never changed between us.

But now, there's so much more to our relationship, and I love every second of it.

I walk slowly, checking on Isaac before I join Paige, shutting the bedroom door behind me. And when I turn, I find her in position, but she's staring at me defiantly in a pair of crotchless panties instead of her bare ass.

"This was supposed to be for you." I smile, my cock hardening at the sight of her lace-covered ass on display for me.

She bites her lip again as she glances over her shoulder, her coy smile shining through. She knows how hot she looks, and she knows I've been a sucker for her crotchless panties since our first session of phone sex.

"How am I supposed to concentrate on your pleasure when you look like that?"

Paige laughs as she wriggles her ass, my attempt to calm her already working. "You'll find a way."

This woman. I bite my knuckles as I groan and stalk toward her, gently slapping her ass when I reach her. "You better be ready, because I plan on making you come. Fast."

"Wha—"

I cut her off, spreading her lips so I can rub my finger through her pussy, circling her clit as my free hand palms her ass. "God, you are a vision, Paige. Bent over like this. Waiting."

She moans in the back of her throat when her body jolts, her pussy so wet that I easily slip a finger inside her. "Always fucking ready."

"Only for you," she rasps. "Fuck me, East. Make me come. Make me forget."

"On it." I wink before working her pussy with my fingers, massaging her clit while rubbing her walls until she's struggling to stay still, her ragged breaths filling the air.

"I'm close," she rushes out at the exact moment her walls tighten, squeezing around my fingers. "East, I'm so—"

Halting my ministrations, I release my cock from my sweats and rub myself through her ass cheeks before lining up with her entrance, loving the way she squirms for me.

She bucks back to take me in, but I pull away, teasing, which elicits her soft mewl. When I line up again, she bucks faster, but I'm still one step ahead, pulling back, my cock throbbing in my hand.

"East, please," she begs and I smile.

"Only because you asked so nicely." I slam into her, and she cries out before burying her mouth in the mattress to stifle her sounds.

With her face in the sheets, Paige rocks her hips, meeting me thrust for thrust as I chase my own release, trying to catch up as she finds hers.

Holding her hips, I grind into her, working her as my balls swell, the sight alone making me groan out loud until Paige shushes me.

She actually *shushes* me.

I slap her ass again, rubbing the mark and reaching around to her pussy, pinching her clit, teasing her in ways I know will usually make her scream, but I get nothing. And while I'm not complaining, because without her sounds, she's still a goddess, I'm greedy. I want it all.

And I know how to get it.

Grabbing her ponytail, I pull her head back and lean in, pressing my lips to her ear. "Let's buy a house," I say out of nowhere, loving her little gasp.

"What?" she whispers, her voice full of confusion.

"A house, Paige." I continue to rock my hips, pounding into her while she processes my words.

When we first got together, I mentioned that I wanted Isaac to grow up in a house, and she understood my reasons, but we both agreed that we'd wait until I'd retired, so we could decide where best to live. And as a bonus, it's nice to have family in the same building, with Paige's dad and my mom. She moved into Paige's apartment when the house got too much for her— with Phil in tow.

I was all for waiting, until Paige smothered her passionate cry just now, making me realize we need more space. I respect the hell out of her for always putting Isaac first, always worrying about him. But I also want to be able to fuck my wife and I want to do it without any restrictions.

"I'm sick of apartment living. I want a house with a gym and a pool and a million other surfaces I can fuck you on. And I want it to be ours." My words are rushed and breathless as my cock drills into her, but I turn her face to see me, making sure she registers the conviction in my expression. This is happening.

"You're choosing now to bring it up?" Paige laughs and her pussy squeezes my cock, making me retaliate with another slap to her ass.

"Yep. Got an issue with that, Wilder?" I suck the flesh below her ear as I cup her pussy, slowing my pace while gently rolling my hips against her.

"Oh God. Oh God."

"Is that a yes?"

"No."

"So, it's a no."

"No. God, Easton. This—" A high-pitched mewl escapes her and I can't help but chuckle.

"Shall I decide for us?"

"You're doing this... Jesus... Yes. There. Oh God."

"Paige?"

"Yes. Okay. Let's buy a house. With every fuckable surface. And a pool house so I can scream your name while you're pounding into me."

"You want a fuck den?"

"Sounds dirtier than I meant it to be, but sure. Although maybe we call it a palace over a den."

A palace? Fuck, I love her but... "I've got another alternative."

"Oh, yeah?"

I push her back down to the bed with her face in the pillow and her ass on full display once more. I groan at the view, before filling her in on my idea. "Bite down on the pillow, Wilder. You're about to see stars."

Thank you for reading Delicate Storm, I hope you enjoyed Easton and Paige's story.

If you want more from the Storm men? Reed's book – Reckless Storm **is now available on Amazon. Keep reading for a sneak peek.**

Books By Katherine Jay

SAN FRANCISCO END GAME SERIES
Beautiful Storm (Luke and Amelia)

Delicate Storm (Easton and Paige)

Reckless Storm (Reed and Hayley)

Careless Storm (Zane and Blair)

Fierce Storm (Salvatore and Keeley)

HOLIDAY ROMANCE
Mistletoe Mail (Mason and Jenna)

SYMPHONY OF SOUND DUET
The Sound Of Silence (Jesse and Willow)

The Sound Of Forever (Jesse and Willow)

HEARTSTRINGS SERIES
When Nothing Else Matters (Summer and Dylan)

Still Here Without You (Joel and Delilah)

It Had To Be Us (Logan and Dani)

Truly Madly Deeply Mine (Wes and Lucy)

A Sky Full Of Stars (Thomas and Lainey)

Ain't No Sunshine (Nate and Cory) – novella

ALL KATHERINE'S BOOKS ARE AVAILABLE ON AMAZON AND
KINDLE UNLIMITED

Reckless Storm
Sneak Peek

Hayley nibbles the flesh of her gloss-covered lips, silently reading her group chat messages. She angles the phone my way, her gaze briefly flitting to mine as she lets me read along.

> Paige: A FAKE RELATIONSHIP?! Yes!

> Amelia: That could work. Side note: Luke's trying to look over my shoulder but I won't let him see what we're discussing

> Paige: Whoops. Are we not supposed to tell the guys? Easton says hi. He loves the idea. But mainly because it takes the spotlight away from him

> Keeley: Paige, tell that brother of mine to grow up. He's a damn football player. He'll always be in the spotlight

> Paige: (Laughing emoji) Well, grumpy Easton is back. Thanks, Keeley. He wants the discussion to revert to Reed

I shake my head as a smile tugs at my lips. But it's fleeting. They want me to fake a relationship? *As if.* I'm not going along with an idea taken straight out of a Hallmark Christmas movie. What do they think is going to happen? That my best friend will see me dating someone else and fall to her knees, begging me to break it off because she's always loved me?

I'm ninety-nine percent sure she already knows how I feel, and it's fucking with my head. *She's* fucking with my head. So yes, it's about time I did something to change that. But that something isn't this.

"You need to shut it down. *Now*," I tell Hayley, running my hands down my face, forcing a laugh. "I wish I'd never said anything to Luke. He's taken my words *way* out of context."

Unfortunately, it's no secret that I have a thing for my best friend, Bria. I wouldn't say I'm in love with her—like my friends so happily like to point out—but there are definitely feelings there beyond that of a traditional friendship.

And it's been that way for *years*.

Bria and I go way back. We attended the University of California together in Los Angeles, and when I was drafted to San Francisco after college, she followed me here, chasing her dream while I chased mine. Now, she's working her way up the ranks at a big accounting firm with a goal to be the youngest partner by the time she turns thirty. And I couldn't be prouder.

But, in order to attain that type of goal, she's always put her career first. As have I. And because of that, I never told her how I felt. It was never the right time.

Not that she's oblivious. She knows. We've just never discussed it. Or let ourselves cross that line.

Except once.

And it didn't end well.

Cut to last week when I decided to get drunk and open my big mouth to the one guy who has trouble keeping his shut—my teammate Luke Bennett, star tight end for the San Francisco Storm, reformed playboy, and one of my closest friends on the team.

Also known as a loudmouth.

I may as well have shouted it from the center of the field during the Super Bowl halftime show. Because that man can gossip.

Now, his wife, Amelia—as much as I love her—has started a group chat about it with some of the girlfriends...wives...sisters...and even goddamn friends of the players on my team, and there's no way back.

Hayley—one of the previously mentioned *friends*—smirks as she undoubtedly prepares to set me straight, something she loves doing.

"According to Amelia, you told Luke your 'love life was fucked' and that you 'needed to fix it.'"

Jesus, I'm a dick. While I have no recollection of that happening, it definitely sounds like me. Not that I'm going to admit that right now. I'm already in too deep. "So what you're saying is that everyone's taking Luke's word for it, because I was too drunk to remember?"

"Yep."

"Meaning...you're not shutting it down?"

"Nope." Hayley's radiant smile lights up her face as she brushes a few wayward hairs away from her eyes, pinning me with her stare.

I met Hayley last year at a joint Thanksgiving and Christmas get-together with my team, hosted by our reluctant coach. We'd been there to fake it for a film crew—for a TV series about our football team—and Hayley happens to be the director's best friend. The director who's now married to the infamous Luke and the two ex-enemies have a baby together. The beautiful Juliet. The reason for my crazy "my love life sucks" rant.

I want that.

Not the accidental pregnancy and subsequent heartache my friends went through, but the endgame. I want a wife; I want kids.

I want Bria.

But I'm beginning to realize that's not likely to happen.

When I don't respond, Hayley raises an eyebrow in challenge and an idea hits me. After Hayley and I first met, we ran into each other a few times, but in the last couple of months, our relationship has morphed from being a friend's friend, to a friend, to close friends, to now speaking daily. Much to Bria's annoyance.

Hayley could be exactly what I need to show Bria what she's missing. But not in the way they're all thinking.

I try to hide my responding smile, but this is too good to suppress and Hayley notices instantly. "What's that look about?"

"I've come up with a plan."

"Oh, yeah?" Her nose scrunches at the thought. While I wouldn't say my plans are as daring as Hayley's usually are, I have been known to have good ideas *occasionally*.

"Instead of this fake dating nonsense, I'm going to tell Bria I have a thing for you and we'll see how she reacts."

Hayley bursts out laughing. "Oh, Reed." She pats my leg condescendingly, her smile innocent as she teases. "If only it was that easy. It won't work unless she *believes* she's going to lose you."

"It's worth a shot though, right?" I comically cringe and Hayley shakes her head, biting back her sympathetic grin.

"Wrong." She waves off my thoughts. "Lucky for you, now *I* have an idea."

Uh, shit. Hayley and her ideas. While I generally love the way her mind works and all the wild adventures she takes me on, I have a feeling I'm not going to like this. Especially when she adds, "You're going to love it."

I force a smile in anticipation, and she snorts, sitting tall and proud.

"I'm going to be your fake girlfriend."

"You're what now?" My eyes bulge as I do a double take. *I did not see that coming.*

"I'm volunteering," she continues as though I was genuinely confused. "I'm an actress; it makes sense for your new girlfriend to be me."

"Ahh, no. That's insane and you know it. Plus—"

"I disagree," she cuts me off, excitement in her tone. "It makes perfect sense. I'm single. You're single. I'm hot. You're insanely gorgeous and you can't deny we'd make a stunning couple." She winks while I roll my eyes jokingly. "It's a no-brainer, Reed. We get along. We have fun. Give me one good reason why it shouldn't be me?"

"Maybe because I don't think it's a good idea to begin with. Fake dating is crazy. Come on, Hayls. Think about it."

"Reed." She hits me with her arresting gaze, her look telling me she thinks *I'm* crazy, not the idea. But she's wrong. I'm being sensible.

"Hayley." I stare back at her, mimicking her stance when she crosses her arms over her chest and pouts.

"Are you saying I couldn't pull it off?"

What? *Dammit.* She's good. Now I feel bad.

"Hayley Jackman from down under. You know I think you're brilliant. And while I'm sure this could be the acting role of your life, you're forgetting one major plot hole." Hayley's smile returns but it won't last long. I'm about to prove why this is a terrible idea. "I can't act."

"But—"

"Or lie," I add, though she already knows this.

"There are ways around that, Reed. Trust me. I've worked on some pretty amateur productions and people still loved them."

I fall quiet, acutely aware that she is unlikely to give up on this. Once Hayley has an idea in her head, it's not easy to get her past it. And I'm usually the one going along for the ride.

"For someone that thought I was insane, you're sure taking a long time to say no."

"I didn't say you were insane, Hayls. The idea is just..." *God, I don't even know.* I release an overexaggerated sigh, knowing she's about to sass me, and beat her to the punch. "It's not the craziest idea I've heard come out of your mouth. But I'm going to need to think about it. I'm still not convinced."

Her eyes light up in victory, reinforcing the fact that I can't say no to her.

"I'll take it," she says, squeezing my leg as she bounces around on the couch. "For now, anyway. I have no doubt I'll change your mind."

Reckless Storm - Reed and Hayley's Fake Dating romance is available now.

CARELESS STORM

A right person / wrong time sports romance

Blair Stevens' thought she had it all — until one devastating moment shattered her world.

Seven years ago, Blair shared a secret love and a future with her brother's best friend, Zane Fitzpatrick. But fate sent them spiraling in opposite directions.

Now she's drifting through life, dating Zane's biggest rival, while he's the NFL's infamous bad boy, making headlines for all the wrong reasons.

Just when she begins questioning everything, Zane reappears, looking at her like no time has passed. And despite her efforts to keep her distance, Zane's unwavering support begins to reignite the strength she thought she'd lost forever.

As the undeniable pull brings them closer together, they're forced to face something bigger.

Because it turns out, Blair's not the only one who's broken. And the only way forward is to face the past... together.

FIERCE STORM

A forbidden, age gap sports romance

He's her boss, her brother's future father-in-law and her best friends dad. She's twenty years younger than him and the one woman he can't get out of his head.

What happens when they give in to temptation?

Find out when the final Storm book releases in June 2026

AVAILABLE NOW ON AMAZON, KINDLE UNLIMITED AND AUDIBLE

ABOUT THE AUTHOR

Katherine writes angsty and emotional, character-driven romance full of banter, steam and the kind of love that's always worth fighting for.

When she's not lost in a fictional world (writing or reading), she's travelling, falling down a binge-worthy television rabbit hole, or letting the perfect song absolutely wreck her.

Katherine lives in Australia with her husband and two boys, which means she's constantly outnumbered, but wouldn't have it any other way.

For more information, visit
https://www.katherinejayauthor.com

If you want to stay up to date with all things Katherine Jay, come and join her Facebook Reader Group – The Angsty Lovers Playlist — for fun, exclusive content and sneak peeks. Or sign up to her newsletter via her website.

Are you following Katherine on social media? If not, you can find her on Instagram, Facebook and TikTok.